Why I Like This Story

Why I Like This Story

EDITED BY
Jackson R. Bryer

CAMDEN HOUSE
Rochester, New York

First published 2019
by Camden House

Camden House is an imprint of Boydell & Brewer Inc.
668 Mt. Hope Avenue, Rochester, NY 14620, USA
www.camden-house.com
and of Boydell & Brewer Limited
PO Box 9, Woodbridge, Suffolk IP12 3DF, UK
www.boydellandbrewer.com

ISBN-13: 978-1-64014-058-5
ISBN-10: 1-64014-058-1

Library of Congress Cataloging-in-Publication Data

CIP data is available from the Library of Congress.

This publication is printed on acid-free paper.
Printed in the United States of America.

Contents

Preface

In his 2014 biography of John Updike, Adam Begley quotes Updike's assertion—made in a 1978 letter to Joyce Carol Oates—that "Nobody can read like a writer." This book stands as an emphatic validation of Updike's statement.

It began several years ago, with a request from a university press to be a reader for a collection of essays on American author Peter Taylor. Among the pieces I read on that occasion was one by Ann Beattie, "Peter Taylor's 'The Old Forest,'" which I thought was a stunning and revelatory essay on one of Taylor's most important short stories. What impressed me about it was that, in one elegantly written and brief piece (five pages in the eventually published book), Beattie managed to achieve several objectives equally well—and they were objectives that heretofore I had regarded as mutually exclusive. She provided an explication of Taylor's story that was extraordinarily useful in unraveling its complexities, subtleties, and virtues; but she also conveyed very unobtrusively yet productively a sense of her personal relationship to its author (he had been her teacher and mentor and they had later become colleagues and close friends). Above all, what differentiated her essay from others on literary subjects was that it was so obviously and uniquely the sort of analysis/appreciation which could only have been written by a fellow writer, someone who knew the territory, who understood how difficult it was to accomplish what Peter Taylor had accomplished because she had tried to do so herself.

Beattie's essay had additional value for me because I had grown impatient with what at the time often passed for literary criticism, writing couched in jargon that obscured rather than illuminated its subject. Her essay was truly a breath of fresh air; and it occurred to me that one way of keeping that fresh air circulating would be to ask some leading American fiction writers to select a favorite American short story and explain why they liked it. Twenty-nine writers responded positively to my invitation. The only instruction they were given was not to write a scholarly essay; the only restrictions I placed were that the stories selected be by American writers and that there not be more than one story by any single writer. Although I was extremely pleased by the submissions I received and while a number of publishers expressed initial interest in the project, I was unable to find a press that would accept all the essays in substantially the form in which they had been submitted— and I felt very strongly that, because in many instances, very successful and busy professional writers had taken the time, on speculation, to write these essays, I owed it to them not to exclude any from the book or insist on major changes in their texts in order to make them acceptable. Very reluctantly, and rather shamefacedly, I put the project aside.

There it remained for several decades until three years ago when, during a chance encounter at the annual American Literature Association conference in Boston, I met Jim Walker of Camden House. I mentioned this then long-dormant project to him, and he expressed enthusiasm for it but encouraged me to augment my original roster of contributors with some younger, more diverse writers who might in turn select stories that would reflect a similar diversity. As had been my procedure originally, I contacted some writers whom I knew personally, and they sometimes led me to others whom I did not know except in the pages of their work.

My invitations included the same specifications I had outlined earlier.

The forty-eight essays published here are thus a combination of those I received when I originally conceived *Why I Like This Story* and those commissioned more recently. They are a diverse group, diverse in ways both predictable and surprising; as a result, the book has in some respects turned out to be somewhat different from what I envisioned it to be. While the essays are perhaps not uniformly useful as full-scale explications of the stories selected, many of the contributors, because they chose to make their pieces personal, often reveal as much about themselves as they do about the story. This is actually not surprising, since reading is so personal, so intimate an experience. It is also frequently possible in these essays to discern the different aspects of storytelling that are valued by different practitioners; in explaining why they chose a particular story, they implicitly but more often quite explicitly tell us what they value in that story—and by extension in fiction more generally. Such information not only helps us appreciate the story but also illuminates the fiction of the author of the essay. In several instances, a contributor's affection for a story is related to the time in the contributor's life when he or she first encountered it. On a few other occasions, but of equal interest, the choice of a story is influenced by the friendship between the author of the story and the author of the essay. And an entirely unanticipated pleasure of the book is that, in five instances—Bausch, Dubus, Garrett, Gass, and Giles—the author of an essay is also himself or herself the subject of someone else's essay.

Another hoped-for value of *Why I Like This Story* is the number of lesser-known stories and writers it brings forward. While some may regret or complain about the absence of a story by Poe, Hawthorne, Twain, Stephen Crane, Sherwood

Anderson, Faulkner, or other acknowledged masters of the form, it should be refreshing to find appreciations of stories by William Carlos Williams, John O'Hara, George Garrett, William Goyen, Jerome Weidman, Kay Boyle, Delmore Schwartz, William H. Gass, and Peter Matthiessen—alongside James, Fitzgerald, Melville, Hemingway, Welty, Paley, O'Connor, Salinger, Updike, Bellow, and Malamud. When one adds the recently added essays on stories by, among others, Andre Dubus, Molly Giles, Deborah Eisenberg, Denis Johnson, Lorrie Moore, Phil Klay, Kirstin Valdez Quade, Stuart Dybek, Edward P. Jones, Jamaica Kincaid, Viet Thanh Nguyen, and Junot Diaz, the selections surely reflect the richness of the American story form from its origins in the nineteenth century to the present day.

These essays should send readers to bookstores or the internet to seek out copies of the stories discussed or perhaps to their own bookshelves to reread stories, memories of which were reawakened by these writers' appreciations of them. If this happens, the primary intention of *Why I Like This Story* will have been accomplished—to place the focus back on the texts themselves. After I read Ann Beattie's essay on "The Old Forest" those many years ago, I immediately reread Peter Taylor's story—and I found enhanced understanding and appreciation of it in the process. May this happen forty-eight times over to readers of this book!

J.R.B.

Kensington, MD

January 20, 2019

Acknowledgments

I am grateful to all the talented fiction writers who wrote essays for this book and to the agents and literary executors who gave me permission to publish the essays by deceased authors. For significant assistance in the preparation of the book for publication, I thank Merrill Leffler, Gerard Holmes, and Mary C. Hartig. My deepest debt of gratitude is to Jim Walker of Camden House—for resuscitating this project and for playing a major role in shepherding it through to publication.

Because of the long gestation period of this project, a few authors published their essays in the interim:

Doris Betts's essay on "Where Is the Voice Coming From?" by Eudora Welty appeared in a slightly different form, as "Killers Real and Imagined," in the Winter 1999 issue of *Southern Cultures*. It is reprinted here with the permission of Lisa Eveleigh, the managing coeditor of *Southern Cultures*, and Jade Wong-Baxter of Massie & McQuilkin, Literary Agents for the Estate of Doris Betts.

R. H. W. Dillard's essay on "Dare's Gift" by Ellen Glasgow was published as "Off to Strange Parts: Ellen Glasgow's 'Dare's Gift'" in the June 2003 issue of *The Hollins Critic*. It is reprinted here with the permission of the editor of *The Hollins Critic*.

Why I Like This Story

"The Fourth Alarm" by John Cheever

Lee K. Abbott

"The Fourth Alarm" was originally published in the April 1970 issue of *Esquire*. It was collected in *The World of Apples* (1973). It is currently most readily available in Cheever's *Collected Stories and Other Writings* (Library of America).

The opening is, happily, vintage Cheever—informal and intimate, deliberate and forthcoming—a paragraph that says, apart from its exposition, that here, fellow citizens, is the story we need to hear today: "I sit in the sun drinking gin. It is ten in the morning. Sunday. Mrs. Uxbridge is off somewhere with the children. Mrs. Uxbridge is the housekeeper. She does the cooking and takes care of Peter and Louise." Not much, to be sure, to fret over, the early tippling notwithstanding. Not a hint of a shootout or the comparably melodramatic to and fro we might elsewhere hanker for. Nothing, in brief, but what Truman Capote called the "gossip" that is literature, the secrets—always dirty, always dire—that we'd rather the world did not know but which are, with only polite apologies to Chekhov, the true engine that makes fiction go. So hold on, for there is more: Our narrator, still another of Cheever's amused and slightly bent men, has a mistress, Mrs. Smithson, who is "seldom in the mood these days," and a wife, Bertha, formerly a sixth-grade social studies teacher but now an actress in an all-nude Equity extravaganza called *Ozamanides II*. Yes, he is a gentleman of more than considerable means whose world, once meet with touch football and Dubonnet, has gone perplexingly (and fetchingly) cockeyed.

Though some might argue, even "correctly," that Cheever's story does not start in proper until the night, some thousand words or more deep into the tale, when Bertha tells our narrator that she has been cast in a production in which "She would be expected to simulate or perform copulation twice during the performance and participate in a love pile that involved the audience," I am here to say that, in part, the vexing of our critical expectations with respect to structure reflects the confounding of our narrator's expectations with respect to his heretofore settled and conventional world. "Oh, how wonderful and rich and strange life can be," Bertha tells him, "when you stop playing out the roles that your parents and their friends wrote out for you. I feel like an explorer." Such wonder and such richness and such strangeness, methinks, demands a fresh form, one which will lead our beleaguered male "explorer" to discover "some marvelously practical and obdurate part" of himself.

Except for the foregoing moment, this is a story with only one scene, such brevity almost an anomaly in the Cheever oeuvre. But like so many other Cheever stories, this is a story that meditates on itself, that asks—good-naturedly, of course; Cheever's nature is preternaturally good—how, given all, likely and not, that has befallen our protagonist, he has ended up alone and all too familiar with "the keenness of love." He is also a man deeply nostalgic for the "innocent movie[s]" of his youth, in particular a feature called *The Fourth Alarm*, a show he even plays hooky to see over and over (and over) at the Alhambra. Its plot——an antithesis of sorts to the other, larger, scene the narrator means still to show us—concerns "the substitution of automobiles for horse-drawn fire engines." You know the rest, I'm guessing. Four fire companies are involved, "its days numbered" for the last of the horse-drawn teams. Then comes "a great fire" that involves, one by one, the first motorized engine and the second and the third. "Back at the horse-drawn company, things were very gloomy. Then the fourth alarm rang—it was their summons—and they sprang into action. . . ." The rest, of course, is an ending as happy as it is sappy: "They put out the fire, saved the city, and were given an amnesty by the mayor." It is a memory revealed while, on stage, "Ozamanides [is] writing something obscene on my wife's buttocks."

Also important to remember at climax is what our narrator calls Bertha's "lullaby," her "peevish" habit of counting *one, two, three* when, frustration mounting, she wants the children to eat breakfast or pick up their toys or go to bed. "I sometimes thought," the narrator reports, "she must have learned to count when she was an infant and that when the end came she would call a countdown for the Angel of Death." In other words, what happens at *four* or after is the brutish and the terrible, the miserable and the graceless, the crude and the tyrannical. In this case, what happens is that, at the urging of the cast, the audience is "commanded" to undress and come to the stage, which our hero does. Though always "very quick to get out of [his] clothes," the narrator immediately encounters a problem: "What should I do with my wallet, wristwatch, and car keys?" Naked, he starts down the aisle, valuables in hand, only to be stopped by a young man, also naked, who shouts—no, sings—"Put down your lendings. Lendings are impure." Of course, our narrator can't. He has to eat and drink and get home, he realizes. He has to drive from the station. He has—well, he is a man with a "literal identification," one who dares not cast off that which would "threaten my essence,

the shadow of myself that I could see on the floor, my name."
Lord help us, there will be no metaphor, horse-drawn or otherwise, to rush in at the last instant to save him, or us, from
the knowledge, certain as sin itself, that these are "fires" of
confusion and loss and displacement and rueful self-awareness
that cannot be extinguished.

What I like about this story is, indeed, what I like about
(nearly) all of John Cheever's short fiction, namely his affection for the equivocal, the crosswise ways that afflict, the hard
landing we all are doomed to suffer—the feeling, so the narrator of "A Vision of the World" tells us, of feeling that we are
characters in a situation comedy: "I mean, I'm nice-looking,
I'm well-dressed, I have humorous and attractive children, but
I have this terrible feeling that I'm in black-and-white and that
I can be turned off by anybody. I just have this terrible feeling
that I can be turned *off.*" In "Just Tell Me Who It Was," the
anomie is "some skepticism about the emotional richness of
human involvements." It shows up in "The Country Husband"
as a "love of parties" which springs "from a most natural dread
of chaos and loneliness." In "The Angel of the Bridge," not one
of his most celebrated stories, it is the "emergence of a new
world, a gentle hint at my own obsolescence, the lateness of
my time of life, and my inability to understand the things I
often see." In "The Geometry of Love," another of his later stories, it is an understanding, no matter the desire for "radiance,
beauty, and order," that reality has "lost its fitness and sym-
metry." And throughout, all is served up in good cheer—the
absurd and the nutty, the provisional and the evanescent. Not
mindless good cheer. No, never that. But the cheer, rising out
of our hearts and peculiar to our inward tribe, that remains
always mindful of, as he writes in the preface to his collected
stories, "one's struggle to receive an education in economics
and love."

Cheever once called the short story "the literature of the nomad," by which assertion I took him, and still take him, to mean that for those of us for whom the story short is the world as written, knowing the stuff we find between margins is knowing enough to get to the next watering hole, the next stand of rushes. In "The Fourth Alarm," we get our peek at the perverse, the dubious, the slipshod, and then we move on, yet once more in love with things that have vanished into the past.

Lee K. Abbott is the author of the short-story collections *The Heart Never Fits Its Wanting* (1980), *Love Is the Crooked Thing* (1986), *Strangers in Paradise* (1986), *Dreams of Distant Lives* (1989), *Living After Midnight* (1991), *Wet Places at Noon* (1997), and *All Things, All at Once: New & Selected Stories* (2006). His stories have been reprinted in *The Best American Short Stories* and *The Prize Stories: The O. Henry Awards*.

"A Father's Story" by Andre Dubus

Elliot Ackerman

"A Father's Story" was first published in the Spring 1983 issue of *Black Warrior Review*. It was collected in *The Times Are Never So Bad* (1983). It is currently most readily available in *The Winter Father: Collected Short Stories and Novellas, Volume 2* (David R. Godine).

In the spring of 2010, when I was thirty years old and expecting my first child, my best friend T__ showed up to one of our early morning runs with a manila envelope. He told me to open it later, when I had some time to read. I tucked it into the glovebox of my car and then we set out on the trail outside of Washington, D.C. T__ and I had a history of running together. We first met at a grueling special operations course where it seemed all we did was run; this was back when he was a twenty-seven-year-old first lieutenant in the Marines and I was still in R.O.T.C., having managed to talk my way into the training.

When we had down time during that course, whether it was before lights out, or on a Sunday afternoon, I remember T__ lounging on a bottom bunk in the barracks, a shower shoe dangling from the foot of his crossed legs as he read Richard Yates or Joan Didion or, as a southerner, anyone along the Faulkner-Styron axis. While the rest of us were tactically or technically preparing ourselves for war—it was 2002—he insisted that reading fiction was the best preparation for any of life's challenges, which, at their core, were always emotional. T— had been a creative writing major at the University of Virginia and, as he later confided to me, had entered the Marine Corps only after experiencing a dark night of the soul in which he nearly abandoned a military career in favor of an application he wrote but never submitted to the Iowa Writers' Workshop.

By the morning of that run, T— had served as my surrogate big brother in the Marines for the better part of a decade. When I was in Iraq he checked up on me every couple of weeks through email. When I was back in the States, he would put in a good word when I showed up at a new posting. And now, nearly ten years later, when he handed me the envelope before our run, I couldn't help but feel he was trying to look out for me once more as I became a father.

That summer, my daughter was due to arrive, so when I opened the envelope and found "A Father's Story" by Andre Dubus, it seemed an obvious pick. T— had a trio of girls. He had also been the first in three generations of his family to have a daughter, so he often wondered if this disadvantaged his understanding of the fairer sex. I grew up in a similarly male household, so I had some of the same early misgivings about how intuitive raising a daughter would be, although I had vague ideas that my role was to serve as her protector.

Luke Ripley, the narrator of Dubus's story, seems to have a similar belief about his role as a father-protector. Ripley is a divorcee who lives a quiet life on a horse farm in northeastern Massachusetts. He is a man of faith, a Catholic, and his closest friend is a priest, Father Paul LeBoeuf, "another old buck," as Ripley tells us. As for Ripley, his life is quiet. He visits Father Paul. He works with his horses and the young people who train them. He spends a lot of time sitting in his front room, watching the world outside: "Then I'm alone again, or I'd appear to be if someone crept up to the house and looked through a window: a big-gutted grey-haired guy, drinking tea and smoking cigarettes, staring out at the dark woods across the road, listening to a grieving soprano."

Although Ripley alludes to the messiness of his life, one which has resulted in solitude and a general sense of isolation, his acceptance of this outcome imbues him with dignity; he's a man who's played at life, lost some rounds and won others. He has several children, but only one daughter. His sons visit him from time to time, and Ripley is sympathetic to the demands of their own lives, but it is his daughter who he misses most acutely. "It is not painful to think about them anymore," says Ripley of his sons, "because even if we had lived together, they would be gone now, grown into their own lives, except Jennifer."

Jennifer, his one girl, is clearly the exception. And it is the nature of that exceptionalism which is the crux of the story.

A few days after he handed me "A Father's Story," T__ admitted that I wasn't the first person he'd given it to, that he'd taken to offering it to any father who was expecting a daughter. "The father-daughter relationship is special," he said. "Dubus really gets at what makes it different." He left it at that. I didn't have a daughter, so I took it on a matter of faith that T__ was right about the story illustrating some great truth, but when I finished reading I wasn't sure what I thought.

After Dubus enters us into Ripley's world—his failed marriage, his children growing up without him, and his friendship with Father Paul, the local priest—he then recounts an evening when Jennifer is visiting. She has gone out with friends. They've been drinking, although not drunkenly so, and Jennifer is driving. She drops all of her friends off and, afterwards, is heading home to her father's, when upon cresting a blind hill she hits a young man walking on the road's shoulder in the dead of night. Without stopping, Jennifer races back to her father for help. She finds Ripley up late drinking at his kitchen table.

Leaving his daughter in the kitchen, Ripley drives alone to the scene of the accident, where he finds the body of the young man his daughter has killed. "His name was Patrick Mitchell, he was nineteen years old, was employed by CETA, lived at home with his parents and brother and sister"; they learn later via a news broadcast that he too had been heading home that night. Even though Patrick Mitchell is a young man with a family like his own, Ripley knows that he has to protect Jennifer. He leaves the body where it is.

As much as Ripley wants to unburden himself of what he's done, to confess, he knows that he cannot, not even to Father Paul, so in this way even his faith is compromised by what Jennifer has done: "Father Paul would not feel that he must tell me to go to the police. And, for that very reason, to confess now would be unfair. It is a world of secrets, and now I have one from my best, in truth my only, friend." He then fakes an accident with the car, running it into a pine in front of St. John's Church in a public display to hide the true reason for its dented fender. The first person to come and see him after he's wrecked his own car is Father Paul. Suffice it to say, for a devout Catholic, the episode weighs heavily on Ripley.

In contemplating his decision to protect his daughter, Ripley thinks on the difference between her and her brothers: "And if one of my sons had come to me that night, I would have phoned the police and told them to meet us with an ambulance at the top of the hill."

Ripley is aware of how the accident has affected Jennifer, noticing how acutely it pains her when her friends tease him about crashing the car. However, he plays the classic fatherly role, covering up her mistakes and shouldering as much of the emotional burden as he can. At first glance, the story seems utterly conventional: a father going to great lengths to protect his daughter. But at closer consideration, Ripley's instincts are not entirely altruistic; Jennifer, in fact, is not the one being protected.

Early in the story, Ripley tells us that he talks with God in the morning while he sits in his kitchen looking out at his horse farm. Without Father Paul, these conversations become more frequent toward the end of the story. The final passage is one such conversation, in which Ripley attempts to explain his decision to cover up his daughter's accident after he admits that he would have turned his sons into the authorities.

"Why? Do you love them less?" God asks.

"I tell Him no, it is not that I love them less, but that I could bear the pain of watching and knowing my sons' pain, could bear it with pride as they took the whip and nails. But You never had a daughter and, if You had, You could not have borne her passion."

God answers, "Then you love in weakness."

It took me several readings, but the revelation of that line is why T__ gave me the story, I think. It was a warning. If I thought my role as a father was to be my daughter's protector, I was only partially right. When I make decisions for both my children, but particularly with my daughter, I ask often whom I'm protecting when I choose the path of caution. If they want to jump off the monkey bars, swim in the open ocean, or head off on a date with a new crush, who am I really protecting if I deny them? Too often, it is myself. This dynamic exists father-to-son, of course it does. But it's far easier for the father of a daughter to slip into a cycle of decisions that he's ostensibly making for her benefit, when it's really his own inability to see her suffer that he's protecting. In this way, it can be too easy for a father to love his daughter selfishly.

In the years since T— gave me the Dubus story, I've given it to one or two other friends who are expecting daughters. When they ask me what the story's about, or even why I'm giving it to them, I say only that it's a warning.

But there's something that I don't say: it's that I feel that passing along the story is something that I owe my daughter, that passing it along is yet another small way to protect her.

Elliot Ackerman is the author of the novels *Green on Blue* (2015), *Dark at the Crossing* (2017), and *Waiting for Eden* (2018).

"Use of Force"
by William Carlos Williams

Julia Alvarez

"Use of Force" was originally published in the November-December 1933 issue of *Blast*. It was collected in *Life Along the Passaic River* (1938). It is currently most readily available in *The Collected Stories of William Carlos Williams* (New Directions).

"U se of Force" by William Carlos Williams is a simple, very-short short story—three pages in most anthologies. Williams, himself a physician, tells the story of a young doctor making a house call in a community where several cases of diphtheria have recently broken out. His patient, a pretty little girl, who seems to be the only child of a working-class couple, the Olsons, refuses to open her mouth for a throat exam. Fearing she may be infected, the doctor forcibly enters her mouth to get a throat culture. But in the process he loses control and realizes his motivation is conquest, not care. He has tried to save her life and fulfill his social responsibility to protect the community but by means that involve a dubious use of force.

One of the things I love about this story is its unpretentiousness. Its craft is truly invisible. I'm reminded of an incident with my father when we visited the Museum of Modern

Art in New York as newly arrived immigrants. We were standing in front of an abstract painting that might have been drawn by a child: a red square and a green triangle posed on a purple background. My father shook his head and whistled, "I could do that!" It was only years later, studying the work of Albers in a history of art course in college, that I understood the technique involved in creating his simple, luminous forms on canvas.

William Carlos Williams's story shares that apparent effortless simplicity. It is not an overtly literary story keeping us at a respectful distance. The style is no-frills, matter-of-fact. No Faulknerian rococo sentences, no stylized deployment of simple sentences as in a Hemingway story. The first-person narrator seems to be speaking the story or typing it out on his clunky Underwood typewriter between patients as Dr. Williams was known to do. Williams avoids the literary use of quotation marks that would make the talk look like "dialogue." The story has such clear, clean lines and represents such a common, everyday situation that reading it, one could say with my father, "I can tell a story like that!"

That is why I always use this story on the first day of my beginning fiction-writing classes. I want to demystify the craft, to dispel the writer's block my students experience when they sit down to write LITERATURE. In fact, I want to discourage them from approaching writing from such a lofty perspective. By college, too many of them have acquired the habits of literary conquistadores: hunting for meaning, discovering themes, imposing theoretical structures, and thus exterminating the native vibrancy of the best stories.

The first thing I point out to them about this story is its wonderful economy. (Another reason I bring this story to the first day of class: we can read it out loud and discuss it in depth in the short space of an hour.) There are no extras here, no background information about the Olsons or the neighborhood or even the doctor. The plot is the classic struggle—one that could be lifted straight from the *Aeneid* or Shakespeare or the tabloids at the grocery store: boy meets girl, girls refuses boy, boy overcomes girl, boy wins. Within three pages—in my *Norton Anthology* version—a whole story gets told. Chekhov, a master himself of compression, would have admired the economy of this short story.

So what accounts for this story's depth? With no clutter, the smallest gesture looms large and gets our close attention. The characters come across in a few, bold strokes: the big, startled-looking mother, who is clean and apologetic. The father, who tries to get up deferentially when the doctor enters, and later, enthralled as well by his little girl, lets her go at the critical moment when the young doctor is about to achieve his goal. And then there's the doctor, who arrives in this cold, damp weather in which this poor Depression family has to stay in the kitchen to keep warm, in a luxurious-sounding *overcoat*. He is a professional, who is going to be paid three dollars for this house call—a considerable fee given this family's humble situation.

These few sharply realized details allow us to see the characters distinctly. We also get to know them by the way they speak. Immediately, we sense the class differences between the doctor and the family by the mother's numerous apologies as she lets the doctor in and her respectful repetition of his title, "Doctor . . . doctor." The parents' ungrammatical speech contrasts sharply with the doctor's pat, professional phrases, his use of "we," "as doctors often do." A professional has entered into a working-class household. There is a hierarchy here, and such power structures are usually kept in place by the use of some kind of force. Class habits dictate that everyone stay in his or her place—even our doctor, who assures us that he is doing "what doctors often do."

Only the child will not stay in her appointed place and obey the doctor's orders, though her humble, compliant parents plead and threaten. ("Abject, crushed, exhausted," the doctor condescendingly brands them.) It is amazing how much power this child commands in the story though she hardly says a word.

Mathilda Olson is the little Infanta in a Velázquez painting transported to a working-class kitchen in Rutherford, New Jersey, during the American Depression. She sits queen-like on her father's lap, the glowing center of the story, with her "magnificent blonde hair, in profusion," which the doctor notices right away. The phrase calls up an image of a sexualized girl child, a Marilyn Monroe type rather than a cute Shirley Temple type. The tag, "in profusion," adds that suggestion of lushness and sensuality, much as the advertising leaflets and photogravure sections of Sunday papers used to touch up photographs of young girls by coloring the lips and cheeks with a rose tint, penciling in each fine eyelash.

While the other characters in the story are known primarily by what they say, the child remains powerfully silent. Only once does she speak, screaming at the doctor at the top of her lungs, "Stop it! Stop it! You're killing me!" That cry has an age-old ring to it: the sound of an overpowered female trying to stop an aggressor, and I believe Williams wanted us to hear that in this girl's voice. The young doctor has already admitted that he has fallen in love with her. He knows he should wait until she has calmed down to get his throat culture if that is all that he wants. But he can't help himself. He has shed his best professional manner and become a man out of control, exercising brute force under the cloak of good intentions. It comes down to a clear and simple moment of violation: he is trying to enter her.

When I suggest the possibility of a kind of rape, some students will resist. Isn't this just a simple story about a doctor examining a little girl? But I remind them that even though this story sounds as if "it really happened," everything in a story is a choice the writer makes. Why didn't Williams make the young patient a boy? Why didn't he make the malady a broken arm that the doctor has to look at? Why a beautiful young girl whose throat has to be exposed for a culture? When the young doctor describes her as rising "to magnificent heights of insane fury of effort bred of her terror of me," she has been transformed in his imagination from a sick child to a heroine in a Greek myth protecting her virtue against some demi-god creep.

But her adversary is just a nice young doctor trying hard to do a good job during what must be a tense time for him. Already "a number of cases of diphtheria" have broken out in town. Many more tired nights and days and house calls in bad weather are in store for him. He is a public servant with a heavy load: a community to be protected against infection. All he wants to do is save a child's life. Poor guy is going to deserve every penny of those three dollars he charges for a house visit! But as sometimes happens in these everyday situations, he suddenly finds himself plunged into his own heart of darkness. It is those moments, I keep telling my students, that suddenly open up to reveal a bottomless bottom, that the best stories are often about.

So, what begins as a doctor's visit turns out to be a battle, for reasons as old as those that started the Trojan War. The child seems to be the aggressor, but really it is the doctor who is transformed into the transgressor. In his hurry and self-importance, with his best professional manner and good overcoat, our young doctor bursts into the Olsons' house, through the front rooms, into the intimacy of their warm kitchen in back. By way of introduction, he gives us only two sentences in the telegrammatic way of doctors reaching out a commanding hand at the operating table, "Scalpel!" "They were new patients to me, all I had was the name, Olson. Please come down as soon as you can, my daughter is very sick." The sentences are run-ons, mimetically recreating the doctor's haste: there is a life here to be saved and our hero doctor is going to be the one to do it.

But although he is a class above his patients and presents himself with the self-assurance of a professional, the doctor, too, has his insecurities. How old is he? I ask my students—and most of them guess that he is a young doctor, fresh out of medical school. Why else would he have to explain that he is following his manual and doing what "doctors often do." Later, somewhat defensively, he assures us, "I know how to expose a throat for inspection." The couple are eyeing him "distrustfully," waiting to see if he proves himself worthy of the money they are spending on him.

A recalcitrant child on the one hand—a young, inexperienced doctor on the other: the war begins. In fact, as the action proceeds, the language of the young doctor becomes more and more peppered with the metaphors of war: "the battle," "the ensuing struggle," "we're going through with this," "fought valiantly," "on the defensive," "attacked," "tears of defeat." He marshals high-flown social-justice rhetoric and professional jargon to cloak the shameful emotions he is feeling: "The damned little brat must be protected against her own idiocy, one says to one's self at such times. Others must be protected against her. It is a social necessity. . . . But a feeling of adult shame, bred of a longing for muscular release are the operatives."

Even though we are in the point of view of the doctor who "loses it," the story is told in the past tense. The doctor has already achieved some perspective and exposed the infection in the heart of his own motives. For Williams, right seeing was a kind of corrective to social and personal ills. That is why his poems focus so intently on the world we must see with clarity and precision: a wheelbarrow, a woman getting a pebble out of her shoe, the glass shards behind the new wing of the hospital. Although the story depends a great deal on what people say for our understanding of what they are like, vision is the central metaphor throughout. From the beginning everyone is sizing everyone else up, looking closely at each other to try to diagnose, not just illness, but character. "Let me see," the doctor says to the child, and to the parents, "Have you looked?" Once he begins to lose it with the child, he scolds her, "Look here . . . we're going to look at your throat." It's not just will clashing with will, but one vision of the world colliding with another vision of the world: a scientific against an emotional world view, an adult against a child, a male against a female, a middle-class professional against a working-class family. It's interesting that when the child first attacks the doctor, it is his glasses that she knocks from his face. From that point on, the doctor begins to operate from "blind fury." The child, too, is "blinded" by tears of defeat and her terror of her secret being discovered. By the end of the story, both adult and child, male and female, doctor and patient are operating out of blind instinct. The use of force makes blind equals of us all.

These fine details of word choice and imagery are, of course, craft at work. But Williams tells the story in such a compact, straightforward manner that we are largely unaware of the craft at work. We, his readers, are seduced into thinking that there's nothing much to this simple tale. The title alerts us that the story might have serious implications. But the philosophical dilemma the phrase poses is one we usually assign to the workings of power on a grander political scale than that of a child's simple medical examination. Perhaps this is Williams's point after all: that the big questions of morality manifest themselves in the small, simple transactions that happen to all of us.

Julia Alvarez is the author of the novels *How the García Girls Lost Their Accents* (1991), *In the Time of the Butterflies* (1994), *¡Yo!* (1997), *In the Name of Salomé* (2000), and *Saving the World* (2006), as well as of collections of poetry, non-fiction, and books for young readers. She received the National Medal of Arts in 2013.

"Leaving the Colonel" by Molly Giles

Rilla Askew

"Leaving the Colonel" was first published in the Winter 1980 issue of *New England Review*. It was collected in *Creek Walk and Other Stories* (1996). It is currently most readily available in *Creek Walk and Other Stories* (Scribner).

I could read this story a thousand times and be delighted every time. Really, I can say this about almost any Molly Giles story, but "Leaving the Colonel" is, for me, nearly infinite in its layers of chilling humor, delight, and despair. I offer it to my fiction-writing students as a last-chance-to-change story, adding that I have it on good authority (the author herself) that I'm wrong in my interpretation—that, in fact, there *is* change here, irrevocable, the moment-after-which-nothing-will-ever-be-the-same. And that's one of the intrigues of the story: you look at it one way, it seems to be one thing. You look at it another, it is something else entirely. In fact, perhaps, the clean opposite to what you first thought.

The story is simple. A bright-tongued woman, unhappy, sloppy, rather continuously sipping bourbon from a teacup, engages in an internal monologue, or rather dialogue, with an imagined interlocutor, the interviewer. She describes for him for the umpteenth time how she is going to leave her husband, the colonel, and also enumerates the reasons she is not able to do it today: she has nothing to wear; she has blackberries to cook, jelly to make, messes to clean up, and of course her daily interview show—the interviewer will want to ask her some questions:

"You've been talking about leaving the colonel for twenty years," the interviewer says.

"You think I can't leave him? I can leave him, my dear. I can leave him like that." She snaps her fingers, sprays tap water from her hand onto his powder blue coat, takes another sip of her teacup bourbon.

"Nothing gets older," the interviewer says, "than an old threat."

And it is clearly an old threat. This is the relentless circular conversation the unnamed woman and her unnamed interviewer have been conducting for twenty years—though she is happy to realize that it cannot possibly be twenty years because the interviewer looks the same as the first day she met him: "He'd been thin and snippy then and he was thin and snippy still. He still had the pegged pants, the blue sports coat, the suede shoes with plaid laces; he still yawned in her face and he still bit his nails. His hair was still crimped in oiled blond waves, there were no lines by his lips, and his cheeks, although sallow, were as smooth as a boy's." With exacting detail, Giles describes an interviewer as real-seeming as any oily game-show host. He has feelings. He has opinions. He has secret yearnings, desires, boredom, ennui. We absolutely believe in him. Yet, when the woman reaches out to touch him:

. . . . as always, he ducked away. Her fingers touched air.
Hot air, she said fondly. That's what you're full of.
Not me. . . . I'm not the one who's been saying I'm going to begin a new life, make something of myself.

The story continues, delightfully, with Molly Giles's signature wit and humor and glorious glittering detail, as a

back-and-forth dialogue between the "deeply unhappy, disappointed woman" and her interlocutor. "You could change,"
the interviewer tells her. "I cannot change," she answers. "You
could try," he says. "I hate my clothes," she responds.

We make no progress—this is the same conversation
they've been having for years. The colonel, who, we are told,
sits all day and night in front of the television with the light
flickering on his pistol—a sinister image—at last makes an
appearance. He is benign in his smiling obtuseness. His pistol
turns out to be a water gun. Is he any more real than the interviewer? Hard to say. Or rather, it is for the reader to say what
is "real" in the story, and what imagined. What is sinister and
what is benign.

At last, the interviewer, having reached the end of his
patience with the woman, and compelled by his own dreams,
tells her he is leaving the show: "I'm leaving you and I'm leaving the colonel and I'm leaving right now."

She doesn't believe him. She challenges him to explain to
her the issues, enumerate his reasons. She insults him, baits
him, berates him. In the end, he demands her final answer to
his final challenge—like the challenge of Rumpelstiltskin, he
demands she tell him his name:

> Asshole, she said. Mr. Jerk Stupid Asshole Junior. That
> is your name.
> When she looked up from laughing he was gone. Well
> go and good riddance, she cried. She swirled the last drop
> of bourbon in her cup.

The story ends with the woman lying down on the kitchen
floor with her bottle: "—she wanted to sleep for a second and
when she awoke she would have a good laugh at herself, her stupid fat self passed out on the floor like some old wino in some
hotel, yes that's what she'd do and then she would leave him."

Except—she won't.

There is nothing in the story to indicate the woman herself is changed. She's no more able to leave the colonel this day than any of the others before, no more capable of changing her life than any alcoholic or addict caught in the throes of addiction, unless something radical within the person changes—but I don't see it here. She'll awaken from her stupor and reach for her bourbon-filled teacup again. And because she needs him, and because she created him, the interviewer will show up again tomorrow morning—apologetic possibly, chagrined almost certainly—to ask his relentless unanswerable questions, to continue their private talk show wherein the woman will "continue to broadcast [her] innermost thoughts to the rest of the world."

This is how I read the story: a chilling and marvelously funny and finally heartbreaking story of an alcoholic woman bumping and blundering about her filthy kitchen in her pink fat dress with puffed sleeves she made herself, talking to the people in her head, filled with resentment and self-pity and snappy humor, lying to herself and to her imagined interlocutor; she is the star of her own show, promising that her life will change, her future will change, she will soon leave this misery—the colonel—and get a life. She will teach domestic arts at a high school. She will join the circus. She will leave, when she finally leaves, "in ranch mink and diamonds, with her hair piled high and something in her suitcase besides bunion pads and size sixteens." Every day, for twenty years, the dialogue, the empty promises, the excuses have been the same. We join the story on this particular day, when she has picked unripe blackberries and scorched them on the stove and made an effort at escape which took her, she says, as far as the swim club, because this is the day her interviewer finally says: "I feel if I don't leave now something might happen and I might never be able to leave you at all." That is what makes this day different from all the other days. That is the answer to the Passover question we are sometimes challenged to ask ourselves about our stories: "Why is this night different from all other nights?"

Molly Giles told me one time when I mentioned to her how much I love this story, and how I teach it and read it as the last irrevocable chance for the woman's life to change: Oh, but the interviewer *does* leave. He's gone. That's it. He's vanished never to return.

And I say, to myself, my students, maybe to the poor hapless unhappy unnamed woman herself: Don't be too sure.

Rilla Askew is the author of the short-story collection *Strange Business* (1992) and of the novels *The Mercy Seat* (1997), *Fire in Beulah* (2001), *Harpsong* (2007), and *Kind of Kin* (2013).

"A Cautionary Tale"
by Deborah Eisenberg

Andrea Barrett

"A Cautionary Tale" was first published in the March 23, 1987, issue of *The New Yorker*. It was collected in *Under the 82nd Airborne* (1992). It is currently most readily available in *The Collected Stories of Deborah Eisenberg* (Picador).

Of the many Deborah Eisenberg stories I cherish, I return most often to "A Cautionary Tale," her brilliant, acid-etched portrait of young people finding their way through an increasingly plutocratic New York. Even among such other gems of her *Collected Stories* as "The Custodian," "Twilight of the Superheroes," and "Some Other, Better Otto," it shines with what, in the words of one character, "in my opinion is, like, an irrefutably fatal dazzle."

The story, simple enough in outline, goes like this: Patty, an ambitious, conventional, earnest young woman, moves to New York, subletting a rent-controlled apartment from a devious college friend. Unwittingly she also acquires the absent college friend's burdensome neighbor, disheveled and impoverished Stuart, who is a crucial decade older than Patty. Over the course of a year, as Patty tries and fails to establish herself as a graphic designer, Stuart loses all his freelance jobs, falls behind on his rent, and moves into Patty's apartment. Not what Patty thinks of as boyfriend material, Stuart is brilliant, literary, self-destructively honest, and deeply hypochondriac as well as actually frail. He reads to Patty from *Tristes Tropiques* when he's in a good mood; quotes Christopher Marlowe after failing to lure her into bed; and—he's a committed socialist— tries to persuade her that her desires for success are unworthy.

Comic scenes ensue; also tragic scenes; also unbearably touching recognitions and reversals. A restaurant owner offers inexperienced Patty a waitressing job; when the restaurant catches on, Patty finds herself making money and meeting interesting people. Hapless Stuart sinks further, while a wealthy couple with co-op ambitions creeps into the upstairs apartment. Meanwhile such fabulously funny and heartbreaking minor characters as Mrs. Jorgenson, who has a habit of falling asleep on the hall floor; building superintendent Mr. Martinez, who longs for the family left at home in Colombia; and Ginger, "the gorgeous but moody prima of a troupe of huge male dancers," play their crucial roles in the plot. Patty and Stuart grow further apart, and eventually part.

Haven't we heard that before? Of course we have: and in versions not only familiar but sometimes maudlin, or sentimental, or trite. Yet in Eisenberg's telling this familiar rite of passage becomes bitingly intelligent, wildly funny, and deeply sad. I can't be sure how she works this magic, but I suspect that one source is her flexible third-person voice, which glides back and forth between a rendition of Patty's inner life close enough to reveal every hesitation and mistaken perception, and an overarching intelligence distant enough to render what young Patty can't yet understand. Henry James couldn't do it better, and this double voice, simultaneously within and without, is really what makes the story *possible*.

You can't read even the opening paragraph without being seduced by its elegant ironies. Not even a single sentence. I always return to this, which reveals an aspect of friendship we've all glimpsed, without being able to understand or articulate it:

> All along, Patty had been unaware that time is as adhesive as love, and that the more time you spend with someone the greater the likelihood of finding yourself with a permanent sort of thing to deal with that people casually refer to as "friendship," as if that were the end of the matter, when the truth is that even if "your friend" does something annoying, or if you and "your friend" decide that you hate each other, or if "your friend" moves away and you lose each other's address, you still have a *friendship*, and although it can change shape, look different in different lights, become an embarrassment or an encumbrance or a sorrow, it can't simply cease to have existed, no matter how far into the past it sinks, so attempts to disavow or destroy it will not merely constitute betrayals of friendship but, more practically, are bound to be fruitless, causing damage only to the humans involved rather than to that gummy jungle (friendship) in which those humans have entrapped themselves, so if sometime in the future you're not going to want to have been a particular person's friend, or if you're not going to want to have had the particular friendship you and that person can make with one another, then don't be friends with that person at all, don't talk to that person, don't go anywhere near that person, because as soon as you start to see something from that person's point of view (which, inevitably, will be as soon as you stand next to that person) common ground is sure to slide under your feet.

Poor Stuart. Poor Patty! Yet the depiction of their doomed friendship is only one layer in a story that is also about the life and death of cities, and the loss of innocence, and, ultimately, about our longing for paradise.

Over the years I have so densely underscored and annotated my copy that I can't always track what I noticed when, but each time I read the story I seem to find more references, implicit and explicit, to this longing. Stuart, that "little humid wad," reminds Patty that "Manhattan's just a playpen for rich people now, but it used to be paradise, Patty, I'm telling you—a haven for the dispossessed." When he reads Levi-Strauss to her, the passage he chooses is about the Caduveo women's dream, expressed in their graphic art, of "an inaccessible golden age." Everywhere there are glimpses of gleaming forests, radiant suns, a "golden sweep of field distantly edged by tiny pointed mountains."

Patty, who thinks of the restaurant where she waitresses as limbo, a place where, despite the rich array of experiences it offers, she is only waiting for her real life to begin, has a cramped, late-twentieth-century, capitalist version of paradise, consisting of little more than a shiny drafting board, a brownstone, and a mysterious handsome escort—but even so, she has her dream. By the end of the story, that wise narrative voice, and the glimpses of alternate versions of paradise as conceived by the other characters, teach us what Patty's too young to know: that the life she's living right now will itself come to seem like very heaven.

Andrea Barrett is the author of the short-story collections *Ship Fever* (1996), which won the National Book Award, *Servants of the Map* (2002), which was a Pulitzer Prize finalist, and *Archangel* (2013), which was a finalist for The Story Prize, as well as of the novels *Lucid Stars* (1988), *Secret Harmonies* (1989), *The Middle Kingdom* (1991), *The Forms of Water* (1993), *The Voyage of the Narwhal* (1998), and *The Air We Breathe* (2007). Her fiction and essays have appeared in *Best American Short Stories*, *Best American Science Writing*, *Best American Essays*, and *O. Henry Prize Stories*. She received the Rea Award for the Short Story in 2015.

"The Wounded Soldier"
by George Garrett

Richard Bausch

"The Wounded Soldier" was originally published and collected in *Cold Ground Was My Bed Last Night* (1964). It is currently most readily available, in a slightly revised text, in the sixth edition of *The Norton Anthology of Short Fiction* (W. W. Norton).

I had been to the University of Alabama, upon the invitation of their Writing Program, so that we could look each other over, as it were. Two days of visits with faculty, with the Dean, and with students. I gave a reading, and answered questions, and there was a polite party at the end of the whole thing. George Garrett had been at the University all fall, as a resident writer, and we were driving north together. He was hard at work on *The King of Babylon Shall Not Come Against You*, and had large parts of it in various disorganized-looking folders, in a satchel, that he had shoved into an overnight bag and put with all his other stuff, when we packed the trunk of the car.

It was almost Christmas. Everybody had been pleasant; the students were particularly kind. We'd said our good-byes at the party, and headed out fairly late in the evening. I'd had a little bourbon, and I could feel it behind my eyes—a warm glow. There were Christmas lights off in the dark, on either side of the road. We drove through a fine mist, talking.

We had been on the road together many times before, and I knew what to expect: stories spinning inside stories, jokes, streams of satire on the various kinds of culture-folly we live with—from bad movies and television, to monstrously shallow celebrities, to the bad councils of local and national governments, and—oh!—all the deplorable pieties of the idiotic present.

Laughs all the way, of course. Lots of those. Great talk, about everything. But mostly laughs. For a while we talked about a novel of Stephen Becker's, set at the end of the Civil War, and then we talked about Becker for a while: his fine translation of André Schwarz-Bart's *The Last of the Just.* We talked about the new books of mutual friends, and about some of the fine people we had just been with. He asked about the book I was writing (*Good Evening Mr. & Mrs. America, and All the Ships at Sea*), which he had heard small sections of. I hadn't made a lot of progress that fall, so there wasn't much to tell about it. It was coming along as my books usually do, by stops and starts. I asked about *King of Babylon*, and he said he was busy re-organizing a lot of it. There were time elements involved. I said I hoped he would read to me from it at some point during the journey, and, characteristically, he waved this away, changing the subject.

Soon we were laughing about politicians, not the big lie but the ten thousand small ones, and all the forms of human folly available to the modern idiot. There was the country's curious madness for *any* kind of celebrity (things had gone completely bat shit; we now had celebrity criminals: the murderer of John Lennon, with his copy of *Catcher in the Rye* on the cover of *People* magazine), and the recent spate of TV freak shows played out in the name of some weird voyeurism that was loose in the land.

Sometime after it was too late to think about restaurants, we checked into a motel. The cold mist was still falling. We walked through it, across the street, to a liquor store, where we bought some whiskey and a six-pack of bottled beer. Next to the liquor store was a gas station with a Food Mart attached, where we got some cold-cut sandwiches, and bags of corn chips. A feast.

In the room, we unwrapped the sandwiches, opened a bag of the chips and a couple of the beers, and I put the TV on. News. We sat watching this, sipping the beer, and eating. The beer was wonderfully cold, and I opened another very quickly after finishing my first. I decided I didn't want any of the whiskey. "You want another beer?" I asked Garrett. "Or should I open the whiskey?"

"No," he said. "I'm beat. I'm gonna turn in."

He lay down on his bed, put his hands over his eyes, and we talked on for a while, me drinking the second beer, and finishing my sandwich. The news ended, and then there was an ad about this Tennessee station's news program. I remarked that it was funny to think how the ads for these TV news teams always made it appear as though their work were some kind of community service, an altruistic undertaking on their part. In answer to this, Garrett took on the voice of a newscaster. "Want a solution to that nagging heart attack? Stay tuned."

I laughed.

"Health threat that might kill you at any minute. Details at eleven."

Finally he went into the bathroom and took a shower, and I had the third beer. A selection from his military fiction called *The Old Army Game: A Novel and Stories* had just come out from SMU Press, and he had given me my copy earlier in the day. I lay down and read the introduction, and the foreword.

He came out of the bathroom, and, crossing to his bed, sighed good-naturedly. "Oh, me."

This is an expression he used in a multitude of circumstances, but often enough when he was tired.

"Me, too," I said. I sat up and brought another bottle of beer out of the bag. "Want to split this?"

"Sure."

I poured half of it into one of the motel glasses, and gave it to him. We talked a little more, winding down. Finally he got under the covers, and was asleep very quickly. I lay sipping the last of the beer, reading in *The Old Army Game.*

I turned to "The Wounded Soldier." I had remembered the story from almost twenty years earlier—I'd first read it in an anthology a professor of mine published with Prentice-Hall: one of those college readers. At the time, I didn't know Garrett. I had only read *Death of the Fox*, the massive, intricately faceted and brilliant first novel of his Elizabethan trilogy. I remember that the thing that most impressed me about the story was its compression; that the same mind that had created *Death of the Fox* had created this astonishingly effective little story.

All the years later, re-reading it in a motel room somewhere on the highway in East Tennessee, it struck me that good fortune had taken me in directions I never would have imagined. Here I was, reading "The Wounded Soldier," and in the next bed Garrett had begun to snore and flute and sigh in sleep.

Here is the story's opening paragraph:

> When the time came at last and they removed the wealth
> of bandages from his head and face, all with the greatest
> of care as if they were unwinding a precious mummy, the
> Doctor—he of the waxed, theatrical, upswept mustache and
> the wet sad eyes of a beagle hound—turned away. Orderlies

and aides coughed, looked at floor and ceiling, busied themselves with other tasks. Only the Head Nurse, a fury stiff with starch and smelling of strong soap, looked, pink-cheeked and pale white as fresh flour, over the Veteran's shoulders. She stared back at him, unflinching and expressionless, from the swimming light of the mirror.

Note the use of the word "wealth" in the first sentence, and the phrase "precious mummy," and the Doctor, with his "waxed, theatrical, upswept mustache." And the description of the nurse, the use of the word "fury," coupled with the smell of "strong soap"—look at how everything in the passage contributes to everything else—and you have a sense of how densely packed this story is.

It seems a perfectly wrought parable about war, and the nature of human responses to its effects, and it wouldn't have to be anything more than that to succeed—but it moves through its events with a shifting, illusory, almost biblical simplicity, and manages to take several unexpected turns, while striking deep into one's own attitudes and suspicions about life, and beauty, and Art, and ugliness. It is a story you never forget. I am and have been convinced, over these last twenty years since I first encountered it, that it is in its understated, disturbing, cruelly apt way a miniature masterpiece, like one of those amazing carved wooden rosary beads from the fourteenth century.

So here I was, re-reading this gem, while its creator, whom I had come to call my friend and whom I loved like an older brother, lay snoring, loud as a horse, in the next bed. It made me smile to think of it. All the thousands of miles we'd traveled together in the last fourteen years, all the good food and drink and talk, and the other pals gathered round us, and the students, too, and Garrett telling stories, or cueing me to tell

them. The tumult of those voices and those happy passages—
and at the heart of it all, the central thing was this gift, this
blessed occupation: writing, our mutual work, the anguish
and celebration that we always had between us, the *defining*
thing every writer lives with, and some writers suffer with.

It seemed rather wondrous to me that the imagination, the
secret heart and soul of the astonishingly gifted writer who was
sleeping so well nearby, was first given to me in the printed
words on a page.

As I finished reading the story again, I felt oddly as though
I had traveled some miraculous distance. And of course, I had.
The story had cast its strange spell, exactly as it did twenty
years ago, when I was starting out and hoping I might be able
to turn myself into a real writer, a writer who might one day
make stories as good and daring as this one is. It had altered
the inner landscape again, and made me forget everything but
itself, murmuring in my head, even as the noise its author
was continually making over there in the next bed grew even
louder.

I closed the book, satisfied, and turned the light out. And
went to sleep.

In the morning, too early—it was still dark—we were
awakened by a terrifying sound: the alarm, a horrible shrill
scream of a buzzing ring, was going off. There wasn't any light.
I groped on the nightstand among the empty beer bottles,
my glasses, and the book, and got the thing turned off. We
laughed about the panic-stricken sound our voices made in the
blackness, through the shriek of the alarm.

"God almighty," I said. "I thought it was the end of the
world."

"I thought it was the end of us," Garrett said.

I lay there in the dark, laughing. "Oh, man," he said.

It was quiet. We could hear the highway outside. Neither of us was going to get any more sleep. I got up and went in and took a shower. He slept on a little.

As we were packing up to continue the journey, I said, "Hey, I read 'The Wounded Soldier' again last night. Man, that's such a great story."

He deflected this with a laugh.

"It is," I said.

"Oh, me," George Garrett said.

Well, it is.

Richard Bausch is the author of the short-story collections *Spirits and Other Stories* (1987), *The Fireman's Wife and Other Stories* (1990), *Rare & Endangered Species* (1994), *Selected Stories of Richard Bausch* (1996), *Someone to Watch Over Me: Stories* (1999), *The Stories of Richard Bausch* (2003), *Something Is Out There* (2010), and *Living in the Weather of the World* (2017), as well as of twelve novels. He won the PEN/Malamud Award for Excellence in the Short Story in 2004 and the Rea Award for the Short Story in 2012.

"Consolation" by Richard Bausch

Ann Beattie

"Consolation" was originally published in the March 19, 1990, issue of *The New Yorker*. It was collected in *The Fireman's Wife and Other Stories* (1990). It is currently most readily available in *The Stories of Richard Bausch* (HarperCollins).

"Consolation" is the sequel to Richard Bausch's exhilaratingly depressing story, "The Fireman's Wife," though it stands on its own and reverberates with enough shock waves that you need not have read part one in order to be stunned by part two. "Consolation" is deliberately not a proper sequel, in which we would meet all the main characters again, but rather a kind of sidebar—a reminder that there are always more characters on the sidelines, and that they, too, have their stories, which inevitably impinge on the stories of the characters we know and, by implication, those we might yet meet. The stories are not exactly a one-two punch—Bausch is too adeptly persuasive a writer, too compassionate (a word George Garrett has aptly applied to Bausch's writing), ultimately, to hit you only in the gut—so although there are moments in "The Fireman's Wife" that make you feel physical pain, "Consolation" reverses the score a bit and is more concerned with phantom pain. Of course, phantom pain is more insidious, and dealing with phantom pain means that the writer has to haunt the reader—along with the character, of course—with what is not, rather than with what is. It's easy to jump out of a closet and scare someone. It is more difficult to make the reader imagine a closet where one doesn't exist, and for the dramatic jump to have transpired long before your story begins. Eudora Welty has dealt with ephemeral, missed moments that nevertheless can be brilliantly conjured up, through the pace of the story and through the writer's language, in "No Place For You, My Love," in which she out*Gatsby*s Fitzgerald. Reynolds Price also comes to mind, with his long, brilliant story about grief, "Walking Lessons." Actually, there is quite a bit of American literature that is about afterwards. Maybe it figures, because our country's identity is the identity of afterwards.

"Consolation" is about a trip a widowed woman takes with her sister, to visit her dead husband's parents, so they can meet their grandson. Bausch's story does not have an ironic title. Though his characters may be caught up in ironies, he presents the stories straightforwardly—or as logically as such complex lives can be revealed in chronological time. They are usually presented simply, in the telling of moment-to-moment events, though they become complex as you begin to sense the structure. What was a realistic painting suddenly becomes a hologram, so convincing, so three-dimensional, that you cannot possibly think the depth is an illusion, and, concomitantly, a surreal quality begins to emerge: the unspoken begins to take on a life of its own. Like other of his stories, "Consolation" does not tell you that everything is OK, but it does tell you that the world is still there. From first story to second, the details permutate; they are different in their specifics, but not in their ability to be disquieting. Gone are the party tiki lights of "The Fireman's Wife," replaced—such as they are—by equally sad exotica: "They drink tropical punch from cans."

The "they" are Milly Harmon, new mother and recent
widow, and her (chronologically) older sister, Meg, who has
accompanied her to Philadelphia so Milly's in-laws can meet
the child born after their son's death. Aside from introducing
us to the characters, the first things described for the reader
are a boy who is swimming and a fat woman lying poolside.
Active and passive, they express Milly's internal conflict: movement is essential; movement may take her, essentially, nowhere.
Which, for a while, looks like the real danger: her in-laws seem
distant, perhaps even uncaring; her sister, who we sense might
do just about anything because she's so desperate and so good
at rationalizing, seems a parody of movement as progress.
Though Milly has decided that after her husband's death she
must proceed, Meg—who has suffered no such tragedy—is so
conflicted over the collapse of her own marriage that it seems
she is essentially along for the ride; this one, or perhaps almost
any other, might offer equal consolation. Meg is not a simple
character, though: she's wise about some things—though the
wisdom has the super-sharp edge of cynicism—and imma-
ture and/or irresponsible about her approach to other important things. Still, Meg is our oracle—or as likely an oracle as
we're going to get in this story. If Milly's panic is imploding,
her sister is exploding—or always about to. Possible parameters are conjured up for us: the active swimmer or the passive
sunbather. Milly, setting a trajectory for herself and her sister,
struggling like some poor creature caught in a spider's web,
desperate to believe in the next big breeze.

We are reminded of and haunted by Milly's husband
Wally's death even when that death is not the overt subject—
perhaps most of all when it is not. We learn that Wally's troubled father leaves the table when "his dinner was still steaming
on his plate." Later, in a brilliant description that links the new
baby to the dead father, there are "fleecy clouds that look like

filaments of steam." The story is much concerned with things that have—so to speak—gone up in smoke: Meg's marriage, on the verge of collapse (she hears about people who have more-or-less reconciled whom she cynically considers "Tied to each other on a rock in space."); Milly, of course, has lost Wally to fire, and Meg's estranged husband may even re-claim his wife, leaving Milly abandoned a second time. Steam might be a perfectly fine metaphor in any number of stories, but it works so well in Bausch's because it subtly directs our attention upward; as we watch it dissipate, we no doubt remember the fire (though we were never present), at the same time we gaze skyward, anticipating the eventual fireworks display at story's end (which also doesn't get staged for us). Much happens off-camera in the story just as it does in real life, but because aspects of the tragedy permutate as they are evoked, they come to seem hyper-real. There is the fact of Wally's death, an inherently dramatic death, but it is in the softer, more diffuse, ghostly vaporous steam that we sense his death reflected again and again. One moment, in effect, repeats itself and masquer-ades as another . . . which leads to another observation:

Throughout the story, there are suggestions of people in costume: Larry, Meg's husband, in his discordant clothing, is described by that very word. But Meg, too, is in costume; she wears a kimono, which she artfully arranges to attract atten-tion. The baby, too, is masquerading: named after his father, he is, instead, nicknamed "Zeke." Harmon, who has brought in an enormous stuffed bear for his grandson (we can't help but think of his dead son, of course, when he "has it over his shoulder, like a man lugging a body"), is said to stand in an "intentionally ramrod-stiff way . . . the stance, he would say, of an old military man, which happens to be exactly what he is." So Harmon resorts to the posture, as if it will be some help to him, just as Larry, in his odd bohemian get-up, tries to emulate a safe but scintillating stereotype of the artist in order to get what he wants. Only Milly, whose childhood nickname was "Stick," seems unconcerned with how she appears physically, and indifferent to appearances, in general, though she is nevertheless concerned with what people think of her ("So much of her own life seems somehow duplicitous to her, as if the wish to please others and to be well thought of had somehow dulled the edges of her identity and left her with nothing but a set of received impressions."). One way or another, all the characters are acting, and as they act, Bausch reveals to the reader more than the characters consciously know. Larry is not only foolishly dressed; more importantly, he displays his emotional wound when his turtleneck is described, "its dark colors bleeding into each other across the front." The masquerades are troubling and troublingly transparent. When Mr. Harmon speaks of the past, he invokes it at first nostalgically ("There used to be a big field out this way—") with regret for what has passed, but in wanting to placate his wife, who remembers her dead son's boyhood in connection with those fields, he insists—hardly to the point, but characteristic of his love of the status quo—that (speaking of the fireworks), "They still put on a good show." Which is what they all strive to do, as Meg announced earlier in the first overt mention of a performance ("Hey," Meg says. "It's your show.").

As the story nears the end, we see everyone's personal show played against the backdrop of the Fourth of July, the fireworks-to-be conjuring up not only war (Mr. Harmon's connection to the military; Larry's chest-wound shirt; even Meg, who describes herself this way, in a moment of despair: "Good lord, I look like war."), but the explosive fire in which Wally died, as well. Literarily, Meg has said more than she knows when she announces, early on, that the Harmons' odd behavior is the result of "the war" ("I think the war got them. That whole generation."). No doubt, but as Bausch demonstrates, there are different kinds of war, and one of them might be the battle you have to wage with yourself to stay sane. At the point of the story when Milly shudders, remembering Wally, Meg calls it right again: "You looked like something hurt you . . . you were thinking about Wally."

No psychic abilities are called for. Of course Wally's death has been the subtext for everything that happens in the story, and that undertow—through image and language and analogy—takes us repeatedly back to the past, even as the story moves relentlessly forward. We have Meg to thank for her words of wisdom, and Meg to pity for the pain her awareness has brought her. An ostensible celebration becomes for her—and therefore, for us—something quite different: "All these years of independence," Meg says. "So people like us can have these wonderful private lives." It's difficult not to expel a cynical snort of agreement with Meg after that observation, but she is speaking not only to assert what she believes (or fears), but to re-state an important element of the story. Which is that the private almost inevitably becomes public—on one level, that's what all stories are about, because what a storyteller does is expose people's lives—but thematically, within the world of this particular story, the smoke never quite clears: it's as if we squint and strain to hear, just as the characters do, hoping for clarification, but fearing it at the same time. Even Meg's husband's ludicrously bad poetry is concerned with his eyes—with his frustrated attempt to see. Things take their course, whether those things be fires, or fireworks displays, and the challenging question—the one it has interested Bausch to explore, here and elsewhere—becomes how one copes.

Certainly, in the larger sense, independence has guaranteed us nothing, but a certain independence of spirit—a reaching out that can result in a firmer bond with another person, rather than separateness—seems to be an idea. When Milly at last hands her baby to its grandmother (we do not fail to notice that this is the baby she was never willing to relinquish to wounded, cynical Meg), something has come full circle. For a moment, everyone has suspended thoughts of separateness and independence. Instead, they have become interdependent, and in that state—like buddies in battle—they can best go forward.

Ann Beattie is the author of the short-story collections *Distortions* (1976), *Secrets and Surprises* (1978), *The Burning House* (1982), *What Was Mine* (1991), *Where You'll Find Me and Other Stories* (1986), *Park City* (1998), *Perfect Recall* (2001), *Follies: New Stories* (2005), *The New Yorker Stories* (2010), *The State We're In: Maine Stories* (2015), and *The Accomplished Guest* (2017), as well as of eight novels and a novella. Her stories have appeared in four O. Henry Award collections, in *The Best American Short Stories of the Century*, and in *The Best American Short Stories*. She won the PEN/Malamud Award for Excellence in the Short Story in 2000 and the Rea Award for the Short Story in 2005.

"Where Is the Voice Coming From?" by Eudora Welty

Doris Betts

"Where Is the Voice Coming From?" was originally published in the July 6, 1963, issue of *The New Yorker*. It was collected and is currently most readily available in *The Collected Stories of Eudora Welty* (Harcourt Brace).

A real event—the murder of civil-rights activist Medgar Evers on June 12, 1963, in his own driveway—sparked Eudora Welty's monologue story "Where Is the Voice Coming From?" She wrote the story at white heat at one sitting the night Evers was shot down in Jackson, Mississippi, where they both lived. By 1999 other real events were bringing a new generation of readers to the story. The victim's surviving brother, Charles Evers, had published his autobiography; the widow, Myrlie Evers-Williams, had become chairman of the NAACP board of directors and written her memoir; and Hollywood had issued a film, *Ghosts of Mississippi*, about why it took thirty years and three juries to convict the white murderer Welty had imagined on paper.

Little of Welty's work has such a sense of art imitating life or so direct a link with current events. In her 1965 article for *The Atlantic Monthly*, "Must the Novelist Crusade?" she warned against stock characters who might only represent ideas—even if these were good ideas. Yet at least one reader sees this story as a move from aesthetics to ethics. This story stands out as a rare comment on her times, and unlike most of Welty's other stories, which were written more deliberately, "Powerhouse" and this one each came out in their essential shape at one sitting. Welty was at work on *Losing Battles* in the summer of 1963 and has told several interviewers that "Voice" just pushed right through that novel. Comparison of her typed draft (then called "From the Unknown") with the version *The New Yorker* got into galleys just two weeks after the killing shows Welty condensing the story while editor William Maxwell and *The New Yorker* lawyers worked to make it less actionable, since a suspect with similarities to her character had been arrested before the story ran on July 6.

A third distinction of the story is that only five other Welty narratives are written in first-person point of view, and none this intensely. *The Ponder Heart*, "Why I Live at the P.O.," "Kin," "A Memory," and "Circe" are all in first person, though Welty has said the last was not spoken aloud but was more a soliloquy or meditation. But "Voice" does seem to be spoken aloud, by the end almost hummed to the twang of a cheap guitar, and its brevity (only two pages when published in *The New Yorker*) makes it a fine dramatic monologue for actors or speech students. In an interview with Linda Kuehl in *The Paris Review*, Welty said she wrote the story to discover who committed the murder, not his name "but his nature," and she believed she had come close to "pinpointing his mind." The killer she envisioned was of the same type Bob Dylan depicted in his song about the same murder, "Only a Pawn in Their Game." His lyrics portray a poor white controlled by his circumstances and by the Establishment.

Both were mistaken. One friend told Welty, "You thought it was a Snopes and it was a Compson."

Instead of being poor white trash, Byron De La Beckwith, the real-life murderer, claimed to be the grandson of a general in Nathan Bedford Forrest's cavalry. He had grown up on a plantation near where Emmett Till, fourteen and black, was also killed, for allegedly flirting with a young white woman, his body dumped into the Tallahatchie River. Yet it was a long way down from an old Delta family that had once owned some of Jefferson Davis's china to this fertilizer salesman called "De-Lay" by his friends, an anti-Semite and member of both the segregationist Citizens' Council and the Klan.

Despite Beckwith's claims to a planter background, this twenty-five-hundred-word interior monologue—boiled down from forty-five typescript pages of revised sections—could have been spoken in his bitter, racist voice. Welty's nameless murderer begins by talking to his wife about another voice, that of a black activist on TV in Thermopylae. He describes to her the route he took through a hell-hot night, to a house not too far across town from his own, envying its outside lights, paved street, and garage—the house where Roland Summers lives.

Summers drives up in his white (of course) car. Like all cowards, the narrator shoots Roland in the back, his envy and rage reflecting that of poor whites described in Lillian Smith's *Killers of the Dream*. The victim's horrified wife runs out to the body; the killer drops his rifle and flees home to his own wife's scorn. When news of the murder breaks, the narrator realizes that he has inadvertently fed a martyr to the civil-rights cause and that he will never be credited with this one most vivid act of his paltry life. He rationalizes the coming race war he predicts, even desires, and by letting escape a few details about his boyhood betrays how warped and small and pitiable his years have been. Gone is the mockingbird that was singing through the hell-hot night just before he pulled the trigger.

Gone is that split second when he and the bird felt briefly on top of the world. Now there is nothing left but his old guitar that—unlike the gun he dropped when he fled—he never lost, sold, pawned except briefly, never gave away; and with "nobody home but me," the killer plays and sings "a-down, down, down, down. Down."

As John Kuehl reveals in *Creative Writing and Rewriting: Contemporary American Novelists at Work* (1967), Welty made changes as the story metamorphosed from life to art. Medgar's name became Roland, the state ceased to be Mississippi, and Jackson turned into Thermopylae with its associations of the brave Spartans. The outgoing governor, Ross Barnett, had originally been mentioned as a lawyer the killer might hire, but Welty cut out that reference after the real Beckwith did hire Barnett's law firm; she replaced it with general resentments of President Kennedy and the federal government. (As it turned out, on the last day of Beckwith's first mistrial, the real Ross Barnett came into the courtroom and shook hands with him in full view of the jury.) Other revisions Welty made with heat and light/dark imagery underscore both the hot night and the hot rifle barrel, so the final singing never rises to the mockingbird's high treble, but seems to slide down the circles of the inferno.

In real life, Medgar Evers, just shy of thirty-seven, son of an illiterate sawmill worker and part-time Pentecostal preacher, was killed just after midnight outside his home on Guynes Street, in the only black middle-class subdivision in Jackson, where poet and novelist Margaret Walker also lived. Other turbulent events in Mississippi preceded the murder. The previous fall, James Meredith had tried to enroll at Ole Miss; he is mentioned in Welty's story. Marches, sit-ins, and demonstrations had been underway in Jackson for two years. As described by John R. Salter in *Jackson, Mississippi: An American Chronicle of Struggle and Schism* (1979), earlier in 1963, six hundred black children had marched in its streets, and riot police had loaded them into garbage trucks and hauled them to the state fairgrounds to be enclosed behind what NAACP leader Roy Wilkins called "hog wire." In Welty's story, these children sing with little new American flags in their hands, which policemen knock loose. (But, says the killer sourly, "children can just get 'em more flags.")

According to Willie Morris in *The Ghosts of Medgar Evers: A Tale of Race, Murder, Mississippi, and Hollywood* (1998) and Maryanne Vollers in *Ghosts of Mississippi: The Murder of Medgar Evers, the Trials of Byron De La Beckwith, and the Haunting of the New South* (1995), Evers had already had a firebomb tossed into his carport that spring of 1963 but would not flee the city. He told the *New York Times*, "I may be going to Heaven or Hell, but I'll be going from Jackson." On the afternoon before the shooting, he notified the FBI that a police car had tried to run him down. This was also the day on which two black students were admitted to the University of Alabama, and Evers had watched Kennedy speak on television about integration. (Welty probably saw this too.) After a rally, Evers came home knowing his three children had also been allowed to watch TV and wait up for him. At the sound of the rifle shot, they hit the floor as they'd been trained. The wounded Evers dragged himself almost forty feet through scattered bloody sweatshirts that said JIM CROW MUST GO. After the bullet from a 1917 Enfield army rifle went through him, through his living room window, through that wall into the kitchen, hit the refrigerator, and ended up on a countertop, someone was heard running away.

As for the real murderer, Vollers reveals that Beckwith was a Shriner, a Mason, state treasurer of the Sons of the American Revolution, a Sunday-school teacher at the Episcopal church in Greenwood. As in Welty's story, the gun was dropped in honeysuckle when the killer fled from the ambush, and it was a fingerprint that matched Beckwith's from the Marine Corps that got him charged. He had been wounded at Tarawa. He had married a WAVE he met during World War II three times and then a woman he met through anti-Semitic organizations. Despite the evidence, two policemen provided him an alibi and helped hang juries in the spring and winter of 1964.

In 1967 Beckwith ran for Lieutenant Governor and came in fifth in a field of six. He was indicted again in 1990, self-published his autobiography in 1991, and on February 5, 1994, was at last convicted of Evers's murder. By then some witnesses were dead; the bullet that had ricocheted so far was missing; the accused was old and sick. A conviction might never have been won if, in the 1970s, Beckwith had not tried to bomb the headquarters of the Anti-Defamation League in New Orleans and, while in a Louisiana penitentiary, boasted to a guard about the Evers case.

The temperament and motivation of real and fictional murderers do coincide, though their backgrounds do not. Adam Nossiter, writing of the Evers murder in *Of Long Memory: Mississippi and the Murder of Medgar Evers* (1994), says that Welty's story "represented wishful thinking by a member of Mississippi's tiny enlightened class" and adds that "Beckwith's kin could have rubbed shoulders with Welty's." Other critics have objected that both the singing mocking-bird and Welty's figurative "wings of a bird" that spread darkly across Roland's bleeding back and pulled him down are images of too great sensitivity to come from the mind of an assassin like Welty's nameless one, and certainly not from Beckwith's. But of course they miss Welty's point. Hitler liked Wagner's music; Raskolnikov wins some pity. Writers have always explored characters they'd not bring home for a weekend, and in *One Writer's Beginnings* (1984), Welty says, "I don't believe my anger showed me anything about human character that my sympathy and rapport never had." What they show in this story, of course, is that the voices in the story come first from Medgar Evers (Roland Summers) and then the unnamed killer (Byron De La Beckwith) and, worst of all, from deep inside the worst part of the reader, of ourselves. Jan Nordby Gretlund writes in *Eudora Welty's Aesthetics of Place* (1994) that Welty "knows very well where the voice comes from," and, finally, we have to admit that so do we.

Why choose this story out of many of Welty's that are better known, more complex, probably more durable? Some fictions are a good teach, a good read, a good speak. In my writing classes at the University of North Carolina, "Where Is the Voice Coming From?" is all three. Read it aloud to beginning writers and you can talk about point of view, characterization, the differences and similarity of fact and fiction, about passionate emotion and how it is transmuted.

But I also owe two personal debts to this story. Its ballad structure suggested to me the ballad shape of a story of mine, "The Ugliest Pilgrim," though that one ends on the upside with the same high piercing note Joan Baez sings at the end of "Old Blue." And the dramatic monologue suggested the method to tell a true child-abuse story from eastern North Carolina in "This Is the Only Time I'll Tell It."

Both Welty's killer and Beckwith, by the way, would hate the changes in—and their legacy to—what Welty called in the Fall 1973 *Mississippi Quarterly* "that world of hate that I felt I grew up with." Evers was buried in Arlington Cemetery. A bronze statue of him was unveiled in the summer of 1992. And Beckwith, at last convicted and—ironically—led from the courtroom by two black policemen, has his own monument in his film portrait by actor James Woods, a performance that film critic Roger Ebert said shows a "vile, damaged man with a shifty squirmy hatefulness." And Welty's story exists in its own right, but will always cause readers to think of the real lives of both real men and to cope with the all-too-real voice of envy and bias inside themselves.

Doris Betts (1932–2012) is the author of the short-story collections *The Gentle Insurrection* (1954), *The Astronomer and Other Stories* (1965), and *Beasts of the Southern Wild* (1973), as well as of six novels. She won the American Academy of Arts and Letters Medal of Merit for her short stories in 1989.

"How Can I Tell You?" by John O'Hara

Frederick Busch

"How Can I Tell You?" was originally published in the December 1, 1962, issue of *The New Yorker*. It was collected in *The Hat on the Bed* (1963). It is currently most readily available in *The Collected Stories of John O'Hara* (Random House).

I return to John O'Hara's "How Can I Tell You?" for the electricity of its dialogue, the pungent lightness of its details, the economy of its construction, and the sense of immensity O'Hara generates beneath its concrete matter-of-factness— what Auden describes in his 1937 "As I Walked Out One Evening":

> O plunge your hands in water,
> Plunge them in up to the wrist;
> Stare, stare in the basin
> And wonder what you've missed.
>
> The glacier knocks in the cupboard,
> The desert sighs in the bed,
> And the crack in the tea-cup opens
> A lane to the land of the dead.

John O'Hara published about four hundred short stories and, since his death, during recurring periods of interest in his work, editors have found and published more. He was one of the most productive and, every once in a while, one of the most brilliant and capable, writers of short fiction in the history of the form. To readers of a certain age, he is identified with *The New Yorker*, where, until August 20, 1949, he published regularly. After that date—it marks the issue in which the magazine ran a negative review of O'Hara's novel *A Rage to Live*—he did not publish there for eleven years. He claimed, in fact, to have stopped writing short stories in 1949 and, according to his Random House editor, Albert Erskine, in his foreword to O'Hara's previously uncollected short fiction in *The Time Element & Other Stories* (1972), did not begin to write them again until 1960, when he and the magazine were once more friendly.

"How Can I Tell You?," a 1962 story, is a good example of what Lionel Trilling called in his introduction to *Selected Short Stories of John O'Hara* (1956) O'Hara's "passionate commitment to verisimilitude," a manifestation of O'Hara's "brilliant awareness of the differences within the national sameness"— terms of praise one could well apply, by the way, to much of the work of Raymond Carver.

In a story called "Summer's Day" (*Selected Short Stories of John O'Hara* [86–92]), written during O'Hara's first great wave of short fiction, he creates Mr. and Mrs. Attrell, who encounter some local citizenry at the beach. The Attrells' daughter, it is revealed in a conversation overheard by Mr. Attrell, hanged herself. Wondering how he can ever again face the local man who spoke up for him and Mrs. Attrell, and wondering how he can in fact face his wife, Mr. Attrell at last realizes "that there was really nothing to face, really nothing." The "nothing" with which Mr. Attrell is faced is both death and the death-in-life, the *nada*, of which Hemingway wrote in "A Clean, Well-Lighted Place." When he is at his best, O'Hara conveys the "nothing" *and* the verisimilitude—Mr. Attrell drives to the beach in "a shiny black 1932 Buick with fairly good rubber and only about thirty thousand miles on it"—in a simultaneousness of effect that creates powerful resonance: the reader inhabits the fictive world's itness and emptiness at once. (It is when O'Hara is unable to establish the truth to his characters of "nothing" that his details overwhelm his work, and he produces banality—in *A Rage to Live*, say, or *Ten North Frederick*, or stories that are smugly seasoned with trendy names and events while offering characters about whose fate we cannot care.)

"Nothing" is at the heart of "How Can I Tell You?" So are the details that make O'Hara at his best such fun to read. A student of American culture would have to consider our mercantile stories—from Melville's seed salesman in "The Tartarus of Maids," and his Confidence-Man, through those archetypal snake-oil salesmen of *The Adventures of Huckleberry Finn*, the king and the duke, to Hemingway's "One Trip Across" and "The Tradesman's Return" (later incorporated into *To Have and Have Not*), to Faulkner's *The Hamlet*, to Welty's "Death of a Traveling Salesman," through Miller's *Death of a Salesman* and Mamet's *Glengarry Glen Ross* to Raymond Carver's "Collectors"—and, surely, "How Can I Tell You?" would have to be part of this list.

It begins with the salesman's litany that knits it together from beginning to middle to end: "A T-Bird and two Galaxies," the selling of which mark a very good day's work. Mark McGranville is a veteran car salesman who in the course of a story laden with verisimilitude comes face-to-face with "nothing," or, more precisely, understands that he has been confronting it all along. (As in so many O'Hara stories and novels—and beginning with the Maugham parable about death that is the epigraph to his first and best novel,

Appointment in Samarra [1934]—death or its cousin, "nothing," is associated with a woman.) A wealthy customer, Mrs. Preston, buys a red Thunderbird, with his initials painted on the door, for her son, a college boy. In the course of the transaction, McGranville and Mrs. Preston exchange crucial information in dialogue that suggests how much O'Hara admired Hemingway and how much students of the story ought to admire O'Hara.

Mrs. Preston, after inquiring about McGranville's mother, says casually that "Your mother's a fine woman, Mark. Any time she's thinking of going back to work again, I hope she lets me know first." So we know that the son of a house cleaner, climbing the narrow and slippery rungs toward middle class "respectability," has been reminded—not only by Mrs. Preston's language, but through the contrast between his life and that of her son—about his origins. In telling Mrs. Preston about his mother's life with his sister, he says, "They have that little ranch-type out at Putnam Park, the two of them. Mary has her job at the Trust Company." And Mrs. Preston replies, "Very nice for both of them."

With her words in his head (and ours), he leaves work at the end of the day thinking that "all three sales should have made him feel better than he felt on the way home, and he did not know why he should find himself wanting a drink and, what's more, heading for Ernie's to get it." That's as deep into McGranville's thoughts as we will get. O'Hara shows him trying to get drunk and unable to, and he performs a little tour de force in writing Ernie the barman: "for all-day drinking, I stick to scatch. You don't get tired of the taste of scatch. Your rye and your bourbon, they're too sweet if you're gonna drink all day. You know a funny thing about scatch." Just as much of the surface of the story resists our desire and, indeed, McGranville's, for more information, so does McGranville's effort to learn what eats at him. He doesn't know, so he can't say. We end up saying it for him.

In fact, "He could not understand why he went through dinner and the entire evening without telling Jean about the T-Bird and the two Galaxies in one day." He does know that she would manifest pride if he told her, "and he was in no mood to share her enthusiasm or accept the compliment of her pride in him." That sense of adult sulking, and of the need to *not* be celebrated because of despair or unworthiness, is a wonderful perception by O'Hara, and is touched upon with perfect glancing accuracy. McGranville cannot get beneath his mood to understand himself. His wife watches and listens. He kisses his children goodnight. He and Jean watch television until bedtime, when they go to their separate beds. There are only a few hundred words of the story left at this point and it begins to unwind, like an anchor chain spinning out, with a low roar and with real danger to onlookers. Jean asks if there is something the matter. He says, "Nope." She says goodnight, and O'Hara—reflecting the formality between them—writes, "'Goodnight,' said Mark McGranville." Ten minutes later, she says, "If you don't want to tell me." And he snarls, "How the hell can I tell you when I don't know myself?" So she knows, and he knows, and we know, and the problem is large and not apprehensible, though invisibly ballasted with Mark's history and the history of class separateness and its burdens. It—"nothing"—looms in the story.

Jean, who is perceptive and unbrilliant, offers to "come over" to his bed. Mark knows that he is too far from her to be reached: he says, "I just as soon you wouldn't." In a separate sentence, a perfect suggestion of the sad cadences of Mark's mind, O'Hara has Mark say, "I don't know what it is." Jean offers herself as a medicament, a sexual tranquilizer: "If I come over you'll sleep better." Mark then—perhaps because her

generosity touches him, and surely because he is bewildered—
explains to her, and to himself, the size of his unnameable
predicament in the only terms they both understand: "'Jean,
please. It isn't that. Christ, I sold two Galaxies and a T-Bird
today—." And their conversation—an enviable, sad, and
beautiful bit of control by O'Hara that makes a writer's mouth
water, has their talk dwindle away into good sales days, the
drink she smelled on his breath, his insistence that he wasn't
hiding his drinking, hers that he did hide the news of his sales,
and then, her "All right. Goodnight" and his "Goodnight," the
sad slide to silence that is part of one's sentence in life.

And they and we are left in the darkness of night and the
inner darkness as Mark listens to his wife sleep and considers—because O'Hara can be a genius with details and because
he knows that desperate people in the dark seize upon remarkably small matters in an effort not to drown in themselves—
that she snores two musical notes, "the first two notes of
'Yes Sir That's My Baby'; the *yes* note as she exhaled, the *sir*
as she drew breath." McGranville reflects—alerting us to his
thought-provoked sleeplessness, their degree of love, and his
perhaps surprising tenderness—how he had often watched her
sleep, thinking that her sleeping face was not a mask but that
"The mask was her wakeful face, telling only her responses to
things that happened and were said. . . . But in the frowning
placidity of sleep her mind was naked. It did not matter that
he could not read her thoughts; they were there, far more so
than when she was awake." We might wonder why it "did not
matter" that he couldn't read Jean's thoughts, until we understand that what matters to Mark is that "they were there": she
was an authentic person, unreachable by him. If that is so, he
is an authentic person, presumably unreachable by her (and
by us). It is the fact of such separateness, the truth of solitude,
that he seems to understand.

He gets out of bed, goes into the living room, and smokes a cigarette, thinking that "He was thirty years old, a good father, a good husband, and so well thought of"—do we hear echoes of Willy Loman's being "well-liked"?—"that Mrs. Preston would make sure that he got credit for a sale. His sister had a good job, and his mother was taken care of. On the sales blackboard at the garage his name was always first or second." "Nevertheless," O'Hara continues, "he went to the hall closet and got out his 20-gauge and broke it and inserted a shell." That "nevertheless" is of course what the story has pivoted on. It was introduced on the first page—the contrast between McGranville's dissatisfaction and the achievement implicit in "A T-Bird and two Galaxies." On the one hand, there is the arduous, long climb from the fringes of the middle class to something approaching its center; there are the emblems of success and even pleasure—the wife, the children, the house, the sister and mother "taken care of." On the other hand, there is what is always on the other hand, waiting to be rediscovered: the "nothing" that one wishes to evade, the emptiness that threatens to fill us.

McGranville returns to his chair. His cigarette has gone out, and he relights it—O'Hara is, here, the master of the small detail—and McGranville becomes a hard, heavy sculpture of confrontation with "nothing": "The shotgun rested with the butt on the floor, the barrel lying against his thigh, and he held the barrel loosely with the fingers of his left hand as he smoked." O'Hara uses the cigarette as a clock. We sense that when Mark is through with it, he will kill himself. Then: 'The cigarette was now down to an inch in length, and he crushed it carefully."

As he does, "Her voice came softly. 'Mark,' she said," and her awareness, her *alertness* (corresponding to his less insightful alertness toward her, in her sleep), make Jean the hero of this story. When she calls him, "He looked at the carpet." O'Hara uses descriptive language to create a musical pause. His timing is superb. Mark finally answers: "'What?' he said."

Jean says, "Don't. Please?"

She calls him back to life, such as it is. "I won't," he says.

The dialogue has the weight of their history in it, and the heroism of Jean's comprehension and care. It says the avowals of love that their daily life cannot. It does not solve what Mrs. Preston has helped to reawaken in Mark, but it carries what comfort there is. The dialogue, like the events of the story, and like the story's protagonists, cannot say what the matter is, and cannot say the solution. These people will not ever name their predicament; there isn't language for it.

Some of the importance of this story for me is its long look into what cannot be said and its confrontation of the silence in which and from which so many of us suffer. I applaud O'Hara's attention to the differences of class, the cost of money, the power of the distances that separate us. I admire O'Hara's accurate use of facts to create a plausible world. I am profoundly moved by the sad, strong, patient suffering of O'Hara's characters, and by the precision in the story's grappling with the silence of his characters' speech. I envy the abilities of this author, I respect his hard work, I am moved at times by his fear of insufficient recognition. I have tried to learn from his life and from his work about my own attempts to write stories about which readers will care.

This story of O'Hara's makes me hear the desert sigh. That sound is the reason I write.

Frederick Busch (1941–2006) is the author of the short-story collections *Domestic Particulars: A Family Chronicle* (1976), *Hardwater Country: Stories* (1979), *Too Late American Boyhood Blues: Ten Stories* (1984), *The Children in the Woods* (1994),

Don't Tell Anyone (2000), *Rescue Missions* (2006), and *The Selected Stories of Frederick Busch* (2013), as well as of seventeen novels and two nonfiction books. He won the PEN/Malamud Award for Excellence in the Short Story in 1991.

"Triumph Over the Grave"
by Denis Johnson

Maud Casey

"Triumph Over the Grave" was first published and collected and is currently most readily available in *The Largesse of the Sea Maiden* (Random House).

In my early twenties, during a lost and lonely year, I worked at the Willed Body Program at the University of California San Francisco Hospital. I got the job through a temp agency called Temporama, a name that made me feel like a clown jumping out of a cake. Mostly, I sat in the windowless basement office answering the phone and filing papers. (It was the early 1990s: landline, no computer.) The tiny office was furnished with a desk and three enormous file cabinets stuffed with paperwork. My job was simple: field calls from people who wanted to donate their bodies to science. On the phone, I spent a lot of time explaining the meaning of *whole body donation* (yes, all of you), why it was bodies were not returned to the families after the medical students were done with them (there's not much left), the ceremony held at the end of every semester in which the cremains of the donated bodies were scattered at sea. I talked potential donors through the Willed Body questionnaire, explaining the medical conditions that prevented acceptance as a donor (Creutzfeldt-Jacob disease, hepatitis, HIV, tuberculosis, extensive trauma at the time of death, advanced decomposition). No, an amputation didn't preclude acceptance. Yes, transportation of your body is paid for by the Program. Yes, that is the number your next-of-kin should call to notify the transport service you are dead and your body is ready for transport to the UCSF morgue.

Many of the people I spoke with were at that time of life marked by emergency rooms, hospitals, funerals, the age of deep aloneness in which they found themselves talking on the phone with a long-term temp from Temporama. These were the people who wanted to talk far beyond the questionnaire, loathe to return to the ache and hum of their empty homes. I was loathe to return to the ache and hum of my own loneliness and so, on slow days (there were a lot of them), we talked; rather, they talked, I listened. They told me about this funeral and that one and then another one, children who visited, children who didn't, their lack of children, an aching knee, athletic pasts, the recent police beating of Rodney King, the upcoming trial of those police officers and the likelihood or unlikelihood of them being charged with the crime, the end of the Cold War, the beginning of the Cold War, the upcoming 1992 election, all the other elections before 1992, long lost love, lost love found, the presence of God, the absence of God, lost keys and lost keys and lost keys. I loved that job.

Thirty years later, when I read Denis Johnson's story "Triumph Over the Grave," I thought of those strangely intimate, digressive, everybody-dead-or-dying phone conversations. Johnson's story has the deceptive looseness of a talkative stranger to whom you are speaking about donating his body, or a talkative stranger in a large restaurant in San Francisco. "Right now," says the narrator, a writer who bears a more than passing resemblance to Johnson, "I'm eating bacon and eggs in a large restaurant in San Francisco." He is passing time while his dying friend, with whom he has been living, has tests done at a hospital nearby. Johnson often pointed to T. S. Eliot's "quasi-musical decisions" as a way of describing his process. He's interested in the sound of sentences, the song of the mind, its texture, its rhythms. "Triumph Over the Grave" is a song about that time of life when you might find yourself talking on the phone with a long-term temp from Temporama. It is a dirge that creates the illusion of improvisation. Is he making it up as he goes along? There are times the story feels so loose as to be boneless; the story reflects the process of its making. Look, says the narrator from where he sits with his bacon and eggs, there's a woman sitting over there, across the restaurant, who reminds me of a friend. He decides to call her, only to discover her husband has died just moments before, and we're off on an associative, wry wander through the end of life. Of *lives*.

The story is a series of digressions on mortality and its discontents: an encounter with a reclusive novelist whose star has faded, now living on a ranch outside of Austin, who once had a book that was made into a movie that almost starred John Wayne, except John Wayne died before the movie could get made; rotting corpse trivia; ghosts; a meditation on vultures. In the midst of all this death, the narrator composes a mini-story ("I'll write a story for you right now") called "The Examination of My Right Knee" in which the narrator, in his early twenties, has dropped tremendous amounts of acid, and has cosmic knee surgery in an amphitheater, during which the orthopedic surgeon appears to turn into a giant and the "Great Void of Extinction was swallowing the whole of reality." The story sounds kind of like a mess and it verges on one, deliberately, but its wild convolutions through time and space are given a shape by the bookend present, the "only now" as Johnson calls it, in which the narrator waits for that dying friend, and then is present for the friend's deathbed visit from his long-lost love who has Alzheimer's and is now remarried but remembers in her haze only her long-lost love. Like so much of the story, it is over the top. Why, then, does it work?

It has everything to do with Johnson's reverence for this absurd splendor known as life. Is it any surprise that, as Johnson noted in an interview in the Fall 2013 issue of the *Yale Literary Magazine*, he returned again and again to the introduction of Walt Whitman's *Leaves of Grass*:

> This is what you shall do: Love the earth and sun and the animals, despise riches, give alms to every one that asks, stand up for the stupid and crazy, devote your income and labor to others, hate tyrants, argue not concerning God, have patience and indulgence toward the people, take off your hat to nothing known or unknown or to any man or number of men, go freely with powerful uneducated persons and with the young and with the mothers of families, read these leaves in the open air every season of every year of your life, re-examine all you have been told at school or church or in any book, dismiss whatever insults your own soul, and your very flesh shall be a great poem and have the richest fluency not only in its words but in the silent lines of its lips and face and between the lashes of your eyes and in every motion and joint of your body. . . .

When Johnson wrote the story, he was dying; when you read the story, he is already dead. "The world keeps turning. It's plain to you that at the time I write this, I'm not dead. But maybe by the time you read it." Much has been made of those chilling last lines and, okay, yeah, it's a neat trick. I love the boo-I'm-a-ghost cheesiness of the last line. The title's irony and the question implicit in it are laid bare. Triumphing over the grave? Maybe if you're resurrected like Biblical Jesus or make art that finds a large audience. As for us humans in our mere mortal bodies: ashes to ashes, dust to dust. (If we donate our bodies to science, useful specimens first, *then* ashes and dust scattered at sea.) "So this is the end," one of the many dying characters in "Triumph Over the Grave" says. A statement, not a question. Death smells, the narrator tells us, of "urine and alcoholic vomit. And the way I'd been rushing at it, if I'd continued toward that kind of end it would have come a lot sooner, in my twenties, if I had to guess, preceded by not much."

You love a story for all sorts of reasons. Folded into this story for me is the thirty years between my stint in the Willed Body Program, when I became a writer, when, as Johnson's narrator says, I began to take the debris of life and "work it into a shape, cast it in a light. It's not that much different, really, from filming a parade of clouds across the sky and calling it a movie—although it has to be admitted that the clouds can descend, take you up, carry you to all kinds of places, some of them terrible, and you don't get back where you came from for years and years." Johnson's humility is palpable, as is his astonishment at having harnessed that rush to death long enough to die, and his abiding tenderness for the wrecks we all are.

"I get in a teacup and start paddling across the little pond and say, 'In seven weeks, I'll land on Mars.' Five years later I'm still going in circles. When I reach the shore in spitting distance of where I started, it's a colossal triumph." This is Johnson on writing stories in a May 26, 2017, interview with David Ulin in the *Los Angeles Times*, but it could just as well be one of the people talking to me on the phone about making it through the day, the weeks, the years. Those people? Long dead, their bodies put to good use, then scattered at sea. There is no triumph over death but Johnson's story nudges us toward something much less grand—the *only now*.

Maud Casey is the author of the short-story collection *Drastic* (2002), as well as of the novels *The Shape of Things to Come* (2001), *Genealogy* (2006), and *The Man Who Walked Away* (2014).

"No One's a Mystery"
by Elizabeth Tallent

Alan Cheuse

"No One's a Mystery" was originally published in the August 1985 issue of *Harper's Magazine*. It was collected in *Time with Children* (1987). It is currently most readily available in *Fiction 100: An Anthology of Short Fiction* (Prentice-Hall).

When I think of great initiation stories, it's always Joyce's "Araby" that immediately comes to mind, and after that Sherwood Anderson's powerful American tale with its distinctive race-track setting, "I Want to Know Why." Between the two of them, these stories, with their near-miraculous fusion of the vernacular and deep and wondering portrayals of the crucial moment in the education of two quite distinctly different adolescent boys, one a turn-of-the-century Irish Catholic from Dublin, the other a country boy from the Middle West, set the highest aesthetic standard for this variety of story. Moreover, they reveal to us what all short fiction in essence cries out to be.

Lyric poetry!

Short stories are as close as I get myself to writing lyric poems, and these two stories come as close as any in creating the effect of the lyric, with its intense recollection of a certain way of having been—usually, it's the memory of having

been deeply in love, with the hope of having that love recip-
rocated—and the shock of the loss of that hope. It's nothing short of miraculous the way these two stories reveal to a
young man just how much of the chaos and near-insanity of
his floundering childhood and youth present a certain pattern
of understanding and loss. A story such as this thrills you with
the intensity of its unfolding, gives you hope that in your own
hopelessness you are not alone, and creates in your blood a
particular emotional effect that we associate usually with only
the finest lyric poems.

But after all of the polemics and lamenting and honest
skull-scratching that we've all suffered through, I have to say,
during the past twenty years with respect to the question of
equality for women in the modem world, the question comes
to mind: what's a *girl* to do? Where does a young woman go to
find a portrayal of female initiation that is as beautifully made
and emotionally unsettling as the Joyce and Anderson stories?

In fact, there's a story of Maine writer Sarah Orne
Jewett's—"A White Heron"—that precedes both the Joyce and
the Anderson, and arguably rivals both of these in its powerful
final effects. And lately, among our contemporaries, women
have produced initiation stories of similar quality right alongside the men. Aside from Richard Ford's "Communist," the
finest coming-of-age stories of the past several decades have,
in fact, been written by women. One of these is Joyce Carol
Oates's "Where Are You Going? Where Have You Been?" and
the other was written by westerner Elizabeth Tallent. It's called
"No One's a Mystery."

Oates's story has been widely anthologized and was made
into a movie. With its dark undertow of a narrative pulling
its heroine closer and closer to a fate so awful that Oates only
hints at it in the end, it captures the worst fears of contemporary girlhood, and in the end leaves little to hope for except

a strong voice to tell about the barren truths of modern life. Tallent's story has been anthologized only a few times; given its compact and forceful rendering of an eighteen-year-old Wyoming girl's coming of age—and the ironic counterpoint of the perspective of her middle-aged rancher lover—the story deserves a much wider audience. Given the relation of its brevity—it's only about a thousand words, less than three pages, in length—to its impact, the story deserves wide recognition as a little masterwork of short fiction.

It goes like this. The unnamed narrator, having just turned eighteen, is riding in a pickup truck on the highway outside Cheyenne, Wyoming, with her married lover, Jack, a man some years older.

He's given her a five-year diary for her birthday and she, rather unconsciously, is musing about what she might say in entries regarding her love for this man. As they're traveling along at a high rate of speed, the man sees his wife's Cadillac coming in the opposite direction and pushes the girl onto the floor of the passenger side and then when the wife's car has passed he lets her get back up on the seat again. The story ends with the girl and the man presenting conflicting visions of what their future together—and apart—may bring.

The poet John Ciardi, one of my undergraduate teachers, used to talk about the two parts of a poem—the wave and the counter-wave. You'd reach a moment in the lyric when it had gone as far as it could go in one direction, and then, like a wave pulled back out to a certain distance from shore by the undertow, the poem broke back on itself, turning the original tendency on its head. Paul Fussell, another one of my old teachers, calls this movement "elegiac action." You can certainly see this—better yet, you can certainly *feel* this—"elegiac action" at work in the Tallent story as the narrator attempts to come to terms with her first understanding of the love affair that has taken up several years of her teenage life. You can feel it deeply after the last exchange between Jack and the narrator as a pulse of emotion and as a sting of awareness and regret.

This comes after one reading. If you bear down on the story and read it again closely, its spare brief surface opens up like a desert flower in a sudden rainstorm. The opening line announces the gift of the diary, with its duration of five years of space—an ironic beginning. It's not until she receives the blank book that the narrator talks—thinks? and possibly writes?—about anything at all related to her affair with the older man. The opening indicates to us that for two years the girl has not thought or recorded anything about her illicit liaison. The presumption is that for the next five years at least she will be paying attention to her own behavior and emotions.

But not yet. For the brief duration of the story, which is told in "real time," that is, in the same amount of time that the characters live it, she will remain unaware, conveying to the reader—the reader of the story, which may or may not be the first entry in her new diary—her perceptions of the next few minutes with a sort of raw innocence much purer, for all of her sexual experience, than that of either the boy in the Joyce or the Anderson stories. Tallent quickly conveys this mixture of innocence and experience in the first paragraph when Jack, her lover, and driver of the pickup truck in which they're riding, sees his wife's Cadillac coming down the highway in the opposite direction and pushes the narrator to the floor of the truck.

She hovers there, at eye-level with the seam of the crotch of his Levis and his zipper glinting "gold" in her view. She doesn't see the wife's car as it passes, merely hears the betrayed woman—also innocent in her own way, we have to suppose— honk twice. The narrator's eyes fall from the view of her lover's crotch to a lower level, where she notices his boots, with their "elk heads stitched into the leather" and the "compact wedge of muddy manure between the heel and the sole." This descent of vision, reminiscent of the fall of the narrator's eye in "Araby" when he sees the object of his infatuation, the girl he refers to only by the phrase "Mangan's sister," standing at the porch railing, takes us from the sexual level to the primal realm of excrement. It's an animal world down here, with the elk heads and the cow manure the reigning materials. But it's also the realm of infancy, and Jack emphasizes this aspect of her place in his life—his child lover—and her own state of being during the past two years—innocent participant in adult games—by responding to her complaint an instant later about the mess of pop-tops on the car floor on which a child might cut herself by saying that no child gets into the car except her.

Leaping forward, you can make the connection between his view of her as a child and Jack's remark about the infant that she imagines they would bear if they married as finger-painting on the bathroom wall with his own excrement. Ranging back again to the first few moments in the truck, we also notice that the Rosanne Cash tape that's playing on the tape deck—the implicit musical background to the entire story, with that brief additional honking of the horn as counterpoint, and the voices of the man and the girl in the foreground—annunciates the father-daughter shadow that lurks behind this illicit love affair. But rather than calling our attention to the incestuous tinge to their romance, the story dramatizes those qualities that we normally associate with the coming-of-age story: the exploration of values and the ceremonial-like passage from innocence to experience that we find in both the Joyce and the Anderson stories.

The pickup zooming along with Jack behind the wheel and the kneeling girl on the passenger side is a small interior location, but as the girl tells us, there is a wider world beyond the truck into which she implicitly puts the story of her two-year teenage love affair with the older Jack. This news comes to us in a striking visual effect. As she tries to imagine what future they might have together, she "cranes" around while kneeling now on the seat "to look at the butterfly of dust printed" on her jeans, and in doing so she glances outside.

"Outside the window Wyoming was dazzling in the heat," she declares. "The wheat was fawn and yellow and parted smoothly by the thin dirt road." More senses than sight come into play: "I could smell the water in the irrigation ditches hidden in the wheat." These lines about landscape suggest more stillness than passage. But the fact is—or is it the irony?—the truck is moving them through time, and the girl has yet to begin to recognize the inexorable passage that will carry her through the next five years of discovery about her self and the world.

The concluding beat of the story is comprised of statement and response between the girl and Jack on the nature of that future. She states as fact her dreams of a perfect marriage. He counter-poses his realistic view of any such situation that she might conjure up and suggests that she has a flawed imagination. Their exchange builds to the stinging pathos of his final comment, which leaves the reader in a certain mood of understanding. Whether or not the girl feels what the reader feels we can't tell. In that regard, we have to look at the story as completely ironic. There is no final epiphanic insight for the main character as there is at the conclusion of the Joyce and the Anderson stories. It's left to the reader to do this girl's feeling for her. But it is a big emotion that we're left with, this sense that the girl, as certain of herself and her vision as she seems to be, has a number of years of trials and tribulations lying ahead of her.

We can feel, too, for Jack, her lover-teacher, the father surrogate who initiates her into the world of loving and love.

All her life lies ahead of her. His best years may have come to an end, even as he hints at the end of the affair, and worse than that for him, the eventual eradication of even any specific memory of him in her life.

Two and a half printed pages. About four minutes of "real" time in which this story unfolds. But four minutes of "real time" at eighty miles an hour. For the narrator the predication of a lifetime to come, and for Jack a life just reaching its zenith, and about to descend. That's quite a lot for one small story to impress upon us, but Elizabeth Tallent's brief lyric miracle quite easily bears all this weight.

Alan Cheuse (1940–2015) is the author of the short-story collections *Candace and Other Stories* (1980), *The Tennessee Waltz and Other Stories* (1990), *Lost and Old Rivers* (1998), and *An Authentic Captain Marvel Ring & Other Stories* (2013), as well as of five novels, a memoir, and three non-fiction books.

"Who Is It Can Tell Me Who I Am?"
by Gina Berriault

Kate Christensen

"Who Is It Can Tell Me Who I Am?" was first published in the Winter 1995/1996 issue of *Ploughshares*. It was collected in *Women in their Beds: New and Selected Stories* (1996). It is currently most readily available in *Women in their Beds: Thirty-Five Stories* (Counterpoint).

"Who is it that can tell me who I am?" King Lear asks plaintively when his once-fawning daughter Goneril mocks him before his hundred knights. It's a cry for identity, and also a plea for connection with and a spark of recognition from a hypothetical *Who*. Lear is homeless, dispossessed, going mad, and his question is entirely personal—it's not general or philosophical or rhetorical like Hamlet's "What a piece of work is man! . . . And yet, to me, what is this quintessence of dust?" Lear wants an answer. He desperately needs an answer. *Who is it that can tell me who I am?*

Gina Berriault's modern version of this hapless, woeful, insistent interlocutor is a young tubercular homeless man in a "badly soiled green parka" who wanders into a library in the Tenderloin district of San Francisco one day. There he encounters Alberto Perera, an elderly librarian, who is immediately afraid that this importuning bum wants to kill him; there have been a series of library arsons and murders of librarians recently up and down the state of California. But the coughing young man has come brandishing, not a weapon, but a poem by the modernist Chilean poet Rubén Dario, scribbled down among a pocketful of scraps of paper. The poem tells various creatures to rejoice in or at least be accepting of their lot in life, and the young man is arguing with the premise somewhat vehemently, and wants Perera to bear witness to this argument and to engage with it. A long conversation ensues, comical at first because Perera continues to think the young man is really there to kill him, and tragic because it soon becomes clear that what the man really wants is for Perera to help him answer, by repudiating the poem's central exhortation to greet the sun from where you lie every morning, a simple and overarching question: Who is he, exactly, if he sleeps on a sidewalk and belongs to no one and nothing? What about his own situation, waking up on the sidewalk? How, like the creatures in the poem being told to rejoice at the rising sun, is he supposed to rejoice in that?

The spider in its web being told to "*Greet the sun*" he can see. The cricket chirping at moonlight he can see. But the final line: "*Dance on, bear*"? Bears don't dance unless there's a chain around their necks and a man with a stick forcing them. "A bear with a rope around his neck, do you see him waking up happy, hallooing the sun?" asks the young man. Besides, as he points out, the poet himself probably woke up in his own bed, maybe even wrote the poem there, not on the sidewalk. So how could he have any idea what he was talking about?

Unable to get Perera to agree with him, the young man scoops his scraps of paper back into his parka's pockets, pauses to cough liquidly and at length into a Palestinian scarf, and leaves.

But not for long, Perera suspects: "Anyone who inquires so relentlessly into the meaning of a poem, and presses the words of poets into the ephemerae of the streets, would surely return, borne up the marble stairs by all those uplifting thoughts in his pockets."

In addition to Perera's ironic detachment, perhaps running parallel to it, is a kind of tragicomic distance between what Perera sees and thinks about the young man, and what we, the readers, understand from Berriault's deft, incisive description through his eyes. For instance, this passage as the young man is leaving: "As he bent to the floor to pick up his scraps, the crown of his head was revealed, the hair sprinkled with a scintilla of the stuff of the streets and the culture. How old was he, this fellow? Not more than thirty, maybe younger. Young, with no staying power."

No staying power. As the story goes on, those words reverberate. More immediately, they serve an ironic purpose, since Perera cannot seem to get his exchange with the young coughing supplicant out of his head. He has struck a nerve in Perera, but in a gentler, more intimate way. Plucked a string, perhaps, as if Perera were a guitar sitting idly in a corner, waiting for someone to come along and play it. Close to retirement, hanging on by his fingernails to his shabby Tenderloin apartment filled with relics of great literary culture, proud of his name and ethnicity, devoted to the job he's about to be aged out of, Perera begins to question the lengths to which he himself is in possession of his own precarious identity.

Born in Brooklyn, the son of refugees from Franco's Spain, Perera has always felt "a kinship with the dispossessed everywhere in the world, this kinship deepening with the novels he'd read in his youth." He eats dinner alone in a scruffy restaurant called Lefty O'Doul's, sharing his communal table with other near-indigent loners, "their winter smells of naphthalene and menthol hovering over the aroma of his roast turkey with dressing." But he assures himself as he eats, thinking of the young man in the parka, "One should not be ashamed of eating a substantial meal while the hungry roamed the streets," since fasting in sympathy with the hungry only causes one's conscience to starve, "unable to survive for very long without a body."

That night, as Perera falls asleep in his own bed, wearing his luxurious if worn nightshirt and his handmade cashmere nightcap knitted for him by his now-dead lover, he wonders "where the poetry stalker might be, the librarian stalker with the excitable cough. Could Dario have imagined that his earnest little attempt to accept God's ways would wind up in the parka pocket of a sidewalk sleeper, trying to accept the same a hundred years later?"

Of course the "stalker" returns days later, still arguing about the poem, and still asking the same essential question that all short stories ask, usually obliquely or implicitly, but in this case, directly, and with Lear's urgency: "What I'd like to know is, what am I?"

And Perera's predictable reply: "You can figure you're a human being." The young man is ready for this. "What else you were going to say is, you're a human being by the sweat of your brow," he mocks—but is work the thing that defines a human being? Animals work too. The young man proceeds to walk Perera through the latter's day, from his job in the library where everything is ordered and catalogued, every book in its place, to the restaurant where he has dinner, to the theater, and finally to the safety and comfort of his own apartment, where he goes to sleep in his own bed, which maybe even has "an electric blanket. Got pillows with real feathers inside, maybe even that down stuff from the hind end of a couple hundred ducks. Nighty-night." And then, devastatingly, the young man contrasts Perera's ability to halloo the sun from the comfort of his own bed—like the spider in his web, like the toad in his hot mud—with his own inability to do the same. "Halloo, says this guy, Alberto Perera, now I get to go to the library again and talk to this guy who can't figure out why he can't halloo the sun with the rest of them."

After a coughing fit seizes the man, making him look "appallingly" flushed despite his pallor while he coughs up something "tormentingly intimate" into his scarf, comes the ask. He wants Perera to let him sleep in the library, to allow him to stay behind in his office after the lights go off and the librarians go home and the doors are locked. Perera objects strenuously, using all his rhetorical powers to convince the homeless man that it would be "*unthinkable*" for him to do so, not to mention impractical and unsafe. If there were an earthquake, he warns, "the whole place could collapse on you." And what if, in the dark of the abandoned library, the young man should fall down the marble stairs and die? "Come morning they open up and find you there. . . . I'll say we spent many pleasant hours discussing Dario's *Filosofia*."

Despite the young man's assurances that the library, dark and labyrinthine and structurally unsound though it may be, is vastly preferable to the streets: "Nobody's going to throw lighter fuel on me and set me on fire in here. Nobody's going to knife me in here," Perera cannot bring himself to allow the man to stay. It is simply against the rules.

"What're you telling me?" the young man asks, contempt in his eyes. "You're telling me to lie down and die?"

"Not at all," answers Perera. "All I'm saying is you cannot spend the night in this library."

Scornfully careful, the fellow placed the porcelain cup on the desk and stood up. "You want me to tell you what that poem is saying? Same thing you're saying. If you can't halloo the sun, if you can't go chirpity-chirp to the moon, what're you doing around here, anyway?"

"That is not what I'm saying," said Perera.

"To hell with you is what I'm saying."

Gone, leaving his curse behind. A curse so popular, so spread around, it carried little weight.

Again, Berriault's sly irony is plain. That popular curse, "so spread around, it carried little weight," is humanity's curse, in both the sense of Prometheus cursing the gods and Adam's curse of the apple. For Perera, a man in possession of a "snob of an umbrella" that never turns inside out, as promised by the sales clerk in London who sold it to him, "not even in Conrad's typhoon," it is a curse that reveals the hollowness of his conceit. "A stance of superiority, that was his problem," he realizes, looking down from his perch atop the comforts of an educated, civilized brain. "And how did he figure he was so smart, this Alberto Perera? Well, he could engage in the jesting the smart ones enjoy when they're in the presence of those they figure are not so smart. He could engage in that jovial thievery, that light-fingered light-headed trivializing of another person's tragic truth, a practice he abhorred whenever he came upon it."

As he wanders about the neighborhood, sloshing through the "neon-colored rain, this headlight-glittering rain, every light no match for the dark, only a constant contesting," Perera thinks of a favorite line from *The Seven Pillars of Wisdom* by T. E. Lawrence: *There is a certainty in degradation.* This, thinks Perera, is the only truth—there is "no certainty in anything else, no matter what you're storing up, say tons of gold, say ten billion library books, and if you think you can elude that certainty it sneaks up on you, it sneaks up the marble stairs and into your sanctum and you're degraded right along with the rest."

A humbling thought, for sure. And if this were a poem, it might end right there, having arrived at a sentiment not unlike Eliot's "These fragments I have shored against my ruins" or Frost's "Provide, Provide." But short stories, since Chekhov at least, are the modern iterations of folk tales and morality plays, whose purpose is to challenge and reaffirm our fundamental understanding of what it means to be human. And the human, in this case, is a *real* human, a real cursing, coughing, soiled, homeless human man.

Over the next few days, Perera looks for his poetry stalker in soup kitchen lines and shelters, even though he knows he won't find him—the young man is a loner, and he's probably hiding on top of that, afraid he'll be arrested for his cough. Even so, Perera begins to collect things and bring them in to his office at the library, a blanket, a thermos of hot coffee, warm socks, handkerchiefs, a thick sweater, things that are more about comforting himself and allaying his own anxieties than they are actual offerings, since he knows the young man won't be back. They have "the same aspect of futility that he saw in the primitive practice of laying out clothing and nourishment for the departed."

And sure enough, the next time Perera sees the young man, in the library one morning as he arrives for work, the man is dead, a corpse lying at the bottom of the marble stairs. According to the "inappropriately young" paramedic at the scene, he just "lay down and died."

Feeling faint, his head in a welter, Perera kneels down by the body to take a closer look at the man's face, "closer than when they sat in the office, discoursing on the animal kingdom. The young man was now no one, as he'd feared he already was when alive. The absolute unwanted, that's who the dead become." Then, when Perera is asked by the young paramedic, "Did this man bother you?" we get a remarkable, exquisite, and devastating answer:

> It would take many months, he knew, before he'd be able to speak without holding back. Humans speaking were unbearable to hear and abominable to see, himself among the rest. Worse, was all that was written down instead, the never-ending outpouring, given print and given covers, given shelves up and down and everywhere in this ware-house of fathomless darkness.
> "He did not bother me," he said.

Perera goes into his office to find the young man's scraps of paper scattered over his desk. "By copying down all these stirringly strange ideas," he wonders, "had the fellow hoped to impress upon himself his likeness to these other humans? A break-in of a different sort. A young man breaking into a home of his own."

He sits at his desk, puts his glasses on, and spreads these scraps out before him "as heedfully as his shaking hands allowed."

It's not enough to say that we're all implicated in Perera's carefully maintained, fragile snobbery, his magical delusion that a cashmere nightcap knitted by his lover and the title of librarian and the bulwark of literary artifacts will save him from this young man's fate, this shared question that we all, at some point, have to ask: "What am I?" Berriault's language, in all its suppleness, its poignant elegance, is so infused with compassion and irony in equal measure that this almost unbearable tragedy is uplifted on a warm breath of fellow feeling.

How Berriault achieves this startling depth of emotional insight is beyond me. Every time I read this story it moves me to a place deeper than tears, and I'm left with the overwhelming sense that the only certainty is not degradation, but recognition. We're human by virtue of our recognition of humanity in others. It is only in our failure to see it that we can be rendered "abominable."

Kate Christensen is the author of the novels *In the Drink* (1999), *Jeremy Thrane* (2001), *The Epicure's Lament* (2004), *The Great Man* (2007), which won the PEN/Faulkner Award for Fiction, *Trouble* (2009), *The Astral* (2011), and *The Last Cruise* (2018), as well as of two books of nonfiction.

"Cathedral" by Raymond Carver

Susan Coll

"Cathedral" was first published in the September 1981 issue of
The Atlantic Monthly. It was collected in *Cathedral* (1983). It
is currently most readily available in Carver's *Collected Stories*
(Library of America).

It was not a Raymond Carver story but a poem that felled
me one April afternoon in 1989. It was called "Afterglow,"
and it was in *The New Yorker* that had just arrived in my mailbox. I read it and I sank into the sofa and I reread it and I
began to cry. I committed the imagery to memory: the wink,
the broad smile, the jaunty slant of the cigarette of the protagonist who in the poem mugs for the camera, unaware he will
soon die. My own vivid memory of that moment—the wan-
ing afternoon sunlight in my apartment, the sleeping infant
beside me, the hideous aged sofa into which I sank—are by
now intermingled with the DNA of the poem itself. At just
under 150 words, the poem is a fully formed narrative, and for
me it served as a gateway to Carver's stories, for which he is far
better known. It led me, eventually, to "Cathedral," a story so
finely chiseled that it is arguably poetry itself.

"His art is an art of exclusion," the critic Irving Howe
observed of Carver's work. Although in a 1983 *New York Times*
review he praised the collection in which this story appears, he

was not entirely a fan of this particular aspect of Carver's writing: "Many of life's shadings and surprises, pleasures and possibilities, are cut away by the stringency of his form," he wrote.

This stringency of form is generally attributed to the red pen of Carver's longtime editor, Gordon Lish. Once his success was established, Carver began to push back on Lish's edits, and their increasingly fraught working relationship is among the more compelling literary dramas of the last century. But that's a complicated subject for a different essay, and as Giles Harvey observed in 2010 in *The New York Review of Books*, "we are likely to end up viewing Lish's involvement with Carver as a footnote, incidental to our appreciation of the finished work."

"Cathedral" was apparently spared Lish's edits. It's hard to say what's the right amount of spare. It's easier to recognize that the brilliance of the story is in its leanness. It can seem a magic trick, a Carver sleight of hand, the way the absence of detail about the narrator magnifies what little information he provides.

As a writer who tends to overcomplicate her plots, I've always been envious of Carver's elegance, not just in the rendering of his characters but of the premises themselves. In "Cathedral," the narrator—whose name we never learn—is unsettled by the visit of Robert, a blind man who is an old friend of the narrator's wife. She used to work for Robert, reading to him, but she hasn't seen him in ten years.

Robert has just lost his wife, and he is passing through their Connecticut town to visit with relatives. With a strong handshake, a booming voice, and the ease with which he answers the narrator's obnoxious questions, Robert is instantly likeable, his character realized with very few strokes.

Carver's narrator is also quickly established, but in his case it's entirely through his bad attitude: "I wasn't enthusiastic about his visit," he tells us. "He was no one I knew. And his being blind bothered me. My idea of blindness came from the movies. In the movies, the blind moved slowly and never laughed. Sometimes they were led by seeing-eye dogs. A blind man in my house was not something I looked forward to."

Carver was not known as a humorist, yet his narrator's discomfort, and the extent to which he feels threatened by the blind man, is based on such ignorance and jealousy that this dark story becomes unexpectedly funny.

Even Carver's strategic deployment of exclamation marks is funny: his wife never had a physical relationship with Robert, but he once asked if he could touch her face—"even her neck! She never forgot it. She even tried to write a poem about it. She was always trying to write a poem. She wrote a poem or two every year, usually after something really important had happened to her."

As for the narrator himself, in actual detail he is an enigma. His name, his age, and his occupation are all withheld. We don't know what he wears, what he drives, where he works; apart from that he doesn't have much choice but to keep working there. He is defined by his petty mean-spiritedness, by his liberal use of exclamation marks, by his comments such as: "A beard on a blind man! Too much, I say."

His wife falls asleep on the couch while he and Robert are watching—or in Robert's case listening to—the television. His wife announces she is going upstairs to change into more comfortable clothes after dinner. ("I didn't want to be left alone with a blind man," the narrator remarks.) She returns wearing a robe, and later, as they watch television and she falls asleep, her robe slips open, revealing "a juicy thigh": "I reached to draw her robe back over her, and it was then that I glanced at the blind man. What the hell! I flipped the robe open again."

The tension peaks. It can't get more cruel than this. From here, the narrator begins to arc toward redemption. The end is so quietly affecting that it might qualify as non-Carveresque, even a little cheesy. The reader can practically imagine the narrator himself complaining about the saccharine end, which makes it all the more apt.

As the narrator and Robert listen to a television show about the construction of cathedrals, he asks whether the blind man even knows what a cathedral is. He does, more or less—or at least he can offer a convincing and educated description of their history and construction. But then, together, they draw a cathedral, the blind man's hand placed over the hand of the narrator as his hand moves about the paper:

"First I drew a box that looked like a house. It could have been the house I lived in. Then I put a roof on it. At either end of the roof, I drew spires. Crazy."

Momentum builds as he continues: "I put in windows with arches. I drew flying buttresses. I hung great doors. I couldn't stop."

Eventually, at Robert's urging, the narrator lets go. He closes his eyes and continues to draw. Even after he is told to open his eyes and take a look at his work, he keeps them closed: "I thought I'd keep them that way for a little longer. I thought it was something I ought to do."

The final sentence of the story, spoken by the narrator: "It's really something."

It's hard to think of a more impactful ending than those three words. A different sort of writer might have elaborated, extended the epiphany, shown apology and neat resolution. But for me, those three words are every bit as powerful as the wink, the broad smile, the jaunty slant of the cigarette of the man in "Afterglow," who took my breath away and led me to Carver's prose.

Susan Coll is the author of the novels *karlmarx.com* (2001), *Rockville Pike* (2005), *Acceptance* (2007), *Beach Week* (2010), and *The Stager* (2014).

"The Magic Barrel" by Bernard Malamud

Nicholas Delbanco

"The Magic Barrel" was originally published in the November 1954 issue of *The Partisan Review*. It was collected in *The Magic Barrel* (1958). It is currently most readily available in Malamud's *The Complete Stories* (Farrar, Straus and Giroux).

I first met Bernard Malamud in 1966. I was an ambitious boy of 23, with a debut novel about to appear and the self-confident conviction that I could and should replace him while he took a leave of absence from his teaching job. He was leaving Bennington College for what turned out to be a two-year stint in Cambridge, Massachusetts; I drifted into town and was hired—astonishingly, I still believe—by elders who saw something in this junior they might shape. By the time the Malamuds returned, I was happily ensconced as their near neighbor in Vermont; over the years we grew close.

The relation was avuncular; though Bennington's faculty is unranked, Malamud was much my senior colleague. It was and is a small school and town, and the Language and Literature Division seemed very small indeed. We attended committee meetings and movies and concerts and readings and poker games together; we shared meals and walks. When I married in 1970, the Malamuds came to the wedding; when they gave a party we helped to cut the cake. With no hint of condescension he described me as his protégé; I asked for and took his advice. My wife's day-book bulks large with collective occasions: cocktails, picnics, weddings, and funerals shared. In times of celebration or trouble—when our daughters were born or had birthdays, during the years I served as Director of the Bennington Writing Workshops, at ceremonies in his honor or when in failing health Bern needed a hand with a suitcase or car—we saw each other often. At his death on March 18, 1986, it seemed to me and to my wife and children that we had lost a relative. The loss endures.

So I can't and won't pretend to critical distance; this is an author I loved and admire. At his best he strikes me as an enduring master of the twentieth century; his best consists of the early novels (*The Natural, The Assistant, A New Life*) and a baker's dozen of short stories. Though lumped—to his disgruntlement—with that of other "Jewish" writers from Singer to Bellow to Roth, the prose was nonpareil. And the terms of appreciation feel oxymoronic as soon as applied: his is a magical realism, a simple complexity, a practiced naturalness. My guess is that, when the dust settles and those critics to whom we look forward look back, the work will loom large within our art's terrain—in the forest a tall tree. For his concerns are timeless not time-bound, his preoccupations lasting and his diction not likely to date.

In 1997 his publishers produced an omnibus collection of short stories, with a jacket photo of a well-dressed Malamud in the New York streets. They are right to call attention to the body of the work, the bulk of it, and to remind forgetful readers of how long and much he wrote. But I prefer the rigorous triage he himself performed in 1983, choosing *The Stories of Bernard Malamud*. It's a telling title: reticent yet declarative, not "collected" or "selected," just *the stories*. No small thing.

In that book "The Magic Barrel" is of course included; it was the title tale of his first short-story collection, the National Book Award recipient for 1958.

The piece itself feels quintessential, and its author wrote a useful lecture on its composition. That lecture—also called "The Magic Barrel"—has been published in its entirety in *Talking Horse: Bernard Malamud on Life and Work* (1996). Were there space enough and time, I would reproduce his notes verbatim; instead I urge the interested reader to consult the essay; it records his painstaking progress from first idea to final draft—from a vague notion that Chagallean imagery should enter into his prose to a discussion with his wife as to his ability to love. "First there is a note in my journal, dated March 8, 1954: It reads: 'Go back to the poetic, evocative, singing—often symbolic short story.'" Then entries span the period from August 21 to September 14, 1954, a relatively rapid time-span, since once he did compose the tale he did so at some speed. The very first notation provides the denouement:

> The young man somehow gets the girl. Not sure what the miracle is but he's got to do something that satisfies everyone but the m.b. He (the m.b.) has to be disappointed yet resigned. Once I work out the meaning of the piece I'll have the ending. Season with Chagall?

What Malamud would later call his "sad and comic tales" assume their definition in this template text. First conceived of as "The Marriage Broker," it engages many of his oft-recurring motifs: beauty and morality, romance and realistic aspiration, paternal love and disappointment, two men at odds with each other. This agon between paired protagonists would be repeated again and again; such stories as "The Jew-Bird" and such novels as *The Tenants* are, in this regard, variations on a theme. The tone is vintage Malamud: rueful yet humorous, fast-paced yet meditative, an Old World circumstance translated to this Brave New World, yet with the bite and flash of inflected speech.

It might be worth repeating that our author was *not* an immigrant and *not* native to or fully fluent in Yiddish; the locale of *The Assistant* remained his native ground. As his notebook indicates, he reached back into Yiddish folklore and literature for a kind of collective memory, but the fashioning of that material was both highly conscious and wholly wrought:

> The idea for the story itself, the donnée, came about through Irving Howe's invitation to me to translate a story from the Yiddish for inclusion in his and Eliezer Greenberg's anthology called *A Treasury of Yiddish Stories.*
>
> My reading in Royte Pomerantzen provided the six marriage anecdotes—two of which were very important.

From literature, then, and collective researched experience stems the particular case. As Malamud observed, "I have never made a study of the main sources of literary material but I imagine they can be divided into two obvious categories: that of autobiography and sources other than oneself." Leo Finkle the rabbinical student and Pinye Salzman, who "smelled frankly of fish," manage somehow to be at one and the same time stock characters and, in their behavior, original. The *luftmensch* Salzman is a familiar type, a weightless man who lives on air, "though I had never met a marriage broker." And Finkle too carries somewhere about him the whiff of personal history—a lonely, romantic, and studious person in a rooming house. What matters here, however, is invention. The fierce and vivid circumstance, the colloquial austerity of language, the unexpected plot-twists that, in retrospect, feel fore-ordained: all these signal mastery.

As does the wit. Much of "The Magic Barrel" is humor-ous—the reeking Salzman, the vaudeville series of slammed doors, appearances and disappearances, the comic disjunction between the advertised and actual truth about the hopeful ladies in the marriage broker's file. There's a series of missed signals that verge on the burlesque. But, as is always the case with this author, the laughter shades to grief: "my sad and comic tales" entail both penury and poverty; when a figure in Malamud's fiction weeps, the tears are real, not feigned.

Which brings me to the story's close, its problematic final line: "Around the corner, Salzman, leaning against a wall, chanted prayers for the dead." Is Salzman's daughter dead to him, or is she somehow also actually dead, or is the mourning general and the Kaddish all-inclusive? Is Salzman deluded; is Leo; is the girl irredeemably whorish or about to be redeemed? Years later, in his final finished book, *God's Grace*, the author would complete his fable of all-levelling catastrophe in a mark-edly similar vein. George the gorilla has been taught both religion and language by Calvin Cohn, the lone survivor of thermonuclear war. When the paleologist also dies, his disciple dons "a mud-stained white yarmulke he had one day found in the woods. . . . In his throaty, gruff voice he began a long Kaddish for Calvin Cohn."

Yet there's salvation in the lovers' story, surely: "Violins and lit candles revolved in the sky. Leo ran forward with flowers outthrust." Here we see Chagall translated from the canvas to the page, and to the young couple at least the story's end looks happy. Malamud himself announced, "Don't worry about the ending. If you think about it it will come to you," but the "desperate innocence" of Salzman's daughter is at least in part offset by her corrupted worldliness. That star-struck creature, Leo, may be embracing ruination when he offers "Stella" a bouquet.

And there's a grace-note, too, of the suspicion that the marriage broker has orchestrated all of this, even at the risk of his own forfeited commission; perhaps he sees in Finkle his daughter's last best hope. Nothing in the scene is simple; nothing means only one thing. "Stella stood by the lamp post, smoking. She wore white with red shoes, which fitted his expectations, although in a troubled moment he had imagined the dress red, and only the shoes white." When Leo "pictured, in her, his own redemption" is that picture accurate or wishful merely; is their happiness provisional or lasting; what wall does Pinye lean against, and why?

At Bennington, in 1984, Bernard Malamud delivered a lecture titled "Long Work, Short Life," which is also published in *Talking Horse*. Its closing assertions are characteristic in diction and stance: self-assured yet modest, a high-priest of aesthetics who's wearing a business suit:

> I have written almost all my life. My writing has drawn, out of a reluctant soul, a measure of astonishment at the nature of life. And the more I wrote well, the better I felt I had to write.
>
> In writing I had to say what had happened to me, yet present it as though it had been magically revealed. I began to write seriously when I had taught myself the discipline necessary to achieve what I wanted. When I touched that time, my words announced themselves to me. I have given my life to writing without regret, except when I consider what in my work I might have done better. I wanted my writing to be as good as it must be, and on the whole I think it is. I would write a book, or a short story, at least three times—once to understand it, the second time to improve the prose, and a third to compel it to say what it still must say.
>
> Somewhere I put it this way: first drafts are for learning what one's fiction wants him to say. Revision works with

that knowledge to enlarge and enhance an idea, to re-form it. Revision is one of the exquisite pleasures of writing: "The men and things of today are wont to lie fairer and truer in tomorrow's meadow," Henry Thoreau said.

I don't regret the years I put into my work. Perhaps I regret the fact that I was not two men, one who could live a full life apart from writing; and one who lived in art, exploring all he had to experience and know how to make his work right; yet not regretting that he had put his life into the art of perfecting the work.

Story after story and chapter after chapter represent this process of revision, a series of stages—sometimes as many as eighteen drafts—from holograph to galley proofs wherein the prose gets reworked. Malamud hand-wrote the third draft of *The Assistant*, for example, after his wife had typed a second draft from the hand-written first. Outline after outline and query after query provide a kind of "lesson plan," as though the habits of the high-school teacher stayed deeply ingrained in the famous professional author; he became his own instructor in the subject and the discipline of art.

Henry James went out to dinner three hundred times a season and kept his notebooks assiduously; why should a chance remark at table have engendered *The Portrait of a Lady*, and the next remark be merely gossip to his ear? Tolstoy read the paper each morning; why should an article about a woman and a train have engendered *Anna Karenina*, and the adjacent article about a man and a carriage, say, have caused him, yawning, to turn the page? The world is full of instances, of stimuli; the question for the writer is more properly perhaps: what causes our response? How may one recognize a subject or, in Malamud's phrase, learn "what one's fiction wants him to say."

For once he did respond to or recognize a subject he left very little to chance. He filled notebook and journal with citations and quotations and articles and buttressing data; if his character went walking, he listed the flowers by season; if he read about the Nez Percés, he listed—for possible use in his character's sojourn in the region—authentic tribal names. He was not some sort of muse-blessed athlete of the pen, a Roy Hobbs write-alike with no hitch in swing or stride. Rather, his notebooks, letters, and his ruminations on art attest to a thoroughly self-conscious and disciplined writer—a picture at important odds with the widespread public notion of this artist as a "natural."

"There's no one way," as he remarked. "There's so much drivel about this subject." Yet in little and large ways over the years he addressed himself unstintingly to problems both of character and craft. He was scrupulous as to procedure, systematic in his methodology and retentive of his "by-blows"; in the age of the computer and the daily-discard of revision it's improbable we'll find again so comprehensive a road-map of one mind's terrain.

This, from *Pictures of Fidelman: An Exhibition.* Here we have the same self-deprecating intensity of effort as that which bedevils Leo Finkle; the locus has shifted from rabbinical studies to painting, but the harsh imperatives of work remain the same:

> The copyist throws himself into his work with passion. He has swallowed lightning and hopes it will strike whatever he touches. Yet he has nagging doubts he can do the job right and fears he will never escape alive from the Hotel du Ville. He tries at once to paint the Titian directly on canvas but hurriedly scrapes it clean when he sees what a garish mess he has made. The Venus is insanely disproportionate and the maids in the background foreshortened into dwarfs. He then takes Angelo's advice and makes several drawings on paper to master the composition before committing it again to canvas.

Angelo and Scarpio come up every night and shake their heads over the drawings.

"Not even close," says the padrone.

"Far from it," says Scarpio.

"I'm trying," Fidelman says, anguished. "Try harder," Angelo answers grimly.

Were there a motto for Malamud's performance as author-teacher, and a single instruction he gave to his students, it resides in the exchange above. "*I'm trying*" says the anguished apprentice; "*Try harder*" the master insists. From the "passion" of one who "has swallowed lightning" to the artist plagued by "nagging doubts . . . and fears" we may limn this writer's terrain. The imagination is allegorical and the plotlines have the force of parable; there's an insistent linkage of morality and art.

One hallmark of the work, of course, is this seeming-seamless blend of fact and fantasy—a magic realism that obtains in ballpark and island and tenement equally. Therefore in 'The Magic Barrel" a photograph proves talismanic; for both the rabbinical student and the marriage broker, the snapshot of Salzman's errant daughter conjures blood-and-flesh. It's no small surprise to recognize that the story was composed more than forty years ago; if Cyril Connolly's definition of a masterpiece—a work that lasts a decade—be applied, then Malamud has managed to trick time.

His essay includes these final assertions as to the tale's origin; they are both wholly clear and opaque:

Some other autobiographical elements are:

    1. the rooming house

    2. in a sense, the time of year: between end of winter and spring is to me a very dramatic time

    3. the tomato, a detail from childhood

And here it's not inapposite to include two notes on *Dubin's Lives*: "One must transcend the autobiographical detail by inventing it after it is remembered. . . . If it is winter in the book spring surprises me when I look up."

To watch Bernard Malamud play poker was to observe him write. For years we shared a poker game in our little town. In the game there were faculty members from Bennington College, musicians, painters, sculptors; there was the local millionaire and the man who ran the gas station; we took turns playing host. Bern came properly dressed to table, arriving on the hour and departing when he'd said he would; well-organized and solemn on those Thursday nights, he pursed his lips in concentration and adjusted his eyeglasses often and joked and chattered sparingly and allowed himself only one beer. The writer was serious rather than sportive; poker relaxed him, he said. But you couldn't tell that, really, from the way he played the game or how hard he studied the hand he was dealt and how he bet, bluffed, pondered, folded, raised. He kept his cards close to his chest.

It's simple truth to say he wasn't a good player, and that he had trouble figuring the odds. But night after night and week after month he defied those poker odds and came up with a perfect low or high full house or aces: he was patient, purposive, and went home a winner. So too with the great gamble of his imaginative word-work, though it was achieved in privacy: he sat at the table, studying, arranging and discarding language until it grew unbeatable, then bet.

For years before his death the Malamuds left Bennington during the harsh, grim winter and went south to their home in New York. Often Bern would call or write me asking for a favor—a note or draft or book or letter had been left behind and now was needed and would I mind collecting it and sending it on down? I had the house-key; I did not mind;

I'd let myself in and find the needed passage and mail it to Manhattan. What was astonishing, always, was the precision of his files: if he told me where a book resided (which corner of which shelf) or a document could be located (which drawer of which cabinet), it came always precisely to hand.

In the case of "The Magic Barrel," clearly, the document itself has not been misplaced. One of the most celebrated stories in our literature, it need not be retrieved. But it comforts me to return, as it were, to his library shelf and find the necessary lines and be by them inspirited and send them on again. In the concluding passage of his own introduction to *The Stories of Bernard Malamud*, the author declares, "I've lived long among those I've invented." And Pinye Salzman, conjured back to life upon the page, has the last word. The Marriage Broker offers his "Professor" a fresh bride and, when his creator demurs, saying he already has one but is "hard at work on a new story," the old invented character withdraws. "'So enjoy,' said Salzman."

An instruction to applaud, a sentence to repeat. "So enjoy," Delbanco says.

Nicholas Delbanco is the author of the short-story collections *About My Table, and Other Stories* (1983) and *The Writer's Trade, and Other Stories* (1990), as well as of eighteen novels and ten books of nonfiction.

"Dare's Gift" by Ellen Glasgow

R. H. W. Dillard

"Dare's Gift" was originally published in the February 1917 issue of *Harper's Magazine*. It was collected in *The Shadowy Third and Other Stories* (1923). It is currently most readily available in *Downhome: An Anthology of Southern Women Writers* (Harcourt, Brace).

After a nearly twenty-year hiatus, Ellen Glasgow began to write short stories again when she was forty-two years old. As an energetic and ambitious young writer, she had renounced the form, declaring to her publisher Walter Hines Page in 1897 that "I shall not divide my power or risk my future reputation." With one reasonably successful novel to her name (although it was actually published without her name on the title page or anywhere else: she was, after all, a well-bred Southern young lady), she went on to declare bravely, "I will become a great novelist or none at all." And she certainly made as determined and serious an effort to do just that as could be expected of anyone. By June of 1916, when Glasgow began writing, as she put it, "a story about a haunted house," she had published eleven novels—and would go on to write nine more before her death in 1945. That story, which became the title story of the only collection of her short fiction published in her lifetime, *The Shadowy Third and Other Stories*, was the first of ten stories that she wrote before abandoning the form again in 1924 or 1925, when she turned her full attention to the writing of her last and finest novels.

It might be possible to conclude from a chronological reading of her novels alone that she had been correct in her belief that she shouldn't divide her power among both novels and stories. In 1913, she had published *Virginia*, which seems more and more (especially to feminist readers) to be a major American novel, and in 1925, she would publish *Barren Ground*, probably her best-known and most widely read novel. And even *Life and Gabriella*, which appeared in 1916 right before she began to write stories, is to my mind a novel deserving of critical rediscovery and positive reassessment. But during the nine years of her story writing, the two novels she wrote, *The Builders* (1919) and *One Man in His Time* (1922), are among her least interesting. Rather than blame the falling off in the quality of her novels to her writing of short fiction, however, I (along with most of Ellen Glasgow's scholarly readers) suspect that the problem lies more with her relationship with Henry W. Anderson—a relationship which, true to Glasgow's independent and rebellious nature, was not only illicit but was also (which was practically as improper for a Virginia woman of her social standing) with a Republican.

On Easter Sunday 1916, she met and soon became passionately involved with Anderson, one of the bright lights of the newly emerging Republican Party in the South, a man who was narrowly to miss being appointed by President Herbert Hoover to the United States Supreme Court. Glasgow had always claimed to be writing a "social history of Virginia" in her work, and the two novels she wrote during the time of her love affair with him are political novels, appropriate enough to that task, but much too strongly influenced by Anderson's ideas and his powerful presence in her life to be true to her own lights, just as *Barren Ground* was to be the unusually bitter response to the break-up of that romantic relationship. The Anderson novels are not without interest—she was a very good novelist even on her worst days—but that fusion of the deepest and most personal aspects of individual inner life with their cultural and social environment which marks her finest work simply does not shape those two books. In them, Ellen Glasgow's keen eye for telling detail and her ear for good prose seem to have been dulled by devotion, and the novels lack both the blood and the irony which she sought in all her fiction.

Yet, the evidence of those two novels notwithstanding, it isn't as though this strong-minded, skillful writer became totally twitterpated for nine years of her writing life. She seems to have turned to short fiction to tell the interior side of her social history, to express the concerns of "the woman within," even as she subordinated those concerns to Anderson's very public and exterior concerns in the novels. The short stories of this period, unmarked by the intrusive presence of his political ideas, are far more akin to her major work than are the novels.

Four of the stories are ghost stories, which must have startled the readers of her solidly realistic novels. (Stuart P. Sherman said of her novels, in a review of *Barren Ground*, that "Realism crossed the Potomac twenty-five years ago, going north!") She appears to have turned to the unlikely literary form of the ghost story in direct response to the emotional trauma of her father's death on January 29, 1916. He, like Anderson, was a powerful man and a public figure, one who laid a heavy hand on Glasgow's emotional life (though perhaps not quite so literally as some modern scholars have been speculating), and his death was the last of a series of deaths in her immediate family which left her alone and lonely in her own home, which had been their home as well. The house, One West Main in Richmond, where they had lived (and which

Glasgow called home for the rest of her life and where she died) seemed to her in the year following his death to be haunted. As she put it in her autobiography, *The Woman Within* (1954), "This was a loneliness peopled with phantoms. . . . The past was present, and past and present were equally haunted. . . . The house belonged to the dead. I was living with ghosts." It is tempting to see the emotional complexity of her stories as the direct result of the tension between the loss of the most powerful man in her life, which left her feeling haunted and alone, and her sudden and very powerful emotional and sexual discovery of another powerful man, but one who was unable to end her loneliness.

Be that as it may, she did write four ghost stories, and the ghost stories she wrote are not really like those of Stephen King or even those of M. R. James. They are a great deal more like those of her fellow Virginian Edgar Allan Poe (whose work she openly admired) or Henry James (whom she found "limited in emotional scope" but whose *The Turn of the Screw* she continued to enjoy) or Oliver Onions (whose work she may not have known at all). She accepted the challenge that any serious writer must face when working in an established and formulaic genre, as Raymond Chandler was to put it many years later, to "exceed the limits of a formula without destroying it." Her ghost stories respect the conventions of the form, but all four of them work psychological and social ground that is far from barren and far richer than that of conventional supernatural fiction. The longest of those stories, "Dare's Gift," is to my mind her finest story and stands alongside her best novels in its subtlety, complexity, and artistry.

Ellen Glasgow may have called "Dare's Gift" a "ghost story" when she announced its completion to her agent Paul Revere Reynolds in January 1917, but by January 1924 she was able to describe it in a letter to Joseph Hergesheimer as "a perfectly true picture of the closing days of the Confederacy." Each description is accurate in its own way, and together they offer considerable insight into the way the story works. It is a ghost story without a ghost. Dare's Gift, the house in the story, is haunted, but not by a ghost; it is, rather, haunted by an idea which is quite as dangerous. Dr. Lakeby, a character in the story, calls it "the idea of the Confederacy," but it is more than just that. As Monique Parent pointed out with a typically French enthusiasm for ideas in her *Ellen Glasgow Romancière* (1962), it *is* *"l'IDÉE de trahison."* The story is about betrayal itself, the sin that Dante placed in the very lowest circle of hell.

The French word *trahison* is particularly appropriate because, in the story, the idea that haunts the house involves both political treason and personal betrayal. In late March of 1865, three weeks before Lee's surrender, this idea reduces Colonel Dare, the elderly owner of Dare's Gift, to "a shell of a man—a shell vitalized and animated by an immense, an inde-structible illusion," and it leads his daughter Lucy to an act of betrayal that continues to haunt the house and injure its inhab-itants for fifty years after it occurs. The ghost story, Glasgow's analysis of the historical aberration of the Confederacy, and her exploration of the varieties of betrayal among men and women fuse at the heart of the story.

The plot is simple enough. In the first part of the story, a Washington lawyer, Harold Beckwith, the narrator, rents Dare's Gift in April 1915, despite some evidence that its inhabitants are often victims of acts of unexpected betrayal, as a place for his wife Mildred to recuperate from her "first nervous breakdown." At the old house, he discusses a very important case with his wife (whom he trusts completely) and reveals information he has found which would cast his side's case in jeopardy, only to have her betray him to the lawyers on the other side. When he questions her, she will only say, "I had to do it. I would do it again." In part 2, Beckwith turns away from the advice of Mildred's Washington specialist to seek the aid of a local physician, Dr. Lakeby, an old man who lost a leg in the Battle of Seven Pines in the late spring of 1862. Lakeby tells him that his wife is the victim of the house: 'The house is saturated with a thought. It is haunted by treachery." He goes on to tell the story, which he witnessed, of Lucy Dare's betrayal of her lover, a Union soldier and escaped prisoner who had come to see her one last time before fleeing to his own lines. The final twist of the plot is that Lucy is still alive fifty years later (in a nursing home, knitting socks for the soldiers in World War I) but has no memory of the events of that day at all.

The story observes the conventions of its genre: the first-person narrator describes himself as a completely rational man ("There is—I admit it readily!—a perfectly rational explanation of every mystery."); he discovers Dare's Gift while hunting on an appropriately autumnal October day at sunset; the house, for all its beauty, is described in vampiric terms—its "rows of darkened windows sucked in without giving back the last flare of daylight" and "a lonely bat was wheeling high against the red disc of the sun"; he ignores evidence that something is wrong with the house (stories of a caretaker who ran away with his wife's sister and of a tenant who gained the hatred of all his neighbors and lost "his belief in human nature"); he notices but does not worry about his wife's "pallor" and her "excitability"; and, finally, he turns to a wise older man who offers a convincing supernatural explanation of the puzzling events of the story. And the story, which is told a year after Mildred's betrayal of her husband, has the calm, meditative tone of the best ghost stories, an almost dreamlike acquiescence to the dark truths of an older time: "Yet, while I assure myself that the supernatural has been banished, in the evil company of devils, black plagues, and witches, from this sanitary century, a vision of Dare's Gift, amid its clustering cedars under the shadowy arch of the sunset, rises before me, and my feeble scepticism surrenders to that invincible spirit of darkness."

What makes this ghost story much more interesting, what allows it to exceed the limits of its genre, are the revelations it makes concerning the sources and pervasive power of acts of treachery and, like *The Turn of the Screw*, the mysteries which it conceals as well as those it reveals. The idea and fact of betrayal haunt the walls and gardens of Dare's Gift; even the house's more recent owners have betrayed its pure lines with "architectural absurdities—wanton excrescences in the modern additions, which had been designed apparently with the purpose of providing space at the least possible cost of material and labour." But the sources of that saturant *trahison* are complex and multilayered.

At the heart of the mysteries of the story is a clash of loyalties, of personal and impersonal loyalty. Dr. Lakeby compares Lucy Dare to Antigone, to another young woman who chose to obey a higher law which leads directly to her death and the death of her lover: as Sophocles put it, "Look what I suffer . . . because I respected the right." Both the blood and the irony of Glasgow's story link directly to Antigone's terrible choice.

I should like to suggest a number of ways in which "Dare's Gift" is less a ghost story or even a ghost story which allegorically analyzes Virginia social history than it is a carefully constructed labyrinth which invites a multiplicity of readings—readings which dissolve into and dissolve one another, which even as they offer new understanding of the nature of betrayal lead beyond that understanding deeper into mystery.

At the simplest level, the ghost story portrays the acting out of ancient blood crimes in the present. Mildred betrays her husband because Lucy betrayed her lover, but Lucy may well have betrayed her lover because her father had betrayed her to his obsession with Confederate patriotism. But her father may himself be victimized by a chain of betrayals leading back at least to Sir Roderick Dare's supposed betrayal of his leader in Bacon's Rebellion in 1676. The individual is caught in a supernatural working out of the sins of (in this case, literally, as it was with Antigone) the fathers.

A less supernatural reading would say that Lucy Dare betrays her lover to the Confederate troops because of her loyalty to the Confederacy, a loyalty which allows her to overcome her own woman's heart, to behave less like her father's daughter than like his son. Her choice is a patriotic one, a choice like Antigone's, to follow a higher law rather than a personal one. Also like Antigone she chooses the dead (the dying Confederacy, her dying father) over the living (her young lover). Mildred Beckwith's betrayal involves a similar choice, a heeding of the demands of justice ahead of those of her love for her husband. The irony and the tragedy lie in the awful consequences of respecting the right when it leads to personal betrayal and destruction.

Dr. Lakeby's interpretation of the idea that haunts the house casts doubt upon that second reading by questioning just what the right should have been in Lucy's case. According to him, Lucy's father had so poisoned her with the false ideals of the Confederacy that she was unable to act properly according to the standards of her true country, the Commonwealth of Virginia. Lakeby, like Robert E. Lee, sees his allegiance to Virginia and to what it means to be a Virginian as more important than loyalty to any federation or confederation to which it might belong. "Lucy Dare was a Virginian," he explains to Harold Beckwith, "and in Virginia—except in the brief, exalted Virginia of the Confederacy—the personal loyalties have always been esteemed beyond the impersonal. I cannot imagine us as a people canonizing a woman who sacrificed the human ties for the superhuman—even for the divine." According to his understanding (and he does have authority as a Virginian of Lucy's generation), Lucy owed respect to the values of Virginia, and that would have meant sacrificing the rights of the Confederacy to those of the heart. She is not then a Sophoclean tragic heroine, but rather an ironic and even pathetic one who sacrifices herself and her love (and her true patriotic obligations) to an illusion. Lucy, he says, "born in another century, . . . might have stood side by side with Antigone. . . . But she has always seemed to me diabolical."

Ellen Glasgow, in more than one place throughout her work, analyzed the deadly effects of the illusion of the Confederacy in ways that might make Dr. Lakeby seem her spokesman in the story, but even as he seems to speak for her (and to fill the role of the older, wiser counsellor of the traditional ghost story), details in the story itself undermine his authority and cast his interpretation into doubt. Embittered by a war wound which cost him his leg in defense of the Lost Cause, and possibly also embittered by Lucy's choice of both her young lover and the Confederacy ahead of him (for it is clear that he was strongly attracted to her), Dr. Lakeby finds the source of the haunting of Dare's Gift in the illusion of the Confederacy and in "diabolical" Lucy herself. Although he is perfectly willing to accuse Lucy's ancestor of betraying his leader in Bacon's Rebellion (a betrayal which is widely believed to have occurred only because the Royal Governor pardoned him after the rebellion failed), he is unwilling to consider in more than a passing way that the sources of her treachery may go back to Sir Roderick or even further back in the family history of the Dares, the line of her forefathers. He does blame her father and the "indestructible illusion" which "nourished him, that gave him his one hold on reality," but he seems eager both to absolve Lucy and to judge her too quickly: "She had drained the whole of experience in an instant, and there was left to her only the empty and withered husks of the hours. She had felt too much ever to feel again. After all . . . it is the high moments that make a life, and the flat ones that fill the years." He is perhaps speaking of himself as much as Lucy in that description, for his life, too, seems to be focused on the past, to be one of memory and regret. Lucy "has forgotten," he says, "but the house has remembered." The house *has* remembered, but Dr. Lakeby has, too.

There is yet another way of explaining the source of the *trahison* that haunts Dare's Gift and injures its inhabitants beyond that offered by Dr. Lakeby and even beyond discovering it in the earlier betrayal of Sir Roderick Dare. "Dare's Gift" is a story in which a man tells the story and relies almost exclusively upon the interpretation of another man in coming to grips with what he is telling. But two women, Lucy Dare and Mildred Beckwith, are the primary actors in the story, the betrayers and possibly the ultimate victims of the idea of treachery that haunts the house. Both choose the impersonal right (Lucy, the Confederacy; Mildred, justice in her husband's case) over the personal (the men they love). Both love their men, but both give over their lovers to the enemy. Both say the identical words when confronted with what they have done: "I had to do it. I would do it again." Ellen Glasgow, by allowing men to mediate their stories, leads an attentive reader to wonder just how much they know of the truth of the women's lives or understand their acts of betrayal.

In the story, men seem to be able to classify women easily, but they are startled when the women break out of those classifications. Dr. Lakeby's lengthy description of Lucy as she looked in 1865 ("pretty rather than beautiful" with a "small oval face" and "gentle blue eyes" and hair "which shone like satin in the moonlight") leads him to conclude that she "appeared cold—she who was destined to flame to life in an act," that she was "one of those women whose characters are shaped entirely by external events—who are the playthings of circumstance." He goes on to say that "In ordinary circumstances Lucy Dare would have been ordinary, submissive, feminine, domestic; she adored children. That she possessed a stronger will than the average Southern girl, brought up in the conventional manner, none of us—least of all I, myself—ever imagined." Beckwith's friend Harrison classifies wives as of two kinds, "those who talked and knew nothing about their husbands' affairs and . . . those who knew everything and kept silent." He adds politely that Mildred is of the second kind. Beckwith himself says of her that "Never once, not even during her illness, had she failed to share a single one of my enthusiasms; never once, in all the years of our marriage, had there been so much as a shadow between us." And yet both of these women act out of character and "would do it again." The classifications simply do not work, just as all of the men's attempts to understand these two women's acts fail to solve the mysteries of the story.

Because the two male observers are allowed both to tell and to interpret the story, the secret inner lives of the two main female characters remain unexplained. The reader is not told what happened to Lucy in the years between her father's death (and Lee's surrender) in 1865 and Dr. Lakeby's visit to her in the "Old Ladies' Home" nearly fifty years later. The reader has only Dr. Lakeby's assurance that Lucy remembers nothing of the night of her terrible decision. Lucy is never allowed to tell her version of the story. Nor does the reader ever hear Mildred Beckwith's story directly (as her husband never does either: "the events of Dare's Gift," he tells us, "are not things I can talk over with Mildred"). Mildred has had her "first nervous breakdown" before the story begins; Beckwith adds no further information about its nature or its causes, only that her doctor, a specialist in women's nervous breakdowns, suggests rest and a change of scene. These omissions lead naturally to certain questions: Is there not a pattern of male betrayal that lies before and behind these particular female betrayals? Could it be that the expectation that a woman be ordinary, submissive, feminine, and domestic, or that she be totally absorbed in her husband's affairs even when she is ill has something to do with their acts of betrayal as well as their breakdowns? What Glasgow was to call "the sheltered life" in her 1932 novel of that name (the old order with its rules and its classifications) closes in around both Lucy and Mildred in this story as thoroughly as it does around Eva Birdsong and Jenny Blair Archbald in that novel, a protective shield of male understanding, forgiveness, and silence that betrays even as it protects. The women in "Dare's Gift" are silenced or choose silence, and the men are complicitous in that silencing whether intentionally or not. Harold Beckwith tells the story to assure himself that "the impossible really happened," but the reader is left to fathom the mysteries of the story beyond the telling of the tale.

Perhaps, for example, there is a larger shadow between Mildred and her husband than he knows. When she settles in at Dare's Gift, she seems to her husband excitable and possessed of an "abnormal psychology," but she herself puts it this way: "It is just as if we had stepped into another world. . . . I feel as if I had ceased to be myself since I left Washington." She does not appear again or speak for herself in the story after Dr. Lakeby gives her a bromide to make her sleep while he tells his version of the story of Lucy to Beckwith. A year has passed when Beckwith begins his narration, but nothing of Mildred's life during that year is revealed; her actions, no matter what their real causes may have been, have become simply the result of her *second* nervous breakdown (whether they are ascribed to the haunted house or not). There is a void in her story quite as meaningful (if briefer in time) as that in Lucy's story. The betrayed caretaker's wife tells Beckwith that Lucy "went off somewhere to strange parts" after her father's death at the end of the war. Perhaps both she and Mildred actually went to stranger parts than those around them know or will allow themselves to believe.

Perhaps, like Antigone, these women were not just acted upon by external forces but, within the context of those forces, actually made individual moral decisions, however terrible the consequences, the actual terms of which we cannot know. Their stories' male narrators, while attempting to absolve the women of guilt by placing it on Lucy's father, "the idea of the Confederacy," or the house, actually betray both Lucy and Mildred quite as much as they themselves had betrayed their lovers, betrayed them by denying them the responsibility for their own actions—and coincidentally avoided any culpability on their own parts as well. The reader is left to wonder and to speculate, to seek the truth that only the women might know but which they never tell (except in those two ominous and minatory sentences: "I had to do it. I would do it again.").

Whether the reader of "Dare's Gift" chooses to read it simply as an effective ghost story or to explore the interstices in the story in search of the mysteries within its central (and apparently fully explained) mystery, it is so carefully written a story that it maintains its own appealing and enigmatic identity either way. One may choose to read it as an analysis of the dangers of unresolved guilt, as social history, as Southern history, as personal psychodrama (surely the tension, the frustration, and the rage in Glasgow's life between her desire for her secret lover and her fear of her dominant father had something to do with Lucy's dilemma), as a feminist recounting of the male's silencing of "herstory," as a philosophical study of the tragic intersection of necessity, chance, and free will, as a revelation of the *trahison* that may be inherent in love, or as a carefully designed labyrinth of possible meanings which cannot finally be solved (like Poe's "Ligeia" or James's *The Turn of the Screw*). The story invites all of these readings and more.

To Harold Beckwith, "the occurrence remains, like the house in its grove of cedars, wrapped in an impenetrable mystery." Like Dare's Gift, "Dare's Gift" is also dangerous and haunting; it, too, is saturated with the idea of treason to which each generation only seems to add its own excrescences; it, too, invites the reader to see through its outward appearances and journey into its interior. A reader who accepts Ellen Glasgow's gift will soon realize that he or she has also accepted her dare as well: to move past the comfortable assurances of her story's use of genre conventions and its own apparent self-interpretation, to go off to strange parts, to enter its impenetrable mystery, the maze where minotaurs may lurk and where one may meet betrayal face to face.

R. H. W. Dillard is the author of the short-story collection *Omniphobia* (1995), the novels *The Book of Changes* (1974) and *The First Man on the Sun* (1983), six collections of poetry, and two nonfiction books.

"The Things They Carried"
by Tim O'Brien

Ellen Douglas

"The Things They Carried" was originally published in the August 1986 issue of *Esquire*. It was collected in *The Things They Carried* (1990). It is currently most readily available in *The Things They Carried* (Mariner Books).

I want to begin with a quotation from Plato's *Republic*—a quotation that Tim O'Brien uses in his book *If I Die in a Combat Zone*:

> "So a city is also courageous by a part of itself, thanks to that part's having in it a power that through everything else will preserve the opinion about which things are terrible—that they are the same ones and of the same sort as those the lawgiver transmitted in the education. Or don't you call that courage?"
>
> "I didn't quite understand what you said," he said. "Say it again."
>
> "I mean," I said, "that courage is a certain kind of preserving."
>
> "Just what sort of preserving?"
>
> "The preserving of the opinion produced by law through education about what—and what sort of thing—is terrible. . . ."

". . . a power that through everything else will preserve the opinion about which things are terrible." Tim O'Brien over the years, writing about our terrible century, has preserved that opinion. He has known which things are terrible and has borne witness, soberly, eloquently, courageously, to that knowledge.

It may be that for Americans, particularly for Americans of O'Brien's generation, no matter that earlier and later there were more terrible things going on in the world, for those Americans, because they took part in it, the most terrible of all things is the Vietnam War. We have shrunk away, have closed our eyes, have cowered before the terrible knowledge of the Vietnam War. Of how we became embroiled in it. Of what we did there. Of how many lives were wasted there: our brothers, our friends, our sons and daughters. Of all the "enemies" we "wasted" there. Of our confusion and bewilderment, of our disgraceful, self-deceiving disengagement. Of what responsibility every single one of us bears. Every single one of us.

But again and again O'Brien has looked that horror in the face. In his novels, *Going After Cacciato* and *In the Lake of the Woods*, in his non-fiction, *If I Die*, and in the novel and the short story both titled *The Things They Carried*.

"The Things They Carried" is a story complete in itself, published originally in *Esquire*. In the novel of which it is the opening chapter there are other stories, complete in themselves, of the lives of soldiers in Vietnam. Linking these is a kind of meditation on the telling of stories: why we tell them and how we cannot understand our world without them. I don't know when, in the course of writing, it came to seem inevitable to O'Brien to use linked stories that, like soldiers delicately making their way through a mine field, tread a line between fact and fiction, in order to explore *which things are terrible*. I don't think it matters. He hit upon his method and it served him well.

In the novel he writes, "If a story seems moral, do not believe it," and "stories are for joining the past to the future." He makes us know that even though the writer understands the softness, the sick odor of "morals" in fiction, even though he labors to find a truth, even though he wants a story to join past to future, he will fail, just as in battle, no matter how brave he wants to be, he will fail. This is one of the terrible things.

The narrative thread in "The Things They Carried" guides us through one short period in the life of a squad of infantrymen walking the mined and lethal fields and paddies and jungles of Vietnam. Incident by incident we learn how the men support one another, how they fail one another, how they fall into bewildered and bewildering brutality, how they see each other die. We follow Lt. Jimmy Cross, dreaming about his girlfriend, as he fails his men, and causes (or perhaps does not cause) the death of one of them. The thread of the story is borne up by a kind of inventory of all the things a soldier—a grunt—must carry on the endless, senseless search-and-destroy missions, walking, wading, crawling through a hostile countryside—the inventory broken into in an extraordinary way by statements about the nature of things or about events:

> they carried M-14s and CAR-15s and Swedish Ks and grease guns and captured AK-47s . . . and black market Uzis . . . and blackjacks and bayonets. . . . Lee Strunk carried a slingshot; a weapon of last resort, he called it.

And:

> They carried Sterno, safety pins, trip flares. . . . Taking turns, they carried the big PRC-77 scrambler radio, which weighed 30 pounds with its battery. They shared the weight of memory. They took up what others could no longer

bear. Often, they carried each other, the wounded or weak. They carried infections. They carried chess sets, basketballs, Vietnamese-English dictionaries, insignia of rank. . . .

And:

Some carried CS or tear gas grenades. Some carried white phosphorous grenades. They carried all they could bear, and then some, including a silent awe for the terrible power of the things they carried.

And:

Ted Lavender, who was scared, carried 34 rounds when he was shot and killed outside Than Khe, and he went down under an exceptional burden, more than 20 pounds of ammunition, plus the flak jacket and helmet and rations and water and toilet paper and tranquilizers and all the rest, plus the unweighed fear.

How can I say why this story seems so important to me, why I turn again and again to Tim O'Brien's work? It has to do, for one thing, with the sobriety of the language, the way it succeeds in conveying, over and over, extremities of bewilderment, suffering, and outrage. I could speak of how carefully O'Brien builds in us a belief in the hopeless love of the lieutenant for his girlfriend. I could speak of the careful delineation of the characters of the men and the vivid evocation of the country. I could speak of economy, of irony, of effective juxtaposition, of eloquence, of all sorts of literary matters, matters that are central to the truth of any story. For it is essential that a story tell itself in a form that is inextricable from its meaning, and O'Brien knows this. But these would not be the most important things I could say. What I want to say has to do with the nature of fiction in our terrible century. It is as if fiction itself is in danger, as if, in the face of our knowledge of how we continue to slaughter each other and to rape our world, the very act of writing fiction threatens to become frivolous, the territory of aesthetes and writers in the commercial marketplace and sentimentalists.

This possibility is what Tim O'Brien takes on in a new and peculiar way, by forcing us to see how fictions are created out of reality and by bringing us face to face with *the terrible.*

Read "The Things They Carried," and then go and find the novel into which it will lead you, and read it, and then find *If I Die in a Combat Zone* and *In the Lake of the Woods.* Read these books and you will understand how a writer can be a member of that part of the city that through everything else will preserve the opinion about which things are terrible, how a writer can look at his own pain and at the wreckage of our century and find a way to write fiction that links past to future and calls "morals" into question.

Ellen Douglas (1921–2012) is the pen name of Josephine Ayres Haxton. She is the author of the short stories in *Black Cloud, White Cloud: Two Novellas and Two Stories* (1963), of seven novels, and two nonfiction books.

"In Another Country"
by Ernest Hemingway

Andre Dubus

"In Another Country" was originally published in the April 1927 issue of *Scribner's Magazine*. It was collected in *Men Without Women* (1927). It is currently most readily available in *The Complete Short Stories of Ernest Hemingway: The Finca Vigia Edition* (Scribner).

In my thirtieth summer, in 1966, I read many stories by John O'Hara, and read Hemingway's stories again, and his "In Another Country" challenged me more than I could know then. That summer was my last at the University of Iowa; I had a Master of Fine Arts Degree and, beginning in the fall, a job as a teacher, in Massachusetts. My wife and four children and I would move there in August. Until then, we lived in Iowa City and I taught two freshman rhetoric classes four mornings a week, then came home to eat lunch and write. I wrote in my den at the front of the house, a small room with large windows, and I looked out across the lawn at an intersection of streets shaded by tall trees. I was trying to learn to write stories, and was reading O'Hara and Hemingway as a carpenter might look at an excellent house someone else has built.

"In Another Country" became that summer one of my favorite stories written by anyone, and it still is. But I could not fully understand the story. What's it *about*? I said to a friend as we drove in his car to the university track to run laps. He said: It's about the futility of cures. That nestled beneath my heart, displaced my confusion. Yes. The futility of cures. Then everything connected and formed a whole, and in the car with my friend, then running with him around the track, I saw the story as you see a painting, and one of the central images was the black silk handkerchief covering the wound where the young man's nose had been.

Kurt Vonnegut was our neighbor. We had adjacent lawns; he lived behind us, at the top of the hill. One day that summer he was outside on his lawn or on his front porch four times when I was outside, and we waved and called to each other. The first time I was walking home from teaching, wearing slacks and a shirt; the next time I was wearing shorts and a tee shirt I had put on to write; then I wore gym shorts without a shirt and drove to the track; in late afternoon, wearing another pair of slacks and another shirt, I walked up to his house to drink. He was sitting on his front porch and, as I approached, he said: "Andre, you change clothes more than a Barbie Doll."

Kurt did not have a telephone. That summer the English Department hosted a conference, and one afternoon a man from the department called me and asked me to ask Kurt to meet Ralph Ellison at the airport later in the day, then Mrs. Ellison at the train. She did not like to fly. I went up to Kurt's house, and he came to the back door. I said: "They want us to pick up Ellison at the airport. Then his wife at the train."

"Swell. I'll drive."

Later he came driving down the brick road from his house and I got in the car and saw a paperback of *Invisible Man* between us on the seat. The airport was in Cedar Rapids, a short drive. I said: "Are you going to leave the book there?"

"I'm teaching it. I thought it'd be phony to take it out of the car."

It was a hot afternoon. We left town and were on the highway, the corn was tall and green under the huge midwestern sky, and I said: "They didn't really ask for both of us to pick up Ellison. Just you."

"I knew that."

"Thanks. How are we going to recognize him? Do we just walk up to the only Negro who gets off the plane?"

Kurt looked at me and said: "Shit."

"We could just walk past him, pretend we couldn't see him."

"That's so good, we ought to do it."

The terminal was small and we stood outside and watched the plane land, and the people filing out of it, and there was one black man. We went to him and Kurt said: "Ralph Ellison?" and Ellison smiled and said: "Yes," and we shook his hand and got his things and went to the car. I sat in back, and watched Ellison. He saw *Invisible Man* at once but did not say anything. As we rode on the highway he looked at the cornfields and talked fondly of the times he had hunted pheasants here with Vance Bourjaily. Then he picked up his book and said: "It's still around."

Kurt told him he was teaching it, and I must have told him I loved it because I did and I do, but I only remember watching him and listening to him. Kurt asked him if he wanted a drink. He did. We went to a bar near the university, and sat in a booth, Ellison opposite Kurt and me, and ordered vodka martinis. We talked about jazz and books, and Ellison said that before starting *Invisible Man* he had read Malraux's *Man's Fate* forty times. He liked the combination of melodrama and philosophy, he said, and he liked those in Dostoyevski too. We ordered martinis again and I was no longer shy. I looked at Ellison's eyes and said: "I've been re-reading Hemingway's stories this summer, and I think my favorite is 'In Another Country.'"

He looked moved by remembrance, as he had in the car, talking about hunting with Vance. Looking at us, he recited the story's first paragraph:

> In the fall the war was always there, but we did not go to it any more. It was cold in the fall in Milan and the dark came very early. Then the electric lights came on, and it was pleasant along the streets looking in the windows. There was much game hanging outside the shops, and the snow powdered in the fur of the foxes and the wind blew their tails. The deer hung stiff and heavy and empty, and small birds blew in the wind and the wind turned their feathers. It was a cold fall and the wind came down from the mountains.

When we took Ellison to his room on the campus, it was time for us to go to the train station and meet his wife. Kurt said to Ellison: "How will we recognize her?"

"She's wearing a gray dress and carrying a beige raincoat." He smiled. "And she's colored."

Wanting to know absolutely what a story is about, and to be able to say it in a few sentences, is dangerous: it can lead us to wanting to possess a story as we possess a cup. We know the function of a cup, and we drink from it, wash it, put it on a shelf, and it remains a thing we own and control, unless it slips from our hands into the control of gravity; or someone else breaks it, or uses it to give us poisoned tea. A story can always break into pieces while it sits inside a book on a shelf; and, decades after we have read it even twenty times, it can open us up, by cut or caress, to a new truth.

I taught at Bradford College in Massachusetts for eighteen years, and in my first year, and many times afterward, I assigned "In Another Country" to students. The first time I talked about it in a classroom I understood more of it, because of what the students said, and also because of what I said: words that I did not know I would say, giving voice to ideas I did not know I had, and to images I had not seen in my mind. I began by telling them the story was about the futility of cures; by the end of the class I knew it was not. Through my years of teaching I learned to walk into a classroom wondering what I would say, rather than knowing what I would say. Then I learned by hearing myself speak; the source of my speaking was our mysterious harmony with truths we know, though very often our knowledge of them is hidden from us. Now, as a retired teacher, I mistrust all prepared statements by anyone, and by me.

Still, after discussing "In Another Country" the first time with Bradford students, I did go into the classroom in the years after that, knowing exactly what I would say about the story. Probably ten times in those eighteen years I assigned "In Another Country" and began our discussion by focusing on the images in the first two paragraphs, the narrator—who may be Nick Adams—bringing us to the hospital, and to the machines "that were to make so much difference," and I talked about the tone of that phrase, a tone achieved by the music of the two paragraphs, a tone that tells us the machines will make nothing different.

The story shifts then to the Italian major. He was a champion fencer before the war; now he is a wounded man whose right hand is shrunken; it is the size of a baby's hand, and he puts it into a machine which the doctor says will restore it to its normal size. Neither the major's hand nor the major will ever be normal. The narrator's knee is injured and the small proportion he gives it in the story lets us know that it will be healed. I told my students, when they were trying to understand a story that seemed difficult, to look at its proportion: the physical space a writer gives each element of the story. "In Another Country" moves swiftly from the futility of cures, to what it is that the physical curing cannot touch; and, yes, the young man who lost his nose and covered his face with a black silk handkerchief is a thematic image in the story, but it is not in the center of the picture, it is off to the side.

In the center of this canvas is death. That is why the narrator, though his knee will be normal again, will not himself be normal. Or perhaps not for a very long time. After the first hospital scene he tells us of his other comrades, the Italian soldiers he walks home from the hospital with; all of them, in the war, have lived with death. Because of this, they feel detached, and they feel insulated from civilians and others who have not been in the war. The narrator is frightened, and at night moves from the light of one street lamp to another. He does not want to go to the war again. So the story now has moved from the futility of cures back to war, where it began with its opening line and the paragraph that shows us lovely pictures of Milan; while, beneath that tactile beauty, the music is the sound of something lost, and the loss of it has changed even the sound of the wind, and the sight of blowing snow on the fur of animals.

A war story, then; and while the major and narrator sit at their machines in the hospital, the major teaches Italian grammar to the narrator. I cannot know why Hemingway chose Italian grammar, but my deepest guess is that his choice was perfect: two wounded men, talking about language, rather than faith in the machines, hope for healing, or the horror of war. I am not saying they ought to be speaking about these things. There are times when it is best to be quiet, to endure, to wait. Hemingway may be our writer who has been the most badly read. His characters are as afraid of pain and death as anyone else. They feel it, they think about it, and they talk about it with people they love. With the Italian major, the narrator talks about grammar.

Then the story moves again, in the final scene. Until now, it has seemed to be a story about young men who have lost that joy in being alive which is normal for young and healthy people, who have not yet learned that within the hour they may be dead. The story has been about that spiritual aging that war can cause: in a few moments, a young soldier can see and hear enough, taste and touch and smell enough, to age his spirit by decades while his body has not aged at all. The quickness of this change, of the spirit's immersion in horror, may cause a state of detachment from people whose lives are still normal, and who receive mortality's potion, drop by tiny drop, not in a torrent.

But in the story's final scene, the major furiously and bitterly grieves, scolds the narrator, then apologizes, says that his wife has just died and, crying, leaves the room where the machines are. From their doctor the narrator learns that the major had waited to marry until he was out of the war. His wife contracted pneumonia and in three days she was dead, and now in the story death is no longer the haunting demon of soldiers who have looked into its eyes. It is what no one can escape. The major reasonably believed he was the one in danger, until he was home from the war. Then death attacked his exposed flank, and breathed pneumonia into his wife. The story has completed its movement. A few notes remain: softly, a piano and bass, and faint drums and cymbals; we see the major returning to put his hand in the machine. He keeps doing this.

Two years after I retired from teaching, and twenty years after that last summer in Iowa City, I was crippled in an instant when a car hit me, and I was in a hospital for nearly two months. I suffered with pain, and I thought very often of Ernest Hemingway, and how much physical pain he had suffered, and how well he had written about it. In the hospital I did not think about "In Another Country." I thought about "The Gambler, the Nun, and the Radio," and was both enlightened and amused, for always when I had talked about that story with students, I had moved quickly past the physical pain and focused on the metaphysical. Philosophy is abundant in that story; but I had to live in pain, on a hospital bed, before I could see that bodily pain deserved much more than I had given it. Always I had spent one fifty-minute class on the story. I should have used two class sessions; the first one would have been about pain.

A year after my injury, in a time of spiritual pain, I dreamed one night that I was standing on both my legs with other people in a brightly lit kitchen near the end of the day. I did not recognize any of the people, but in the dream they were my friends; one was a woman who was deeply hurting me. We were all standing, and I was pretending to be happy, and no one could see my pain. I stood near the stove. The kitchen door to the lawn was open, and there was a screen door and, from outside, Ernest Hemingway opened it and walked in, looking at me across the length of the room. He wore his fishing cap with a long visor. He walked straight to me and said: Let's go fishing. I walked with him, outside and down a sloping lawn to a wharf. We went to the end of the wharf where a large boat with an inboard motor was tied. Then we stood in the cabin, Hemingway at my right and holding the wheel with both hands; we moved on a calm bay, and were going out to sea. It was dusk and I wondered if it was too late to go to sea, and I had not seen him carrying fishing rods, and I wondered if he had forgotten them. But I worried for only a moment. Then I looked up at his profile and knew that he knew what he was doing. He had a mustache but no beard and was about forty and still handsome.

The next night a writers' workshop I host gathered in my living room. When they left I sat in my wheelchair in the dining room and remembered my dream, and remarked for the first time that Hemingway had his head, and I had my missing leg, and the leg I do have was no longer damaged. Then I remembered reading something that John Cheever either wrote or said: during one long dark night of the soul, Ernest Hemingway spoke to him. Cheever said that he had never heard Hemingway's voice, but he knew that this was his voice, telling Cheever that his present pain was only the beginning. Then, sitting in my chair in the quiet night, I believed that Hemingway had come to me while I was suffering, and had taken me away from it, out to sea where we could fish.

A few months later, in winter, I wrote to Father Bruce Ritter at Covenant House in New York and told him that I was crippled and had not yet learned to drive with hand controls; that my young daughters were no longer living with me; that I hosted, without pay, a writers' workshop, but its members could afford to pay anyone for what I did, and they did not really need me; and I felt that when I was not with my children I was no longer a useful part of the world. Father Ritter wrote to me, suggesting that I tutor a couple of high-school students. In Haverhill there is a home for girls between the ages of fourteen and eighteen. They are in protective custody of the state, because of what people have done to them. In summer I phoned the home, and asked if they wanted a volunteer. Someone drove me there to meet the man in charge of education. A light rain was falling. At the home I looked through the car window at a second-story window and saw an old and long-soiled toy, a stuffed dog. The man came out and stood in the rain and I asked him what I could do. He said: "Give them stories about real people. Give them words and images. They're afraid of those."

So that fall, in 1988, we began; and nearly eight years later, girls with a staff woman still come to my house on Monday nights, and we read. For the first seven years I read to them; then they told me they wanted to read, and now I simply choose a book, provide soft drinks and ash trays, and listen. One night in the fall of 1991, five years after my injury, I read "In Another Country" to a few girls and a staff woman. This was the first time I had read it since my crippling. I planned to read it to the girls, then say about it what I had said so many times to students at Bradford College. I stopped often while reading the story, to tell them about images and thematic shifts. When I finished reading it, I talked about each part of it again, building to my explanation of the story's closing lines:

> The major did not come to the hospital for three days. Then he came at the usual hour, wearing a black band on the sleeve of his uniform. When he came back, there were large framed photographs around the wall, of all sorts of wounds before and after they had been cured by the machines. In front of the machine the major used were three photographs of hands like his that were completely restored. I do not know where the doctor got them. I always understood we were the first to use the machines. The photographs did not make much difference to the major because he only looked out of the window.

Then, because of my own five years of agony, of sleeping at night and in my dreams walking on two legs then waking each morning to being crippled, of praying and willing myself out of bed to confront the day, of having to learn a new way to live after living nearly fifty years with a whole body—then, because of all this, I saw something I had never seen in the story, and I do not know whether Hemingway saw it when he wrote it or later or never, but there it was, there it is, and with passion and joy I looked up from the book, looked at the girls' faces and said: "This story is about healing too. The major keeps going to the machines. And he doesn't believe in them. But he gets out of his bed in the morning. He brushes his teeth. He shaves. He combs his hair. He puts on his uniform. He leaves the place where he lives. He walks to the hospital, and sits at the machines. Every one of those actions is a movement away from suicide. Away from despair. Look at him. Three days after his wife has died, he is in motion. He is sad. He will not get over this. And he will get over this. His hand won't be cured but some day he will meet another woman. And he will love her. Because he is alive."

The girls watched me, nodding their heads, those girls who had suffered and still suffered; but for now, on this Monday night, they sat on my couch, and happily watched me discover a truth; or watched a truth discover me, when I was ready for it.

Andre Dubus (1936–1999) is the author of the short-story collections *Separate Flights* (1975), *Adultery and Other Choices* (1977), *Finding a Girl in America* (1980), *The Times Are Never So Bad* (1983), *The Last Worthless Evening* (1986), *Selected Stories* (1988), and *In the Bedroom* (2002), the novel *The Lieutenant* (1967), the novella *Voices From the Moon* (1984), and two books of nonfiction. He won the PEN/Malamud Award for Excellence in the Short Story in 1991.

"Like Life" by Lorrie Moore

Pamela Erens

"Like Life" was first published and collected in *Like Life* (1990).
It is currently most readily available in *Like Life* (Vintage).

D o I "like" "Like Life," the title story of Lorrie Moore's second collection? The story, by the way, has a lot to do with
liking and loving and what we do or don't like and/or love. It's
a bleak and frightening tale that is also bracing and funny and
immensely smart. "Like" seems a tame word for my reaction
to it. I relish it, am in awe of it; I never tire of rereading it.

Moore's stories often deal with extremity. "People Like
That Are the Only People Here," one of her most famous,
limns the horror of being a parent with a dangerously ill
child. "You're Ugly, Too," which appeared in John Updike's
anthology *Best American Short Stories of the Century*, suggests
that being a single woman in search of a minimally acceptable partner is a situation hardly less dire. But "Like Life"
gets at something more broadly existential: the irreducible
terror at the heart of human existence, the way we are never
completely safe, housed, and loved. The story makes me feel
the way I used to when, as a child, I believed that a skeleton
lived in the bathroom shower; that my parents, late to relieve
the babysitter, had died and would never return. Perhaps I
go to it as an inoculation, a way of experiencing a small and

localized amount of terror so that I can tolerate it in the rest of my life.

Written in the 1980s, "Like Life" takes place in a futuristic New York City of the 1990s, where pollutants have rendered the water undrinkable and citizens, especially young men, are dying of unnamed illnesses (the AIDS crisis is clearly an allusion here). There is also a serial killer on the loose, and to top it off it is February, when "a thaw gave the city the weepy ooze of a wound." The physical city repeatedly appears as toxic and repulsive: "fetid," "wet," and "decaying." A sunset is "a black eye yellowing." Mamie, a 35-year-old children's book author and illustrator, recently had a mole on her back removed and fears being the next victim of the plague. The title of the story contains an allusion to terminal illness. The doctor refers to Mamie's removed mole as "precancer," and Mamie asks him: "*Pre*cancer? . . . isn't that . . . like *life*?" The doctor "took her wrist and briefly squeezed. 'It's *like* life, but it's not *necessarily* life.'"

Perhaps the doctor is telling Mamie that she needn't live as if tragedy and demise are around every corner, but Mamie feels afraid and threatened even in her own home. She lives in a converted beauty parlor that stinks of turpentine from the labors of her husband of fourteen years, Rudy, whose lack of success as a painter is turning him bitter and aggressive. (There is a startling moment where Mamie describes the "acrid, animal smell hot under his arms. He could smell like that sometimes, like a crazy person.") For unstated reasons Rudy sleeps with a hatchet, which he once raised above Mamie's head during the confusion of a nightmare. Long ago, Mamie and Rudy were in love, but she can no longer find in herself any passion for him, or even, most of the time, tenderness, despite his frequent kindness and charm. She fantasizes about leaving him and shops around for an apartment of her own, unable to afford anything. Almost nothing happens in this longish story, if deep longing, despair, rage, and radical unease are nothing. Then, near the end, there is a genuine plot development that takes one's breath away and brings everything we've read into almost unbearable focus.

I see that my exegesis so far strongly supports my statement that "Like Life" is a bleak story, and not so much my claim that it is also delightful. As is usual with Lorrie Moore, the delight is partly in the fresh and vivid language. A star Mamie sees outside her window is "an asterisk to take her away briefly to an explanation" and her marriage seems to her "like a saint, guillotined and still walking for miles through the city, carrying its head." The delight is also in Moore's receptivity to the absurd. The absurdity is often of the banana-peel type: unsuspecting innocent tripped up by lowly reality. As readers we can't help but identify and experience a relieved laughter, a sense that our own clumsiness and vulnerability have been sympathetically acknowledged. As a fellow writer, I take a sly pleasure in the account of Mamie's interactions with her editor:

> "Mamie? Great stuff," he liked to say. "I'm sending the manuscript back with my suggestions. But ignore them." And always the manuscript arrived three weeks later with comments in the margin like *Oh please* and *No shit.*

Earlier, when Mamie is looking for an apartment, a realtor filling out her application acts as if even her full name, Mamie Cournand, is an affront: "*What?* Here. You fill this out." We've all been there, just going out about our business, when someone sees fit to pull us down a peg. We know Mamie doesn't deserve it. By analogy we didn't either.

If Mamie were merely the ongoing victim of society's minor bullies, we would tire of her, but she also has a skewed self-awareness that is quite endearing. At the coffee shop she frequents after delivering work to her editor, "usually she ordered a cup of coffee *and* a cup of tea, as well as a brownie, propping up her sadness with chocolate and caffeine so that it became an anxiety." Her sense of character is acute. Of Rudy, she muses:

> Years ago she had come to know his little lies, harmless for the most part and born of vanity and doubts, and sometimes fueled merely by a desire to hide from things whose truth took too much effort to figure out. She knew the way he would tell the same anecdotes from his life, over and over again, each time a little differently, the exaggerations and contradictions sometimes having a particular purpose—his self-portrait as Undiscovered Genius—and sometimes not seeming to have one at all. "Six inches from the door was an empty shopping cart jammed up against the door," he told her once, and she said, "Rudy, how can it be six inches from the door but also jammed up against it?"
> "It was full of newspapers and tin cans, stuff like that. I don't know."

Don't we all know someone like this? Maybe that someone is ourselves.

But Mamie's perceptiveness, rather than grounding her, only adds to her growing dread that something is sinister and off-kilter about her world. And maybe there is. At the very beginning of the story, we learn that "[a]ll the movies that year were about people with plates in their heads." In these movies, alien spirits take over the bodies of human beings, people believe they are other people, people meet their doppelgangers. The focus on simulacrums and imposture continues throughout. Mamie is tormented by the idea that much of what she experiences is fake. She is not sure she knows who her husband really is; there's a pointed passage about how he always seems to be doing imitations of someone else: "[I]t was a little scary, as if he were many different people at once, people to turn to, not in distress, but like a channel on television, a mind gone crazy with cable. He was Jimmy Stewart. He was Elvis Presley." Mamie also sees their beauty-parlor living quarters, where out of penury they use napkins for toilet paper and dishwashing liquid for shampoo, as ersatz: "We're camping out here, Rudy. This is camping! . . . This is not life. This is something else."

But what *is* life, and how can Mamie find it? She remains unsure that anything she dreams up—divorce, a new apartment—promises to deliver it.

"Like Life" forces the reader into a continuous oscillation: its bleakness is never without a certain brave jauntiness, its humor is never without a sting. At its sharpest, that sting has to do with Mamie's buried rage. Most of the time she behaves meekly and as if stunned, but the focus on the interactions with the realtor and the editor suggests she files away and nurtures her hurts. Her insights about Rudy are the insights unearthed by a deeply disillusioned lover. Her anger is too deep to be burnt clean by irony or surrender, and the residue is projected outwards, onto the filthy weather, the "sidewalks foamed to a cheese of spit," and the "hating eyes" of the homeless. Perhaps we are even to take the sexual bullying of her husband as an externalization of Mamie's own growing desire for violence. Mamie has a conversation with a co-worker who (giving us yet another twist on the story's title) claims she doesn't have a love life, she has a *like* life. Mamie's reaction is to envy her: it sounds "nice" and "peaceful" to be "free from love." Would Mamie's rage dwindle and the world itself appear less rage-filled if she could be unbound from her soured feelings for her husband? The logical endpoint of rage may be a wish for death, one's own or someone else's. Despite how many times I've read this story, only when I returned to it again recently did I note a thread I'd previously neglected: *Mamie is looking for a place to die.* Perhaps it was simply too upsetting to think that this character, of whom I'm very fond, will, in fact, develop cancer; I always believed she had a case of hypochondria (the mole was only "precancer"; it was removed). But the signs are too relentless to ignore:

> On nights when she [Mamie] did sleep, her dreams were about the end of life. They involved getting somewhere, getting to the place where she was supposed to die, where it was OK. She was always in a group, like a fire drill or a class trip. Can we die here? Are we there yet? Which way can it possibly be?

Almost the last line of the story is "If one were to look for a place to die, mightn't it be here?" In this light, Mamie's frantic searches for an apartment seem less about her desire to leave her husband—though there's that too—and more about wanting a safe burrow to pass quietly away in. It's jarring that as much as Mamie fears death (the way I'd always previously read the story) she may be wishing for it even more.

At a moment of crisis and self-doubt Mamie's husband cries out to her to "give me one good reason why we should go on living." Mamie is not sure she has an answer. This is the terrible question the story asks of readers as well. One could walk away from "Like Life" believing that its author has reached a point of no return, that after writing her way into such despair there will be no more stories to create. But—apart from the fact that Lorrie Moore has gone on to produce several more excellent books of fiction—that would be discounting the humor on the page, humor that Mamie is often impervious to but that boomerangs back to us. Humor is one of the qualities most difficult to convey out of context, and possibly the examples I've given won't hit everyone's funny bone. The wit in "Like Life" is the cumulative result of tone, energy, word choice, double entendre, precise observation, and above all a quirkily jaundiced point of view. And it provides a possible answer to Rudy's question. Maybe jokes are a good enough excuse to go on. Or the oddities one can see on any stroll down a public street.

Or maybe the story itself is the answer. Like the commercial horror movies beloved of adolescents and the adolescent-at-heart, "Like Life," in its masterful mix of the frightening and the ridiculous, allows us to experience our fears—of sickness, violence, and the people we're closest to—in a form that is unabashedly artificial and therefore endurable. With the "like-lifeness" that is art, perhaps we can manage to keep stumbling through our lives, day by day.

I've never known quite how to read the last three paragraphs of "Like Life." These paragraphs follow the dramatic turn that makes this story not just a tour de force of language and mood but also a revelation of what the mechanics of fear and loathing can do to a human soul. I don't want to write about this turn, or these last paragraphs, here, for fear of spoiling the pleasure of a first encounter for readers unfamiliar with the story. I love the ending, it makes the hair on my arms stand up, but I'm not quite sure what Lorrie Moore had in mind. That's all right; I don't need to know. I probably don't want to know. I can't predict what Mamie is going to do, and I can't say what she feels, except, because I'm told, that she's still terrified. Just as I am, reading this story. And going back to it again and again because it tells me I'm not alone, because I find a crazy, painful laughter in its dark unfolding.

Pamela Erens is the author of the novels *The Understory* (2007), *The Virgins* (2013), and *Eleven Hours* (2016).

"Ghost and Flesh, Water and Dirt"
by William Goyen

George Garrett

"Ghost and Flesh, Water and Dirt" was originally published (as "The Ghost of Raymond Emmons") in the February 1951 issue of *Mademoiselle*. It was collected in *Ghost and Flesh: Stories and Tales* (1952). It is currently most readily available in *The Norton Anthology of Short Fiction* (W. W. Norton).

It is ironic that, for a number of reasons, William Goyen, one of the most original and innovative voices in twenti-eth-century fiction, especially the short story, should now need some words of introduction. Not that the man, poet, playwright (five produced plays), and editor (McGraw-Hill), as well as fiction writer, and his work—six novels, five collections of stories, three other works—were or are unknown. Not by any means. In Europe, thanks in part to able and gifted translators, especially in France and Germany, his work has been highly honored and is widely studied. Here at home in America, aside from the many other writers who are on record as his admiring readers, he early earned and has maintained the mixed blessings of a kind of cult status. In her wonder-fully perceptive introduction to Goyen's posthumous *Had I a Hundred Mouths: New & Selected Stories, 1947–1983* (1985), Joyce Carol Oates celebrates the originality of his work ("A story by William Goyen is always immediately recognizable as a story by William Goyen."). And she focuses on the paradoxical conflicts out of which his singular method grew. He is "the most mysterious of writers," she writes: "He is a poet, singer, musician as well as storyteller; he is a seer; a troubled visionary; a spiritual presence in a national literature largely deprived of the spiritual." On the one hand, he is lyrical and visionary. On the other, he is deceptively "artless": "So fluid and artless are the stories that they give the impression of being 'merely narratives of memory.'"

I like to think that William Goyen was a deep and altogether benign influence on me as a writer. As a reader, I first began reading him about the same time, 1946, that he began publishing stories in *The Southwest Review*, reading purely for the pleasure of it; he was for me a joyful discovery at just the time when I was discovering everything all at once. And over the long years he has been a constant companion. The influence on my writing was always more a matter of exemplary inspiration than any kind of imitation. To the best of my knowledge and recollection I have never written or even tried to write anything like William Goyen's work, though I surely envied him the options he exercised. Some writers open doors and windows for other writers. Others seem to help other writers just as much to find themselves by closing off certain possibilities. Goyen did what he did so well that it would have been folly to try to follow him closely. On the other hand, the full range and unique qualities of his voice challenge any writer to seek and find his own particular voice and variety.

I should add that besides helping me along in the neverending quest to find my best voice and best subjects as a writer, besides affording me the richest pleasures as a reader, William Goyen was, briefly but strongly, a personal influence and example as well. He surprised me more than once by coming to readings I gave when he happened to be in the neighborhood. He filled in for me for a semester at Princeton when I had to be away, and as a teacher he was a great and good influence on some of my best and favorite students there, people like the young Madison Smartt Bell. Later, on turf that had once been my own, at Hollins College, he was more than helpful to young writers like Cathy Hankla and Allen Wier.

Though rich in variety, his stories are all filled with his voice—the voice he created out of the common language of his East Texas tribe—and haunted by the selfsame music, a music he made out of the poetry of his place and his people. William Goyen was, after all, a composer who won awards for his music. And in any number of interviews he compared his stories to songs and invited the reader (and sometimes baffled critics) to think of his fiction as, among other things, music. In the preface to *The Collected Stories of William Goyen* (1975), he wrote: "I've cared about the buried song in somebody, and sought it passionately; or the music in what happened. And so I have thought of my stories as folk song, as ballad, or rhapsody."

Each of his stories, dark or lighthearted, shares this kind of caring, and, thus, all are marked by an indelible identity. Thus, any of his stories might well fit here. Everything he ever did, while always fresh and original, shares and demonstrates the unique qualities of his voice. There is nothing that Goyen allowed himself to publish that is in any way inferior, less than fascinating in ways and means, that is insignificant in substance. I love his speakers, his people, ordinary East Texas folk riddled with extraordinary thoughts and feelings, speaking in a language that he first borrows directly from them, then returns enhanced by its essential poetry. My particular favorite has long been the title story of his first collection—"Ghost and Flesh, Water and Dirt." Part of my special interest and pleasure is derived from and heightened by the tape cassette recording I have (from American Audio Prose Library) of William Goyen reading this story, a tape I have often played for classes and workshops where students sat and listened closely with a rare, rapt attention, dazzled by his voice and the rhythm and music of it. I usually withhold the text until they have heard the story straight through, until they have *experienced* the story.

Not plotted in a conventional sense, "Ghost and Flesh, Water and Dirt" is a brief story covering most of the adult life of a woman, Margy, from a little Texas town, Charity (the imaginary version of Goyen's hometown, Trinity). She is haunted by the ghost of her dead husband Raymon Emmons, a railroad man who killed himself, and (as we learn) the ghost of their daughter Chitta, who was killed falling off a horse. ("O I was broken of my sleep and of my night disturbed.") At the urging insistence of her close friend, Fursta Evans, Margy goes off by train to California where, with World War II underway, she works "in an airplane factory" and where she meets a sailor, Nick Natowski, "a brown clean Pollock from Chicago, real wile, real Satanish," has a passionate love affair with him until he goes off to war and is lost at sea: "O what have I ever done in this world, I said, to send my soul to torment? Lost one to dirt and one to water, makes my life a life of mud."

Goes back home to Texas and to a surprise: "Come back to this house, opened it up and aired it all out, and when I got back you know who was there in that house? That old faithful ghost of Raymon Emmons." A whole life, in fact several lives, in a few poetic pages, told to us in the resonant, credible voice of Margy. Who also, from first to last, considers the subject of telling life stories to each other: "Honey, why am I talkin all this? Oh all our lives! So many things to tell." Abruptly, near the end, we discover that we are not eavesdropping on a dense first-person monologue, but are being addressed directly as a particular person (ourselves a character in the story) in a particular place—"settin with you here in the Pass Time club, drinkin this beer and telling you all I've told." And Margy gratefully celebrates her life and offers us a closure, a kind of fairy-tale moral to the experience: "Us humans are part ghost and part flesh—part fire and part ash—but I think maybe the ghost part is the longest lastin, the fire blazes but the ashes last forever."

If Keats was right, where, in one of his letters, he said that poetry should surprise "by a fine excess," Goyen has written a folk tale that moves into poetry. Goyen wears the skin and bones and knows the thoughts and feelings of Margy the way she says Nick Natowski was "tight as a glove in iz uniform." There is, in this complete engagement with character, humor but no cuteness, no hint or telltale stain of condescension (a very common flaw in contemporary short fiction). Nothing is wasted, no unnecessary gestures; yet it is in no way minimal. And in his mastery of the first-person narrative (it seems as easy as pie when Goyen does it, and it just isn't), he can build toward the kind of closure that the contemporary story and mindset seldom allow.

Goyen loved the people he wrote about, and that is rare enough at any time; and he loved the form of the short story, how in a small room he could come to a great reckoning. Now he is a ghost himself, and we miss him and his way of doing things like nobody else, telling tales that nobody else can or does, speaking for people who seldom are listened to. But, like the ghost of Raymon Emmons—"All night long he uz talkin and talkin, his speech (whatever he uz sayin) uz like steam streamin outa the mouth of a kettle, streamin and streamin and streamin"—he speaks to us still and for as long as we can believe in the magic of words and books. "Ghost and Flesh, Water and Dirt," like the other twenty-five stories in *The Collected Stories of William Goyen*, does not need my endorsement; but I am honored and happy to recommend it to any reader (surely there are some somewhere) who is looking for something wonderful, original, and, yes, beautiful to experience. Think of this particular story as a gateway to his other work, an excellent introduction. After the experience and engagement and pleasure, his stories remain wonderful and strange. They are deeply simple and highly sophisticated, impeccably written line by line.

"Saw pore Raymon Emmons all last night, all last night seen im plain as day."

George Garrett (1929–2008) is the author of the short-story collections *King of the Mountain* (1957), *In the Briar Patch* (1961), *Cold Ground Was My Bed Last Night* (1964), *A Wreath for Garibaldi and Other Stories* (1969), *The Magic Striptease* (1973), *To Recollect a Cloud of Ghosts: Christmas in England* (1979), *An Evening Performance: New and Selected Stories* (1985), and *Empty Bed Blues* (2006), ten novels, eight collections of poetry, three plays, and seven nonfiction books. He won the PEN/Malamud Award for Excellence in the Short Story in 1990.

"The Tree of Knowledge"
by Henry James

William H. Gass

"The Tree of Knowledge" was originally published and collected in *The Soft Side* (1900). It is currently most readily available in *Henry James: Complete Stories 1898–1910* (Library of America).

Henry James's short story, "The Tree of Knowledge," might have been more literally and less sacredly titled "The Bush of Belief." At the center of the pleasant little paradise, which seems to be sculptor Morgan Mallow's life, stands that artist's complacent certainty about his genius, a confidence which he has faithfully sustained through a productive although unheralded life. Mallow's entourage is as small as his fame is restricted, and consists of a wife so devoted she receives no other name than Missus, their only offspring, Lancelot, and finally this son's godfather, Peter Brench, a literary figure we have learned to call "the friend of the family," and a man who counts among his numerous discretions (including a prolonged though muted adoration of Mrs. Mallow) his refusal to publish his own literary endeavors.

These players form a box—the boundaries of a garden, if you like—of the most traditional kind: husband, wife, son, friend of the family. The dynamics of their relationships are determined by a diagonal that triangulates the box so that sometimes we are dealing solely with the family trio, while at other times with the romantic triangle of friend, wife, husband. The tale is itself of the simplest. Each individual, in ignorance of the true convictions of the others, is endeavoring to maintain the group's belief in the genius of its center—its grand master—and therefore each member's reason for being. A comedy of errors ensues and epiphanies abound.

The story is told from Peter Brench's point of view, and therefore is in the service of this careful man's proudly held convictions, some of which are stated early and openly while others emerge with some shyness: (first) that he has managed to maintain his friendship with Morgan Mallow while never for a moment compromising the principles of his taste by lying or deception, not easy since (second) Brench considers Mallow to be a charming man but, as an artist, a shallow pretentious hack; (third) that Mrs. Mallow's allegiance to Morgan Mallow's genius is the basis of her love for him; (fourth) therefore that Brench can be loyal to his love for Mrs. Mallow only by protecting her opinion of her husband as well as he has hidden his own; (fifth) that the son shares her idolatry and her error; (further, sixth) that Lancelot, despite the hopes the Mallows have for him as a painter, has no more talent than his father, if as much; (seventh) that Peter's reluctance to publish maintains "the purity of his taste by establishing still more firmly the right relation of fame to feebleness"—that, in sum, although Peter Brench has "the misfortune to be omniscient," "it is ignorance that is bliss." And therefore it is folly to be wise.

The Mallows put on Italian airs as if they were tunes on a phonograph, and James takes obvious delight in describing the pretensions which furnish their Eden; however, its serenity is threatened by another misconception: that Lancelot Mallow (such a disastrous name) has been born to the brush rather than to his father's chisel. The Mallows embrace the difference because Morgan had always been a bit disappointed he'd rounded and smoothed so many stones rather than coloring and brightening canvas, and his son's success in this line would do much to right that hereditary wrong.

Peter Brench does what he can to prevent it (he throws money in the young man's path—a common enough gesture in James), because he fears that the Paris experience (for that is where Lancelot is headed), by educating his eye, will reveal his father's achievement to be as banal as his own talent is manifestly *manqué*. Before Lancelot spurs his horse toward the center of the painter's world, Peter and Mrs. Mallow have this delicious exchange:

> "Don't you believe in it?" asked Mrs. Mallow, who still, at more than forty, had her violet velvet eyes, her creamy satin skin and her silken chestnut hair.
>
> "Believe in what?"
>
> "Why in Lance's passion."
>
> "I don't know what you mean by 'believing in it.' I've never been unaware, certainly, of his disposition, from his earliest time, to daub and draw; but I confess I've hoped it would burn out."
>
> "But why should it," she sweetly smiled, "with his wonderful heredity? Passion is passion—though of course indeed *you*, dear Peter, know nothing of that. Has the Master's ever burned out?"

Peter Brench smothers all honest response to ask whether Mrs. Mallow thinks her son is going to be another Master, and receives an armload of rationalization in reply:

She seemed scarce prepared to go that length, yet she had on the whole a marvellous trust. "I know what you mean by that. [She does not know, of course.] Will it be a career to incur the jealousies and provoke the machinations that have been at times almost too much for his father? Well—say it may be, since nothing but clap-trap, in these dreadful days, *can*, it would seem, make its way, and since, with the curse of refinement and distinction, one may easily find one's self begging one's bread. Put it at the worst—say he *has* the misfortune to wing his flight further than the vulgar taste of his stupid countrymen can follow. Think, all the same, of the happiness—the same the Master has had. He'll *know*."

Peter looked rueful. "Ah but *what* will he know?"

"Quiet joy!" cried Mrs. Mallow, quite impatient and turning away.

Henry James, as if he had been tutored by his brother, makes his entire story turn on the distinction between belief and knowledge (truth and opinion); and then upon the differences among (a) knowing a fact, (b) understanding what someone means, (c) exercising a skill, (d) affirming a faith, and (e) having an experience—for each of which the word *know* will sometimes serve.

Lancelot learns that indeed he is a dauber, a muff: "But I'm not such a muff as the Master!" For, as Peter Brench is more than disconcerted to discover, the son saw through his father as sun through clear glass early on. And, as Brench's beliefs continue to come to grief, he learns that Lancelot's mother, the silken and satiny Mrs. Mallow, whom his love has lived to protect . . . that she has also known all along. Each member of this saintly trio has conspired to keep from the others the downcasting truth lest it remove *cher maître* like a title from the Master, and shatter the blessed ignorance which holds the little group together.

So it not unexpectedly turns out that Peter Brench, the omniscient one, has not known, has only believed; and in caring for Mrs. Mallow as Mrs. Mallow cares for the Master, he has mirrored her love without receiving, as she has, any in return. His errors, in fact, have been many, because he wrongly supposed Mrs. Mallow loved, in the Master, the genius that the genius believed he had, when it was not the artist but the man; it was not the quality of the result, but the passion in the process, that drew her to Morgan Mallow and held her there.

Peter Brench had a horror of error; he did not wish to risk making a fool of himself; hence his own general silence: no protestation of love, no public productions. And in the end, he knew none of the kinds of knowledge aforementioned: not Morgan Mallow's faith in his talent or his joy in creation, not Lancelot's recognitions, not Mrs. Mallow's passion for passion. To keep his intelligence unsmudged, he cleaned the implement but failed to use it.

James's satirical intent in this piece is clearly evident and broadly stated. The names of the characters are signal enough. Morgan Mallow cannot possibly be anything more than a soft bog; Mrs. Mallow has lost sight of her own self, hence has no name of her own; and "Lancelot Mallow" is a ludicrous combination. What might have been a shrewdly observant "Peter Bench" is wrenched just enough to spell out confusion, so that when this gentleman says he has "judged himself once for all," his name belies the accuracy of that boast.

Critics have been no kinder to this story than the art world has been to Morgan Mallow. One dismissed it as "a bore." Most writers on James ignore it altogether. Summaries of it in volumes pretending to be inclusive are curt and unflattering: "The usual narrator is given an external appearance which might have served to clothe a minor character in a better tale."

The kind of knowledge which gives James his epistemological misgivings always concerns the nature of moral good and evil. Belief is grounded in gossip and depends upon the interpretation of social intentions. Its unreliable nature leads invariably to ambiguous conclusions, and guilt is spread over everyone like grease over toast. The screw which can be given one more turn is a regular feature. If Peter Brench is mistaken about Mrs. Mallow and her son, and they, in turn, are wrong about him as well as one another, might not Morgan Mallow be in no doubt really about his own deficiencies, and be keeping up the charade of his purity and ambition for everybody else's sake, for how can he disabuse the faithful of their belief in him? The story does not turn this far, but it gives us the mechanism for its movement.

Moreover, what gives Morgan Mallow his dignity, despite his hollow pretensions, is the fact that his passion for art appears to be genuine if none of its products is.

There is, nonetheless, the suggestion that both Mallows might more readily succumb to mammon's temptations than their ideals should approve, if ever they were offered the opportunity; and James has great fun with the wealthy Canadian couple who wish to commission Mallow to do a tomb for their three children. Here, the word *moral* is deployed like a skirmish line in front of an absent army:

> Such was naturally the moral of Mrs. Mallow's question: if their wealth was to be assumed, it was clear, from the nature of their admiration, as well as from mysterious hints thrown out . . . as to other possibilities of the same mortuary sort, that [*sic*, what?] their further patronage might be; and not less evident that should the Master become at all known in those climes nothing would be more inevitable than a run of Canadian custom.

The reader should be ready to believe that the arty ideal the Mallow clan embraces, they embrace because no prettier mate has made itself available. They have gone to bed with what they must.

James leaves us in a quagmire of doubt. Peter Brench believes that Mrs. Mallow believes that Mr. Mallow believes in his genius, although later he is led to believe that she has never believed in him any more than Peter Brench has. So it is not only possible that Morgan Mallow knows his failings too, as his wife knows, as his son knows, as the family friend knows, as the world, in its treatment of his work, seems to know; but that the Master's purity from profit is also a pose, though as genuine as circumstances demand, and that were the world to come to his door with wealth and glory to confer, he would not turn the world away as he might a salesman with only encyclopedias to sell; rather he would graciously accept the proffered laurels, and sharpen his chisel and endeavor to keep up with this welcome run of intercontinental custom.

Mrs. Mallow believes that her husband has a passion for art if he hasn't the genius we suppose he supposes he has, but she believes that Peter Brench hasn't such devotion, and cannot have known "quiet joy." Although joy has been denied him, we know that Peter has his passion and has been more faithful to it than most husbands. He knows quietness, and if his passion has been sterile, at least it has not peopled parlors with a "little staring white population" of mis-scaled statuary.

If the suspicions the story stirs in us are sustained during still another turn, we may wonder if Morgan Mallow's commitment to art isn't more a matter of necessity than devotion. Then Mrs. Mallow would be wrong about the pure part of her husband's nature. A plot that has turned itself to the point of Peter Brench's epiphany and disillusionment might be turned almost interminably.

To eat of the fruit of the true tree of knowledge might not be, in our secular world, such a bad thing. Just beware of the berries on the bush of belief.

We readers don't know—can't know—why, when, what, or whether. We can only believe what we believe. And understand how well we've been warned.

William H. Gass (1924–2017) is the author of the short stories collected in *In the Heart of the Heart of the Country* (1968) and the novellas and stories collected in *Eyes* (2015), of the novels *Omensetter's Luck* (1966), *The Tunnel* (1995), and *Middle C* (2013), the illustrated novella *Willie Masters' Lonesome Wife* (1968), *Cartesian Sonata and Other Novellas* (1998), and nine nonfiction books.

"Sur" by Ursula Le Guin

Molly Giles

"Sur" was originally published in the February 1, 1982, issue of *The New Yorker*. It was collected in *The Compass Rose: Short Stories* (1982). It is currently most readily available in *The Unreal and the Real: The Selected Short Stories of Ursula K. Le Guin* (Saga Press).

I never go anywhere without bringing something to read, and I was waiting in line at the DMV the first time I read "Sur." The story made me so happy that I laughed out loud. People turned and stared. It was as if they had never heard a laugh in the DMV before. I laughed again, tore the story out of the magazine I'd stuck in my purse that morning, and assigned it to my graduate writing class that night.

My students didn't like the story much. I was a lazy teacher then and I am a lazy teacher now. When I love something I just want to hand it over, gift it out. I don't want to talk about it. I don't want to explain it. I just want the lucky recipients to see the shine, feel the heat, enjoy the light, savor the flavor. Swallow it whole and take it home with you, that's been my teaching style. It's never worked but it's hard to abandon and so it is difficult even now to say what makes "Sur" such a brilliant, brave, and beautiful story, but it is and I will herewith try to tell why.

The idea, for starters, is delicious. Nine genteel South American ladies tell their friends and families they are going on retreat to a convent for six months, but instead they hire a steamer, sail from Chile, and trek to Antarctica, arriving at the South Pole in 1909, three years before Amundsen. They build an elegant ice cave where they study, cook, play guitar and banjo. They embrace the hard work of sledge hauling and become their own dogs. They live on dried fruits and potatoes that have been freeze dried "according to an ancient Andean Indian method." They shake their heads at the mess previous explorers have left behind—a "graveyard of seal skins, seal bones, penguin bones and rubbish, presided over by the mad, screaming skua gulls"—and delight in the free beauty of the orca whales, the floating rainbow clouds, multiple suns, and constant white light of the Great Ice Barrier. One woman creates a walled studio out of transparent sheets of ice and carves exquisite water sculptures. All of them make friends with the void, the abyss, the empty heart of lightness; they fly through its terrors and sing "like sparrows." They survive snow blindness, frostbite, and childbirth and do so with gaiety, grace, and goodwill. As the unnamed narrator explains, in her modest and sensible Victorian voice, "the nine of us worked things out amongst us from beginning to end without any orders being given by anybody." All women are equal; all are "crew."

Only a few of them, however, make the long final trek to the Pole itself. Once they arrive, they camp briefly, make a cup of tea, confer, and agree to leave no mark. Some man "longing to be first" might see their little flag or snow cairn and it "might break his heart." So the ladies quietly step back into the blizzard, leaving no footprints, and return to the domestic responsibilities of their families at home. "Of the return voyage," the narrator says, her sadness palpable, "there is nothing to tell. We came back safe."

Safe, sound, silent, and unsung. They have had a secret adventure, the best sort of adventure, and they have earned that holy glory known to anonymous artists since the beginning of time. They have learned that although humankind is often small and mean, "the sky, the earth, the sea, the soul" are large. They have overcome every hardship with resourcefulness, harmony, hard work, and faith in their enterprise. They have spent six months living exactly the way they've wanted to, that is, living a life of "danger, uncertainty, and hope," and they have done so with courage and grace. They have succeeded in creating a world where peaceful intelligent cooperation actually works.

I love "Sur" and all I can say is: I hope you will too.

Molly Giles is the author of the short-story collections *Rough Translations* (1985), *Creek Walk and Other Stories* (1996), *Bothered* (2012), *Three for the Road* (2014), and *All the Wrong Places* (2015) and the novel *Iron Shoes* (2000). Her stories have received an O. Henry Award and two Pushcart Prizes.

"FRAGO" by Phil Klay

Julia Glass

"FRAGO" was first published and collected and is currently most readily available in *Redeployment* (Penguin).

I've always had a low tolerance for violent movies. A band of college classmates once dared me to attend a late-night screening of *Texas Chainsaw Massacre* and took bets on how soon I'd leave; I fled before the end of the opening titles. When it comes to the suspension of disbelief, I'm a pushover. Turn down the lights and I am in: I am in *deep*.

The experience of enduring contrived horror, especially theatrical carnage for its own sake, has never been entertaining to me. It horrifies me, pure and simple. Yet for years I went to war movies, and what is war if not the apogee of horror? It may seem necessary or unavoidable, call for courage and cunning and stamina and sacrifice and nerves of steel—the conventional tropes are endless—but to wage war is to flout the sanctity of life. Respect for history, however, demands that we look war square in the face. I remember how apprehensively I stood in line for *Apocalypse Now*, *Platoon*, *Full Metal Jacket*, *Das Boot*, *The Deer Hunter*, *Glory*, *Gallipoli*—but I watched them from beginning to end (if now and then shielding my eyes). A few of them I saw twice. These were the war movies of my twenties and thirties; most of them focused on Vietnam.

At least for Americans, it was a time of relative peace, a lofty place from which to probe our collective conscience.

But when, at thirty-nine, I had a son, war movies became unbearable. Every soldier onscreen was a onetime infant, a child whose mother stood to suffer inconsolable loss. (*Saving Private Ryan?* Not in a million years.) Then, just months after having my second son, I and my family lived through 9/11 in Lower Manhattan—and watched our country go to war. As we all know, American soldiers—and by national identity, the rest of us—have been continuously at war now for nearly two decades.

A few years into our long-term "engagement" (interesting how betrothal and battle share that word), American novels and stories about our many wars, past as well as present, began to proliferate. Perhaps not since Tim O'Brien's seismic story collection was published in 1990 had the literature of war felt so present, so urgent, and so important. Though it may seem perverse, I do not have the same maternal aversion to war on the page that I do to war on the screen, and suddenly I found myself drawn to reading one fictional war story after another; among the most memorable from the past decade are *The Sojourn*, *The Boat*, *Billy Lynn's Long Halftime Walk*, *March*, *Yellow Birds*, *You Know When the Men Are Gone*, *A Pigeon and a Boy*, *To the End of the Land*, *Girl at War* (and I cannot omit *A Soldier's Heart: Reading Literature Through Peace and War at West Point*).

Most of these books I picked up after reading reviews, but Phil Klay's *Redeployment* chose me. There are random days when my authorial conscience reminds me, *You want to sell books? Go buy some.* On one such day, I arrived at my bookstore right on the heels of a brand-new debut story collection: stories about the war in Iraq. I took it home and read it from beginning to end in every spare moment I could find over the next week. When I finished, I stared at the kind-looking man pictured on the back flap, and I thought, *Who the hell is this guy? How do I tell everybody in the world about this book?* Fortunately, unsurprisingly, the book didn't need me to make itself known.

As reviews and awards would affirm, there isn't a weak story in the lot. Nor is there a duplicate. Each story is told from a distinct perspective, through the eyes not just of soldiers on both the home and battle fronts but of a chaplain, a foreign service officer, a marine in Mortuary Affairs, a veteran who served in PsyOps. The book is like a kaleidoscope aimed at this war so few of us understand anymore—if we ever did. Through these stories, we understand at least what it's like to have been a part of that war.

As a teacher of fiction writing, I give students about a dozen short stories per semester. I pick stories that I hope will startle, challenge, move, and delight them in unexpected ways. I also assign the stories in pairs; they will have something in common but also differ in dramatic ways. Lately, I begin each workshop with what has become my favorite duet: Klay's "FRAGO" in concert with J. D. Salinger's "For Esme, with Love and Squalor." Both are war stories. Both show soldiers before and after battle. Time, however, stretches far and wide in "Esme," with a major, significant chasm in the middle. It's a long, slow burn of a story in which the true drama plays out offstage, while "FRAGO" ignites and sizzles out like a flare, its drama front and center, occurring in the space of a day. And while the astute elegance of Salinger's language gleams across its hidden brutalities like a soft, ironic light, Klay's is just plain brutal. What you read is what you get. (Only on a second reading of *Nine Stories*, thirty years after my first, did I understand that Salinger's book is also a collection of war stories. His war is a subject between the lines, veiled behind a scrim.)

Of the twelve tales in *Redeployment*, I chose "FRAGO" not because it was my favorite (not initially) but because it's a brilliant example of a story that plunges readers instantly and unstintingly into a foreign culture and language, demanding close attention to an unfamiliar experience without explicit guidance or translation. The narrator and all other significant characters are Americans, but they are also US Marines on a mission: one that is routine yet risky. They operate and communicate in methods and modes all their own.

I know of few first paragraphs more in-your-face, more you-are-there than this succinct opening salvo: "LT says drop the fucking house. Roger that. We go to drop the fucking house."

This other "we," we leisurely readers—supine in bed or hammock, leaning quietly over a sleek library table, in an armchair by a fire; at worst, maybe standing in the crush of a sweltering rush-hour subway clutching an iPad—are about to be taken on a raid: "HUMINT says the place is an IED factory filled with some bad motherfucking hajjis, including one pretty high up on the BOLO list. SALUTE report says there's a fire team-sized element armed with AKs, RPKs, RPGs, maybe a Dragunov." We may not be storming the beaches of Normandy, but lives are at risk and bullets will fly. As will the military acronyms, aphorisms, and insider slang, the language of men trained to kill and, by consequence, to swim in the dark absurdity of putting themselves in harm's way.

The oo-rah vernacular of "FRAGO" is both aggressively and misleadingly cryptic. I say "misleadingly" because for all the undefined terms peppering the pages—IFAK, DFAC, SITREP, CASEVAC, UXO, PPE, CCP, KBR, MRE, EPW . . . FOBbits, anyone?—the sequence of events and the suppressed emotions are vivid as hell (literally so). In the stealthiest way possible, they are also heart rending. Some of the terms you guess at from context, others you let go. But the esoteric nature of this world and its particular physics as well as its lingo, the extent to which it unsettles you: *that* is part of the point. It is not Klay's intention to let you get comfortable here, no sir: not even in your word brain. But he does intend to tell you a story you cannot turn away from.

This is a story, by the way, that begs to be read aloud. The pace of the prose is the pace of the men as they follow their orders. Read this out loud now, and listen:

> When we get to the house, the other squads set a cordon and we tear down the road and bust in the back door. M870 with lockbuster shells. Boom, and we go.
>
> Back door leads to the kitchen. Right, clear. Left, clear. Overhead, clear. Rear, clear. Kitchen, clear. We roll through, don't stack, just roll. Slow is smooth. Smooth is fast. Corporal Sweet's fire team clears houses like water running down a stream.
>
> Next room there's AK fire as soon as we go through the doorway, but we're better shots. End state is two hajjis, no survivable wounds, no injuries on our side, just another day in paradise.

I ask my students to read to their classmates passages from whatever story I give them. Typically, I have to goad or tease them into reading. But this story? When I ask for volunteers, up shoot their hands. The pleasure of the language is visceral and bracing.

Among the chaotic comings and goings, the wounds inflicted and sustained, the vulgarities and the fuck-ups, the core relationship here is the one between the narrator, a war-wise sergeant whose name we never learn, and a greenhorn private under his command: "Sweet's SAW gunner is PFC Dyer, and Dyer's excited because here's a chance to finally pop his cherry and shoot somebody. He's nineteen, one of our baby-wipe killers, and all he's killed so far in the Corps has been paper."

It is, for the most part, a one-way relationship founded on vigilance: when everyone's life is on the line, you can't let the newbie fuck up or freak out. And, as we can guess—or as you'll know if you break down and google FRAGO—things on this mission do not go as planned. (*FRAGO, or fragmentary order: a hasty or sudden change to a previous operational order.*) The surprise involves two torture victims, their teenage captor, and a video camera.

"Lance Corporal McKeown looks at the camera and says, Al-Qaeda makes the worst pornos ever." Even the most unthinkable cruelties (perhaps especially those) must be cloaked in humor. Humor is a form of endurance.

In a moment of peril, Dyer gets his wish and shoots an insurgent who was hiding behind a bed—though only after the bad guy shoots one of the good guys first. And yes, this is how you see it, not just because this is how you have to see it but because there's evil stuff going down in this house.

What happens from this moment on is a minor narrative symphony in which a dozen men do what they've been trained to do in a variety of urgent situations occurring all at once. The narrator is the conductor of this symphony, our guide in this underworld wrought by politics, power, poverty, and failed diplomacy. But you do not think about such abstract notions as you read this story. Watching these men do what they get paid to do day after day, you see the mad beauty to all the things they know, to their terse slang, their mutual mockery, their unflinching attention to protocol under pressure.

Klay has also published a number of powerful Opinion pieces in the *New York Times*, most notably an essay called "What We're Fighting For," published in early 2017, an implicit rebuttal to cavalier statements made by a new Commander in Chief. It's a patriot's fierce account of difficult choices made in the heat of battle, including acts of courage in which mercy is still an option. It provides a glimpse of experiences Klay and his fellow soldiers had in Iraq that clearly found their way into "FRAGO." I sent it to a friend of mine, a distraught mother whose son, after returning to the States from earning a history degree at Oxford University, made the surprise decision to apply for the Marines' Officer Candidates School. I hoped it would help show her what kind of men her smart, good-hearted son would be joining— and why.

In an earlier essay, "After War, a Failure of the Imagination," Klay laments and challenges a frequent remark that servicemen hear from civilians: "I could never imagine what you've been through." Someone who utters this platitude to a vet may think that it conveys praise or awe, but in fact it creates a shield, a defense against talking about war, asking questions— when all of us should compel ourselves to do just that.

All good fiction offers the reader a mirror as well as a window. You see out into a world you've never seen—or see anew—but somewhere, you also recognize something of yourself. Or you are able to imagine another self you might inhabit. You don't just get into the story; the story gets into you. From the writer's side, as Klay states, "It's a powerful moment, when you discover a vocabulary exists for something you'd thought incommunicably unique. . . . This self-recognition through others is not simply a by-product of art—it's the whole point. . . . Believing war is beyond words is an abrogation of responsibility." Reading this statement, I realized that to engage with war stories is not just to respect history; it's to respect and to *hear* those who fight our wars for us. *Tell us what it was like.*

What Klay does so well through all the stories in *Redeployment* is take us inside the hearts and minds and bodies—the physical, mental, and moral vulnerability—of those who work in a war zone, whether behind a desk or a gun. And it is the vulnerability that grips me again and again.

The last few pages of "FRAGO" are about what happens when the men return to base, stopping at the hospital to see a wounded comrade before they head to the DFAC for dinner:

> We're quiet as we get close, and then McKeown says, Sergeant, that was really fucked up.
>
> But now's not the time to have that conversation, so I say, Yeah, that's the most blood I've seen since I fucked your mom on her period. And then the guys laugh and bullshit a bit, and it breaks the mood that was settling.

The sergeant's focus, however, is on Dyer, for whom the day was the initiation he thought he longed for. Dyer is not in good shape, though perhaps only the sergeant perceives this. With a fatherly gesture, he tells Dyer that he "did good today."

Eating in the DFAC, though it's just an immense cafeteria, is a treat for these men, "something that's not an MRE or the Iraqis' red shit and rice." And because it happens to be Sunday (reminding us that no day is sacred for soldiers), it's also cobbler day. Several flavors, with ice cream, are laid out on a serving table. "The 04 says the cherry's the best. Roger that. I get the cherry. Dyer gets the cherry. We all get the fucking cherry."

And of course it would be *cherry.*

Dyer can only stare at the dessert before him, the ice cream melting into the fruit.

"No good," the sergeant tells us. "I put a spoon in his hand. You've got to do the basic things."

When I finished this story for the first time, I thought immediately of soldiers as onetime infants, carefully spoon-fed by their mothers; by fathers, too. We have all heard about the unique loyalty of warriors, their willingness to sacrifice everything for one another; it's a bond we can envy without wanting to know it firsthand. Soldiers speak about how this intense fraternity is what they miss most when they return home, how there's nothing like it in civilian life. But what Klay shows in this chink of a moment is the intimacy in that bond, the almost maternal tenderness nestled covertly in the real-man shtick. I felt myself fully and lovingly inside both men, as if Klay, at the end of the story, had opened a door to a peaceful place in the middle of this war, and he invited me right through.

I wanted so much more of these characters. I thought about both men for a long time, as I do each time I finish this story. Reading it anew is something I look forward to as much as anything I do at the start of a brand-new class—my new band of recruits, PFC storytellers hoping to beckon readers through a door of their own, hoping to move them even half this much.

Last year, more than twenty years after swearing off war movies, I decided to take a chance and go see *Dunkirk*. My younger son, at sixteen, had developed a love of history and was studying World War II. Rarely will he go to the movies with his parents, but this was one that none of his friends wanted to see. I decided to see it for another reason as well: a memory of my late father. Dad's father and grandfather were both West Point graduates, but because of poor eyesight, he couldn't follow. (He even tried to memorize the eye charts.) My grandfather served in both world wars, and though he died when I was small, Dad carried his stories forward; he loved to talk to me and my younger sister about World War II, what he knew of it as an avid student but also as the son of a soldier. One night at dinner, when I was in middle school, he told us the story of Dunkirk. Not a man to shed tears, he began to weep as he told it. So the story of Dunkirk is also, to me, a story about my dad, not just a story about the world. I think my father still yearned to have been a soldier, and I think he wanted his daughters to imagine, along with him, what that might have been like.

I asked my son if I could grab onto him should the movie become hard for me to take. Begrudgingly, he agreed. ("Jeez, Mom, okay!") But I was fine, and of course I was moved. I felt firsthand the emotions that had overtaken my dad that night at dinner.

Perhaps every good war story is a cautionary tale about what should never be, just as it's about what regrettably, undeniably, tragically, is. You read the story (or you watch it) and hope that no one you love ever has to experience the horror it reveals—but you think about what it means to endure and survive that horror, to help others survive, and then to tell it. You see the tenderness as well as the violence; you see human nature at its deepest and widest, highest and lowest extremes. You imagine yourself a soldier.

Julia Glass is the author of the short-story collection *I See You Everywhere* (2008), as well as of the novels *Three Junes* (2002), which won the National Book Award, *The Whole World Over* (2006), *The Widower's Tale* (2010), *And the Dark Sacred Night* (2014), and *A House Among the Trees* (2017).

"My Father Sits in the Dark"
by Jerome Weidman

Herbert Gold

"My Father Sits in the Dark" was originally published in the November 1934 issue of *Story*. It was collected in *The Horse That Could Whistle "Dixie" and Other Stories* (1939). It is currently most readily available in *The Norton Book of American Short Stories* (W. W. Norton).

Jerome Weidman had a long career as a novelist, playwright, short-story writer, reporter, and contributor to *The New Yorker* and other popular magazines. His early novel, *I Can Get It For You Wholesale*, was both a best seller and shocking for its time. There were other commercial successes. His book for the musical *Fiorello!* won a Pulitzer Prize. He was a working professional, a writing writer, with unashamedly commercial intentions. He once told me that his legal training—speed typing—was a major contribution to his career.

I didn't expect to discover that he has also written a miniature masterpiece in "My Father Sits in the Dark," a very short story published first in *The New Yorker*. Jerome Weidman's known strengths as a writer were accurate dialogue, reminiscent of John O'Hara and Hemingway but with a New York Jewish accent, and the ability to depict upward-striving Jewish life in the familiar world of immigrants and their children.

This story—poetic, cadenced, unstructured, modest in length, carried by intense feeling without a moment of self-pity or inflation—was written early in his career.

It is merely a young man's account of spying on the older man who would be an utter stranger if he were not his father—that's all it is. The narrator watches; the old guy sits there alone, unaware. Neither utters any declaration of feeling. There is silence in the room, all around; silence envelops them. The father has no sense of the turbulence in the son's watching.

And the wonderment of connection between son and father, of love, lost opportunity, melancholy, the mystery of time passing and age—the arbitrariness of our souls on earth—is given something like a name. Of course there is no name and it cannot be named. And that's all and enough. As in William Saroyan's early story, "The Daring Young Man on the Flying Trapeze," there is the sudden flare of something like genius.

"My Father Sits in the Dark" is not a calculated work by a writer setting out to compose a well-formed product. It is a pure cry by a son yearning to peer into the soul of his father and to see his father's soul peering out to him. Surely many sons reach toward their fathers and find the distance too great, too far; surely many fathers have sought to reach their children across the space of family loneliness, and many fathers fail. Fathers and sons have tried to write this tale many, many times. When it works, when it happens without bathos, self-pity, or self-justification, it's a miracle. When the story comes out pure and fine, it's heartbreaking. When it tells more than the writer's story but also tells the reader's, we're in the vicinity of heartbreak, the suspicion of masterpiece. "My Father Sits in the Dark" is in that neighborhood.

When I think of why this simple account can move a reader so deeply although there is very little story, very little

happening—the title tells most of it—I have to assign the
effect to notions before which a report like this one is inadequate. The triumph is one of voice, a son's pure voice, and
a rhythm in the telling which is Weidman's gift on this occasion. I can only believe it is a controlled and autobiographical
prayer. He dipped into the well of family, childhood, his deepest yearnings; he came up clean. I could demonstrate the point
by quoting the entire story to show how it grows, swells, and
completes itself. But probably the task here is not to cite the
entire story, so let me quote only a few passages:

> My father sits in the dark. . . . If only I knew what he
> thinks about. If I only knew what he thinks at all, I might
> be able to help him. He might not even need help. It may
> be as he says. It may be restful. But at least I would not
> worry about it.

I have quoted, but I cannot quote correctly when I cite out
of context. I am omitting the rhythm which builds an image,
a longing, an emotion; the questions about mortality, communication, and the suspension bridge between the generations:
a son's need, a father's need. The emotion is musical, melodic,
not too vague for words but too precise for words. Yet words
are all the writer has, so here Weidman uses the words to make
chords, drumbeats, syncopations, harmonies:

> I can see the deeper darkness of his hunched shape. He is sit-
> ting in the same chair, his elbows on his knees, his cold pipe
> in his teeth, his unblinking eyes staring straight ahead. He
> does not seem to know I am there. He did not hear me come
> in. I stand quietly in the doorway and watch him. . . .
>
> My father sits in the dark.

Here again I have not quoted exactly, because I have added the hypnotic phrase from elsewhere in the story, *My father sits in the dark.* This might be called sampling.

> "You mean there's nothing wrong? You just sit in the dark because you like it, Pop?" I find it hard to keep my voice from rising in a happy shout.
>
> "Sure," he says. "I can't think with the light on."
>
> I set my glass down and turn to go back to my room. "Good night, Pop," I say.
>
> "Good night," he says.
>
> Then I remember. I turn back. "What do you think about, Pop?" I ask.
>
> His voice seems to come from far away. It is quiet and even again. "Nothing," he says softly. "Nothing special."

The themes of communication/miscommunication, often the miscommunication a kind of communion, sometimes in contemporary times the communication a kind of dreary courtship of the young, compose some of those writers' preoccupations which would be worn out if they were not so essential to our understanding of family life. Probably we can't ever understand family, the connections among parents and children, but we struggle to reckon with blame and yearning without any real hope of redeeming the past. In this tale or rhapsody Jerome Weidman provides a rhythm and melody, a song of a story, that can console us, parents and children, at least while we are under its spell.

Jerome Weidman, a social detailer, a chronicler of habits and talk and the furniture of his times, here gives us very little social detail. Since nothing much happens—although the immigrant trajectory is suggested, the poverty of immigrants in New York and its ghettos—the story raises an unusual problem of interpretation and explication. There is hardly anything to interpret. There is little to explicate. The way to understand this story is to read it, probably read it aloud, and then say, "Well, do you see now?"

And because the writer's nerve was steady and sharp, and his feeling intense, and his yearning fresh, the answer from most listeners will be: Yes, I see. Yes, we see.

In the unnecessary interest of full (partial) disclosure, let me stipulate my relation to Jerome Weidman. I came to know him a bit when he came to live in San Francisco as a fairly elderly party, but still writing. At that time he was a talkative and gossipy man preoccupied with his early days among the likes of Somerset Maugham, Lillian Hellman, John O'Hara, various show folks and New York literary personages, contributors to *The New Yorker* magazine. He told amusing anecdotes, and then told them again. He had been writing so long in the naturalist manner that he talked in the same style with such filler as, "So he said 'hello,' and then I said, 'Hello, Mr. Maugham,' and then he said, 'Would you like some tea?' and I said, 'Sure, thanks very much,' and then he said. . . ." I tended impatiently to interrupt. "Jerome! Get to the point!" He would pause and then say, "So then Mr. Maugham asked, 'Have you had a good trip?' and I said, 'Yes,' and then he said. . . ."

Therefore, when I read this story, knowing the old writer, it refreshed my sense of the miracle of the human spirit beyond how any striking story does so. I saw a different Jerome Weidman. Within the carapace that the years put upon a man, there was still this brooding child, asking his father the meaning of life by not asking it and not being told the untellable. So thank you, young Jerome.

Now please forgive a bit of anonymous name-dropping. A friend, a very good writer, once commented about someone we both know, a writer who is very popular among teachers of contemporary literature, his books much-taught and much-discussed: "People love teaching him, there's so much to explain. Since he doesn't do the work of getting at feeling, the teacher can feel his own soulfulness overflow as he *explicates*."

This story is in the category of very little to teach. The best learning from it would be a simple reading aloud its rhythms, its dark and hopeful pressing against the father in the dark of the kitchen. A teacher can point and say, "Listen." But that doesn't fill a 50-minute hour, so perhaps the lecture needs to speak of the immigrant experience, the yearning of son for father, the life of Depression-era New York (working-family non-glamorous New York), the power of incantation in simple American English, the nature of a tale told around a fire to listeners in awe because the act of communion is occurring.

Alas, since I'm asked to write about a story here, I've been obliged to explicate a little, untangle what doesn't need untangling. What I really want to say is: Listen to Jerome Weidman speak in "My Father Sits in the Dark" and let the voice and time reverberate.

Herbert Gold is the author of the short-story collections *Love and Like* (1960), *The Magic Will* (1973), and *Lovers & Cohorts: Twenty-Seven Stories* (1986), of approximately seventeen novels, and of approximately eight nonfiction books.

"The Jilting of Granny Weatherall" by Katherine Anne Porter

Jack Greer

"The Jilting of Granny Weatherall" was originally published in the February 1929 issue of *transition*. It was collected in *The Flowering Judas and Other Stories* (1930). It is currently most readily available in *Katherine Anne Porter: Collected Stories and Other Writings* (Library of America).

An old woman lies dying. Her daughters, her memories, the chipped flint and bone of her life, appear to her and then disappear, like glimpses of the past, like false promises.

I first read this story as a young man, and was struck by its tough language, its brevity, its look-you-in-the-eye truth. Now, so many years later, I ask myself, why do I like this story?

First, listen to the language, to the opening sentences:

"She flicked her wrist neatly out of Doctor Harry's pudgy careful fingers and pulled the sheet up to her chin. The brat ought to be in knee breeches."

The sentences are short, hard. The central mind of the story, Granny Weatherall herself, contrasts immediately with the younger doctor's "pudgy careful fingers." As communicated so directly by her name, Granny Weatherall is accustomed to toughing her way through the countless nagging annoyances of life. But now, in the present of the story, her toughness is unraveling. She is like a tough braided rope coming apart, like a hard thing coming loose:

"Her bones felt loose, and floated around in her skin, and Doctor Harry floated like a balloon around the foot of the bed."

Katherine Anne Porter finds the right objective correlative for Granny's lightheadedness—the doctor floating over the bed. Perhaps as well as any story I know, "The Jilting of Granny Weatherall" captures immediate experience—what it means to *be* in the face of approaching death.

I have often thought that the highest purpose of serious literature is ontological: to help articulate, and to help us understand, what it means to *be*. The defining moments of ontological reckoning are instances of realization, what James Joyce called epiphanies, what Virginia Woolf experienced as enduring flashes, fixed eternities. And in many ways the most defining of these moments is the moment of death. Death is a true thing—no one can bluff it; no one can escape it. While Poe thought the death of a beautiful woman the most poetic of subjects, in "The Jilting of Granny Weatherall" Katherine Anne Porter presents us with a different kind of poetry, something closer akin to Emily Dickinson's stark reality in "I heard a Fly buzz—when I died."

Rather than a poignancy born of sentimentality, the reader finds a piquancy born of irony but with a deep humanity that separates it from satire. We feel for Granny Weatherall precisely because she does not seek our sympathy.

"Get along and doctor your sick," said Granny Weatherall. "Leave a well woman alone. I'll call for you when I want you. . . . Where were you forty years ago when I pulled through milk-leg and double pneumonia? You weren't even born. Don't let Cornelia lead you on," she shouted, because

Doctor Harry appeared to float up to the ceiling and out. "I pay my own bills, and I don't throw my money away on nonsense!"

Despite the nearness of the doctor and her well-meaning daughter, Cornelia, Granny Weatherall is remarkably alone. In the subjective flux of the narrative, the doctor, Cornelia, in fact everyone, essentially floats away. It is in this aloneness that we find Granny's central core, and in her isolation that we recognize our own. One thinks of Tennessee Williams, who once remarked that we are all sentenced to solitary confinement within our own skins.

The clear-eyed language ensures that Granny Weatherall's aloneness will not be weepy.

> "What'd you say, Mother?" [her daughter Cornelia asks.]
> Granny felt her face tying up in hard knots.
> "Can't a body think, I'd like to know?"
> "I thought you might want something."
> "I do. I want a lot of things. First off, go away and don't whisper."

Go away. This seems Granny's central message, and in many ways represents her central flaw. For her, much of life has become an interference. In her rage for order, she seeks a numbing emotional insulation, captured in the story's deft descriptions of the concrete:

> It was good to have everything clean and folded away, with the hair brushes and tonic bottles sitting straight on the white embroidered linen: the day started without fuss and the pantry shelves laid out with rows of jelly glasses and brown jugs and white stone-china jars with blue whirli-gigs and words painted on them: coffee, tea, sugar, ginger,

cinnamon, allspice: and the bronze clock with the lion on top nicely dusted off. The dust that lion could collect in twenty-four hours!

Here is the beast in the jungle: the lion that is time, and time finally out of control—dust gathers, no matter how conscientious the duster.

The lion appears in a world of order, laid out here among a series of clever colons. This order stands in direct contrast to all that has begun to loosen and float; and despite the neat jars and her own industriousness, Granny finds the thief of time lying among her things: "While she was rummaging around she found death in her mind and it felt clammy and unfamiliar." Yet even death does not knock Granny from her tough-minded willfulness: "She had spent so much time preparing for death there was no need for bringing it up again. Let it take care of itself now."

In fact, throughout the story Granny is not preparing to die—this again is a central irony—"Her father had lived to be one hundred and two years old and had drunk a noggin of strong hot toddy on his last birthday." Granny, who is still two decades away from one hundred, calls out to Cornelia for a hot toddy. She is not ready to die. She does not yet have time for death. Much remains to be done, and no one else appears up to the job:

> It was good to be strong enough for everything, even if all you made melted and changed and slipped under your hands, so that by the time you finished you almost forgot what you were working for.

Strong enough for everything, and yet in the end everything melts and slips. Granny Weatherall, hard as a pine knot, is rotting, dying by degrees.

As she descends she confronts herself, and the writing takes us there, inside her consciousness, in a most remarkable way. The third-person narrative, interior from the start, becomes more and more private. At length the reader comes to the most private hurt of all, enshrined in her still-sharp memory, her being left at the altar as a young bride-to-be. "What does a woman do," Granny asks, "when she has put on the white veil and set out the white cake for a man and he doesn't come?"

The reader is brought inside this private insult, and studies this wound, just as Granny studies it: "For sixty years she had prayed against remembering him." Now she does remember him, the one who left, the one who did not show: "Wounded vanity, Ellen, said a sharp voice in the top of her mind. Don't let your wounded vanity get the upper hand of you. Plenty of girls get jilted. You were jilted, weren't you? Then stand up to it."

This voice appears in the story without inverted commas, the interior voice, the voice that has no doubt spoken to her these sixty years, urging her on, coping with her wound. Katherine Anne Porter has taken us where many other writers have tried, to Yeats's foul rag and bone shop of the heart, the place where the final secrets are kept.

Counterpoint to the interior voice is that of the faithful and underappreciated daughter, Cornelia. Cornelia's statements, mostly unadorned and without ancillary description, signal a reality outside that of the interior voice. "She's saying something," the narrative reads, and we would not know the speaker, if not for Granny's response: "I heard you, Cornelia. What's all this carrying-on?"

Cornelia's voice, the voice of the physical world, grows farther and farther distant from the world of the interior voice: "Cornelia's voice staggered and bumped like a cart in a bad road. It rounded corners and turned back again and arrived nowhere." Two paragraphs later, "Cornelia's voice made short turns and tilted over and crashed. 'Oh, Mother, oh, Mother, oh, Mother. . . .'"

"'I'm not going, Cornelia [Granny says]. I'm taken by surprise. I can't go.'"

These voices—the interior voice, the exterior voices of Cornelia, the doctor, the priest, and the other children, and the voice of Granny herself when she speaks—all fade in and out, weaving a tapestry of entangled emotion. Granny mistakes one voice for another, one person for another. "Is that you, Hapsy?" she asks, looking for her favorite daughter, but the answer comes: "Oh, no, I'm Lydia. We drove as fast as we could."

Even when Cornelia cries, it comes to Granny as a kind of misunderstood speech: "Cornelia knelt down and put her head on the pillow. She seemed to be talking but there was no sound."

At the very center of the story lies a hole, a vacuum, a nothingness. The strongest metaphor for this throughout the piece is George, the man who left, the bridegroom who wasn't there: "Yes, she had changed her mind after sixty years and she would like to see George. I want you to find George. Find him and be sure to tell him I forgot him." Granny thinks how she had gone on to find another husband, John, and how John had given her children, and she had had a home "like any other woman." She has gained everything back, she thinks: "Tell him I was given back everything he took away and more." And yet, something more eludes her, and the vacancy at the center of her life persists: "Oh, no, oh, God, no, there was something else besides the house and the man and the children. Oh, surely they were not all? What was it? Something not given back."

Perhaps it is pointless to define the thing not given back. One could say it was her heart. Her soul. In any event, this emptiness, this thing taken from her, becomes the vacant crater around which her being circles: "Since the day the wedding cake was not cut, but thrown out and wasted. The whole bottom dropped out of the world, and there she was blind and sweating with nothing under her feet and the walls falling away."

True to the ontological dimensions of the story, the final betrayal occurs again at the (metaphorical) altar. She begins to realize the immediacy of her own death:

> . . . Granny closed two fingers around Jimmy's thumb. Beads wouldn't do, it must be something alive. She was so amazed her thoughts ran round and round. So, my dear Lord, this is my death and I wasn't even thinking about it. My children have come to see me die.

Breaking through her hide-tough determination comes this indisputable fact of her impending end. She begins to address, directly, "my dear Lord." A sentence or two later she asks for more time: "Oh, my dear Lord, do wait a minute. I meant to do something about the Forty Acres."

But there is no more time. There is only the light, and it is fading: "The blue light from Cornelia's lampshade drew into a tiny point in the center of her brain, it flickered and winked like an eye, quietly it fluttered and dwindled." The eye is that of death, of the divine presence. The point of light (another excellent correlative) is, finally, all that is left of her being: "Granny lay curled down within herself, amazed and watchful, staring at the point of light that was herself."

In the approaching darkness, as she nears the end, the metaphorical altar, she seeks a final signal, perhaps the final balm for the aching vacancy at her core: "her body was now only a deeper mass of shadow in an endless darkness and this darkness would curl around the light and swallow it up. God, give a sign!" This last is spoken out directly by the interior voice. It is the final plea, the last chance not to be left alone at the altar. The story's final paragraph relates Granny's final jilting:

> For the second time there was no sign. Again no bride-groom and the priest in the house. She could not remember any other sorrow because this grief wiped them all away. Oh, no, there's nothing more cruel than this—I'll never for-give it. She stretched herself with a deep breath and blew out the light.

What shall we make of Granny Weatherall's final act? It is an act of defiance, true to the toughness of fiber evident throughout the story. It is also in some sense a sacrilegious act, a failure to surrender to the divine will. As Dylan Thomas wished for his father at the end, Granny Weatherall appears to "rage, rage against the dying of the light."

In terms of the story, the irony is complete, and the narrative unflinching.

Why do I like this story so much? I like the metaphorical language, the concrete correlatives that reflect the mind's attempt to make sense of the incomprehensible. For example, the way Cornelia's voice "staggered and bumped like a cart in a bad road . . . and arrived nowhere." The way the exterior world floats and moves and melts.

I like Granny Weatherall's toughness of spirit: "and, Doctor Harry, do shut up. Nobody sent for you." I like the creative tension between Cornelia, largely evoked by indirection ("tell it slant," Emily Dickinson said) and her ailing mother: "Cornelia was dutiful; that was the trouble with her. Dutiful and good: 'So good and dutiful,' said Granny, 'that I'd like to spank her.'"

"What'd you say, Mother?" [Cornelia asks, dutifully.]

Most of all, I like the way Katherine Anne Porter has entered the human mind. I am grateful for the journey. I think, even, of the Mona Lisa. When seeing the Mona Lisa for the first time one realizes it is not the smile that so captivates, but the eyes, watching you, as though Leonardo da Vinci had in some way painted a conscious mind on canvas. As with the Mona Lisa, Katherine Anne Porter has created her own remarkable canvas, on which she has captured consciousness.

Jack Greer is the author of the collection of short stories *Abraham's Bay & Other Stories* (2008) and co-author of the nonfiction book *Chesapeake Futures* (2003).

"The Bridegroom's Body" by Kay Boyle

Doris Grumbach

"The Bridegroom's Body" was originally published in the Summer 1938 issue of *The Southern Review*. It was collected in *The Crazy Hunter: Three Short Novels* (1940). It is currently most readily available in *Three Short Novels* (New Directions).

K ay Boyle's long short story (she called it a short novel, others a novella) "The Bridegroom's Body" has been reprinted often since its first appearance in the *Southern Review*. It was 1938, she was thirty-six and had published in that year a review of William Faulkner's *The Unvanquished* in *The New Republic* in which she wrote: "The weaknesses there are, the errors, the occasionally strained effects, are accomplished by the same fearless, gifted hand." Those words could easily be turned back upon herself, but still, "The Bridegroom's Body" is a memorable and curious story as, sadly, some others of Boyle's are not.

I have said the story is curious. So it is, for it contained a strong feminist theme many years before such fiction became popular and by a writer who declared she had no feminist feelings whatever, indeed gave ample evidence that in her personal life she much preferred men to women. Curiouser still is that, although the intent and meaning of the story seems to me to be crystal clear and unambiguous, forty-three years after she had written it Kay Boyle firmly repudiated its unmistakable message.

Listen to the story, and then see what you think:

Lady Glourie, the protagonist and point of consciousness of the story, is "a woman of thirty five or six with a big pair of shoulders, strong as a wood yoke." She smokes constantly, allowing her cigarette to hang from "her unpainted lip." She is apparently the only woman (the swanherd's ailing wife is never seen and the farmer's wife and daughter are similarly absent from the visible action of the story) living on a vast, rural estate in southern England. She dresses always in tweed skirts, cardigans, suede jackets, and "the heavy brogues a man might have worn." Her hair is "cut short as a man's hair on her ears and neck." When she writes it is with "a bold strong man-like hand."

Her young son and daughter have gone away to school, so she and her boorish, indifferent, heavy-drinking, and uncommunicative husband, Lord Glourie, live alone in their great barren stone house, visited often in the evenings by equally boorish neighbors, the male gentry who hunt and fish with him, or on weekends by many hunters up from the city for duck shooting. Well into the late hours of the night the men gather downstairs in the great hall, shouting, drinking, laughing loudly, keeping Lady Glourie awake upstairs until early morning.

She is surrounded by men, a manservant waiting on their table, a male cook, the virile, womanizing young sheepherder-farmer who lives in a farmhouse on the land, and the aging swanherd, Lucky, whose wife is about to give birth to their first child. He yearns for a son, only a son, because swanherding is traditionally handed down from father to son.

The estate's main distinction is a large lagoon on which live great flocks of swans. Miles of fields are filled with sheep, their hooves in the swampy, sodden grass of early May eaten away by soft, black rot. Significant as this animal foot disease is to the story of isolated, crippled human spirits, it is the spring mating ritual of the swans that provides the undercoating to the story. We are witness to this ceremony: young male and female swans, cobs and pens, try to establish their territory while older, cruel, even murderous, cobs invade the nests and try to kill their male rivals.

Lady Glourie decides to hire a nurse from London for the final weeks of Mrs. Lucky's pregnancy. Awaiting the arrival of the unknown woman, and yearning in her long loneliness for the presence of another woman, she fantasizes about what the nurse might be like, old or young? her name? what they will talk about. She plans to place fresh flowers in her room, to take her on visits to the swans and the sheep so that she will not think that everything on the place "has succumbed to the sound of glasses, bottles, guns, to the smell of stone and fish dying with hooks through their gills." She may even read to her poems she wrote as a girl at school.

And when she tells Panrandall, the farmer, about the coming of the nurse (for his young daughter has worms and may be helped by her), she feels "the relief and the faint sense of excitement a lover feels when he has at last, after a long time of waiting, brought the loved name into a conversation of other things."

Curious. Knowing nothing whatever about the nurse, Lady Glourie is aware of her "faint sense of excitement" that a lonely woman might well have felt at the thought of the arrival of an unknown woman. But why, we wonder, in terms of "a lover" and "a loved name?"

When Miss Cafferty arrives, she turns out to be very young and pretty, a homeless but cultivated, middle-class Irish girl who seems to Lady Glourie to be almost a child. She wears a thin, unsuitable "schoolgirl's" coat, she is seated for her meals in an absent child's place, she listens to Lord Glourie's interminable lecture on swans "as a child might"; her arms are like a child's, her face "oddly childlike"—all this on one page.

The men on the place seem much taken with her, or so Lady Glourie imagines they must be: she spots footprints of Miss Cafferty's "narrow, high-heeled shoe" near the farmer's cottage. Lord Glourie is openly admiring, or so it appears to Lady Glourie's narrating eyes. For we are privy to no observations or thoughts but hers. On one skillfully composed page, about her belief in the nurse's affair with the farmer, Boyle uses words that hint at but do not confirm her suspicions: the woman had seemed to saunter in the rain, his arm about her, *probably* exactly as it was, *doubtless* their mouths together, *might* be anyone's but must be hers, etc.

At first glance, the reader, expecting conventional narrative developments, misses these ambiguities. And there are other seemingly unrelated and guileless meanders. Lord Glourie instructs Miss Cafferty about the affectionate, monogamous relationships of cob to pen. Lady Glourie interrupts,

> speaking rapidly, as if to save or hide them all from the implication. "We've seen them, Glourie and me here. One autumn a couple of cobs paired off together, went through all the song and dance of meeting each other on the water and dipping their heads under . . . and then sank under the surface for the pairing. And in the spring, mind you," said Lady Glourie, staring with inexplicable sorrow into the fire, "the two cobs took turns sitting on the empty nest they'd built together."

Lord Glourie's response to this extraordinary ("inexplicable") story is to tell Miss Cafferty, with annoyance, that pens have done the same thing. Last year, he thought it was, in

the spring he saw the two females, making "a sight of themselves . . . laying infertile eggs and sitting a month on them
trying to hatch them out!" Lady Glourie remembers that
Lucky thought they ought to introduce the two cobs to the
pens, and Miss Cafferty responds, in a tone that is low and
passionate, "Do you think that would have helped? . . . Do
you think that would have changed anything at all?" We are
misled into thinking this is all offhand chattering, like the
earlier lecture on swans. The story moves to its climax. Lord
Glourie's savage jealousy of the farmer and Lady Glourie's
suspicions (and thus ours) of the nurse and the farmer,
indeed her resentment of her husband's attention to Miss
Cafferty, are mistakes, misleading. On the last, dark night,
Lady Glourie, standing in the muck of the lagoon, fights off
the vicious old cob in order to rescue the body of the young
bridegroom he has killed.

Alone in the lagoon, Miss Cafferty has witnessed the
death. She loses control when Lady Glourie arrives: "Her hand
moved, seemingly without warmth or volition," into Lady
Glourie's. And then she watches, terrified, as Lady Glourie
goes out through the mud to rescue the dead body from the
hovering old cob. "Lady Glourie, my darling, my darling," she
cries out, and goes toward her, "reeling and staggering through
the muck. . . . 'If he touches you, I'll kill him.'" Flinging herself on Lady Glourie, she cries, "Are you hurt, my darling, are
you hurt?"

In the last moments of this scene, the truth, hinted at but
missed by the reader, is revealed. Miss Cafferty had gone out
for her night walks because she could not sleep ("Night after
night I've walked the country alone"). This night she happens upon the terrible fight between the male swans but is too
frightened to call for help. She believes she is responsible for
the bridegroom's death.

That is not all. In the course of her outburst she confesses
to Lady Glourie the motive for her nocturnal walks:

> "I came out thinking about you. Let me say it! . . . I came
> out to think about you alone where there might be some-
> thing left of you somebody hadn't touched . . . some mark
> of you on the ground . . . I couldn't sleep in the room, I
> couldn't bear closing the door after I'd left you, just one
> more door closed between what you are and what I am!"

What pours out of the distraught nurse is almost unbearable
to read. She goes on: "Night after night I've walked the country alone instead of walking it with you . . . asking you to give
me everything I haven't." Stunned as we are by this confession, we are even more amazed by what Boyle assigns to Lady
Glourie's thoughts: "For now the words seemed no longer
Miss Cafferty's . . . but these were things she had heard once
or once imagined and had for a long time only dimly remembered, and this declaration was shape given them at last in the
moving and terrible statement of memory."

She tries to quiet the nurse, but in the final sentences of
the story Miss Cafferty's confession flows on unchecked:

> "Don't you think I see you living in this place alone, alone
> the way you're alone in your bed at night, with butchers,
> murderers—men stalking every corner of the grounds by
> day and night? . . . Don't you think I fought them all off
> because of you, because I knew that fighting them was tak-
> ing your side against them? . . . Every night since I've come
> here I've walked out in the rain through the fields or up on
> the cliffs thinking of how I could tell you, or ever make you
> see your beauty, or how I could ever make you know . . .
> Every night I've asked everything of you . . . asking you to
> escape from this. . . ."

Her heartbreaking confession is cut off by the appearance of Lucky and Lord Glourie, who find the two women looking at each other. Lord Glourie is annoyed at how wet they are. Lady Glourie "looked down at the nightdress clinging to her own strange flesh and suddenly she began shaking with the cold."

Lord Glourie's lantern-light has fallen between the two women "like a barrier falling." The last moment is a tableau, "lit as if someone had switched on the illumination in a room." We are left with this unresolution, with questions about why Lady Glourie at this moment feels her flesh to be *strange*, what "barrier" has fallen, what sudden understanding between the two women has been illuminated, why it is that Lady Glourie is shaking. This is the story that Kay Boyle, in a letter to scholar Sandra Whipple Spanier, who was doing a book about her almost fifty years later, wrote: "There were no lesbian under-tones or over-tones" in it. "Never for a moment" did she intend to suggest that a lesbian affair was offered as a solution to the women's loneliness. Spanier sees the last sentence as evidence that Lady Glourie "is shaken by the other woman's declaration of love." Almost cynically, it seems to me, Kay Boyle dismissed the emotional relationship in the story by saying that she did not know what happened to the two women "but I'm pretty sure they did not find salvation in each other. Miss Cafferty was probably shipped back to where she came from because of delinquency in performing her duty toward the swanherd's wife, and Lady Glourie probably went back to knitting the sweater for her son." I have called the story curious. The most curious thing about it is that its author, a most self-aware and skilled writer with a most "fearless and gifted hand," and who said this was one of her stories she loved best, had not a clue to what it was about. Homosexuality was "an aspect of love I was never moved to experiment with," she told Spanier. Not having been moved to it herself, she could not imagine her characters were.

I suppose one might well conclude that the writer, in many cases, is the last person to understand the implications of her own work.

Doris Grumbach is the author of the novels *The Spoil of the Flowers* (1962), *The Short Throat, The Tender Mouth* (1964), *Chamber Music* (1979), *The Missing Person* (1981), *The Ladies* (1984), *The Magician's Girl* (1987), and *The Book of Knowledge* (1995), of six books of memoirs, of a biography of Mary McCarthy, and of a children's book.

"The Doorbell" by Vladimir Nabokov

Olga Grushin

"The Doorbell" was first published in 1927, in Russian, as "Zvonok," in *Vozvrashchenie Chorba*. It was first published and collected in English in *Details of a Sunset and Other Stories* (1976). It is currently most readily available in *The Stories of Vladimir Nabokov* (Vintage).

Vladimir Nabokov was not American-born, nor a native English speaker—Russian-born, he wrote in three languages, with English coming in third after Russian and French—but he considered himself very much an American writer. "I am as American as April in Arizona," he famously said in a *Paris Review* interview in 1966; and while some might quibble as to exactly how American April in Arizona might be, in many fittingly modern ways Nabokov epitomizes what it means to be an American writer from a foreign cultural background, an increasingly widespread type today (of which I myself, incidentally, am an example).

"The Doorbell" is an early story, written in Russian and published in 1927 in a small émigré magazine in Berlin, where Nabokov spent most of his exile years after leaving post-revolutionary Russia and before arriving in America in 1941. He wrote some twenty-five stories before the age of thirty, most of which had already begun to explore the themes he would develop at length in his novels—memory, time, loss of one's country, loss of one's beloved—all subjects that seem quite relevant, once again, in today's America of multiculturalism, restlessness, and upheavals. "The Doorbell" was translated into English by Nabokov's son, Dmitri, under Nabokov's own supervision, and included in 1976 in *Details of a Sunset and Other Stories*.

Standing at a modest nine or ten pages, "The Doorbell" possesses the deeply nostalgic overtones of Nabokov's longer fiction, as well as a surprising wealth of meanings and a sense of playfulness with which it subverts several of the reader's expectations. A man, driven out of Russia by the revolution, has been leading a vagabond life of adventure and occasional soldiering all over the world. Now, having "grown hardier, rougher," "lost an index finger," and "learned two languages," Nikolay Galatov comes to Berlin, more or less on a whim, to find a woman from whom he was parted in Petersburg seven years ago. His last recalled glimpse of her is decidedly romantic—his farewell words, "Good-bye, dearest," and the train starting as she walks alongside it, "tall, thin, wearing a raincoat, with a black-and-white scarf around her neck." His search for her, too, bears an unmistakable whiff of a past love affair: "A chill of excitement came over him at the idea that he was in the same town as she."

He does not have her present address, does not even know whether she still lives in Berlin, has only her name—that of her second husband, a late German industrialist—to go by, yet within a few hours of arriving in the city, he manages to find her, with a fairy-tale felicity of "a card trick," in a plot twist conceived with a typically Nabokovian sleight of hand: as Nikolay wanders the streets of Berlin at random, he stumbles upon a dentist's sign, suddenly recognizes the name from his own childhood dental visits, and, thinking that the man might be of help in his quest, visits his office. Disappointingly, the dentist turns out to be someone else, merely a namesake, albeit also from Petersburg; and then, with the dreamlike ease of resolution, he happens to recall a certain Madame Kind who paid him a recent visit and promptly supplies Nikolay with her address. It is at this point, while the reader is still processing the double salvo of the two preceding surprises (wrong man, right woman), that the story twists again, as the amiable man (incidentally, a recognizable Jack-in-the-Box figure in Nabokov's fiction, a magically appearing, entirely altruistic facilitator of fate) asks whether the woman is a relative, and Nikolay replies: "My mother."

It is already evening when Nikolay, unannounced, rings his mother's doorbell, his heart pounding, wondering how she will receive him—whether tenderly, sadly, or "with complete calm"—yet when she opens the door at last, their reunion is awkward, tense, strange from the very first moment. The encounter starts in the dark, for the lights are out in the entire building, and is then illuminated uncertainly, flickeringly, by candlelight. She seems to be expecting someone else, and the sudden appearance of Nikolay wrings from her a cry "as startled as if a strong hand had struck her." Her apartment is foreign, full of "awful middle-class trappings"; she herself is virtually unrecognizable, perfumed, dressed in a glossy blue dress, her formerly dark hair bobbed and bleached, her face made up "with excruciating care." "Everything about her was unfamiliar, restless and frightening." Her table is set for an elaborate meal, sparkling with crystal and crowned with a cake with a ring of candles in it. Oblivious at first, then with an increasing sense of some "doomful thing coming from afar, menacing and inevitable," Nikolay proceeds to treat her to a continuous stream of overly jolly and disjointed anecdotes of his adventures, afraid to ask her anything about her own life, ignoring the fact that she is barely listening, puzzled when he counts the candles on the cake and discovers there are twenty-five of them (he himself, we learn at this point, is already twenty-eight).

It is then that they are interrupted by the buzzing of the doorbell. He wants to get the door, still talking cheerfully about some African episode, disregarding her anxious objections—"Nonsense, Mother. They'll come, they'll see your son has arrived, and very soon they'll evaporate"—but she does not let him answer the bell, whispering frantically, "Don't you dare!" and pulling at him, whereupon her "twenty-five guests," as he calls them, proceed to knock, ring some more, and depart. The mother begins to weep. "It's all over now," she sobs. "I'll be fifty in May. Grown-up son comes to see aged mother." Nikolay, confused—"a real nightmare," he thinks as he chuckles uneasily—contemplates again the cake with the twenty-five candles, the two wineglasses, and the gift box with a silver cigarette case inside, looks at his mother, crying "so girlishly," grunts, and announces that he is moving on, feeling "an urge to head north now, to Norway, perhaps." She offers no objections but sees him to the door, asking him to write often, discovering, in passing, that he is missing a finger ("Blown off by a bullet," he laughs); he takes leave of her with words that echo their farewell at the start of the story, "Goodbye, my dearest"; and, once the door shuts behind him, "she flew, her blue dress rustling, to the telephone."

Nabokov never offers an explicit explanation, yet the situation is unmistakable: the forty-nine-year-old woman is expecting a lover young enough to be her son (and, in fact, younger than her actual son), for whom she has prepared a romantic dinner, when her real son arrives instead. She is obviously trying to conceal her age from her visitor (hence the candlelight, the careful makeup, the dyed hair, the youthful dress), and has likely neglected to mention the existence of a grown son as well. The prodigal son, returning with fate's worst possible timing ("Why did you have to come right at this moment . . . tonight!" she cries), threatens to throw her entire life into disarray.

The basic premise is simple, yet the story is not; it lends itself to a score of possible interpretations and misinterpretations. One academic writer sees the mother's financial circumstances as reduced and the woman driven to the life of a courtesan (blatantly not the case), while another reviewer, likewise erroneously, assumes her to be waiting for a middle-aged suitor. More interesting than these crude misunderstandings, however, is the wide divergence of opinions as to the character of Nikolay, with several critics viewing him as a negative type, a boorish, egotistical intruder of the kind that abounds in Nabokov's fiction, and the nature of his mother, seen by some as tawdry and cold, and by others as poignant and tragic.

Nabokov certainly embraced ambiguity in his fiction, and the entire story is delightfully full of casually dropped, understated clues, which need to be pieced together to decipher the puzzle of his characters' motivations. Did Nikolay intend to leech off his mother or to ensure her comfort? Did he mean to stay in Berlin for a while, or was he always going to leave the very next day? Was he a heartless son at fault in their estrangement, or was she truly as chilly and distant as he remembers her (his impression as a boy was that "she did not have much use for him")? Had he failed to stay in touch, or had she? (There is a mention of an advertisement he once half-heartedly placed in an émigré paper, which she, it later transpires, saw and to which she was still "on the point of" replying—"always on the point," as Nabokov comments, in one of those tiny details that in a lesser writer's hands would become mere fodder but which are never accidental in his complex universe.) Is she genuinely in love with her twenty-five-year-old visitor, or only trying to bribe him with gifts, a wealthy aging woman buying some vulgar gigolo's attentions in a pathetic bid for affection? And in the end, is she crying over her lost youth or her lost country? Is she anxious about being abandoned by her recent lover or grieving over her severed bond with her son?

A few red herrings are, indeed, thrown at the reader here and there: Nikolay, we are informed, is "running out of funds" on the way to Berlin and does have an embarrassed exchange about money with his mother (who is, to all appearances, comfortably well-off and becomes alarmed by a suspicion that he has come to ask her for help, quickly refusing it even as he denies that he needs it). Yet I see him as an essentially well-meaning, appealing active type, a *doer*, quite distinct from a more familiar Nabokovian *artist*, a creative, introspective neurotic much more given to selfishness. Nikolay is largely a poetic figure, exaggeratedly so in many ways; Nabokov himself pokes gentle fun at the man's thirst for adventure: "ah, those years, that stupendous roaming about the world, the obscure ill-paid jobs, chances taken and chucked, the excitement of freedom," "pure Jack London" ("total Meyne Reid" in the Russian version).

In fact, he may be seen as a somewhat two-dimensional hero from an adventure novel, his life a succession of clichés of flying bullets and wild animal chases, who, blinded by the romance of his recent African past and hoping to recover the nostalgic romance of his remote Russian childhood, is perfectly, and tragically, oblivious to his mother's mundane life in bourgeois Germany, ruled by middle-class conventions and a terrible, tangible fear of a lonely old age. His streak of insensitivity is undeniable (and quite masculine in nature), yet in the end, when he does understand the situation, I believe that he nobly chooses to leave, inventing his desire to go north on the spot, and even, magnanimously, absolving her of any guilt for their abrupt parting by shifting the onus of the decision fully onto himself: "Don't be cross with me because of my wanderlust!"

The mother is more enigmatic in her role as "the other" (we only ever see her through his eyes). There is a certain cheap theatricality about her, apparent in the vulgar furnishings of her apartment, the tastelessness of her intended gift to her lover, the shine of her dress, her dyed "artificial hair," her handkerchief dropped "just the way it was supposed to, in that pretty scene"; and yet Nabokov supplies her with a tragic past of her own (a widowed countess whose first husband, an admiral, shot himself) and offers a number of clues to prove that she does indeed love her son: at his arrival, she tenderly calls him "Nicky, Nick" and prattles, "It's you. You've come. You're really here. It's good," while at their parting, she cries out at the discovery of his missing finger, feels its "smooth stub" and gives it "a cautious kiss." Her despair at the end is as palpable and real as his excitement at the beginning.

On the other hand, there is also an undeniable, if implicit, judgment of both characters present in the very situation. The bond between mother and child is supposed to be one of the most sacred human bonds imaginable (Nabokov himself, not coincidentally, was very close to his mother and wrote of a nearly mystical connection the two of them shared), and the fact that this amiable young man entirely lost touch with his mother for seven years, barely thought of her for a while, and fails even to "picture her face" clearly, seeing her through an idealized mist instead, as well as the fact that she was less than attentive to him when he was a boy, come to reflect off each other in a number of echoes and ironies, ultimately resulting in the tragedy of their nightmarish reunion. Ever a visual writer who brilliantly employed the effects of light and dark, Nabokov uses the total darkness in which they first meet as an obvious metaphor for their essential otherness to each other. The image of the birthday

cake, too, figures twice in the narrative and serves as an interesting focal point for failed celebrations and ruined fantasies, both
childish and romantic: upon seeing it on her table, Nikolay
reminds her, with a heartrending offhandedness, how she once
ruined a birthday of his (he was turning ten, but she had put in
only nine candles; "I bawled my head off"); now, in a kind of
mirror punishment for her shortcomings as a mother, he exacts
his unintentional vengeance by ruining the birthday celebration
she has planned as a woman, not a mother, for someone else. As
the flip side of the same coin, had he been more dutiful as a son,
had he not drifted out of her life, he would not now be facing an
entire childhood worth of memories soured by the aftertaste of
their disastrous encounter.

The gradually revealed complexity of the two characters
is fascinating; and like a many-faceted diamond, the central
juxtaposition between them can be turned, shifted, considered from different angles to reflect other layers of meanings,
to symbolize other possible conflicts—most obviously, the
dramatic gulf between the past (as characterized by Nikolay's
naïve, vague attempts to recapture his childhood, his frag-
mented recollections, his abbreviated anecdotes) and the
present (the woman trying to arrange her romantic life, her
surroundings depicted in concrete, physical, prosaic terms),
but also, more tenuously yet not implausibly, given the mul-
tidimensional richness of Nabokov's fiction, conflicts between
man and woman, between Russia and Germany, even between
the conventions of the adventure genre and the romance genre
or poetry and prose. One can also expand on the theme of the
severed bond with one's mother by reading into it the greater
tragedy of being exiled from one's motherland. (Russia is, of
course, often referred to as "Mother Russia"; Nabokov does
not allow himself such heavy-handed allusions here, yet the
description of Nikolay escaping Russia, in the story's opening

paragraph, is curiously anthropomorphized, with Nikolay much like a youth who leaves the warmth of his family upon entering adulthood, and Russia—referred to as "she"—attempting to hold him by various enticements, until at last she "let go of him").

Still, deeper layers of meaning aside, for me the main appeal of the story remains in its vivid portrayal of essential human solitude. Nabokov has a perfect touch when describing abbreviated conversations, terminated connections, unvoiced emotions (he explores similar situations elsewhere, for instance, in "The Reunion," a 1931 story about an equally unsatisfying meeting between two estranged brothers, or his first English-language novel, *The Real Life of Sebastian Knight*), and his mastery is on full display in this sad tale of two people who appear to love each other, who should be close because of their blood ties and shared past, yet who brush past each other in a terribly unsettling, painful way before each retreating back into his or her loneliness. Yet there is a hopeful note here, too: like Proust, Nabokov sought meaning in preserving moments of heightened perception, and Nikolay bears an unmistakable, if inverse, resemblance to Lev Ganin, another appealing but flawed protagonist, from Nabokov's 1926 debut novel, *Mary*, likewise a Russian exile in Berlin who relives an intense love affair in recollections but decides to avoid reconnecting with its flesh-and-blood object.

Returning to the past is impossible, yet one can, briefly, warm oneself by recapturing its beauty, its life, in brightly illuminated glimpses, in fragments of smells, tastes, sounds, in echoes of strong feelings, before letting go forever; and Nikolay, while failing to re-establish lasting ties with his mother, is yet, generously, granted a vibrant vision of his forgotten past when coming upon the dentist's sign, "an unexpected recollection" that "virtually scalded him," like the celebrated Proustian madeleine, which, in turn, leads to the gift of an intense, rich hour during which he sees his surroundings in an entirely new light: "Beautiful city, beautiful rain!" And while the vividly experienced hour would not fully make up for the heartbreak of the subsequent human failure, it is yet a poetic note of grace that sounds, clear and sonorous, through this poignant story, both a deceptively simple study of feelings and a small jewelry box in which one can already find a few gems polished in Nabokov's more mature works.

Olga Grushin is the author of the novels *The Dream Life of Sukhanov* (2005), *The Line* (2010), and *Forty Rooms* (2016).

"Good Country People"
by Flannery O'Connor

A. R. Gurney

"Good Country People" was originally published in the June 1955 issue of *Harper's Bazaar*. It was collected in *A Good Man Is Hard to Find* (1955). It is currently most readily available in *A Good Man Is Hard to Find and Other Stories* (Harcourt Brace Jovanovich).

The first thing to say about this story is that it's funny— funny as a crutch, to use a cliché the author might either appreciate or wince at. It happens to be the first work of hers I ever read, and I remember coming to it not expecting to laugh. I was a big reader of *Time* magazine in those days, and I think they told me that Flannery O'Connor was Southern, Gothic, deep, and Roman Catholic. Furthermore, I knew that she had a mysteriously degenerative disease called lupus, and had recently died of it at a relatively early age. So naturally I was expecting to read something shadowy, profound, and grim. "Good Country People" certainly is all those things, but it is also very funny.

I read it because I had to. In the mid-1960s, I was teaching an Introduction to Literature course in the Humanities Department at M.I.T., and "Good Country People" happened to be one of the stories in the designated anthology. I tossed this story onto the syllabus rather arbitrarily, but when I finally got around to reading it for class, it blew me away. I could tell from the classroom response that it blew the students away too. And it has stayed with me ever since.

It is first and foremost a good yarn. If you try telling it to people who haven't read it, they follow it easily and eagerly. In the 1960s, I even told it, in a somewhat censored version, to my four young children during a long trip in the car, and it apparently stayed with them too, since elements of it still come up in family conversations. Reading it again now, I see new and different things in it, but the clean thrust of its narrative line remains very impressive.

There's no point in retelling the plot here, except to say that the story is basically about the conflict between a genteel, platitudinous mother who manages a farm and her sullen, intellectual, rebellious daughter—two recurring types in O'Connor's fiction, as I learned as I read more of her. The mother is somewhat subversively abetted by the nosey wife of her tenant farmer, while the daughter attempts to rebel against the stultifying atmosphere by seducing an itinerant Bible salesman who comes to their door. You might wonder what's so funny about that? On an immediate level, the comedy comes from the constant clash between the mother's sentimental vision of the world as opposed to the daughter's cynical take on it, as well as from the subordinate characters who undermine and twist both perspectives.

But the issue is more complicated than that. It has to do with what seems to be the religious dimension in the story. How can something be funny and seriously religious at the same time? Flannery O'Connor, of course, is a tricky writer who takes us down strange and murky paths, but she always gives us slyly helpful markers along the way. For example, the sentimental mother in "Good Country People" is called Mrs.

Hopewell, whereas her more realistic subordinate is a Mrs. Freeman. The sulky daughter was originally christened Joy, but has defiantly changed her name to Hulga. The Bible salesman, who turns out to have an eye for the vulnerable women, calls himself Manley Pointer. With all these moral signposts, we find ourselves, like it or not, in a vaguely allegorical world, almost as if we had come upon a southern and contemporary version of John Bunyan.

Yet the religion dimension is much more subtly present than it is in traditional allegory. One of the implications of the story, for example, is that mere names are inadequate or false labels for the complex human beings they are attached to. Mrs. Hopewell is hopelessly trying to cheer herself up. Mrs. Freeman is hardly free, having only three gears—neutral, forward, and reverse—"for all human dealings." Joy is certainly joyless, and if Manley Pointer is able to point like a compass toward the true north of other people's deficiencies, he is certainly not "manly" in the way he is expected to be.

In the same way, the clichés and truisms that people use in daily conversation to explain events or occurrences are seen to be as inadequate as names:

> "Why!" [Mrs. Hopewell] cried, "good country people are the salt of the earth! Besides, we all have different ways of doing, it takes all kinds to make the world go 'round. That's life!"
> "You said a mouthful," [Manley Pointer] said.

The clichés tumble over themselves here, and cancel each other out. Indeed, the title of the story, "Good Country People," which Mrs. Hopewell uses to describe those who are simpler and more innocent than she herself, is a particularly untrustworthy phrase. Neither Manley Pointer nor Mrs. Freeman is in any way "good," and if "country" means simple, they are hardly that either. In fact, both have an instinct for the jugular, which one wants to call evil. The real innocents, the closest we come to "good country people," turn out to be the supposedly more educated and sophisticated mother and daughter.

This theme of the untrustworthiness of the world and the foolishly limited labels we slap on life is embodied most effectively in the story of Joy-Hulga. Having lost a leg in a hunting accident as a child, she re-christens herself Hulga, a name which she believes is a tough-minded and accurate moniker for who and what she actually is. She goes on to earn her PhD in Philosophy, but now is unable to teach because of a weak heart. Because of her physical disabilities and her sense of confinement in a life that she loathes, she believes herself to be beyond illusion. "We are not our own light!" she cries at her mother, with her mouth full, one night at supper. And later she tells the Bible salesman: "We are all damned, . . . but some of us have taken off our blindfolds and see that there's nothing to see. It's a kind of salvation."

Of course, from the author's perspective, nihilism is no salvation at all, as Hulga soon discovers. She sets about to seduce Manley Pointer, the Bible salesman, out of a kind of perverse desire to destroy his innocence and reduce him to her own level of disillusionment. In the end, however, she turns out to be the violated one, and it is her own innocence that is molested. The seducer has become the victim, and Pointer's Holy Bible is simply a hollow shell containing a bottle of liquor, a box of condoms, and a pack of pornographic playing cards. Hulga is last seen abandoned in the hayloft of the isolated barn, helpless and humiliated: "[Y]ou ain't so smart," the salesman jeers at her. "I been believing in nothing ever since I was born!"

O'Connor may be a Catholic writer, but she is hardly explicit in her Catholicism. This story, along with so many of her others, derides those who are proud enough to think they have the answers, and illustrates how incapable we are of achieving salvation on our own. We can't help but laugh at the fatuous pieties of conventional wisdom mouthed by Mrs. Hopewell and at the self-deluding intellectual nihilism of Hulga. We see similar limitations in the supposedly more realistic characters: Mrs. Freeman's lugubrious dependence on the difficulties of others hardly sets her free, and Manley Pointer's perverse hypocrisies suggest that he is impelled to steal other people's souls because he has none of his own. But if we are ceaselessly reminded of our own limitations, and made constantly aware that "we are not our own light," then where is the light to turn to? The story leaves these questions up in the air.

Or does it? How can we read "Good Country People" without speculating about what happens after it ends? Surely any reader would go on to imagine the one-legged Hulga struggling down the rickety ladder from the hayloft and crawling across the fields for home. We would also envision her trying to explain the loss of her wooden leg to her mother and Mrs. Freeman. It seems to me this would be as humbling an experience as climbing the steps of Saint Peter's on one's knees, before confessing one's sins to a priest.

Hulga might be viewed as a kind of heretic, who has baptized herself into a vain skepticism and put her trust in a false prophet with a fake Bible. But for all her sins, she is still a seeker after truth, and by implication, may ultimately find peace through the offices of an established institution long accustomed to the workings of the world. You might want to argue that Roman Catholicism is a cliché itself, time-tested and time-worn, but it is a cliché imposed on the world by God and history. It is under no illusions about such sins as pride, lust, sin, anger, and despair, and offers age-old sacraments for us to confront and deal with them.

But this sense of religious salvation, which we arrive at in the story primarily through a kind of philosophical triangulation beyond the actual events presented on the page, must have something to do with the sense of humor in "Good Country People." The strangely comic tone of the story is what has stayed with me over the years, and I am compelled to ask once again, as I asked my M.I.T. students thirty years ago, why and how is this strange tale of a silly mother and her dying daughter so damned funny?

Here are some possible answers: first of all, in its basic situations, the story manages to do a twist on a number of standard comic chords. In Hulga's conflict with Mrs. Hopewell, for example, the author reworks the standard parent vs. child antagonisms which we are all familiar with. Hulga locking herself in the bathroom, clumping late down to breakfast, sardonically putting down the fatuous chatter of her mother reminds us of all those other rebellious American offspring who have populated American culture from Tom Sawyer through Holden Caulfield on down to the latest family sitcom on television. Mrs. Freeman, similarly, reminds us of the typical wise-cracking neighbor, leaning on the refrigerator, making with the jokes, while her daughters, "Glycerine and Caramel," are funny in the way so many pairs of sisters are funny, from Cinderella's stepsisters on down. Another old chord resonates through the last movement of the story, namely the Hulga-Pointer seduction scene. In some ways, it is a weird and humorous twist on the old dirty jokes about travelling salesmen and farmers' daughters. Here, in a series of reversals worthy of Molière, the innocent is revealed to be guilty, the seducer is seduced.

In other words, "Good Country People" is a story that plays comically with clichés, which are the woefully inadequate ways we have of decoding a mysterious and unpredictable world. The story's title is a cliché; its plot reworks and plays with a number of narrative clichés; its characters fall back on clichés as a substitute for wisdom, and they get into trouble because they view each other in terms of clichés. Clichés contain just enough truth to fool us, and in our yearning for answers and solutions, we allow ourselves to be easily fooled by them. By inference, the only way out of this dilemma might be to turn toward another cliché, the one true and reliable one: the Roman Catholic Church.

Finally, I remember—from another course I taught at M.I.T.—that Kierkegaard describes a particular kind of comedy that he categorizes as "religious." He suggests that if we view the world from the infinite perspective that only religion can give us, then the exertions of people, whether for good or evil, can be seen as humorous when measured against the workings of an infinite, perfect God in an ultimately benign universe. You could say that Dante looks at things this way and therefore calls his poem a Comedy. Chaucer might achieve a similar feel in *The Canterbury Tales*. Shakespeare achieves it in his late comedies. Possibly, with a little work, we could say that Flannery O'Connor does, too, at least occasionally, in stories such as this one.

A. R. Gurney (1930–2017) is the author of the novels *The Snow Ball* (1984), *The Gospel According to Joe* (1974), *Entertaining Strangers* (1977), and *Early American* (1996), as well as of more than fifty plays, most notably *The Dining Room* (1982), *The Cocktail Hour* (1988), *Love Letters* (1988), and *Sylvia* (1995). He was elected to the Theater Hall of Fame and to the American Academy of Arts and Letters.

"Jubilee" by Kirstin Valdez Quade

Jane Hamilton

"Jubilee" was first published in *Guernica* on June 17, 2013. It was collected and is currently most readily available in *Night at the Fiestas* (W. W. Norton).

I more or less remember two things: first, a demanding, pitiless professor from my college years shaking his head in shocking bewilderment, wondering at how hard-hearted his beloved Jane Austen must have been to visit so much suffering upon her heroines. And two: my sister once remarking that a famous young male writer, who had been pronounced Great, wasn't mature enough to write great novels. My sister said he was too full of rage to write with dispassionate clarity. If some day he gained the distance on his characters that, say, Alice Munro or Willa Cather had, then maybe he could be called Great.

Rage is a staple fuel for a writer; it is plentiful, exhilarating, and cheap. The white carbs, the potatoes, fries, and donuts of the writer's emotional food group, what's required to climb the mountain. One of the beauties of rage is how it can be conjured in an instant; it is borne from the smallest injustice or hurt, and also it will flame up from gross violations to the body and spirit. Rage, in sum, is not special. But controlling the heat and the sprawl of it—that's another story.

I'm guessing that "Jubilee" could well have been written from a point of white-hot rage, and therefore been in danger of a hectoring, didactic tone, the ideas overwhelming the characters. However, Kirstin Valdez Quade isn't interested in writing directly about oppression or social justice; she doesn't seem to want to place blame, to stick it to the man. Rather, in "Jubilee" she wants to get at how social standing, income inequity, and race affect the inner life of one young woman. Although Quade is herself still a young writer, she is preternaturally mature. She understands that by precisely chronicling Andrea's distress, by mapping her inner landscape, the outer world then will be precisely revealed. As for a hard heart, I suspect that Quade is tender for all real-life intents and purposes, yet she spares her heroine no misery. Quade and Jane Austen both are master torturers in their work.

"Jubilee" is the story of a young Latina woman, Andrea, the daughter of a farm worker; her father is now a supervisor of a blueberry farm and orchard. When a writer sets a narrative in an orchard there are specific challenges. Does she ignore the freight of Orchard? Must there be Eden and the inevitable fallen world? The damn snake? Can't the setting simply be an orchard for its own sake? There are choices, in other words, that she will have to make.

Andrea is a bright, ambitious woman who's just finished her freshman year at Stanford, a woman who is in the midst of realizing her aspirations. Race and class animate the fury in her heart and soul on any given day, and when we see her showing up at an orchard party that she's not exactly been invited to, her fury is at full tilt. Quade doesn't merely begin her story at the party; she unleashes the tornado that is Andrea into the story, Andrea funneling her way through the event. It is William Lowell's shindig, the landowner and employer of her father, the company throwing the annual party to celebrate the success of the orchard. Andrea explains to her Hispanic plus-one, Matty, "they own everything. Not just blueberries, either. They grow practically every stone fruit ever invented. Even the dumb ones, like nectarcots." (Quade grants Andrea a jaundiced scorn that is funny, but also throughout the story the dignity of astute observations.)

The laborers at the orchard have been given the day off, all except Andrea's father, who is one focal point of the celebration, the authentic Mexican! Serving tacos from his food truck, a business he has on the side. The party is Mexican themed, Andrea notes with derision, the tent decorated with papel picado flags, little piñatas on each table, margaritas in the guests' hands. Her culture is reduced to decor. Andrea is burdened by seeing all of the world in a multiplicity of codes. The objects, clothing, table decorations—everything means one thing or another, or both, the meaning of a single object often at war with itself. The food truck's menu has been upgraded for the Lowell party: tacos with "Kobe beef, wild-caught salmon, free-range chicken, and vegetarian, all on blue corn tortillas." (The lack of parallelism is the set-up for an attempt at a joke that follows: "A vegetarian on a tortilla. Ha.") For Andrea, the Momofuku-ized bullshit tacos are a perversion, the dressing up of the humble tortilla, the phony—no, but wait! There is high value deliciousness and elegance on display in that food—No, no, stop! She must not admire the elegance. After all, her culture and its own attendant goodness is being whitewashed. In a few lines and a couple of tacos, the reader understands the ledge on which Andrea teeters, understands her stubborn pride and her longing.

Everywhere the codes are flashing. Signs of white versus non-white; elegance versus trashy taste; intellect versus ignorance; the oppressor versus the worker. (It's hard not to think that Quade had real pleasure writing, in her word-perfect prose, the glory that is Andrea's suffering—the complexity, the facets, the gleam of the heroine's misery.) Her anguish is made up of equal parts hatred and the terrible irritant that is love. Andrea both longs for what seems out of reach to her, she hates the world she wants, she hates herself for wanting what she ostensibly hates, but—in truth—she loves the Lowells too. She loves the ideal of the family and the practical grace they are able to bestow on others. She thinks she doesn't care what the Lowells think of her; she in fact cares immoderately. Andrea hates their dominion; she also wants them to be in charge. They are, in her mind, not only the rightful rulers, they are just and good. Matty, her date, the moral center of the story, observes, "You're fucked up, you know? You're fucking obsessed."

Her own warring feelings are so intense that she of course cannot help going wrong at every turn during the party. It's a feat for a writer to put so many tensions in one character, to load her to the brim; and indeed there's the danger of burdening a heroine with too much changeable feeling. And yet Quade with great ease doesn't so much justify Andrea's feelings—but allows for them. Complicating matters further, there is the Lowell daughter. Parker has also just finished her freshman year at Stanford; she is a thin girl with skin so translucent the veins at her temples are visible. Andrea wants to be in Parker's club; she hates Parker and everything she stands for. She wishes to be an empathic friend to Parker; her rage prevents her from being discreet and comforting. She wants handsome Matty to be her arm candy to impress Parker; she's repulsed by him, by his wormy black moustache. She's afraid of exposure, afraid to be seen as striving, and unworthy; she wants to show everyone her real self because she's proud of her family, proud of where she's come from. On the one hand, she feels she should be equal to the Lowells, now that she's at

Stanford; on the other, she knows she will never be in their club. All this fury is serenely delivered in twenty-four pages.

One of the saddest moments in the story comes in a flashback, Quade now and again leavening Andrea's rage with a quiet sorrow. Andrea realizes that the certificates of honor she's received from the Chicano Student Association aren't anything that students would receive in the real Stanford world, that is, the white world, the authentic world. The certificates are "just part of all the extra efforts made on behalf of minority students."

Back to the wrath: how sharply Quade shows the effortless way Parker seems to move through the world: Parker at the orchard party wearing a floral shift with Converse sneakers, and no socks. How galling, the sneakers that on a rich girl are automatically ironic, cool, and therefore classy. The gold Tiffany heart at Parker's throat is a little call and response with the sneakers: "Something about the necklace combined with the Converse suddenly enraged Andrea." Parker moves through the air is if on wings; for Andrea the world is sludge she's got to pull herself through. The J.Crew dress which she cannot afford has the price tags in place (down her sweaty back) so she can return it after the party. She worries that the tags will be seen, and she'll be exposed as unworthy, cheap, out of place. That, of course, feels to her like the story of her life, the dress as a metaphor. Always, always she has been afraid of exposure.

She remembers picking blueberries when she was a girl, set loose into the orchard with Parker, seven-year-olds joyful in their task. Joyful, until Parker's father tells Andrea she must stop. After all, he could be prosecuted for violating child labor law, a little Mexican girl on his property, picking blueberries. And yet Parker, the white girl, is allowed to keep picking, Parker gathering fruit for her mother's pie. Why can't the Mexican girl pick fruit with her father, when the white girl—whose lawyer father isn't even a real farmer—can carry on? The memory, the bitter irony, continues to sting through the years in part because Andrea chooses to recast the memory, Parker's father yelling at her, as she tells it, even as she knows that William Lowell gently removed her from the scene. It is through Andrea's eyes that Quade, in an astonishing feat, manages to give every single character dignity, each character, no matter their ethnicity or privilege, rendered with compassion.

When Andrea learns about Mrs. Lowell's affair, she must suffer further. The violation of the Lowell code, the fact that they aren't upholding the edifice, is nearly intolerable. Still, it is that tear in the Lowell fabric that gives Andrea pause: "In Andrea's mind Parker underwent a faint oxidation, taking on a patina, for the first time, of vulnerability." There is suddenly an opening for friendship. Is there a real chance the classmates can come together? Andrea, acknowledging that all people suffer, nonetheless makes a mess of her overture to Parker, leaving only wreckage in the wake of that moment.

What do you ultimately give your heroine when you have walked her step-by-step into one landmine after the next, the heroine leveling not her opponents but herself? And when the story is set in an orchard? Quade doesn't torment Andrea indefinitely, doesn't quite keep the fall in perpetual motion. She grants her character a way back into the garden—a place of her childhood, a place where goodness is recovered, at least temporarily. With a swift sure stroke the writer relieves the suffering by a gorgeous fulfillment. It is by erasure, the self forgotten, that Andrea is, as in the beginning, at one with the natural world.

Jane Hamilton is the author of the novels *The Book of Ruth* (1988), which won the PEN/Hemingway Award, *A Map* *of the World* (1994), *The Short History of a Prince* (1998), *Disobedience* (2000), *When Madeline Was Young* (2006), *Laura Rider's Masterpiece* (2009), and *The Excellent Lombards* (2016). Her story "Aunt Marj's Happy Ending" was reprinted in the 1984 volume of *The Best American Short Stories.*

"Winter Dreams" by F. Scott Fitzgerald

Edmund Keeley

"Winter Dreams" was originally published in the December 1922 issue of *Metropolitan Magazine*. It was collected in *All the Sad Young Men* (1926). It is currently most readily available in *The Short Stories of F. Scott Fitzgerald: A New Collection* (Scribner).

During my early encounters with F. Scott Fitzgerald's work, beginning with a senior thesis that I wrote as a graduation requirement at Princeton in 1948–49, I was haunted by a persistent question. How could the author of what Fitzgerald himself called that "picaresque ramble" of a novel, *This Side of Paradise*, and that too prolonged and sometimes artless cautionary tale called *The Beautiful and Damned*, with its often obtrusive "attempt to convey a profound air of erudition" (Zelda Fitzgerald's phrase in her 1922 review of the book)— how could that same author produce, just three years later, a third novel as structurally tight and as splendidly artful as *The Great Gatsby*? The question became all the more compelling when I learned at another time that Fitzgerald actually wrote the first draft of *The Great Gatsby* during 1923, the year following the publication of *The Beautiful and Damned*, a draft rewritten and completed a year later. He was just twenty-seven years old when he began to work on his durable masterpiece.

How could Fitzgerald have learned so much so well in such a short span of time and at such an early age? His college friends, Edmund Wilson and John Peale Bishop, offered some early criticism, but he clearly knew more about the writing of fiction from the start than they did. His undergraduate work on scripts for the Princeton Triangle Club musicals was of dubious lasting value, and according to his own testimony he got no help from those who were paid to teach him the virtues of literature either during or after his days at Princeton. His apprenticeship as a professional writer came while he earned his living under the pressure of writing story after story, each seemingly out of the same mold, for one or another popular magazine.

I found an answer to these questions when I had to begin assigning my students background reading in the under-graduate creative writing program that was first established in Fitzgerald's university some twenty years after he failed to earn his degree there as an English major. In my fiction workshop I used several stories from Fitzgerald's short-story collections to illustrate, along with a number of other sources, various aspects of the craft we were exploring, and in the course of my search over the years for new material I discovered not only how much Fitzgerald had written before he turned twenty-seven but how mature several stories published shortly after *The Beautiful and Damned* turned out to be under close study. It became clear to me that Fitzgerald had actually learned a great deal about the craft of fiction from writing his heart out more or less in isolation day after day, year in year out, what-ever the distractions outside his private workshop. And his early maturity was the product of his having worked hard—in what a 1934 letter of his calls "a dirty, sweating, heartbreak-ing effort"—to find a theme that so touched the center of his being as to bring forth the gift of both a shaping preoccupation and a defining voice. The story that still appears to me to best illustrate this early development is "Winter Dreams," which first appeared in December, 1922.

The "winter dreams" of the title belong to Dexter Green, and it is his obsession with those dreams, his tenacious desire to possess "glittering things," that gives shape to the portion of Dexter's life that the story outlines: not his career as a whole, the narrator tells us, but the story of one of the mysterious "denials and prohibitions in which life indulges" for those who grow up and finally live too long in the neighborhood of illusion. Both the obsession and the denial come to be embodied in the figure of Judy Jones, who goes after whatever she wants, including one man after another, "with the full pressure of her charm" and her capacity for making men "conscious to the highest degree of her physical loveliness." She also makes sure that she knows at the very start how rich or poor her potential lovers are.

Dexter meets her for the first time as a "proud, desirous little boy" of fourteen when she arrives at their local golf course with her nurse and tries to hire him as a caddy, an encounter that perturbs him enough to cause him to give up caddying on the spot, a move that the narrator tells us "was unconsciously dictated to by his winter dreams." And when he meets Judy again on the golf course almost ten years later, he now a highly successful entrepreneur and she now not only careless at golf but at all else in her life, he again succumbs to her charm and what he sees as her passionate energy, and he commits himself from then on "with varying shades of intensity" to surrender a part of himself to her however she chooses to treat him. He is happy with her for a season, humiliated by her for another season or two, loses her to others, regains her when she learns that he is about to announce his engagement to somebody else, loses her again when her latest "flare for him" endures for just another month, continues to carry her image untainted for years until he finally discovers, at age thirty-two, that she, now Judy Simms and mother of several kids, is "treated like the devil" by her philandering husband and, though only in her late twenties, has faded as fast as a snap of the fingers.

Much has been written about the relationship of this story to *The Great Gatsby*, some of it initiated by Fitzgerald's own notation that the story is a "sort of 1st draft of the Gatsby idea," some of it by a perhaps legitimate impulse among Fitzgerald's critics to point out not only the obvious similarities but the more subtle differences between Dexter Green and Jay Gatsby and even between Judy Jones and Daisy Buchanan. What I might want to add to that discussion in this context would be to say that as a writer I still live with the old-fashioned prejudice that a writer is likely to know at least as much as a critic about his or her own intentions and that his or her intentions matter. I therefore take Fitzgerald at his word: "Winter Dreams" is governed by an idea—a theme, a central focus—that is developed further in *The Great Gatsby*, and I take that idea to be the glowing presence in a few people, often unlikely people, of what Nick Carraway calls Gatsby's "heightened sensitivity to the promises of life," his "extraordinary gift for hope," and his "romantic readiness."

These are the qualities that in the end distinguish Gatsby from those who raised a foul dust in the wake of his dreams. They are also the qualities in lesser measure that drive Dexter Green of "Winter Dreams" to embody his image of possibility in the person of glittering Judy Jones, the "most direct and unprincipled personality with which he had ever come in contact," qualities that appear to die in him when he learns seven years after parting from her that she is no longer even pretty but "all right," with "nice eyes," a woman who is liked by "most of the women" and who "stays at home" while her husband "runs around." With this news Dexter finds that something in him has gone, a "thing that will come back no more" because, along with even the capacity for grief, it is now behind him "in the country of illusion, of youth, of the richness of life, where his winter dreams had flourished."

Gatsby never loses his heightened sensitivity and gift for hope, and that is what allows Nick Carraway to tell us that Gatsby "turned out all right at the end." Not so Anthony Patch of *The Beautiful and Damned*, who is missing the "part of him" that even "hard-minded" Dexter Green surrenders to his image of possibility, and not so Dick Diver in *Tender Is the Night*, who begins with a portion of Gatsby's gift but loses it some time before he retreats into "one town or another" in upstate New York, a victim of Fitzgerald's theory of emotional bankruptcy. The idea, the commanding theme, is also there in aspects of the portrait of Monroe Stahr of *The Last Tycoon*, who had "flown up very high to see, on strong wings, when he was young," and after looking on all the kingdoms had "settled gradually to earth," and it is also there in some form in several of Fitzgerald's best short stories. But the most effective early dramatization of it is in "Winter Dreams," and it is to the character of that dramatization that I will devote the rest of my remarks here.

Beside Zelda's criticism of her husband's attempt to convey an "air of erudition" in *The Beautiful and Damned*, I would place Fitzgerald's early weakness for conveying his perception of his characters through overt authorial statement rather than by allowing them to present themselves as much as possible through the subtleties of dialogue and gesture and self-revelation. Also, in "Winter Dreams" the author moves one step toward a more objective—and therefore dramatic—rendering by offering his commentary largely through the perspective of Dexter Green, almost as effective as his later use of the morally astute narrator Nick Carraway, ready from the novel's start to guide our perception of Gatsby and those in his wake. The intensity of Dexter's winter dreaming, especially after it focuses on Judy Jones, is conveyed by the heightened language that Fitzgerald brings to Dexter's first image of her as an adult:

> Dexter looked at her closely. . . . She was arrestingly beautiful. The color in her cheeks was centered like the color in a picture—it was not a "high" color, but a sort of fluctuating and feverish warmth, so shaded that it seemed at any moment it would recede and disappear. This color and the mobility of her mouth gave a continual impression of flux, of intense life, of passionate vitality—balanced only partially by the sad luxury of her eyes.

The concluding phrase, "sad luxury," might seem a gratuitous oxymoron were it not to capture precisely the element of hopeful excess in Dexter's perception of his arrestingly beautiful Judy and to provide the reader a fleeting glimpse of the unhappy reality under the surface of his image.

Again, when Dexter meets Judy one on one, and the meeting leads to her "casual whim" of inviting him to a dinner that ends up giving "a new direction to his life," the ecstasy, along with a hint of danger, in that first private meeting is conveyed by the language of Dexter's vision of her swimming in the lake:

> There was a fish jumping and a star shining and the lights around the lake were gleaming. . . . Watching her was without effort to the eye, watching a branch waving or a sea-gull flying. Her arms, burned to butternut, moved sinuously among the dull platinum ripples, elbow appearing first, casting the forearm back with a cadence of falling water, then reaching out and down, stabbing a path ahead.

That "stabbing a path ahead" tells us much about Judy that lies beyond Dexter's exalted vision of her in the rest of the passage. And when Dexter runs into Judy while he is engaged to another woman and agrees to take her home, the charged language of Dexter's thinking as he scans the architecture of her street subtly conveys the sad news of a winter dream that still cannot perish despite Judy's mischievous treatment of him, along with the inescapable fact, stated earlier, that "no disillusion as to the world in which she had grown up could cure his illusion as to her desirability":

> The dark street lightened, the dwellings of the rich loomed up around them, he stopped his coupé in front of the great white bulk of the Mortimer Jones house, somnolent, gorgeous, drenched with the splendor of the damp moonlight. Its solidity startled him. The strong walls, the fine steel of the girders, the breadth and beam and pomp of it were there only to bring out the contrast with the young beauty beside him. It was sturdy to accentuate her slightness—as if to show what a breeze could be generated by a butterfly's wing.

The strategy of contrasting the gleaming rhetoric of Dexter's inner dream world with the cruder reality in front of his eyes allows Fitzgerald much room for irony in this story, and it also generates moments of bright dialogue that anticipate the brilliant dialogue of *Gatsby*. It is in dialogue that we get the sharpest image of the real Judy Jones, beginning with the "beautifully ugly" girl of eleven whose smile is "radiant, blatantly artificial—convincing" and whose first exchange with the fourteen-year-old Dexter is to call him "Boy!" as though he is her servant. During their first adult encounter, she offers Dexter the kind of succinct self-revelation, even if coated in charm, that all but a committed dreamer would take for a warning: "I live in a house over there on the island, and in that house there is a man waiting for me. When he drove up at the door I drove out of the dock because he says I'm his ideal." After their first dinner, the dialogue between the two establishes the essential difference in their ways of looking at the world, hers formed by careless if ambitious superciliousness, his by honest if naive romanticism, both characteristics that will doom their hopes in the end:

> "Do you mind if I weep a little?" she said.
>
> "I'm afraid I'm boring you," he responded quickly.
>
> "You're not. I like you. But I've just had a terrible afternoon. There was a man I cared about, and this afternoon he told me out of a clear sky that he was poor as a churchmouse. He'd never even hinted it before. Does this sound horribly mundane?"
>
> "Perhaps he was afraid to tell you."
>
> "Suppose he was," she answered. "He didn't start right. You see, if I'd thought of him as poor—well, I've been mad about loads of poor men, and fully intended to marry them all. But in this case, I hadn't thought of him that way and my interest in him wasn't strong enough to survive the shock. As if a girl calmly informed her fiancé that she was a widow. He might not object to widows, but—"
>
> "Let's start right," she interrupted herself suddenly. "Who are you, anyhow?"
>
> For a moment Dexter hesitated. Then:
>
> "I'm nobody," he announced. "My career is largely a matter of futures."
>
> "Are you poor?"
>
> "No," he said frankly, "I'm probably making more money than any man my age in the Northwest. I know that's an obnoxious remark, but you advised me to start right."

There was a pause. Then she smiled and the corners of her mouth drooped and an almost imperceptible sway brought her closer to him, looking up into his eyes. A lump rose in Dexter's throat. . . .

And finally, before Judy's last month-long flare for Dexter dies out, we have words spoken by her that, even with their artificial coloring, their calculated insincerity, seem at the same time to anticipate with subtle irony what Dexter will later learn of her painful fate during his ultimate epiphany:

"I'm more beautiful than anybody else," she said brokenly. "Why can't I be happy?" Her moist eyes tore at his stability—her mouth turned slowly downward with an exquisite sadness: "I'd like to marry you if you'll have me, Dexter. I suppose you think I'm not worth having, but I'll be so beautiful for you, Dexter."

The art of "Winter Dreams" strikes me as an early turning point in Fitzgerald's fiction. What is at work there—controlled narrative focus, rich rhetorical nuance, subtly evocative dialogue—was perfected in the novels that followed it, but its sharp illumination of one of Fitzgerald's central themes and its sophisticated mode of crafting and dramatizing that abiding preoccupation fully justify the important place it now appears to have in the Fitzgerald canon. Few American writers have written that well that early in what Fitzgerald's 1934 letter calls "the heartbreaking effort extending over a long period of time when enthusiasm and all the other flowers have wilted"—that phrase perhaps speaking both to the loss of his own winter dreams and to the single enduring recompense of his art.

Edmund Keeley is the author of the novels *The Libation* (1958), *The Gold-Hatted Lover* (1961), *The Impostor* (1970),

Voyage to a Dark Island (1972), *A Wilderness Called Peace* (1985), *School for Pagan Lovers* (1993), *Some Wine for Remembrance* (2001), and *The Megabuilders of Queenston Park* (2014), as well as of ten nonfiction books, two poetry collections, and sixteen volumes of translations, primarily of Greek poetry.

"In Dreams Begin Responsibilities" by Delmore Schwartz

Joyce Reiser Kornblatt

"In Dreams Begin Responsibilities" was originally published in the December 1937 issue of *The Partisan Review*. It was collected in *In Dreams Begin Responsibilities* (1938). It is currently most readily available in *In Dreams Begin Responsibilities and Other Stories* (New Directions).

We all dream our parents' courtship, if they had one; we all fantasize their first fateful encounters, tender or passionate or violent. The family drama begins without us, and rankled by exclusion, undaunted by chronology, we invent the means to witness the intimate exchange from which we are forever barred. Some of us write down these fantasies of origin, and a few are masterpieces: Delmore Schwartz's story "In Dreams Begin Responsibilities" is one such treasure.

From what might have been a hackneyed device—a young man dreams he is watching a silent movie in which his father and mother court—and a melodramatic premise—the young man wishes he could thwart the marriage which will yield "only remorse, hatred, scandal, and two children whose characters are monstrous"—Schwartz creates an ingenious and haunting narrative which stays with us the way a significant dream does. Resonant, ambiguous, transparent, and mysterious, this story rewards our scrupulous attention, each reading and re-reading revelatory and disturbing.

Schwartz's narrator begins his tale in uncertainty—"I think it is the year 1909"—and it is not just factual confusion he is announcing, it is not just dream-terrain he is signaling. In his scholarly way, Freud postulated what shamans and seers from other cultures have always known: the dream is a coded description of the dreamer's soul, and the soul of Delmore Schwartz's narrator is a tormented mix of self-loathing, sentiment, rage, and compassion.

From the first paragraph of this classic story, those disparate elements project themselves onto the screen that is the teller's mind: "This is a silent picture, as if an old Biograph one," the word "biography" there in the detail of cinema history, alerting us to the doubleness of every image in this dreamscape—theater, film cast, usher, and audience are all rendered in vivid detail by a witness observing his own psyche's show. As Gestalt psychologist Fritz Perls observed, everything in a dream is an aspect of the dreamer, constructed by the dreamer and deconstructed by the dreamer as well. It is all an interior event, a darkened theater, a cast of one.

The narrator adjusts to the bad light and the anachronistic technology—what a good metaphor for memory's fading archives—and by the second paragraph, he knows the date and more: "It is Sunday afternoon, June 12, 1909, and my father is walking down the quiet streets of Brooklyn on his way to visit my mother." Lost in the details of his father's animated presence, surrendering to the "obvious and approximate emotions on which the audience rocks unknowingly," the narrator reveals both his pleasure at being part of that unconscious collective and his contempt for the nostalgic dangers to which we all succumb: "It is always so when one goes to the movies, it is, as they say, a drug."

Drugged then, he assumes a posture of reliability we know to be false even as we find ourselves enthralled by the somnambulistic scenes which accrue a kind of old-fashioned narrative authority. Here come the characters and the setting: the father walking down the Brooklyn street, the mother's house, her family—father, sister, brother—and then, Part II like a curtain raised after a brief intermission—"finally my mother comes downstairs, all dressed up," and the Oedipal drama, if one is inclined to read the story that way, asserts itself. "At this point," the narrator says, "something happens to the film, just as my father is saying something funny to my mother; I am awakened to myself and my unhappiness just as my interest was rising."

The self-censoring, the guilt-inducing super-ego appears in many forms to the narrator: his own unhappy self, his critical grandfather, the judgmental voices in the audience, the annoyed old lady in the seat beside him, the flashlight-wielding usher whose instrument of control evokes the gun and the policeman's baton and searchlights of prison yards (much like that "long arm of light" in the story's first paragraph), the fortune-teller the parents will encounter as the day proceeds. Although many of these critics ostensibly urge the dreaming son back to his movie-dream, all arrive as breaks in the narrative of the parents' romance, as interruptions to the son's voyeuristic desires.

When he's able to lose himself again in the intimate events of his dream-story, it is an ominous re-entry: "the darkness drowns me," the contents of the unconscious menacing now, killer-rich. In the next moment of the text, "my father and mother depart from the house," take the step, literally, into the future which is now the irrevocable past. The narrator shares with his father "some unknown uneasiness," and, as his mother relates the story of a novel she is reading, shares as well his father's need to counter sentimentality at every turn: "and my father utters judgments of the characters as the plot is made clear to him. This is a habit which he very much enjoys, for he feels the utmost superiority and confidence when he approves and condemns the behavior of other people."

Not only father and son dwell in this kind of split-screen reality. The writer of the story, Delmore Schwartz himself, via the creation of this self-reflexive, self-conscious voice, distances himself from the characters he is creating, and invites the reader as well into that postmodern stance in which the father's "brief 'Ugh'—whenever the story becomes what he would call sugary"—becomes the reader's guarded skepticism of the act of reading itself. In this way, "In Dreams Begin Responsibilities" is a kind of battle between old and new theories of writing/reading, much as Grace Paley works out in her "Conversation with My Father." In both stories, the generations war over meaning itself, over the consequences of one philosophy or another, over the ways in which love devolves into moral combat. Both stories explore the ways in which this combat shapes and limits creative work, the stories themselves examples of the fractured, self-interrogating narratives with which we have become more and more familiar in the second half of the twentieth century and the beginning of the twenty-first.

But here, in Schwartz's fitful dream, it is, in part, 1909. Here the shops still close on Sunday—"Is not Brooklyn the City of Churches?"—and "the streetcar leisurely arrives." Yet beneath the surface of the parents' ordered and custom-driven romance, the weeping son sees the seeds of future conflict and despair. He sees it in his father's braggadocio—"But my father has always felt that actualities somehow fall short."—and his mother's determined cheerfulness. At Coney Island, "the sun's lightning strikes" again and again, but neither of them are at all aware of it: with all the beachgoers, they partake of a false sense of security and "gaze absentmindedly at the ocean, scarcely interested in its harshness." Not their unborn modern son: "But I stare at the terrible sun which breaks up sight, and the fatal, merciless, passionate ocean. I forget my parents." Roused in his dream to terror and ecstasy—"that moment is intolerable"—the narrator dreams himself a trip "to the men's room," his own tortured sexuality foretold by the dream of his parents' past.

He returns to them on the "ceaseless circling of the merry-go-round," to his "father . . . on a black horse, my mother on a white one." We choose our symbols and they choose us, the polarized couple who believe they are in love creating in a Sunday outing the parameters of a lifetime: "My father suggests the best one on the boardwalk and my mother demurs, in accordance with her principles. However, they do go to the best place," the father asserting his power again and again, the mother pretending and posturing, going along. Seeing what they do not see, the son finds her acceptance of his father's proposal horrific, "and it was then that I stood up in the theater and shouted: 'Don't do it. It's not too late to change your minds, both of you. Nothing good will come of it, only remorse, hatred, scandal and two children whose characters are monstrous.'"

Simultaneously, the censors arrive in the theater, the son is silenced, "and so I shut my eyes because I could not bear to see what was happening." What is it the son cannot bear? The bad match, of course, the foreshadowing of family misery. But perhaps as well the union between the father-rival and the desired mother, an aspect of the dream the dreamer fails to note. He identifies with the photographer who takes the parents' posed picture: "He feels with certainty that somehow there is something wrong in their pose." Though the parents object to such scrutiny and control, "the photographer charms me. I approve of him with all my heart, for I know just how he feels, and as he criticizes each revised pose according to some unknown idea of rightness, I become quite hopeful." Through aesthetics, the dreamer/writer finds a means to confront the intimacy of his parents without despair, but it is a short-lived celebration.

In the final section of the story, the depressed parents argue over whether to enter the fortune-teller's booth: "my mother wishes to go in, but my father does not." The father "consents angrily," but when the fortune-teller arrives, "in terrible anger, my father lets go of my mother's arm and strides out, leaving my mother stunned." The son, too, is stunned, by the very narrative he has created, by the intensification of his desire to thwart the marriage and his horror that he might succeed. He shouts in the theater again, but this time it is not a warning against the warning that he cries out: "What are they doing? Don't they know what they are doing? Why doesn't my mother go after my father? If she does not do that, what will she do? Doesn't my father know what he is doing?"

The usher arrives to quell the outburst: "Why don't you think of what you are doing? You can't act like this even if other people aren't around." This, in a crowded theater, the injunction bringing us back to the solitary nature of the dream, to the fantasy of its peopled world, so that even the usher himself dissolves in our recognition that he is an aspect of the dreamer, a constructed conscience—just or punitive, each reader will decide alone—and an arbiter of emotional excess not even permitted, it appears, in dreams. "Why don't you think of what you are doing?"

The usher/warden/patriarch is the voice of consequence, real or imagined, wise or bullying: "'You will be sorry if you do not do what you should do, you can't carry on like this, it is not right, you will find that out soon enough, everything you do matters too much,' and he said that dragging me through the theatre into the cold light, and I woke up into the bleak morning of my 21st birthday." What are we to make of this initiation into manhood? How are we to read the dreamer's future now, "the windowsill shining with its lip of snow, and the morning already begun"?

The writer offers the ambiguous reading—crystal ball or narrative text, they are the same prognosticating artifacts—in that final phrase, "the morning already begun." Morning yields to mourning, the new day of legal maturity is also the onset of grief, and the movie ends with a future as uncertain as the past in which it began—"I think the year is 1909." What is certain is the power and brilliant crafting of Delmore Schwartz's story, one which many a "postmodern" writer has looked to for guidance and courage and ongoing inspiration.

Joyce Reiser Kornblatt is the author of the novella/short-story collection *Nothing to Do with Love* (1981), as well as the novels *White Water* (1985), *Breaking Bread* (1987), and *The Reason for Wings* (1999).

"Goodbye and Good Luck"
by Grace Paley

Beverly Lowry

"Goodbye and Good Luck" was originally published in *The Little Disturbances of Man* (1959) and is currently most readily available in *The Collected Stories of Grace Paley* (Virago).

In my twenties, I had a secret friend. We'll give him a quick name, say Jack. This was a lot of years ago, back in the early 1960s. Those days, the radio was full of Petula Clark singing "Downtown," where, the song promised, "Everything's waiting for you." I don't know if everything was what I expected when I took the D-train south to Greenwich Village to visit Jack, but I know this, he gave me a lot. Taught me things—new language, other foods—told me stories. Once I started making the trip to see him, I never wanted to stop.

He was somewhat older than me but not much. He seemed older . . . partly, I think, because he was Jewish, born and raised in Brooklyn. These things gave him—to my conflicted Southern mind—an exotic kind of authority and a high level of culturally earned wisdom. I was the one with the formal education. I'd graduated from college; he'd barely gone. But he'd read more, had firmer opinions. He couldn't believe I'd grown up in Mississippi and hadn't read Faulkner, even though I went to college in the very town where, at that time, the great man yet lived.

Those days, being a writer wasn't on my mind the way it had been in high school. Now that I was grown up, I wanted to be an actor. (I had some splashy ideas.) Jack was an actor. Mondays—his night off from a bartending job—he taught a late-night class upstairs in a rehearsal studio in the theater district. I attended a few classes, did some scenes, and so in the beginning Jack was my teacher and in a lot of ways I remained in the learner's position—like a hopeful first-grader with a new lunch pail—from then on.

Because he worked at night and I was free afternoons, our schedules gave us the opportunity to be together, and once or twice a week for a long time we were. Long afternoons, we roamed downtown streets, sat in the park watching children dash in and out of the big water fountain, went to museums, ate the occasional street-vendor hot dog, and became—more than anything else—friends.

We talked books and sometimes bought them. And somewhere along in there, Jack decided to take me on, and teach me about books the way Fitzgerald did Sheilah Graham. He made lists. I read whatever was on them. Sometimes he read aloud to me, but in truth, I didn't so much like it when he did. But Jack was insistent and wildly energized—not to mention, fiercely in charge, and so I sat, and—five flights up in his floor-through Village apartment with the bathtub in the kitchen, suppressing all contrary impulses—listened. Then when he got into the story—an actor after all—he'd draw me in, reading the voices, making the most of meaningful pauses, occasionally stopping to point out phrases he thought were brilliant or funny, that I might have missed.

Those days were high literary times for urbanites and the American Jew—the mostly *male* American Jew. Bernard

Malamud, Saul Bellow, Philip Roth. From books and stories Jack pressed on me, I learned about Passover, Yom Kippur, and the bar mitzvah, about rituals and nuance; the ceremonial difference between leavened and unleavened bread, atonement, pork chops, other ways of thinking and seeing, the Holocaust. I remember riding the subway one afternoon, hanging from a strap while reading a heart-crushing scene from Henry Roth's *Call It Sleep*, thinking if living in this world was my only choice maybe I didn't want to. When I read "Goodbye, Columbus," I identified with the heartless narrator instead of Brenda Potemkin, because it was what women did in those days: bonded with male writers and characters, so as not to be dismissed or taken for a housewife-ish birdbrain, interested only in chatter and her eggs, whether by lunar rhythms or scrambled in a pan.

I wasn't sure it was possible and I can't even say I was entirely aware of the idea at the time, but I think I was working at the notion of becoming an unfamiliar—to me anyway—version of womanhood, of transforming my good-girl Southern self into a woman who was both dangerous and smart. This seemed risky. The smart, dangerous women I'd known were crazed loudmouths who never put out one cigarette without lighting another. They drank hard and lost their looks early and lived alone.

But times, I thought, were different now. Didn't the songs say so?

After the urban Jews, we read all over the map, even back home to Mississippi and Faulkner. Jack gave me a syllabus; I stuck lovingly to it. "Start with the trilogy," he instructed, "*The Hamlet, The Town, The Mansion* . . . in that order." We laughed out loud at V. K. Ratliff and Mink Snopes and the horses, admired the living fire out of Eula Varner on the road. We had fun. I learned.

"Sit down," Jack commanded, one—as I recall—hot summer afternoon. He held a slim volume. As if I were his analysand I took up my regular position, flat on my back on his single bed while he sat tall in a straight-back chair. Once I was sufficiently attentive he read me the title: *The Little Disturbances of Man.*

Jack's personal canon included a few women writers, in particular Hortense Calisher and Doris Lessing. Calisher's *False Entry* woke me up to language and its ability to transcribe the senses into art. In gorgeously difficult prose, that writer re-imagined the world I lived in—New York, the upper west side—and described the color of the air outside my own apartment building, when as far as I could tell, air was clear or not and that was the end of it. Lessing's Martha Quest books taught me that even the life of an ordinarily smart housewifely kind of woman could become the subject of serious fiction: of literature, even.

Oh, I thought, you can write about this? Women can write this way? Who knew?

Not that I was writing yet. Jack taught me the first thing to know how to do, to read like a writer.

He smoked. I didn't, but in those days I liked watching men do it. Sexy stuff, back then, and he knew it. Whether or not he pulled on his cigarette for actorish punctuation and emphasis, I don't remember. It was a long time back and many lives ago. But he might have. He probably did.

He turned a few pages, then read the title of the first story in the book, "Goodbye and Good Luck," the first story Grace Paley ever wrote.

"I was popular in certain circles," the story begins, "says Aunt Rose. I wasn't no thinner then, only more stationary in the flesh."

Did he stop? Point out the delicious exactitude of "stationary in the flesh"? The daring freshness of the triple-layered narrative: the "I" of the story told by Aunt Rose, the reference to the story within the story, not to mention the presence of the as yet unnamed listener, Lillie, who in truth is the one re-telling the story as she heard it from Rose. Or did I notice on my own?

"In time to come, Lillie, don't be surprised—change is a fact of God. . . ."

He read in full Bronx dialect, which he could move into as easily as I could V. K. Ratliff's nasal redneck twang. The story drew me in. In no time, I became wholly absorbed into the third-hand telling of the story, as Rose Lieber tells Lillie and Lillie tells us how in middle age Rose falls scandalously in love with the famous Yiddish actor Volodya Vlashkin, the Valentino of Second Avenue. How Vlashkin—tall, courtly, married— helps Rose become a ticket-seller at the theater where he plays, and sets young Rose up in a room near the theater so that he can come by for visits between shows.

My heart thumped. By the time Rose tells Lillie how she moved out of her home and into the rented room, I had stopped thinking about literature and learning. I was done with restraints of intellect, all the silly censors that warn us to keep our wits about us when engaged in the pursuit of hard thought. Every time Jack said "Vlashkin," and the unexpected *l* tiptoed yet again soft and easy behind the hard distinctive heel-tap of the *V*, I felt what Rosie did for the Great Man, for whom she threw over everything, including dignity and her mother's approval. And, in the same way I had watched pic-ture shows at the Paramount theater in Greenville, Mississippi, where I grew up, I longed for a happy ending. For Ann Blythe to marry Mario Lanza. For Cary Grant to find Deborah Kerr, for Robert Francis not to die and for the movie life to go on and on forever.

It will not happen, I told myself. A grown-up serious person does not go around expecting a fairy tale. The dangling man dangled, Malamud's Frank Alpine had himself circumcised, Brenda Potemkin's heart was cruelly cracked in two. Still, I hoped and longed and waited. I look at the story now, thinking how long my heart seemed to have stopped that day. Only ten pages? By the time Jack read the last paragraph I was breathless with hope and dread:

". . . give me a couple wishes on my wedding day," Rose tells Lillie. "A long and happy life. Many years of love. Hug Mama, tell her from Aunt Rose, goodbye and good luck."

That rare brave thing, a happy ending without mush. An *earned* happy ending. It made me weep then, and it does now.

Jack gave me a copy of *The Little Disturbances of Man* as a special present that day. I still have it. Since that hot, important afternoon, I have re-read "Goodbye and Good Luck" many times and have never looked at or thought of it without hearing the special way Jack the actor said "Vlashkin," and that in turn makes me remember all that I learned from him. In literature if not in life, anything can happen, I knew, after he read that story to me. People can end up happy or sad, scared, dangerous, sexy, wild, dangled or flummoxed. They can surprise themselves, maybe more than anybody. They can one day just up and . . . go.

Things change. By the time Jack died I hadn't seen him in years. He was not my Vlashkin, nor I his Rose Lieber. But I think of him often and sometimes wonder if he ever came to understand how much he gave me. Because I eventually met Grace Paley and became a long-distance friend, I could call her by her given name, as did everyone who knew her. And so I say also with sadness, Grace died some years ago as well. Petula Clark hasn't had a hit song in forever. The names of all the downtown trains are different. I gave up acting a long time ago, partly because Jack said I should write, instead. The story remains.

Beverly Lowry is the author of the novels *Come Back, Lolly Ray* (1977), *Emma Blue* (1978), *Daddy's Girl* (1981), *The Perfect Sonya* (1987), *Breaking Gentle* (1988), and *The Track of Real Desires* (1994), as well as of two biographies and *Who Killed These Girls? Cold Crime: The Yogurt Shop Murders* (2016).

"Flight" by John Updike

Jill McCorkle

"Flight" was originally published in the August 22, 1959, issue of *The New Yorker*. It was collected in *Pigeon Feathers and Other Stories* (1962) and is currently most readily available in *John Updike: The Collected Stories* (Library of America).

The first assignment I always give a new class is to come in with a description of "Home." I don't give any suggestions beyond that, and the results vary wildly. One student gave a geographical description of his home state complete with state bird and flower and motto; another said that when he thought of home he thought of incense and cat shit (certainly an answer that prompted many questions) and another, a favorite, was the description of the shelf beneath the register in a Chinese restaurant where he napped as his parents and various relatives hustled about making a living. The exercise is designed to make students think about those early years, the details about the people and place that serves as backdrop to those earliest emotional reactions to the world. Then I assign John Updike's story "Flight" because I think it is a perfect example of all the memories and feelings the exercise was attempting to spark.

In an interview with Charles Thomas Samuels in *Writers at Work*, Updike said: "I suppose there's no avoiding it—my adolescence seemed interesting to me. In a sense my mother and father, considerable actors both, were dramatizing my youth as I was having it so that I arrived as an adult with some burden of material already half formed." Updike then proceeds to discuss the theme of "flight or escape or loss, the way we flee from the past, a sense of guilt," and he goes further to recount the final scene in the story "Flight":

> I think especially of that moment in "Flight" when the boy, chafing to escape, . . . finds the mother lying there buried in her own peculiar messages from far away, the New Orleans jazz, and then the grandfather's voice comes tumbling down the stairs singing, "There is a happy land far far away." This is the way it was, is. There has never been anything in my life quite as compressed, simultaneously as communicative to me of my own power and worth and of the irremediable grief in just living, in just going on. . . . I really don't think I'm alone among writers in caring about what they experienced in ,the first eighteen years of their life.

I have to say that in this particular interview Updike gives voice to all of my feelings and beliefs as a writer, and in the story "Flight" he breathes life into those memories we all have of adolescence and the bundle of complicated emotions. Updike goes further to discuss how the sensibility of the writer then steps in as a kind of shield to the way the adolescent experiences the world. I think that this careful, critical eye probably comes to all adults and with it robs the freedom of pure emotional response. I push students to leave their literary references and interpretations, their psychology and philosophy texts, at the door and instead to enter the world as they knew it then. All too often in the name of sophistication and education students turn their backs completely on the very things that shaped them and thus come out with stories that (though academically sound) are thin and lifeless. What they latch onto in a story like "Flight" is the strong sense of honesty, the willingness to see the real person without all of the camouflage and pretenses.

Why are adolescents so horrified when their parents show up in full view of all the other kids? The parents are a window into the life behind the person and offer total exposure. Likewise the hometown offers a glimpse into the person. I now and always will feel a responsibility and a connection to my hometown: bad news leaves me sad and defensive; good news fills me with pride. I always tell students that I rely on the landscape of my hometown because it's what I know best, though the picture that comes to my mind is not of Lumberton, North Carolina, at present, but Lumberton in the early 1970s. Updike, when asked about his southeastern Pennsylvania roots, said: "I know how things happen there, or at least how they used to happen. Once you have in your bones the fundamental feasibilities of a place, you can imagine there freely."

The first time I ever read "Flight" I fell in love with Allen Dow. Even now I catch myself thinking, *Here I am, Allen. I'm the girl for you.* I'm certain that I'm among thousands of readers who share this love. There is so much in Allen to be recognized. Updike has beautifully captured the tear we all feel between who we are (the parents and grandparents, the town housing our roots) and who we want to be. I love the way that Allen thinks of himself in the third person. It's the writer, yes, but it's also the human spirit struggling to be recognized. We've all been there. It's that private kind of fantasy daydream that we all have but rarely discuss with another person.

When I first read this story in college it tapped every part of me that wanted to be a writer. Allen represents our desires and vulnerabilities. He represents the struggle we recognize in adolescence and then live with forever. In his mother Allen sees the dashed dreams and disappointments; he sees himself both as her vicarious flight out of Olinger and as her competitor. How far can he fly away without rejecting all that makes him who he is?

In this story, I marvel again and again at the merging of detailed specific moments into the larger philosophical commentary. Allen recounts a wonderful story about how his great-grandfather, as he lay dying, requested a particular kind of apple from the far edge of the meadow only to have Allen's grandfather bring him a different kind that was growing close to the house. The great-grandfather refused it; the grandfather went and got what he wanted the first time but Allen's mother has never forgiven her father the "savage insult." Allen asks:

> What had his father done to him? The only specific complaint I ever heard my grandfather make was that, when he was a boy and had to fetch water for the men in the fields, his father would tell him sarcastically, "Pick up your feet; they'll come down themselves." How incongruous! As if each generation of parents commits atrocities against their children which by God's decree remain invisible to the rest of the world.

Just read that quotation aloud to a class of college students and listen to the stories that follow. It becomes clear in the reading and discussion of "Flight" that Updike has successfully put into words all of those confusing anxious moments that most folks try to leave behind in the junior high classroom and yet are hopelessly connected to and shaped by for life.

Everything Allen does is directly linked to his mother, who is directly linked to his grandfather: "My mother felt that she and her father alike had been destroyed by marriage, been made captive by people better yet less than they. . . . the inheritance of frustration and folly that had descended from my grandfather to my mother to me, and that I, with a few beats of my grown wings, was destined to reverse and redeem." Allen's first love (Molly) is both tainted and encouraged by the fact that his mother remembers Molly's mother as "the smuggest little snip south of the pike" and someone who is "old Olinger stock. . . . They have no use for hillbillies." Allen says that every time he saw his mother cry, he had to make Molly cry; that he never made love to Molly technically because he feared that if he "took her virginity she would be mine forever."

Just as in that wonderful memory scene in the opening of the story where Allen's mother is telling him he will fly all the while holding tightly to the hair on his head, pulling him back into her own place, he is left straddling the center line, attempting to balance his flight from the very place that created him with the guilt of surpassing those left behind. The detail of the old Philco radio comes to serve as a revealing symbol of Allen's world in this house in Olinger. The radio takes his mother off to New Orleans, representing her escape from reality. This object is a permanent part of the household: "I had once drawn a fish on the orange disc of its celluloid dial, which looked to my child's eye like a fishbowl." And it is a fishbowl Updike has created—the town, the house, the fragile adolescent soul—and within this very specific fishbowl, we find the universal vision that simultaneously makes us feel big and small, blessed and damned, trapped and free. In short, this story makes us feel the power of adolescence and all the strong feelings that shaped us before we actively began interpreting and analyzing and categorizing our thoughts and feelings.

It has been wonderful in recent years glimpsing the older Allen Dow. Most memorable for me is the end of the story "His Mother Inside Him," which appears in the collection *The Afterlife*. His mother has died and he is hit with a panic "not so much the fear of death as the sensation that his life was too *small*—he smiled to think that his mother had reached this point at the age of thirty, whereas he was all of sixty. As they tell you in seventh-grade health class, girls develop more rapidly than boys." Once again, we are called back to adolescent knowledge; not only does Updike make his point but in the process a window is opened to the way life was, suggesting that no event is ever purely removed from all that has gone before it.

And that is why "Flight" is one of my very favorite stories, as a writer and as a teacher of writing. It is a story with the power to move me to another time and to move me with all of the power of childhood memories. I am left feeling both elated and heartbroken, larger than life and microscopic. When students examine the world of Allen Dow, they are amazed to see how easily they can reconstruct their own Olinger and house and field trip and first love; their parents and grandparents and a random Sunday afternoon. They find themselves embracing the very memories that they have tried to ignore, details that they feel have nothing to do with the success that is waiting for them just beyond graduation. What a wonderful lesson for all.

Jill McCorkle is the author of the short-story collections *Crash Diet* (1992), *Final Vinyl Days and Other Stories* (1998), *Creatures of Habit* (2001), and *Going Away Shoes* (2009), as well as the novels *The Cheer Leader* (1984), *July 7th* (1984), *Tending to Virginia* (1987), *Ferris Beach* (1990), *Carolina Moon* (1996), and *Life after Life* (2013).

"A Silver Dish" by Saul Bellow

Alice McDermott

"A Silver Dish" was first published in the September 25, 1978, issue of *The New Yorker*. It was collected in *Him with His Foot in His Mouth and Other Stories* (1984). It is currently most readily available in Bellow's *Collected Stories* (Penguin).

I love this story because it begins as every story, every poem, every play, every novel ever written might well begin: "What do you do about death?" That's Bellow for you: six words in, and we are confronted not only with the existential, the essential question, but with the straightforward, no-nonsense voice of the man who asks it: Woody Selbst, of Selbst Tile Company ("offices, lobbies, lavatories"), "a modern person, sixty years of age, and a man who's been around."

Bellow then puts a fine point on the question: "How, against a contemporary background, do you mourn an octogenarian father, nearly blind, his heart enlarged, his lungs filling with fluid, who creeps, stumbles, gives off the odors, the moldiness or gassiness, of old men. I *mean!* As Woody put it, be realistic."

In his *Lectures on Literature* Nabokov refers to the storyteller as a master magician, and I love this story because all that is masterful about Bellow's work, all that is magical, is on display as he swiftly conjures Woody's biography: two years in the seminary, mother a Christian convert, father Morris a Jew, "vital and picturesque," who "relished risk or defiance," and who is now one week in his grave, dressed in the Hawaiian shirt Woody himself had brought home from a tilers' convention in Honolulu. A week in, Woody, this practical man, has been "too busy to attend to his own feelings except, intermittently, to note to himself, 'First Thursday in the grave.' 'First Friday, and fine weather.' 'First Saturday; he's got to be getting used to it.' Under his breath he occasionally said, 'Oh, Pop.'"

Notice the sleight-of-hand in that last sentence: all the grief "A Silver Dish" will evoke and illustrate and grapple with is contained therein.

I love this story because, with Woody's life and obligations and proclivities defined, with the essential question asked and attendant images supplied (Woody recalls seeing a Buffalo calf snatched by a crocodile on the banks of the Nile, remembers the animal's parents' "brute grief"), Bellow the magician sets the church bells ringing:

> But it was Sunday that hit him, when the bells rang all over South Chicago—the Ukrainian, Roman Catholic, Greek, Russian, African Methodist churches, sounding off one after another. . . . He was still in bed when he heard the bells, and all at once he knew how heartbroken he was.

Anyone who's tried it, or who has read the tepid attempts of lesser writers, knows how static, how lifeless the *he sat and contemplated the past* story can be. But Bellow follows this realization with the simple line, "While the kettle was heating, he put on his Japanese judo-style suit and sat down to reflect," and soon Woody's "bell-battered" soul is ranging far and near, out of the apartment he has built for himself on the top floor of his warehouse, into the past, his mother's refined Christianity, Woody's own days in the seminary, his "picturesque" father

Morris, a quintessential Bellow character, a conniver, a thief, a crook.

I love this story because even as the reader resists Morris's sleazy, slippery charms, or recoils from his intractable misogyny ("Morris said that if titties were not fondled and kissed, they got cancer in protest. It was a cry of the flesh."), we, like Woody, are seduced by the sheer animal, physical, comic humanity of Morris's character. Let there be no doubt: it is a presence, a humanity Bellow bestows upon his creation not only by portraying Morris through the loving eyes of his heartbroken son, but by the careful attention the author himself pays to the man, to these lives, through the precision of the prose:

> Mischief was where Pop came in. Pop passed straight through all those divided fields, gap after gap, and arrived at his side, bent-nosed and broad-faced. In regard to Pop, you thought of neither sincerity nor insincerity. . . . Pop was physical; Pop was digestive, circulatory, sexual. If Pop got serious, he talked to you about washing under the arms or in the crotch or of drying between your toes. . . . Pop was elemental. That was why he gave such relief from religion and paradoxes, and things like that.

I love this story for the terrible, vivid, tragicomic drama of its central event, delivered to Woody's recollections via the "great lake of quiet" that settles over his kingdom when the church bells stop: a long-ago journey with Morris through a Chicago blizzard to beg Woody's Christian patroness for a loan. Out of Woody's reflections arises a scene so alive, so present, it invites the reader to forget momentarily its seated context. The tram itself is "the color of a stockyard steer." "When Woody wiped the vapor from the glass, the wire mesh of the window guards was stuffed solid at eye level with snow." Two black coal heavers in the seat ahead "smelled of sweat, burlap sacking, and coal.

Mostly dull with black dust, they also sparkled here and there."
And amidst all this vivid detail, character and story persist: "And
Pop rehearsed his pitch on the Western Avenue car. He counted
on Woody's health and his freshness. Such a straightforward-
looking body was perfect for a con." The present moment of the
silenced church bells persists as well:

> Woody, now sixty, fleshy and big, like a figure for the vic-
> tory of American materialism, sunk in his lounge chair, the
> leather of its armrests softer to his fingertips than a woman's
> skin, was puzzled and, in his depths, disturbed by certain
> blots of light within him, blots of light in his brain, a blot
> combining pain and amusement in his breast (how did *that*
> get there?).

Pain and amusement. How indeed?

The sheer physicality of this recollection makes it indelible. Bellow's textured depiction of place and weather, heat and
cold, sights and smells (At the patroness's house, "There were
Bibles and pictures of Jesus and the Holy Land and that faint
Gentile odor, as if things had been rinsed in a weak vinegar
solution."), as well as the expert dramatic timing that gives us
a climactic scene evocative of both old Westerns and the Old
Testament, is as good an example of the conjurer's art, or, in
this case, the con man's art, as literature provides. It is the art
of distracting the reader, delighting us with time and place and
detail and character, anecdote and story, all the while setting us
up for the kill: for the devastating drama of the story's denouement, a scene that reverberates—much as "the last of the bells
still had the bright air streaming with vibrations"—with all
that has been recalled, transforming the tragicomic into something profound and moving and utterly elemental. Magic.

Years ago, my literary agent, who was then Saul Bellow's
literary agent, invited me (for my future edification, she

said) to listen in on speaker phone to a conversation between Bellow and an attorney who was "vetting" another Bellow story, in case it should expose the author to claims of defamation. In lawyerly monotone, the attorney asked of each character depicted, "Is he/she real? Is he/she based on a real person? Might this character be reasonably construed to be have been based on a real person?"

Bellow answered each question thoroughly, politely, with what struck me then as heroic, even elegant patience and restraint. I, on the other hand, felt an escalating sense of outrage. For God's sake, I wanted to cry out, look at the story, read the prose, acknowledge the gift of the thing itself: a marvelous tale about human beings, about what it is to be human, brilliantly told.

I recall that conversation, and that feeling, whenever I come across readers who dismiss Bellow's work because it leaves unchallenged another era's misogyny or ethnic stereotypes, or moral, even amoral, certainties.

I love "A Silver Dish" for its honesty and courage and wit, for its willingness to confront the essential question in its first six words, for its compassion, for the rough, physical humanity of its characters, for its marvelous prose. I love it because no matter how many times I read this story, full of admiration for the master magician's art, I reach the end ("In his great pity, Woody held Pop, who was fluttering and shivering.") and know, with Woody, how heartbroken I am—for Woody, for Pop, for all of us in whatever era we find ourselves as we take part in that inevitable struggle: the struggle to know what to do about death, what to do about love.

Alice McDermott is the author of the novels *A Bigamist's Daughter* (1982), *That Night* (1987), which was a Pulitzer Prize finalist, *At Weddings and Wakes* (1992), also a Pulitzer

Prize finalist, *Charming Billy* (1998), which won the National Book Award and the American Book Award, *Child of My Heart* (2002), *After This* (2006), which was a Pulitzer Prize finalist, *Someone* (2013), and *The Ninth Hour* (2017).

"Flying Home" by Ralph Ellison

Clarence Major

"Flying Home" was originally published and collected in *Cross Section: A Collection of New American Writing* (1944) and is currently most readily available in *Flying Home and Other Stories* (Vintage).

The short story "Flying Home" is an important contribution to American literature not only because it defies convention and succeeds in terms of style, technique, and its use of aspects of Negro culture but because it is the stuff of fine literature. I always enjoy reading the story; and although its subject matter and themes are not joyous, it leaves me feeling good, enriched, better about the promise of humanity.

The story also succeeds in exploring Negro consciousness and what is often called racial conflict in the Deep South without being didactic. And perhaps most importantly, "Flying Home" also succeeds in its use of folklore and myth. Folklore and myth blend in as intrinsic parts of the story.

The scene is Alabama in the 1940s near Tuskegee Institute, where, at that time, Ralph Ellison was a music student. There was in fact an air school at Tuskegee like the one in the story. It was established by the War Department in response to complaints about discrimination against black men in pilot training. Here black pilots were being trained for the war, yet few

would ever see combat. Most black soldiers were placed in service companies. So, in a sense, Todd, the young Negro pilot in
the story, is an anomaly—and he thinks of himself and is seen
as such.

The subject matter of "Flying Home" is simple: a conversation between an old black man and young black man in a
field where the young man's airplane has crashed. The themes
are powerful and universal: crisis, ambition, shame, pride, racism, redemption, recovery, and deliverance.

The myth of flying has long roots in African American
culture. In the folklore there are many examples of characters
flying away from earthly troubles. The legacy of these myths
found their way into the literature. Two examples are the
1930s Broadway play *All God's Children* and Toni Morrison's
novel *Song of Solomon.*

"Flying Home" is really both a complex and a very simple
story involving just a few characters: the protagonist, Todd,
a young Negro pilot; Jefferson, an old Negro sharecropper;
Jefferson's grandson, Teddy; Todd's mother and girlfriend;
Dabney Graves, a mean-spirited old white man who owns the
land Todd's plane has crashed on; and Jefferson's ox, Old Ned.
Only Todd, Jefferson, and Teddy are central to the action.

The story starts out in the voice of a very personal third-
person limited narrator for the first ten pages. Then Ellison
switches to first person for a brief time to cover the material set
in Todd's past and having to do with his mother and girlfriend
and also with the lurking terror of the KKK. At first glance
these five pages seem to be a conventional flashback. Ellison
then switches back to third person for two pages to end the
story. This is something that in creative writing workshops students are often told not to do.

Flashbacks are difficult things to handle because they
interrupt the flow but Ellison has managed to transform this

flashback into an interesting story within the frame of the larger story. In fact this frame holds many such little stories.

Ellison makes expert use of myth as part of the compositional scheme for his story. Perhaps the most apparent one is the story of Icarus and his father Daedalus. The correlation between Todd's fall and the fall of Icarus is obvious without being corny. Icarus after all is flying to escape bondage on Crete. Some readers might find a parallel between King Minos of Crete and Dabney Graves, and another one between Jefferson and Daedalus—especially since Jefferson tells a story of flying in Heaven. And in a way Todd's effort to fly is an escape from the bondage of racism.

Other analogies and prototypes are possible. The phoenix bird is certainly one possible model for Jefferson's story of dying and going to Heaven. It may also be a conscious motif for the image of the bloody buzzard flying up out of the carcass of the dead horse. It is also a useful model for Todd's story itself.

The phoenix is essentially a mythical bird about the size of a buzzard. It's found in many cultures and countries—Turkey, Persia, China, and Egypt—and in the folklore the legend usually has it that when the phoenix saw death approaching, it made itself a nest of special aromatic woods and resins. The bird's story is essentially a re-creation myth that attempts to explain why life continues. Out in the open sun the bird sat calmly in its deathbed. When the sun reached its full intensity the nest caught fire and flames shot up, burning both the nest and bird to ashes. Then out of its own ashes another phoenix rose. In some cultures the new bird comes up out of the marrow of the dead bird.

The Christian version signifies a belief in life after death and a belief in eternal life. It is easy to see how the phoenix would have great appeal for Ellison, and why it is such an appropriate model for a young man who falls from the sky and is finally lifted up, both physically and mentally, and returned to his culture. Todd is renewed and given a new sense of life.

In psychological terms the bird represents our own inner private phoenix, which enables us to survive all the little deaths we encounter each day. This is just another way of talking about getting through one's problems, which are, as James Baldwin often said, always coming.

The two biblical prototypes for "Flying Home" are the Fall from Grace and the Prodigal Son. I see more of a correlation between the Prodigal Son and "Flying Home" than between the Fall and Ellison's story.

In relation to "Flying Home" the Fall has its points but they are limited. The Fall of man and woman has to do with the birth of the Christian Devil, or evil. It's a myth that tries to explain how evil came into the world. It is one of the early Israelite doctrines describing the temptation and transgression of the so-called first man and first woman and how—to put it simply—they messed up and got kicked out of the Garden of Eden. It in itself essentially expresses a longing for and a speculation about a state of primordial existence before human self-consciousness, or should we say, full-consciousness. Todd in a sense does come out of a state of deadness into one of consciousness through his contact with old Jefferson. But to carry the analogy beyond this point into a moral area of sin and redemption would imply that it was wrong for Todd to be flying in the first place. To do so would echo Booker T. Washington's advice to the Negro: start where you are with what you have. In other words, go slowly; do not push forward too quickly.

The Adam and Eve story also attempts to make clear why we die and why it is necessary to work, and perhaps the most striking thing about the myth is its attempt to show why women must be subjected to men. The often overlooked most important implication is that human beings gained self-consciousness and intelligence through an act of defiant disobedience. The story makes no attempt to explain Original Sin, just as Todd's story makes no attempt to justify why he is a pilot in a culture that does not want him to be one.

But the Prodigal Son is more accessible as a prototype. In the New Testament, Christ tells the story of the Prodigal Son. In short, it is the story of a young man who, after going out into the world and squandering his share of the family fortune, is accepted back into the bosom of the family by his father. The father forgives him for his foolishness. But here again to carry the analogy too far and to believe that Ellison meant to suggest this analogy would be to imply that Todd should not have attempted to fly. But it is likely that Ellison was aware of not only T. S. Eliot—whose poetry he was studying at Tuskegee—but James Weldon Johnson's poem "Prodigal Son," which uses the biblical story as a model. Given the fact that Ellison was so well read, he may have also been aware of the many Sea Island legends of prodigal sons actually flying—but not airplanes—back home after much misadventure in the world beyond.

"Not a machine," Todd says of the airplane, "a suit of clothes you wear . . . It's the only dignity I have." One of the values of Jefferson's talk with Todd is that he comes to realize that the crashed airplane is not necessarily his only viable source of dignity. Until now he has used the aircraft as an extension of himself.

When the buzzard hits the windshield, causing Todd to lose control of the aircraft, Todd thinks: "It had been as though he had flown into a storm of blood and blackness." The coming-home aspect of this thought is obvious. And it is the incident of the buzzard that triggers Jefferson's highly relevant story of the horse and the buzzard, which may be seen to represent death. Todd's symbolic death and rebirth, culturally speaking, is not without "loathing," but alongside the loathing he also feels admiration for the buzzard he sees flying so gracefully in his world of the sky.

Jefferson's grandson, Teddy, calls the buzzards "jimcrows." The name is significant in that it is an upfront reference to the Jim Crow laws put in place during Reconstruction. These laws created the legal means that made much of life worse for many Negroes in the South than it had been during slavery. These laws legalized segregation between people of noticeable African descent and people known to be white. The name Jim Crow comes from a racist minstrel song of the mid-nineteenth century. The laws were not struck down until the 1960s, many years after "Flying Home" was written. So the existence of Jim Crows laws in the context of the story makes Teddy's play on the term all the more important.

The buzzard itself occupies a central role in African American historical culture. Jefferson's buzzard story also echoes the famous 1940s song, "Straighten Up and Fly Right," sung by Nat King Cole. In that story a buzzard takes a monkey for a ride up in the sky:

> The buzzard took a monkey for a ride in the air
> The monkey thought everything was on the square

There is another notion connecting Todd and the buzzard. Jefferson is teasing Todd about the possibility that he might get shot down—mistaken for a crow. The implication here is, for a black man, you are flying too high. Much of what Jefferson says echoes the grandfather's deathbed oath in *Invisible Man*. In both cases, it is a mixed message. On the one hand Jefferson is proud of Todd, proud to see him up there in the sky, like a white boy, flying a big metal bird; but on the other, he is fearful for him, fearful that he is not conscious enough of the restrictions white men have placed around his life.

Todd also briefly thinks of himself in symbolic terms as a buzzard: "Maybe we are a bunch of buzzards feeding on a dead horse, but we can hope to be eagles, can't we?" The buzzard tends to fly higher than most other birds, but part of the symbolic lesson here is that even the buzzard has to come down to earth to feed. And the moral of the Negro fable Jefferson tells about the horse and the buzzard is that in basic matters we are all on the same level, no matter how high and mighty we may feel we are in relation to others. And the hope of being an eagle, in the end, is a reality as Todd is lifted out of his fallen state.

When in America we speak of race we often mean culture. Even before reflecting on his own fallen condition, when Todd comes to consciousness his first thought has to do with skin color or race. Are the faces looking down at him black or white? In this context race is implied by color, yet Ellison knew perhaps better than most American writers of the period that skin color had only a relative relationship with the culture of race in America. Ellison was once speaking at a university and said to the gathering of students: all of you white kids are part colored and all of you black kids are part white. And the students seemed to understand the essential truth of the statement. Classification by race is perhaps the most fatal and tragic flaw in America. Ellison has Todd respond the way he does because Ellison understood this tragedy.

Yet "Flying Home" is ultimately not about race. Todd looks toward Jefferson and the boy, "realizing and doubting at once that only they could release him from his overpowering sense of isolation." Isolation, then, is certainly one of the great themes of the story. It is an inner isolation earned at the expense of Todd's quest for dignity, his need to be respected, even honored. While in this quest Todd is "poised between two poles of fear and hate," which makes his actions and thoughts ambiguous and deeply ironic. There is nothing unusual about irony in African American life or literature. Irony is the cornerstone of African American life. The seeds of what Todd feels and needs at the end of the story were present at the beginning when he observed: "the closer I spin toward the earth the blacker I become." And also at the beginning, Todd's fall from the sky itself is ironic—ironic because it brings him into himself, into his history, into his culture. When Jefferson and Teddy finally lift Todd onto the stretcher, he is lifted culturally and spiritually. He becomes that dark bird gliding into the sun "like a bird of flaming gold."

Clarence Major is the author of the short-story collections *Fun & Games* (1990) and *Chicago Heat and Other Stories* (2016), as well as of nine novels, fifteen poetry collections, and ten nonfiction books. His short story "My Mother and Mitch" won the Pushcart Prize in 1989.

"Blessed Assurance"
by Langston Hughes

Edward Kelsey Moore

"Blessed Assurance" was first published and collected in *Something in Common and Other Stories* (1963). It is currently most readily available in *Collected Works of Langston Hughes*, vol. 15, *The Short Stories* (University of Missouri Press).

Black kids of my generation who showed even the slightest literary inclinations were very likely to be handed a collection of Langston Hughes's work. Because I was identified early on as one of those kids, I was familiar with Hughes's more frequently anthologized works, including "The Negro Speaks to Rivers" and "I, Too," by the time I was seven years old. Two more decades would pass, though, before I found my way to Hughes's brilliant short story "Blessed Assurance." When I encountered this funny, sad, and strange story as a young adult, I instantly fell in love with it.

Published in 1963, "Blessed Assurance" addresses race and the relationship of black Americans to white American society, like many of Hughes's poems and short stories. But "Blessed Assurance" is also the most directly and undeniably gay work Hughes published during his lifetime. From the point of view of John, a distraught father, Hughes candidly observes masculinity within the black community, within the black church, and within one particular family.

> Unfortunately (and to John's distrust in God) it seemed his son was turning out to be a queer.

From that opening sentence, it is clear that Hughes is setting "Blessed Assurance" apart from his other work and from other stories of its time period that dealt with homosexuality. Hughes is not dropping hints or leaving it to the reader to guess the cause of John's distress. He dives right in.

John is a man struggling with the unwelcome realization that his son is gay. He personalizes his son's sexuality to the extent that he suspects that God Himself must surely be involved in the conspiracy to make John's life miserable. Later in the first paragraph, Hughes lets it be known, as he does repeatedly throughout the story, that there is far more to John than bitterness and homophobia. John refers to his son as "queer" in an era long before that term had lost its power to offend. Still he can't help but show the pride he takes in his son, referring to the boy as a "brilliant queer" and acknowledging that he has done extraordinarily well in school. John is frightened and deeply worried because he knows the difficulties that lie ahead for his son as a black man and he is overwhelmed by the thought of what the consequences will be for someone both black and gay: "John was more disturbed about his son's transition than if they had been white. Negroes have enough crosses to bear."

John's anger and disappointment battle with his concern for his son throughout the story. Looking back at his family's past, John searches for a place to cast blame for his son's homosexuality. Maybe it is his wife's fault. It was his wife who insisted on naming their only son Delmar, after her father. He imagines that his son would surely have turned out straight if he'd been named John Jr. There were no effeminate men on John's side of the family, he notes. To make matters worse, Delmar has acquired the girlish nickname "Delly."

John keeps a list of crimes against masculinity that his son has committed over the years. Delmar doesn't steal or do drugs like more appropriately macho boys. He is kind to his younger sister. He does his household chores without complaining. He has an aptitude for artistic pursuits. He prefers tennis to football. Rather than attend the black college that his father graduated from, Delmar wants to leave the country and enroll in the Sorbonne. He keeps his clothing clean and the outfits he wears are too color coordinated. John's only solace comes from the fact that his son has not yet committed even more embarrassing offenses like wearing an earring or rhinestone-rimmed glasses.

In response to Delmar's failings, John offers his son what he sees as helpful criticism. John says, "Delmar, those school togs of yours don't have to match so perfectly, do they? Colors *blended*, as you say, and all like that." He warns him that the other boys will think he is a "sissy." We learn that Delmar perceives his father's behavior as bullying when he is brought to tears by John's pleas that Delmar not hold his cigarettes "like a woman."

Even the greatest kindness John extends to Delmar in the story, an offer to pay for Delmar's ticket to Paris so he can achieve his dream of studying at the Sorbonne, is tempered by the shame John feels for having a son who others can tell is gay. John's fraternity brothers are coming to his home to visit him in the fall, and even though John finds Delmar's desire to go to Paris embarrassing, he would rather have Delmar across the ocean in a dormitory than have him on hand to parade his effeminacy in front of the real men who will be John's houseguests.

When it appears that John will fit comfortably into the role of Delmar's torturer, Hughes reveals still more about John. The wife who burdened Delmar with his less than macho name has left the family. She has run off with an "uncouth rascal" who has more money than John, drives a Cadillac, and (John believes) has mob connections. Emasculated and humiliated by his wife, John has been left to assume the role of caretaker for Delmar and his younger sister, Arletta. John describes his wife's lover as "burly," suggesting that he feels his wife has left him and their children for a bigger and more powerful man. Now, in John's view, Delmar is poised to bring more shame to the family.

Music fuels the latter half of the story, and Hughes employs it beautifully. Delmar is a gifted singer. He is in the Glee Club at school and is the star of the choir at Tried Stone Baptist Church: "Delly had a sweet high tenor with overtones of Sam Cooke. The women at Tried Stone loved him." Hughes's comparison of Delmar's voice to that of Sam Cooke is a masterful touch. Sam Cooke, the singer of the smoothly romantic hit "You Send Me," began as a gospel singer and became well known for music that had an overtly sexual appeal. Readers of the 1960s, especially Hughes's black readers, would certainly have understood just why the women of the church loved Delmar.

Like everything about Delmar, his musical ability evokes conflicting emotions in his father. Yes, Delmar's voice causes women to swoon, but that same gift has also attracted the attention of the Minister of Music at the family's church, who, during a choir trip to New York, took Delmar with him on an excursion to Greenwich Village. The Minister of Music has written a composition based on the biblical story of Ruth and he has dedicated the piece to Delmar.

To his horror, John discovers at the church choir's spring concert that the Minister of Music has decreed that Delmar will sing the part of Ruth. John and his daughter walk into church and are treated to the spectacle of Delmar singing an original composition honoring Ruth's great devotion to another woman as set to music by Delmar's admirer: "*Entreat me not to leave thee. Neither to go far from thee.*" Instead of enjoying a choir concert spotlighting his son's magnificent, swoon-inducing voice, John feels that he is being forced to witness Delmar starring in a drag show at the family's church. John's reaction: "I'll be damned!"

Along with Hughes's powerful use of music, there are other charming touches that make the later part of the story soar. Hughes has given the Minister of Music the delightful name Manley Jaxon. Attaching the name Manley to the "saffron robed" Minister of Music is loaded, as is the spelling of Manley's last name. His name is most likely an allusion to Frankie "Half Pint" Jaxon. A popular singer in the 1920s and 1930s, Frankie Jaxon performed, often in drag, with many of the great Harlem Renaissance-era jazz musicians. Hughes is having a lot of fun here, and it comes across beautifully on the page.

John's humiliation is heightened when Manley Jaxon has the most feminine reaction possible to Delmar's singing. The Minister of Music faints. And he manages to pass out in a dramatically feminine manner: "Not only did Dr. Jaxon fall from the stool, but he rolled limply down the steps from the organ loft like a bag of meal and tumbled prone onto the rostrum, robes and all." Delmar's sister makes matters even worse for her father with her commentary. "'Some of the girls say that when Delmar sings, they want to scream, they're so overcome,' whispered Arletta. 'But Dr. Jaxon didn't scream. He just fainted.'"

Seeing Manley Jaxon overcome by Delmar's singing of love and devotion, John is forced to place his son's excursion to Greenwich Village with the Minister of Music in a new and much more disturbing context. With Manley Jaxon's help, his "brilliant queer" son has used his singing talent to throw his sexuality in his father's and the entire church's faces.

After Jaxon faints, the pastor of the church stands to assert his authority, but Delmar refuses to cede the spotlight. He continues to sing: "Delmar's voice soared to a high C such as Tried Stone Baptist Church had never heard." The church is transfixed by Delmar's voice, but John is appalled. It seems to John that Delmar has wildly overstepped the place he is allowed to occupy as an effeminate male. The boy has claimed this moment for himself in front of everyone. He has refused to hide and demonstrate what his father sees as the appropriate amount of shame for his lack of manliness. "'Shut up, son, *shut up*,' he cried, 'Shut up!'" Delmar goes on singing above his father's tirade.

After Delmar has finished his performance, the pastor makes his appeal to the ushers to bring forth the baskets for the offering and asks the deacons to raise a hymn. Now the pastor leads the congregation into "Blessed Assurance." Although only the opening verse of the song is quoted in the story, readers who are familiar with the hymn know that its refrain is "*This is my story, this is my song. Praising my Savior all the day long.*" The preacher might be leading the hymn, but Delmar has already let it be known that this is *his* story, *his* song. Delmar has proclaimed himself a "brilliant queer" on what is, to his father, the biggest and most high-risk stage possible. John continues to suffer as the congregation joins in singing "Blessed Assurance." His final words of the story are "God *damn* it!"

It is tempting to see this story as autobiographical. Hughes had a highly contentious relationship with his father. He lived his life as a closeted gay man. Like many black artists of his generation, he escaped the racial discrimination of the United States by moving to Europe during his youth. He also wrote these words in "Note on Commercial Theatre":

> But someday somebody'll
> Stand up and talk about me,
> And write about me—
> Black and beautiful—
> And sing about me,
> And put on plays about me!
> I reckon it'll be
> Me myself!
> Yes, it'll be me.

What I love about "Blessed Assurance" doesn't require it to be autobiographical. It's enough for me that its six brief pages are packed with tension, warmth, and fun. Each beautifully constructed sentence of the story brings the characters, the time, and the place vividly to life. With an economy of words, Hughes creates fresh and surprising characters who feel intimately and sometimes uncomfortably familiar.

The first time I read "Blessed Assurance," I was convinced that Hughes had written it as a present to me. I should know better now than to believe that Hughes wrote the story for me, a toddler at the time of its publication, to find decades in the future. But with every re-reading, I am reassured that he wrote it with me in mind. Langston Hughes's brilliant writing allows other readers to enjoy his gift to me as well.

Edward Kelsey Moore is the author of the novels *The Supremes at Earl's All-You-Can-Eat* (2013) and *The Supremes Sing the Happy Heartache Blues* (2017).

"Big Black Good Man" by Richard Wright

Sabina Murray

"Big Black Good Man" was first published (as "Big, Black, Good Man") in the November 1957 issue of *Esquire*. It was collected in *Eight Men* (1961). It is currently most readily available in *Eight Men* (Harper Perennial).

At a recent event at the Asian American Writers Workshop, I was delighted to see one of my former students in the audience. She is now a journalist, which is not much of a surprise given that she always had good questions. Indeed, she had one for me. She asked, "So what is up with cultural appropriation?" I am one of a select few who is asked this with fair frequency. As an instructor of creative writing, I get this question from students unsure of how to populate their short stories and novels if they can't use characters that reflect the world they live in. I get this from other writers, who want to write relevant, important books and are unsure of how to proceed if certain populations are off limits to other populations. I ask this of myself while walking the dog, in the shower, and looking in the mirror. And I always have the same response: "Cultural appropriation is like pornography. You know it when you see it." But having a ready response does not dispense with the need for discussion.

As widely covered in the news and other venues, costumes and uniforms create unique opportunities for cultural appropriation. In the first of these examples, costumes are—quite literally—a chance to be someone else. Cinco de Mayo with its usual parade of idiots in sombreros and the furor over the white girl who chose to wear a cheongsam to prom and then posed with her hands in some sort of prayer gesture (not Chinese at all, yet still an act of cultural appropriation) no doubt inspired my desire to write this. Uniforms attempt to make everyone uniform, which most often involves a departure from self, and in some cases uniting under something as offensive as the ferociously grinning Cleveland Indians logo. And there are many interesting arguments to be made around fashion, sensitivity, celebration, representation, and race. One interesting thing about hearing people weigh in on how they feel about cultural appropriation is that a lot of them aren't sure. Fashion undermines itself as a serious medium within its ardent embrace of the superficial. Having a background that draws from a near-invisible minority—Filipinos—I can see the lure of recognition. Bruno Mars stirs a prickling nationalism in me and I wonder how I would feel should a Madonna or a Gwen Stefani or a Beyoncé show up on stage in a Maria Clara. I think, to be honest, I would find it funny.

But cultural appropriation is real and I'd like to meditate on it, particularly as a fiction writer who is more often populating books with characters than commenting on culture. And because I feel that it is an issue that is so brilliantly explored in Richard Wright's story, "Big Black Good Man," which examines all the possibilities of racial identity without succumbing to didacticism and polemic. The story dialogues with a political truth that propels it to an even greater level than its clear aesthetic merit. Stories afford us entertainment, but also the space to think about a thing and realign our understanding. My reading and appreciation of a story is shaped by this.

A few years ago, my editor Elisabeth Schmitz sent me a book by one of her other authors. Elisabeth does this frequently. I tore open the envelope with my usual enthusiasm. The book, a novel, was *Wash* by Margaret Wrinkle. The subject is slave breeding in Tennessee, and the novel has three narrators: a slave owner, the "traveling Negro" Wash, and Wash's lover. And of course you're asking, if you don't already know, and the answer is white. Margaret Wrinkle is white. She is also brave. She is also a good writer, and I sped through this book. I was curious about how the reviews would go, about who would review it. The next week's *New York Times Book Review* held a treat: the selected reviewer was Major Jackson.

There is no better commentator on race than Major Jackson, an intellectual and a gifted writer, most often of poetry, but sometimes he generously lends his perspective to critical pieces. Jackson opened his review with, "One of the challenges white writers face in creating black characters is the avoidance of caricature and stereotype. If cultural appropriation must take place, the thinking goes, then authors should treat black narratives . . . with kid gloves. If they fail even in the slightest, readers are sure to voice criticism and, maybe, justifiably, rain down judgment and reckoning." Jackson concluded, "Wrinkle's novel does not allow us to draw easy correlations but invites us to consider the painful inheritance and implications of such a horrendous moment in American history. Rather than disapproving opprobrium and diatribes, this debut occasions celebration." He supported the portrayal of these black characters by this white woman. This was not the first time Jackson had grappled with the thorny issue of racial representation in literature and poetry. In his highly illuminating essay, "A Mystifying Silence: Big and Black," Jackson wonders if "hypercritical vigilance actually

endangers writers' freedom to fully characterize with great can-
dor the complexity of their full humanity." He goes on to state
that poetry has the power to enact empathy, and in its ability
to "inhabit the consciousness of others . . . widens our humanity." The essay, a response to racist poetry and literature, laments
"the dearth of poems written by white poets that address racial
issues" and goes on to conclude that "without the complete,
wide-ranging and far-reaching racial dialogue as a literary and
cultural legacy . . . discussions of race and ethnicity will forever
be a spectator sport."

This line of thought can read as an invitation to engage in
just the sort of behavior excoriated by those sensitive to cultural appropriation. Could there be such a thing as good cultural appropriation? Or is the benevolent version not cultural
appropriation?

In the mid-1970s, the great Nigerian writer Chinua
Achebe delivered a lecture at the University of Massachusetts at
Amherst, where I now teach. This lecture, "An Image of Africa:
Racism in Conrad's *Heart of Darkness*," was quickly brought
to print and is now included in the Norton Critical Edition
of Conrad's famous Congo work. Achebe asserts that *Heart
of Darkness* is so steeped in racism that it is no masterpiece.
Conrad's Congo is "a metaphysical battlefield devoid of any
recognizable humanity." Despite Conrad's firm and obvious
stance against the Belgian colonizers' brutal treatment of the
locals, the writer's treatment of the Congolese natives in the
work renders whatever is of merit in the narrative as tainted
beyond rescue. As stated by Achebe, Conrad's Africans are
largely voiceless victims, and, when they do speak, deliver brokenly passionate exhortations to cannibalism, or offer the inel-
egant and hard to argue with, "Mistah Kurtz, he dead." The
kinship alluded to throughout the story is of no value because
of how the African "kin" are realized in the piece. Achebe in

his essay implies that no one should teach *Heart of Darkness*. And many people don't teach *Heart of Darkness*, and students often don't want to read *Heart of Darkness*, and some appeal to this legacy of Achebe's to support their decision.

I do teach *Heart of Darkness*. I do. Frequently. And I don't do this *despite* what Achebe had to say, I do this *because of* what Achebe had to say. Achebe, in a complex transactional move, provides the African voice that was previously missing. More pertinently, Achebe and Conrad have taught me, an instructor, two important realities: the first being that racist literature provides the perfect place for vital discussions of race to take place, and the second that once you invite Africans into your story, you had better let them speak. Perhaps the safe way out of this second assertion is not to invite the Africans into your story in the first place (hard to see how that would work in *Heart of Darkness*, but perhaps Conrad was trying to do this, attempting to have the Africans' extreme presence and extreme absence in the story simultaneously: if there's a writer who can pull this off, it's Conrad) but is that really an acceptable response? Isn't that, well, cowardly? Steering clear of anything that might be accused of cultural appropriation could be inspired by a desire to be respectful of other cultures, but I do detect the whiff of cowardice in anything, particularly in art, that values safety above all. Art should not be safe, not for the writer, and not for the reader.

While we're on the topic of unsafe literature, here's a brief excerpt from one of my favorite examples:

> He was bending forward and loosening his shoelaces when he heard the office door crack open. He lifted his eyes, then sucked in his breath. He did not straighten; he just stared up and around at the huge black thing that filled the doorway. His reflexes refused to function. It was not fear; it was just simple astonishment. He was staring at the biggest, strangest, and blackest man he'd ever seen in all his life.

"Good evening," the black giant said in a voice that
filled the small office. "Say, you got a room?"

Yes, the story is "Big Black Good Man." The "giant" is a sailor,
who becomes a regular at a dockside Danish hotel, and we
stay firmly planted in the night porter Olaf's perspective for
the duration of the story as he explores the escalation of his
baldly racist fear of his lodger. Olaf is a well-traveled poly-
glot who speaks English, French, German, Danish, Dutch,
Norwegian, and Spanish. He has also spent ten years living in
New York, and before his guest, who gives the story its title,
shows up, he expresses an articulate, embracing love for sailors,
who "reminded him of his youth" and are "direct, simple, and
childlike." What they want is "women and whiskey," and Olaf
finds that "[n]othing could be more natural than that." This
is voiced right before he encounters his guest, a sailor who is
not natural or childlike, and reminds him of nothing familiar, although he appears to conform to all the positive qualities associated with sailors as stated by the narrator. The guest
is a "thing," a "vision," and, the observation that unflaggingly
asserts itself, a "giant." Olaf suffers a crippling fear, a "primitive hate" for the "black mountain of energy, of muscle, of
bone" and the "vast clawlike hands that seemed always to hint
of death." Wright's feat as a writer here is to empathize with
Olaf's prejudice and dehumanizing of the "giant," to invite
the reader to borrow this perspective and to be disturbed by
inhabiting such proximity. There is a skillful use of tension and
some indelible images that make, without addressing the obvious racial content, a good story. But what makes this an essential read is Wright's use of Olaf's perspective.

We become complicit in his racism and we are forced to
confront, at close range, Olaf's dehumanizing logic that makes
him feel "how puny, how tiny, how weak, and how white" he

is. His sense of powerlessness is crippling. From this initial interaction, the story escalates through a series of misunderstandings. For a night porter and a hotel guest, the stakes are high. At one point the "giant" has his hands wrapped around Olaf's throat. Later, Olaf has armed himself with a gun and is ready to shoot. But the story ends in a volley of words, with Olaf—coming to understanding—stating, "You're a good man too. . . You're a big, black, good man," and as the giant too comes to understanding, he responds, "Daddy-O, drop dead."

Throughout the story, the point of view never wavers. We are Olaf, and the distortion of visual material and logic is all the work of Olaf's consciousness. The story is harrowing and it is vital. But just for fun, I'll pose a question: Is Wright—an African American, racially kin to the "giant"—guilty of cultural appropriation?

I think not.

The problem is that Wright's inhabiting a white perspective is not a problem; it is the default setting, the reality. The problem is that—despite whatever our racial background—we inhabit a white perspective all the time. If you're not white, at least in the United States, it's sort of like being bilingual, but using "white" for the majority of your experiential transactions. This is nothing new, but it is of the utmost importance to try to get a fresh sense of this as it relates to cultural appropriation. One has only to hear the Pulitzer Prize-winning poet Natasha Trethewey tell, wearily, of the many occasions she has heard people try to engage her with how the South is marked by the loss of the Civil War, and her response, "My people won that war." Is that statement—provocative, brilliant, and true—an invitation to engage in cultural appropriation? One has to. Perhaps that's something different: involuntary cultural appropriation. Or is that just empathy?

These are interesting times. White people wanting to empathize with non-white people—at least among readers of literary fiction—is at an all-time high. I would say that this is, by and large, a good thing, but it does give rise to a few curious realities. In his recent *Lit Hub* article, "Why I'm Done Talking About Diversity," Marlon James turns a sharp wit to the wheel of cheese that is Diversity. He discusses the prevalence of panels where people of color are brought to talk about issues of diversity when they are the precise people who are beyond benefit of such a discussion, noting how well diversity works with segregation. James writes, "You would think our sole purpose as writers at these panels is to broaden the understanding of white people, when we could, you know, talk about writing." The truth of the matter is that in discussions of race, there's a desire to bring in a minority member to make it appear that positions have been rendered safe. But the desire to render things safe without actually solving the problem is not a solution but another problem.

"Big Black Good Man" is one of my favorite stories because I believe that fiction should engage with culture and that it is essential that it do so. I see "Big Black Good Man" as a story that you can read each year and each time come away with more understanding. Fiction should never be safe, and "Big Black Good Man" is unapologetically dangerous. As with all good art, it is fearless.

Sabina Murray is the author of the short-story collections *The Caprices* (2002), which won the PEN/Faulkner Award, and *Tales of the New World* (2011), as well as the novels *Slow Burn* (1990), *A Carnivore's Inquiry* (2004), *Forgery* (2007), and *Valiant Gentlemen* (2016).

"Travelin Man" by Peter Matthiessen

Howard Norman

"Travelin Man" was originally published (as "Traveling Man") in the February 1957 issue of *Harper's Magazine*. It was reprinted in *Midnight Turning Gray* (1984), and is currently most readily available in *On the River Styx and Other Stories* (Vintage).

When "Travelin Man," a story by Peter Matthiessen, was published in *Harper's Magazine* in 1957, it won an O. Henry Prize. It was one of the earliest of Matthiessen's publications. Eventually, the story appeared in a small press edition, *Midnight Turning Gray*, and, finally, in *On the River Styx*, the excellent Random House collection which includes what are in my judgment Matthiessen's best stories, "Lumumba Lives" and "On the River Styx." In my copy of *Midnight Turning Gray*, Matthiessen inscribed, ". . . from a fledgling author." Hardly. Though in a hint of melodrama here, a touch of heavy-handed symbolism there—very few instances, really—"Travelin Man," beautifully balanced as it is, can feel like a *young* story—the author was just thirty. What is remarkable, however, is that "Travelin Man" already contains Matthiessen's mature themes—his preoccupations with race, landscape, the powerful articulation of the unlettered voice—that would inform his writing for the next fifty years. In a conversation partly about "Travelin Man" in particular, his stories in general, in the Lennox Hotel in New York City, I asked Matthiessen how large Faulkner loomed for writers of his generation. (Matthiessen was born in 1927.) "For some of us, very large," he replied. "He cast a wide shadow. That shadow falls over 'Travelin Man' to some extent, I suppose, as well as my first published story, 'Sadie.' But keep in mind, I've always written about race, about backwater peoples, about the way landscape penetrates people's lives, their psyches. It's all throughout the Watson books."

Minor literary influences aside, "Travelin Man," too, already contains Matthiessen's inimitable use of *landscape.* I don't mean just physical description of a given topography, not just a "sense of place." I mean that no writer since Conrad has so inventively and insistently involved landscape with his characters' fates as Matthiessen. In "Travelin Man," for instance, the Carolina coastal swamps and Deep River not only house the action of the story, but are themselves an intensifying agent. Matthiessen's landscapes are bold acts of the imagination. They are as complicit in the narrative strategies and dramas of his novels and stories as any protagonist—or antagonist—in, say, Dostoyevsky. That is, his landscapes are a way of *thinking.*

As for plot, "Travelin Man," is in a sense a prison drama that doesn't take place in prison. Traver, whose "skin was the mud black of the coastal Gullah," has escaped prison. We are with him on every page of the story. If—ten years later— someone on his former prison block would ask, "Whatever happened to Traver, anyway?" the warden might hand him a copy of "Travelin Man."

The story opens with a scene suggesting an allegory of the earth bearing up humanity itself:

Toward dusk, a black man slithered from a drainage ditch. He moved swiftly on his belly, writhing out across a greasy bog and vanishing into the sawgrass by the river. The grass stirred a moment and was still. A rail bird rattled nervously, and a hunting gull, drawn inland, cocked a bright, hard, yellow eye. Startled, it dropped a white spot on the brown waste of the bog and banked downwind.

Even as the bird lightens itself, rises spirit-like from the earth, the moment—no matter that it is simply one beat in a million-year-old rhythm—contains a kind of *gravitas*, even a foreboding. (Of birds, Matthiessen writes like the eccentric eighteenth-century naturalist Mark Catesby drew; they both provide an ornithological *experience*, not merely a fine recapitulation of what is observed in the wild.) In addition, this paragraph contains what will prove to be yet another Matthiessen hallmark, the astonishing ability to impart zoological information in poetically compressed prose of startling beauty. Matthiessen's novel *Far Tortuga*, for instance, offers image after image of Caribbean natural history, each crafted with photographic clarity. ("On a coral rock protruding from the sand, a bleeding tooth snail budges, and a ghost crab, half hidden, extends dry eyes on stalks.")

In "Travelin Man"—as in much of Matthiessen's fiction—one gets the impression that the landscape only grudgingly allows human beings to eke out a little breathing room. (When there is breathing room—the vast Caribbean in *Far Tortuga*, for example—human beings find a way to collide with each other, out in the middle of "nowhere.") Matthiessen loves to bring a "marginalized" landscape—mangrove swamp, backwater archipelago, hurricane-battered island—front and center. These comprise Matthiessen's menacing paradises; in them, nature is constantly on high alert, circling, diving, waiting, going in for the kill, tolerating or repelling interlopers;

the *action* of nature is often lethally plaited into the action of desperate human striving. (Traver is striving for freedom.) Matthiessen's landscapes also have a fixedness, a timelessness, whereas people in those landscapes often seem incidental, exiled, "on the lam," at cross purposes with each passing moment, uneasy in their skin—*fugitive.*

The black man's name, Traver, is a shortening of 'Traveler," which his "wayward" mother had nicknamed him. Traver escapes prison; he is hunted down like an animal; he is shot, he dies. In broad outline that is the story. Much of the action consists of Traver navigating a near Mesozoic labyrinth— swamp, muck, ooze, mangrove; the soundtrack is mosquitoes buzzing, as if in our brains. The atmosphere is highly agitated, fraught, primeval.

Yet about one-third of the way through "Travelin Man," Matthiessen provides some of Traver's biography (as it directly relates to landscape), heartbreaking because resident in these passages is a foretaste of freedom:

> He had come to Ocean Island because here he could survive. As a boy he had labored on the rice fields and the dikes, and he knew the name and character of every pond and ditch and slough. He knew where to snare rabbits, stalk birds, ambush deer, and where the wild swine and cattle were which he might outwit and kill. On the salt shores there were razor clams and oysters, and mullet in the canals, if a fish trap could be rigged. He would not starve. He could even eat raccoon and otter and, if necessary, he could eat them raw.
>
> He could survive here, too, because he would not be caught. The island had been unused for years, even for gunning. If he were tracked to this forsaken place, he could always find shelter in the swamp. Hounds could not help them here, and the whites did not know the swamp as he

did, how to move quickly in it without risking the deep
potholes and soft muck. He could elude a wider search than
the state would send into the swamp after a black man. For
this was black man's country, slow and silent, absorbing the
white man's inroads like a sponge. A white man loomed
large on Ocean Island, but a black man was swallowed up
in it, and disappeared.

The character of Traver introduces a "type" of man that
has haunted Matthiessen, long engaged his scrutiny. Traver, by
dint of necessity and perhaps by inclination, literally travels
light. He uses whatever tools are at hand to try and survive.
("Traver opened the knife blade and lay still. Traver was hardened to hunting and being hunted, and the endless adaptation
to emergencies.") Matthiessen uses his investigation into this
"type" to brilliant and memorable effect in one of the most
enigmatic characters in contemporary fiction, Lewis Moon, in
the novel *At Play in the Fields of the Lord*. A mercenary, Moon,
suffering from—or perhaps, not suffering from—the most
severe form of disaffection, inhabits the jungle rivers of South
America, seems to daily reinvent his life. Moon is at once
comic, violent, existential, shiftless, uncannily ethical, living
each moment as it comes, living it to the hilt. In this sense,
Moon, like Traver on the run, embodies the present tense. In a
conversation recorded in Sagaponack, New York, and eventually published as part of "The Art of Fiction" series in the 45th
Anniversary Issue of *The Paris Review*, Matthiessen spoke of
Moon's lineage:

> Lewis Moon was drawn from at least three people. The first
> was a young Navaho hitchhiker I picked up in New Mexico
> when I was traveling the Southwest doing research for *Wild-
> life in America*. We wandered together across Arizona, and
> I dropped him off somewhere in the empty desert country

of southern Nevada. In all those miles, over two or three days, we spoke scarcely a word. He seemed to have no destination—an enormously alienated, sullen, angry guy. Since then I have spent a lot of time with Indian people, and I realize now that part of his alienation and anger was that he was a traditional from the remote mesas who scarcely spoke English and was ashamed of that. He might have feared I'd think him stupid or backward, which is how some of the acculturated Indians treat these traditionals. Though I'd carried him hundreds of miles and fed him, too, he could not even say thanks when he got out. He just rapped the window, looking straight ahead, and I dropped him off on the road shoulder at this desolate place in the desert buttes without a sign of human habitation. Maybe our culture clash was just too much for him, and he wanted out right then. I only hope he knew where he was going. He was nineteen or twenty, all tied up in anger, as I had been myself at that same age.

I met the second guy in a bar in Belém, at the mouth of the Amazon. He was a French-Canadian ship's carpenter who'd been shunted off a freighter's stern off Trinidad when the deck lumber cargo shifted in high seas. It was night, nobody saw this, and he swam and floated in the ocean for eight hours before he was miraculously spotted. We talked all evening. He told me about the strange places he had been since—a man consumed with wandering. He showed me the small kit that he kept with him, everything he owned in life, pared down almost to nothing—a waterproof packet containing a map, a cutoff razor, a change of underwear, and very little else. He said, "It's easier to throw away stuff and replace it. I'm always ready. I don't stay put and I owe nothing, so if a guy tells me he's headed somewhere, and there's a seat, I go." As a merchant seaman, he had made good money and, when he was picked up out of the sea more dead than alive, he understood something about life and death. He had a family in Canada, and he wrote his wife, "I love you, but I won't be home again. I'll send money when I make any. You're welcome to the house." A solitary and indifferent figure, cryptic and memorable.

This man and that young Navaho were joined in Lewis Moon. The third man, inevitably, was me. I brought with me as much as I understood back then about loneliness and anger, which was quite a lot.

My point is obvious. In terms of literary trajectory, Traver foreshadows Lewis Moon. Certainly they are very different men, but what their disparate predicaments and qualities share is that Matthiessen writes their marginalized lives with tremendous skill and affection.

Naturally, to isolate any aspect of a story might risk refracting the whole, a sluggish academic convenience which, to my mind, is the death of the spirit. Yet I return here to landscape, because Matthiessen's are animated with such vivid immediacy. In a particularly memorable scene in "Travelin Man," Traver slogs along, hounded by a white hunter, all in his desperate attempt to circumnavigate fate in the swamps of his childhood. "Then fiddler crabs snapped faintly on the flat," Matthiessen writes. "Where he had passed, their yellow claws protruded, open, from the holes." Humankind passes by—Matthiessen then allows a reader to linger behind a moment. It is as if his fiddler crabs are scissoring open holes in the humid fabric of existence, letting readers gulp air as, a few pages farther along, we surface from Traver's harsh demise.

It is a death, by the way, forecasted late in "Travelin Man," when Traver "mourned a blues":

Black river bottom, black river bottom
Nigger sinkin down to dat black river bottom
Ain't comin home no mo'

Howard Norman is the author of the short-story collections *Kiss in the Hotel Joseph Conrad and Other Stories* (1989) and *The Chauffeur: Stories* (2002), of the novels *The Northern Lights* (1987), *The Bird Artist* (1994), *The Museum Guard* (1998), *The Haunting of L* (2001), *Devotion* (2007), *What Is Left the Daughter* (2010), *Next Life Might Be Kinder* (2014), and *My Darling Detective* (2017), and of several books of Canadian native folklore in translation and of nonfiction.

"Pet Milk" by Stuart Dybek

Leslie Pietrzyk

"Pet Milk" was first published in the August 13, 1984, issue of *The New Yorker*. It was collected in *The Coast of Chicago* (1990). It is currently most readily available in *The Coast of Chicago* (Picador).

This six-page masterpiece of a story is, more than anything, a story about memory, so it's appropriate that I recall with perfect precision where I was the first time I read it, when it was published in the pages of *The New Yorker* magazine. It was April, and I was on the verge of graduating from my college outside Chicago, ready/not-ready to head out into the world clutching my hard-fought English/Creative Writing B.A. I had recently bought a subscription to *The New Yorker*, writing a check for what was a serious sum of money out of my student budget. Subscribing to *The New Yorker* felt like an impossibly adult thing to do, and I marveled that somehow I had managed to turn into an adult, sort of, and how maybe this might be what becoming an adult was, finding a magazine nestled in your apartment's mailbox. April was spent worrying about my boyfriend, wondering if he was going to stick with me after graduation, though I knew he wouldn't because, well, he had told me he wouldn't. Maybe we could hold on through the summer, but after that, well. Well. This situation felt impossibly both like an adult's problem, yet also extraordinarily childlike, as I waited for him to change his mind.

I remember the nubby slipcover of the couch where I curled up to read my new magazine, the yellowish light slanting off my roommate's lamp, the heavily patterned rug that no one ever vacuumed, the window that looked out onto a wall of red brick. I remember reading the two pages of "Pet Milk" and reaching the bottom of the second page and sighing, staring out the window, unaware of the rows of brick, and sighing again, then transferring my stare to the author's name: Stuart Dybek (at this time, the author's byline appeared at the end of the story). I carefully ripped out the pages, which are now buried in a box in the back of a closet. The experience of reading this story at this exact time and place in my life is that vivid and specific.

And yet. Many years later I had occasion to look up "Pet Milk" online in the archive of *The New Yorker*, where I learned that it was published not in April as I remembered, but in August, which isn't even a school month. It appeared a full year and a half *after* I graduated from college, my boyfriend long gone, my freshly adult life (and magazine subscription) shifted to Washington, D.C.—and so my vivid and specific memory is absolutely wrong. Yet it's also absolutely right, because this experience of living inside a powerful memory is what "Pet Milk" so elegantly captures, and I'm not sure it's important if a memory is true, or if any memory actually can be entirely true, or if all memories are simply and utterly true even if maybe they never really happened.

"Pet Milk" by Stuart Dybek is my most favorite short story ever. As reprinted in his collection *The Coast of Chicago*, it is a mere six full pages, and the "plot" is slight. But the complexity of its effect leaves me breathless, the way food and memory mingle and intertwine, allowing Dybek to capture how a certain time in one's life feels urgent and sharpened, composed of vivid memories that feel immediately of both the past and the present, of something that's already dissipating even as we're amid it. Yet, the story also cares about the lived moment: As the waiter Rudi advises the narrator who's staring contemplatively into his beverage: "It's not a microscope. . . . Drink."

The story opens in the present with the male narrator drinking instant coffee the way his Polish grandmother did, using canned, evaporated Pet milk in place of cream (which is exactly what my own Polish grandmother might have done though she didn't). The narrator's "cream" swirls through the coffee, and he's lost in those drifty swirls, letting his thoughts follow their meandering path, a mirror of the snowflakes floating outside the window. He's reminded of the past, specifically of his girlfriend Kate and their first adult jobs out of college. These swirls of the past collect into a magical brew: we learn about a neighborhood Czech restaurant the two of them patronized, where Rudi the waiter introduces them to the King Alphonse, an after-dinner drink also involving cream: "We'd watch as he'd fill the glasses halfway up with the syrupy brown liqueur, then carefully attempt to float a layer of cream on top. If he failed to float the cream, we'd get that one free." (There's an unspoken understanding that the narrator will nudge the table or distract Rudi to get a King Alphonse on the house.)

Ultimately, the narrator remembers his twenty-second birthday, a passionate evening that starts with oysters at the restaurant but that quickly shifts to him and Kate making love on an empty El train car streaking to Evanston, where her apartment beckons. Out the window, as the express train passes through a station, the narrator sees a 16-year-old boy catching sight of the two of them, the boy grinning, about to wave before the train whisks away, and in the final lines of the story, the narrator thinks, "It was as if I were standing on that platform, with my schoolbooks and a smoke, on one of those endlessly accumulated afternoons after school when I stood almost outside of time simply waiting for a train, and I thought how much I'd have loved seeing someone like us streaming by."

It's startling to notice how many writing rules Dybek breaks in this short miracle of a piece. No wonder I was subversively intrigued when my young writer-self first encountered the story: how did the author understand he could break those rules? That he could ignore the maddening mutterings rising from the workshop table, "You can't . . ." and "Are we allowed to . . .?" Maybe that's what being an adult was, successfully understanding which rules applied when, and which rules applied never.

The male narrator is nameless, becoming both mysterious yet also more deeply known, someone so familiar it's ludicrous that their name would be a word inside your head. The reader knows nothing at all about this guy in the present of the story, what sort of job he has or where he lives, what he looks like or how old he is now; we have no idea what happened to Kate or Rudi. Nothing is at stake here. Nobody in the story changes. The story starts with a frame, or so we think, but we get exactly *one* bland sentence of the present action: "Today I've been drinking instant coffee and Pet milk, and watching it snow" (which, by the way, is not necessarily a kick-ass, enticing opening line—yet another rule smashed to smithereens). That single sentence is literally all we see of the narrator in the present, as we immediately travel into his past through layers of flashback, not once returning to that cup of coffee or that snow. (How many times have I intoned to the workshop table, "Never start a story with a flashback"? How about a story that's *only* flashback?) Finally, the story concludes by introducing another unnamed character, the boy on the train platform, who's used solely to bring us to the climactic moment of the story, when the writing teacher surely would advocate relying on an already-established character or referring to an image that has been set up, like, say, that falling snow. So many writerly sins! And I'm imagining that every reader will offer all the forgiveness in the world to this extraordinary story, and its swirl of time and memory.

I'm biased toward this story because in my writing, characters are always eating or drinking, and there, and here, and as in real life, food is both food and more than food. I admire here how exotic the Pet milk in the coffee feels to the modern reader, a near-forgotten ingredient, used in my circles pretty much exclusively to make the Libby's pumpkin pie recipe at Thanksgiving. (The Libby's label actually calls for Carnation evaporated milk, but in honor of this story I always grab Pet.) Yet this same Pet milk is a comforting memory to the narrator, even as it's simply an everyday product to the Polish grandmother, who likely saves money by eschewing real cream. The other beverage in the story is the King Alphonse, a drink I've found on exactly one menu in my life, at The Musso & Frank Grill, the oldest restaurant in Hollywood. (Of course I ordered it!) Here, the swirling imagery of the rising cream and the King Alphonse play the same role as the Pet milk does in coffee: it's the "regular" drink now for Kate and the narrator, yet it's something so special that one tiny jiggle of the table breaks the floating layer of cream down into the booze, and the entire enterprise crumbles. It's all precarious, Dybek suggests: the true love romance with Kate that isn't going to last, the train's journey that will end at Howard Street, these jobs, the narrator's elderly grandmother, the memories. The best we can hope for, perhaps, is the wisdom Rudi the waiter brings to these young people, helping guide them into understanding that they are living in magic, that we all are: "Drink," he says.

How can we live within the magic while knowing that to recognize the magic puts an end to it?

I look for such paradoxes to create tension in my own work, and this story is a master of paradox. How can the reader feel immersed in the past while reading these details and images as if they are happening right now? The poetic language of the story and the eye for specific Chicago details feel authentic, well-observed, yet the reader is aware that memory is inherently imprecise and unreliable. We understand that this time in the narrator's life is lost forever to the past, yet somehow it continues to exist—through memory, and also through the written word, but really through the reader's contribution: it's inevitable that we overlay onto this story memories of our own early experiences, as I did at the beginning of this essay. Time passes in these short pages, lots of it—years and years—and yet the exact present action of the story is, literally, a man sitting and staring into his coffee for, well, we don't even know how long. Perhaps it's no more time than the flash of the train rattling by, giving us the tiniest glimpse of something we've never seen that also feels familiar.

What keeps me returning to this story is the absolute intensity of experience that comes from reading the work itself, which I urge you to do. Even now, at the end of this consideration, the story catches me anew: I confess to drafting this essay in a coffee shop, my mind confident in its East Coast snobbery and easily lured into imagining there's no f-ing way a cup of Starbucks could ever set anyone forth on a similar mental journey through the past and present. Yet we don't know that. We don't. In "Pet Milk," as in all of life, the potential for magic exists in the normal, in the everyday, and in the memories created during these everydays—whether remembered accurately or inaccurately through a haze of longing. There was nothing inherently special about Pet milk, a product found in any grocery store baking aisle. Who's to say that right here or down the street or in a mall or somewhere, there isn't a person sitting in a Starbucks right now, or ten years from now, gazing into a paper cup, languishing in drifty thoughts of the past, their mind swirling through layers of memory?

Dybek's right: How I would love to see someone like that.

Leslie Pietrzyk is the author of the short-story collection *This Angel on My Chest* (2015), as well as the novels *Pears on a Willow Tree* (1998), *A Year and a Day* (2004) and *Silver Girl* (2018).

"The Pedersen Kid" by William H. Gass

Annie Proulx

"The Pedersen Kid" was originally published in volume 1, issue 1, of *MSS* in 1961. It was collected in *In the Heart of the Heart of the Country and Other Stories* (1968). It is currently most readily available in *In the Heart of the Heart of the Country and Other Stories* (NYRB Classics).

Not long ago I read a collection of essays by contemporary British writers, edited by Antonia Fraser, *The Pleasure of Reading* (1992). The childhood experiences that brought these writers to books were remarkably similar: illness with long weeks abed, parents who read aloud, awkward appearance or shy character that sent the child to the refuge of books. Many wrote that they were perversely attracted to frightening or sordid books, disliked books with youthful chum characters, and, above all, quickly developed an insatiable greed for the worlds and people found between book covers that was only tempered in adulthood by a maturing sense of value and perhaps the knowledge that one could not read everything.

I suffered no serious childhood illness, but my mother read to me and invented stories. I learned to read when I was four and assigned characters and personalities to the letters of the alphabet, particularly the capitals, which I saw as heroic—and to numbers, eight with its treacherous personality, seven in a sweeping cape. I was drawn to the Gustav Doré illustrations of Dante's *Divine Comedy*, turned again and again to Ugolino gnawing Ruggieri's head. I despised the girl mysteries and I read obsessively. When I was eight Jack London's *Before Adam* came my way, a vivid story of a prehistoric clan dominated by the brutal Red Eye who took females by force and intimidated or killed the other males. The black buckram cover influenced my choice of library books for years until I read Nordhoff and Hall's *Mutiny on the Bounty* bound in tropic beach-sand beige. I read ferociously all that came my way.

I suppose the indiscriminate wolfing of books might have gone on, but high-school Latin slowed reading down and I began to turn over in my mind the images and ideas that rose from the page and the words and sentences that carried them. I noticed there were styles and architectures of writing aside from rational and logical unfolding, that there were meanings that lay not on the page but in my own perception. In those days I valued fiction less than accounts of the lives of Chinese poets or books about cheiromancy, farrier's tools, windmills.

In the late 1960s I crossed some kind of line. In the hours it took me to read William Gass's long story "The Pedersen Kid" I understood for the first time that fiction possessed curious powers, though of what they consisted and how they were manifested I barely sensed and could not explain. At first this story gave me the sensation of examining a fine cabinet, looking for the subtle joinery of the story's parts, the inlay of punctuation, searching out secret panels. Although I had experienced the reader's tranced condition many times before, this was the first occasion I became aware of it and myself in it, experiencing season and place as strongly as though I, too, lived inside the story with these terrible people; I read in a chill blue light that emanated from the page itself. I knew nothing of the author then, did not know he seined the world through philosophy's nets, nor that he had written a celebrated novel, *Omensetter's Luck*, knew nothing of his critical essays, nor theories of fiction, only that here was a piece of work that gave very much.

As the years passed it was clear enough that the powers of fiction were, in the hands of more ordinary scribblers, quite dilute. I read Gass's other stories, *Omensetter's Luck*, *On Being Blue*, critical essays, and then his novel *The Tunnel*, rising like a great pyramid from the plain of American literature, even a few reviews by meat-and-potato critics who categorize Gass as an acquired taste, not for olives, but monkey brains. But what follows is neither a discussion of Gass's writings nor literary commentary, but an anecdote of personal recognition.

"The Pedersen Kid" remains for me one of the two most powerful stories I have encountered (the other is Seumas O'Kelly's "The Weaver's Grave"). By powerful I mean that my mind has returned to these stories again and again for many years with undiminished interest.

"The Pedersen Kid," like Gaul and the Trinity, is divided into three sections. There are no quotation marks to set off the dialogue, so that sometimes the speech between characters serves as silent observation or interior monologue, adding complex, chromatic layers to the exchanges between characters. The wide gaps within and separating certain sentences, a device of poets I did not recognize when I first read the story, pictorially indicates the physical stillness of the adolescent narrator Jorge—waiting, listening, figuring; and these gaps imply not hesitation but a canny sorting-out, a gauging of strategic position. All the characters, even the pecked-hen mother, are cunning, all, mother, father, son, hired man, horribly linked to one another in a dyscratic form of the midwest rural family.

Old Magnus the father is a brilliant hider of whiskey bottles; yet the cringing mother knows where one is secreted and fetches it to resuscitate the neighbor's child, the half-frozen Pedersen kid discovered in the snow near the corn crib, now naked and unconscious on the kitchen table, his skinny behind in the slick and sticky bread dough. An expectation flares in Jorge and Big Hans that the fetching of the whiskey means the mother will finally confront Magnus, and when that expectation fades they anticipate Magnus's rage when he learns the hen has scratched out his bottle. And Big Hans, hired man and instigator, how sly he is, rubbing and rubbing the naked Pedersen kid's body under the guise of warming him.

The savage climate, the landscape empty of everything but random snowdrifts and two remote farms, is at once the arena where the events of the story occur and the force that drives the events. It is a story that twists the rural myth of good neighbors, for Magnus hates old Pedersen, "that cock. That fairy farmer." Everything is counted and measured with hard, suspicious eyes: the distance between the two farms, the strength of the blizzard, the strangeness of the Pedersen kid's journey, and Big Hans's discovery of him.

Although Jorge is clinically interested in watching the Pedersen kid die, he is relieved that Big Hans found him or he, Jorge, losing at the drift game, might have stepped on the rotting corpse in the spring. The Pedersen kid revives and utters an ominous list: Mackinaw, cap, yellow gloves, and gun. And so we learn someone has put the Pedersen family in their cellar.

In the second section Big Hans and Jorge carry guns, Magnus a bottle of whiskey, and they go with horse and sleigh into the intense cold that follows a blizzard, steering through the deep prairie drifts toward the Pedersen farm to tell them the kid is saved, to find out what has happened. The road disappears, the horse bogs in a drift, and now Magnus drops his bottle in the snow and forces Jorge to paw for it, an impossible task like the tests set for youngest sons in *Märchen*. The horse lunges and breaks a trace, and when it pulls again the sleigh runner must crush the bottle beneath it.

Difficulty piles on danger: the stunning cold, the smoke-less chimney, the discovery of a dead horse—not Pedersen's horse—Jorge fooling with the gun and aiming it, the digging of a futile tunnel to evade the eye of Yellow Gloves, Jorge's bold run across the open yard to the house where he shouts All Clear, and then the shots.

The reader must play the drift game as well, treading on the seemingly solid surface only to sink and feel something awful beneath the feet. The sleigh of the story rips into a hole. Did Yellow Gloves or Jorge or both shoot Big Hans and Magnus? I was satisfied it was Jorge, for in thinking how he would bury the dead he adds "and even ma if I wanted to bother."

Some years later when I read the story again I saw I had missed everything. In the final section of "The Pedersen Kid" Jorge is alone in Pedersen's kitchen, drowsy with the heat of the fire he has made, the Pedersens probably dead in the cellar, Big Hans and Magnus probably dead outside, and he envisions the one with yellow gloves riding the stolen Pedersen horse to the other farm, envisions the man entering the home kitchen where once more the story begins, where Big Hans and ma and the Pedersen kid repeat their actions but in the company of the gloved character. Jorge thinks, "They'd disappear like the Pedersens had. He'd put them away somewhere out of sight for at least as long as the winter. But he'd leave the kid, for we'd been exchanged, and we were both in our new lands."

This mobius-strip scene is working in the reader's mind when the story vaults again, back to Jorge in the Pedersen farm kitchen, Jorge to whom it seems the unseen one has returned, the stolen horse circling through the drifts of the featureless plain and the snow (for the storm has begun again as well), coming home to Pedersen's barn. Jorge scrabbles around, trying to put out the fire before the rider notices the smoke: "The wind whooped and the house creaked like steps do. I was alone with all that could happen."

I was alone with all that could happen.

There it was, what I had not seen years earlier, a profound, disturbing, and exhilarating sentence that applied to the characters, the writer, and the reader, for each is alone with all that can happen. Characters can be exchanged. The unknown and unknowing one can ride up on his circling horse, a black horse can or can not have two brown hind legs. Oppressors are shot or imagined shot. The beginning begins again, the end is the beginning. The seemingly solid narrative sways, twists on itself, not just in a Ripley's believe-it-or-not exclamation that anything is possible, nor through the shifting focus of varieties of truth as in Akutagawa's "In a Grove," nor in deconstructionist denial of Meaning in a narrative undercoated with many meanings, nor through the magic realism of, say, Kafka's "A Country Doctor," nor through the convoluted and elaborate fictional mazes constructed by Turkish novelist Orhan Pamuk, nor as the story-wrenching falcon of fiction multiplied to sky-darkening flights, but something slyer, more ironic and funnier than all of these, a situation of deep play and high risk that depends in considerable measure on the interpretive construction of the reader.

For me "The Pedersen Kid" illustrates the difficult and absurd effort in telling any story because of all that could happen. This rich, dark joke that lurks behind fiction has my attention.

Annie Proulx is the author of the short-story collections *Heart Songs and Other Stories* (1988), *Close Range: Wyoming Stories* (1999), *Bad Dirt: Wyoming Stories 2* (2004), and *Fine Just the Way It Is: Wyoming Stories 3* (2008), and of the novels *Postcards*

(1992), which won the PEN/Faulkner Award, *The Shipping News* (1993), which won the Pulitzer Prize and the National Book Award, *Accordion Crimes* (1996), *That Old Ace in the Hole* (2002), and *Barkskins* (2016). Her stories have been reprinted in the 1998, 1999, and 2000 editions of *The Best American Short Stories* and in the 1998 and 1999 editions of the *O. Henry Awards: Prize Stories.*

"Bartleby, the Scrivener"
by Herman Melville

Joanna Scott

"Bartleby, the Scrivener" was first published in the November-December 1853 issue of *Putnam's Monthly Magazine*. It was collected in *The Piazza Tales* (1856). It is currently most readily available in *Herman Melville: Pierre; Israel Potter; The Piazza Tales; The Confidence-Man; Uncollected Prose; Billy Budd* (Library of America).

It would not be enough to say that I love Melville's story "Bartleby, the Scrivener" because of its sentences, so I will attempt to explain what about those sentences holds my attention. Why do I find that this story has never failed, upon multiple readings over several decades, to fascinate me? What is there to learn from a story that is simultaneously hilarious and heartbreaking? How do Melville's sentences generate such a complexity of meaning?

Before I continue, I want to reflect generally on the nature of the sentence itself. Disregarding the long-standing argument about the relationship between sentences and ideas (does a sentence record a complete thought, or must we form a sentence in order to understand what we are thinking?), along with the fact that the sentence as we conceive of it today is relatively new (up through medieval traditions, punctuation was used to help a speaker phrase and shape the language when reading aloud; modern punctuation was developed in the Renaissance and sentence structure codified by the mid-seventeenth century), let's consider the plasticity of the sentence. Even as we attend to the rigid demands of grammar, a sentence's shape turns out to be remarkably flexible. Within the closed unit of a sentence, the possibilities are endless, as long as we follow the rules of grammar and arrange the words in such a way that they make sense.

Bartleby, the scrivener, became famous with one short sentence: "I would prefer not to." There doesn't seem to be much to say about this particular sentence. It uses simple grammatical construction without any punctuation other than the end point of the period. Its longest word is only two syllables. It is a clear, adamant refusal. It seems easy enough to understand.

In contrast to his scrivener, Melville's narrator prefers to get things done. He characterizes himself as an "eminently *safe* man." He is a Wall Street lawyer (the subtitle of the story is "A Story of Wall Street") who prides himself on his "grand point[s]" of "prudence" and "method." He is confident of his ability to understand—and to make himself understood—until Bartleby comes along and announces that he "would prefer not to." The sentence, it turns out, is not as clear as it appears. It forces the narrator to doubt himself: either he did not hear Bartleby's answer correctly, or Bartleby misunderstood the meaning of the request. Once he confirms what was said, the narrator reacts more strongly to the unfinished aspect of Bartleby's sentence than to his refusal. "What do you mean?" he thunders. "Are you moon-struck?" Our reasonable narrator, whose "snug business" consists of drawing up wills and titles for rich men, can't stand the evasiveness of his ghostly scrivener. With the plaster-of-paris bust of his hero Cicero—the influential, forceful, coherent orator and lawyer

of Ancient Rome—watching over his shoulder, Melville's narrator is stunned. He is used to clarity and certainty. Suddenly,
meaning is elusive.

Bartleby's sentence ends with the marker for the infini-
tive; the actual verb is missing, leaving readers to fill in the
blank. What is it, exactly, that Bartleby prefers not to do?
The answer seems obvious, but it keeps changing. The list
of tasks unfolds over the course of the story. Will Bartleby
"examine a small paper"? Will Bartleby "not speak"? Will
Bartleby "answer"? Will Bartleby go to the post office, or say
anything about himself? Again and again, his response is "I
would prefer not to."

The narrator keeps pressing. He has to know . . . something; it hardly matters what. Won't Bartleby say anything
about himself? Why won't he speak to his friendly employer?
The narrator can't fathom meaning that is not explicit. Bartleby
tries to add clarity by gently spelling out the missing parts of
his sentence, adding the words that have already been implied.
He announces that he would prefer "to give no answer." He
would prefer "not to be a little reasonable."

When asked why he did not write, Bartleby explains that
he has "decided upon doing no more writing." The narrator
can't believe it. No more writing? Is that what he said? A scrivener who was hired to write prefers to do no more writing!

Here's our Cicero-inspired narrator, in response: "'Why,
how now? what next?' exclaimed I, 'do no more writing?'"

Let's take a look at the grammar. The urgent questions are
written as one syntactical unit. The internal punctuation is
more emphatic than functional. Take out the narrative fram-
ing, and this is what we get: *Why, how now? what next? do no
more writing?* Even as I try to type it out, Microsoft keeps trying to auto-correct the grammar. The line is full of errors. The
final predicate has no subject. The questions aren't properly

divided with upper-case letters. It seems to indicate that our narrator has started to fall apart.

Melville published this story anonymously in *Putnam's Magazine* in 1853. His most recent major publication was *Pierre; or, The Ambiguities*, a novel which moves between a country estate and urban settings. There are no ships or white whales in *Pierre*. Reviewers were appalled. One reviewer in the *New York Day Book*, under the headline "HERMAN MELVILLE CRAZY," reported that Melville was "really supposed to be deranged" and hoped that he would be kept "stringently secluded from pen and ink." In an article that ran in the *Herald* in September, 1852, the reviewer wondered why Melville had deserted "the blue waters of the Pacific" in favor of the "mere wordy anatomy of the heart." The reviewer weighed in more generally: "Modern readers wish to exercise some little judgment of their own; deeds they will have, not characters painted in cold colors, to a hair-breadth or a shade."

Ah, Bartleby, how coldly you are painted. You are pale and silent and cadaverous. You do nothing but stare at a "dead brick wall," refusing to write. The narrator compares you to "the last column of some ruined temple." Above all, you are not ordinary. The word that the grub-man in the Tombs uses to describe you is "odd." The narrator has a better word: "'I think he is a little deranged,' said I, sadly."

Melville makes sure we dwell on that word. "Deranged? deranged is it?" asks the grub-man.

Who isn't deranged in this story? Of the two other copyists in the narrator's office, one, Turkey, is known to spill his sand, split his pens, and throw his papers about "in a very indecorous manner." The other, Nippers, grinds his teeth together and hisses and can't decide whether to raise or lower his table lid. The office-boy, Ginger Nut, stores the shards of nut-shells in his desk. Nuts indeed, all of them, not least the narrator himself, who fears chaos and invites chaos. Why, how now? what next? do no more writing?

What is more absurd than asking a man to spend his life copying sentences word for word? Yet until Bartleby arrives, the narrator has never stopped to question his work. Only in the face of his scrivener's refusals does our prudent, methodical lawyer grow more self-reflective—and more confused. He tells himself that both he and Bartleby are sons of Adam. What can he do with "such a helpless creature"? He won't be cruel, he won't abandon his scrivener, but he has to do something about the situation. Does it count as cruelty if he finds other chambers for his business and leaves Bartleby behind?

Bartleby is as impossible to ignore as the fact of mortality. He refuses to work. He refuses to answer. He refuses to write. Each refusal compels the narrator to think harder about the scrivener. In the process, the narrator's views grow more contradictory. Bartleby is an "intolerable incubus." No, he's a "poor, pale, passive mortal." No, he's a ghost. It becomes increasingly difficult for our reasonable narrator to think straight and come to a conclusion.

I'm not the first to notice all the dangling modifiers in "Bartleby, the Scrivener." They begin to appear at the point in the story when Bartleby first makes it clear that he is going to stand fast in his refusal to work. The narrator's explanation for not firing Bartleby on the spot is that he isn't an ordinary human. Bartleby must stay. But something must give in order to make space for the scrivener. That something is the common rule of grammar that prohibits us from mixing up our participial phrases: "So calling Nippers from the other room, the paper was speedily examined," announces the narrator in exasperation, erroneously conflating himself—who is calling Nippers—with the examined paper.

Early dangling modifiers pave the way for others later in the story. The most significant is given its own paragraph:

Going up stairs to my old haunt, there was Bartleby silently sitting upon the banister at the landing.

Wait a second! The narrator is the one going up stairs to his former office, yet the subject being modified is Bartleby. Why didn't anyone catch Melville's mistake before the pages were sent to the printer? It's the kind of mistake that would keep me up at night. Did Melville lose any sleep because of this sentence? I doubt it.

By breaking the rule governing modifying phrases, Melville allows a telling slip on the narrator's part. According to the logic of the sentence, the two men, employer and employee, are blurred together in a paradoxical set of images. Both the narrator and Bartleby are going up the stairs. Both are sitting on the banister. Look at them. Look at the way language can embody our groping effort to make sense of absurdity.

The reviewer in the *New York Day Book* hoped that the deranged author of *Pierre* would be kept forcibly from writing. Melville, however, was not easily silenced. He changed our literary history by adapting the rules governing sentence structure for his specific purposes. We all know from Cicero to consider the "how" of rhetoric, along with the "what." A good, forceful argument must be carefully shaped, progress logically, and include evidence. But any formula is only an abstraction. Every great writer, in one way or another, increases the power of individual words by arranging them in unexpected syntactical designs. The author of "Bartleby, the Scrivener" can be irresistibly persuasive and logical with one sentence, and with the next sentence he can move the words in a different direction, offering new ways of thinking about such topics as the pressure of mortality, the limits of reason, and the value of imaginative expression.

There were severe financial stresses and failures in Melville's life, and he had to endure plenty of public insults in response to his work. But maybe we should thank the reviewer who called Melville deranged and who hoped that the author would be kept from picking up his pen. Melville did just the opposite. After being called deranged, he made the word his own. He put it in action, providing an unforgettable context with sentences that are anything but ordinary.

Joanna Scott is the author of the short-story collections *Various Antidotes* (1994) and *Everybody Loves Somebody* (2006), as well as ten novels, including *The Manikin* (1996), which was a finalist for the Pulitzer Prize. Her stories have been selected for the 1993 edition of *The Best American Short Stories* and for the 1993 and 2015 Pushcart Prize.

"Old Boys, Old Girls" by Edward P. Jones

Rion Amilcar Scott

"Old Boys, Old Girls" was first published in the May 3, 2004, issue of *The New Yorker*. It was collected and is currently most readily available in *All Aunt Hagar's Children* (HarperCollins).

The students filed into the class wearing blue jumpsuits. There were three of them, black men in their late teens and early twenties—youthful offenders in the parlance of the prison system. They took seats in chairs designed to be too flimsy to do any damage if thrown, around a table too heavy to be lifted by a single person, and thus unable to be used as a weapon.

I was a guest in their class, in their house. My first time inside a prison. Two of the students immediately expressed their enchantment with the mechanics of writing, but more so the magic of becoming taken with a story while reading— "movies for your mind" one student dubbed it.

The third student—let's call him K.—was a quieter sort, avoiding eye contact lest he be called on. Later I found out he signed up for classes mainly to get out of his cell, for something to do amidst the monotony of prison. He rarely completed the work, and that was fine.

After we talked some, I opened a book of my stories to read a bit. When I glanced up between sentences, I could see

K. smiling and laughing at the story's humorous turns. K.'s teacher sat to the right of me, also smiling, amused by K.'s change in demeanor. K. locked eyes with his teacher and without a second thought, righted his face, turning his smile not into a scowl exactly, but into something steelier than a grin.

Inside the prison, I imagine, a smile isn't very rich currency. In Edward P. Jones's short story "Old Boys, Old Girls" from his second collection, *All Aunt Hagar's Children*, one of the first lessons Caesar Matthews learns upon entering prison for a murder charge is not to avoid smiling—he knows this from the brutal life he's lived to this point—it's that to survive in the prison environment one must practice total domination. So upon meeting his new cell mate, on the advice of a lifer, Caesar demands the bottom bunk despite being indifferent to which bed he'd rest his head upon. That lifer, Cathedral, tells him: "Listen man, even if you like the top bunk, you fuck him up for the bottom just cause you gotta let him know who rules. You let him know that you will stab him through his motherfuckin heart and then turn around and eat your supper, cludin the dessert. . . . Caes, you gon be here a few days, so you can't let nobody fuck with your humanity." When his cellie refuses to hand over the bunk, Caesar initiates a several-days-long brawl that ends in victory for Caesar, now a ruler of a kingdom made of concrete and steel bars. When he later meets a new cellmate, Caesar greets him by knocking him unconscious and urinating on his belongings. A preemptive note: We are not equals and no dissension or disrespect will be tolerated.

Cathedral, hell, the whole damn prison system, is fucking with Caesar's humanity.

Though Caesar has learned to trade his humanity for violence, he is really just a child with a wound. Part of the magic of Edward P. Jones—aside from his labyrinthine sentences that move forward, backward, and even sideways in time—is that his two story collections chronicle the same characters in black Washington, D.C., at different points in their lives. The D.C. of Edward P. Jones is not "the Washington they put on post cards and in the pages of expensive coffee-table books," as the narrator of "Young Lions" from Jones's debut collection, *Lost in the City*, puts it. His D.C. is the pre-gentrification Chocolate City, often poverty-stricken, often forgotten in the shadow of monuments and the seats of national power. When we first meet Caesar in "Young Lions," he is winding his way down the path of thug life, spurred on by the rejection of his father, Lemuel. The narrator of "Young Lions" tells us: "His father was the kind of man who, if he looked out his office window and saw his son, would come down the stairs three at a time and hold him until someone called the police."

In "Young Lions," we watch as Caesar commits several robberies—including the meticulously planned fleecing of a mentally handicapped woman; he shoots a man in the face; and as the story ends, Caesar brutally beats a woman who wanted little more than to be in love with him. It would seem that Caesar has sacrificed his humanity on an altar of a cold and cruel criminality, but that unravelling follows the untimely loss of his mother, the pain of which Caesar tries to ease by growing close to Angelo, a ne'er-do-well cousin. Soon Caesar is spending his time cutting school and hanging around Angelo's apartment. This is too much for Lemuel Matthews, who smacks his son and physically tosses him onto the sidewalk, lamenting that he's slaved away just to "raise another Angelo." It's here that any hope of Caesar living a respectable life fades away; the wound, that rejection by his father, casts a pall on all things in Caesar's life.

When "Old Boys, Old Girls" opens, Caesar is entering prison for a second murder, never having had to answer for the first. Or as the narrator tells us: "It was almost as if, at least on the books the law kept, Caesar had got away with a free killing."

I've heard people speak of the verisimilitude of Jones's jail scenes, as if the sentences are life sentences and the act of reading them transports the reader to prison, and we all become lifers sitting with Caesar and Cathedral and Multrey discussing the best way to live in cages like animals in captivity. Here is where I think readers misunderstand Jones's magic. There is indeed something transporting about this story, but it's not due to a buildup of true-to-life details.

Absent are the mice many prisoners report as their constant companions. If there are maggots in the food, we don't hear about them. There is no mention of the walls with their drab colors that discourage dreaming. Jones ignores the frequent searches, the noise, the clink of the steel gates, a sound that my father, a defense attorney, says rattled him every single time he heard the jail door close behind him in his forty-something years practicing law. Yes, Caesar Matthews is one of 1.4 million people in a U.S. prison—37 percent of those being black men despite black people making up about 12 percent of the country's population, according to Department of Justice statistics. It's a situation so dire and rife with inequality that it would not be a stretch to label every single Caesar Matthews a political prisoner. In Maryland, the state that incarcerated K., 72 percent of the prisoners are black men, the highest percentage in the country. But the sociological reality of Caesar Matthews and the hundreds of thousands like him is not Jones's concern in "Old Boys, Old Girls." The verisimilitude is entirely in how deeply Jones gives us the internal life of Caesar, a man numbed by, to paraphrase the narrator, all the world has done to him, but more so by what he has done to himself.

Caesar cycles through his time in prison, and as he grows older he loses friends to murder and insanity, and with age he also loses some of his cachet and prison menace. Soon Caesar—still cold, still numb—finds himself spit back out in the world, living in a room in a building in black D.C. on the 900 block of N Street and working in a restaurant on F Street. In his building Caesar discovers living a few doors down, Yvonne, an *Old Girl*—"whores, young or old, who had been battered so much by the world that they had only the faintest wisp of life left." Yvonne is not any "Old Girl," but by coincidence Caesar is neighbor to his old girlfriend, a woman who disappeared from Caesar's life before his incarceration. He begins spending time with her again, talking and nothing more, listening to her spit out her philosophy on the uses and abuses of bullshit: "People should stand up and say, 'I wish you were dead,' or 'I want your pussy,' or 'I want all the money in your pocket.' When we stop lyin, the world will start bein heaven." She never recognizes him, it appears, as the boyfriend she left so many years ago. Another figure from Caesar's pre-incarceration days, his estranged brother, finds Caesar at the restaurant and pleads with Caesar to come to dinner with him and their sister. Previously, Caesar ignored letters his siblings sent him while in prison, regarding them as allies of his father, the source of his deepest wound.

Here "Old Boys, Old Girls" reveals itself as something of an alternate version of the story James Baldwin tells in "Sonny's Blues."

In that story, the narrator, a math teacher, struggles to understand his younger brother, Sonny, a jazz musician and a drug addict, as he returns from prison. "Sonny's Blues" is told entirely from the perspective of Sonny's older brother as he falls out with Sonny, loses touch and then reconnects. Sonny writes his brother a letter after a long estrangement asking to meet when he returns to New York. All throughout the story Sonny's brother wonders after his sibling's internal life and as the story ends, he gains an understanding of his brother by listening to him perform his beloved jazz music.

Like Sonny and his brother, Caesar and his siblings are divided by class distinctions. Against his better judgment, Caesar agrees to Sunday fried chicken dinner with his siblings out on the "Gold Coast," a wealthy, but still black, part of Washington, D.C. Caesar and his siblings share very little conversation outside of platitudes. They ask him few questions about his life and he offers nothing. There is no unfurling of the soul in the manner of Sonny playing his music and his brother receiving the transmission from within. Though Caesar's siblings verbally express joy after seeing him, they never truly listen to him, so when Caesar lets his guard down and plays with his niece, grabbing at her foot, his sister watches him with a disgust that pains him. His sister, Caesar believes, has mistaken him for a child molester. He thinks back to teaching his sister how to ride a bike, assuring her he'd never let her fall; now in her eyes, since she knows little about Caesar aside from his status as an ex-convict, he's the one who is fallen.

If it could be said that Caesar has a recovery from his fall, it's upon coming home and finding his old girlfriend, Yvonne, has passed away, felled by her own hand. Caesar performs what seems like a selfless act, cleaning her room and arranging her body peacefully on the bed. However, the things we do to maintain the dignity of the dead are ultimately about maintaining the dignity and humanity of the living.

Jones writes: "Before finding Yvonne dead, he had thought he would go and live in Baltimore and hook up with a vicious crew he had known a long time ago. Wasn't that what child molesters did? Now, the only thing he knew about the rest of his life was that he did not want to wash dishes and bus tables anymore."

Caesar leaves his home, the place of Yvonne's death, and decides to hand over his next moves to chance. He flips a coin, but instead of letting it determine his fate, he decides a flip he doesn't like would not count. For so long things outside himself—the prison system, old wounds—had ordered his life. Now it's Caesar and Caesar alone who is in charge of his destiny.

It isn't so much the death of Yvonne that brings about a new day for Caesar; it's Caesar's ritual cleansing of her body, his loving arrangement, his decision to thaw his heart and connect despite his many wounds that for him bring about a new era of intentionality and humanity.

Rion Amilcar Scott is the author of the short-story collection *Insurrections* (2016), which won the PEN/Robert W. Bingham Prize for Debut Fiction.

"The Secret Life of Walter Mitty" by James Thurber

Mary Lee Settle

"The Secret Life of Walter Mitty" was originally published in the March 18, 1939, issue of *The New Yorker*. It was collected in *My World—and Welcome to It* (1942). It is currently most readily available in *The Secret Life of Walter Mitty* (Penguin Classics).

One evening in December 1944 a group of foreign correspondents, some of whom had just come back from France, sat with friends in the warmth and deceptive safety of the Connaught Hotel in London having drinks. One of the correspondents was late. He came running in and said, "I've just made a great discovery."

Of course, in that atmosphere of waiting for news of the Battle of the Bulge, and of V2 dodging, an alertness which is the positive use of fear, we all froze.

"Walter Mitty is to our generation what Spengler's *Decline of the West* was to the last," he said. Maybe he was right. There is an element of Joseph Conrad's Lord Jim or James Thurber's Walter Mitty in those who volunteer to go to war. It is a major part of survival.

But that evening, as so many evenings, we were doing what we had found to be the real business of war, waiting: waiting for action, waiting for disaster, waiting for it to be over. We were doing it in elegant comfort. There was no heroism for any of us beyond ears fine-tuned to the sky—not Conrad's stamina in a storm, only the demanded patience of the grey days.

This was far from the only time Walter Mitty was recognized in World War II. Bomber pilots in the Pacific theater made *Ta pocketa pocketa pocketa pocketa pocketa* an official password, and painted the "Mitty Society" emblem, two crossed Webley Vickers 50.80 heavy automatics, on their fuselages. That was in honor of Walter Mitty. Who but Kilroy has entered more quickly into folklore?

"The Secret Life of Walter Mitty," set on one uneventful morning in the life of a shy henpecked dreamer of a certain age ("Don't forget your overshoes."), is just seven pages long. It encompasses his life, my life, and maybe your life. Mitty's wife is drawn so deftly and with so few strokes that Thurber gives us permission to sympathize with her. Let's face it—she is married to (in his outer husk of daily life) a nerd. His inner life is a mystery that she only sees as "You're tensed up again."

Outer Mitty stumbles, is embarrassed, buys puppy biscuits, remembers to get overshoes, can't park his car, gets yelled at by a cop, hides dreaming in a hotel lobby waiting for his wife.

Ah, but Inner Mitty! Inner Mitty is the greatest pistol shot in the world, the one doctor who can save a millionaire after "coreopsis has set in," takes flight through the sky in the worst storm in twenty years of Navy flying, saves everybody, gets World War I wonderfully mixed up with World War II, but never mind—all this in seven pages where Thurber never tries to lead the reader, never, to use a word Mitty would love, "spins." He simply tells, not only in "The Secret Life of Walter Mitty," but in "You Could Look It Up," in *My Life and Hard Times*, and in *My World—and Welcome to It*, what our world is like.

Why do we choose a favorite? A short story? A novel? It is not because they are "better" stylistically or more profound (but what could be more profound than the sharing of a shy man's dreams?). I think it is because we have been singled out for secret recognition. We read a story. We smile. We look with some self-compassion into another heart when we thought we were alone.

Only a few American writers have honored us with characters who have entered the galaxy of memorable people who survive the story they may have been born in—and the memory of them is as true as factual memory. A friend on a train— Sister Carrie on a train; a cousin on the river—Huckleberry Finn on the river; an embarrassed adolescent memory of our own, of when we appeared in slightly wrong clothes, in acts of innocence which show themselves as naive social ambitions— the great *naif* of American letters, Jay Gatsby.

I once made an experiment on a class. They had read *La Rouge et Le Noir* by Stendhal. They didn't "like" it. They hated Julien Sorel. They were meeting their first anti-hero. The first question I asked in the class was, "WHEN did you first identify with Julien Sorel?" Every student answered the same way, at the moment of embarrassment when Julien is sitting on a stool in the grand drawing room of the de la Mole household. He had become for them completely alive—one of them— one of us.

So yes, I, too, who was in a war, identified with Walter Mitty. I, too, and all of us, were drawn into mundane, authoritarian dailiness, like Mitty, who was cast down out of the "remote, intimate airways of his mind" by his wife. In my case it seemed to be sergeants.

The best American comedy has a strong sense of compassionate indignation as its driving force. Thurber's stories have it, a hint of darkness. T. S. Eliot recognized this quality in Thurber as "serious and even somber . . . unlike so much humor, it is not merely a criticism of manners—that is, of the superficial aspects of society at a given moment—but something more profound." Thurber touched on this in an interview when he said that his work was "reality twisted to the right into humor rather than to the left into tragedy."

It is not surprising that it is Eliot who saw this so early. Like Poe—only in the timing, God knows, because he was recognized in France long before he was acclaimed in America—Thurber was recognized early in England as a writer who, in A. L. Rowse's words, is "part of the English language."

Mark Twain's novels balanced this quality of darkness with wit, and sometimes hilarity, but sometimes, as in "The Man That Corrupted Hadleyburg," his work tips over into blackness. James Thurber does this, too. He can be mean, his fury can drown his wit. But when he is in balance, prejudiced, grumpy, human James Thurber is one of the greatest writers of pure American prose of the twentieth century.

His training in precision and length was the newspaper trade. You can see that training in his stories, especially in his fables, where it is a lesson to us all. He is a midwestern minister who cloaks his moral tales, his parables, in comic "legends." But I would rather see a child who is learning to read, read "The Bear Who Let It Alone," than the twee-baby pap they have already outgrown at birth.

A graduate "creative writing" student might well hang above the desk, as I did for years, Thurber's Moral: "Don't get it right, just get it written." It is etched in my mind when I work with Conrad's "Above all, to make you see. That—and no more, and it is everything."

I hope for our sanity that we all share a secret inner life in one form or another. Believers in reincarnation, or ancestor braggarts, both Mittys once removed, never chose old Joe Soap who fell down drunk and hit his head, they (we?) have to have at least a royalty, a hero as undefeated, as inscrutable as Walter Mitty.

Thurber's reputation has suffered, I think, from the almost incestuous mutual admiration of the pre-World War II *New Yorker* writers, and also from a more serious thing. The Pantheon of American classics is a solemn place. Thurber flaunted its deepest prejudices. He was and is one of the funniest writers of American prose. He made a lot of money in his lifetime. And he hasn't been dead long enough.

So it is time to rescue him from his success. Perhaps, once again, we can go back to where his "serious" reputation started. That verbose, Spencerian and most English of prose writers, Winston Churchill, called James Thurber "an insane, depraved artist." Let his redemption start there.

Mary Lee Settle (1918–2005) is the author of fifteen novels, including *Blood Tie* (1977), which won the National Book Award, and the five-book *Beulah Quintet*, as well as of eight books of nonfiction.

"Sonny's Blues" by James Baldwin

Joan Silber

"Sonny's Blues" was first published in the Summer 1957 issue of *The Partisan Review*. It was collected in *Going to Meet the Man* (1965). It is currently most readily available in *Going to Meet the Man* (Vintage).

"Sonny's Blues" is a story about pain—well, maybe most stories are—but "Sonny's Blues" is especially direct about it. It begins with the arrest of a younger brother for drugs, includes the death of a two-year-old daughter and the killing of an uncle, and concludes with paragraphs about what art can ever do with that. As Sonny himself says, when he hears a woman singing gospel at a street meeting, "It's *repulsive* to think you have to suffer that much."

Most people read "Sonny's Blues" in college (it's in many anthologies, as it should be), but I didn't read it for the first time till I was older. I had the sense to be stunned by it and am still. By now I've written about its use of time and discussed with classes its shrewdness in point of view, and for all the times I've read it again, I've never gotten through a reading dry-eyed. It's the least dismissible story I can call to mind.

It begins with the narrator, a high-school teacher in Harlem, reading the news of his younger brother's arrest for heroin. He and Sonny, a jazz musician, have been at odds for years. "He must want to die, he's killing himself, why does he want to die?" the brother asks a neighborhood junkie who knew Sonny, and the answer is, "Don't nobody want to die, ever. . . . It's going to be rough on old Sonny." "And I didn't write Sonny or send him anything for a long time," the narrator tells us.

On his release, Sonny stays with his brother and his family, as he settles tentatively back into the world. Watching Sonny warily, the brother leads us into scenes from earlier times. The first is his mother telling him, "Your Daddy once had a brother. . . . You didn't never know that, did you?" He was killed on a nighttime highway in the South by a car of drunken white men whose joking went wrong, witnessed by the father on the road. The narrator has his own regretful memories of haranguing the teenage Sonny about where he was ever going to get with this piano obsession. The final and most important switchback is the re-mention (we heard it very briefly early on) of the narrator's daughter Grace—"she only lived a little over two years. She died of polio and she suffered." The account of her death—and the grief of both parents—shows Baldwin doing what few writers can do: bringing the excruciating to us in full power, without a shred of inauthenticity or special pleading. Baldwin's details are brief, and they include the child's mother hearing her fall and the child's screams when she can finally get her breath. "I think I may have written Sonny the very day that little Grace was buried. I was sitting in the living room in the dark, by myself, and I suddenly thought of Sonny. My trouble made his real."

To me, this is the crucial line of the story. *My trouble made his real.* It argues for why the complexities of plot are needed—the brother can't understand a thing without having his own devastation too—and it supports the remarkable ending, in which Sonny at the piano, working his way into the inventions of his music, is understood to be proof that "the tale of how we suffer, and how we are delighted, and how we may triumph is never new, it always must be heard. There isn't any other tale to tell, it's the only light we've got in all this darkness."

I used to teach the story as a way to talk about point of view—to consider why the brother tells it and not Sonny. I learned to warn students not to think Sonny would make an unworthy narrator, just because we've heard about him as an addict. The entire story is an argument for the fact that there is nothing wrong with Sonny's insight or powers of expression. How fondly Sonny is regarded through all of it, how respectfully he is treated as a character—how strongly that still goes against our accepted beliefs.

Of course, the story changes each time I go through it. At this moment, Baldwin has been re-introduced to America in the terrific film *I Am Not Your Negro*, in which the Haitian filmmaker Raoul Peck uses words from Baldwin's unfinished manuscript about the civil rights era, news clips of mob and police violence we've half-forgotten, and footage of Baldwin speaking, sounding astute and prescient.

Baldwin was often asked to be a commentator on race—I remember seeing him on TV—and I certainly read his essays (as well as some of the novels) when I was young. He was the "articulate" (remember when they used that word about Obama?) African American whose phrases were heard by a mixed audience. He was also close to openly gay, at least by the time I caught up with him. (His second novel, *Giovanni's Room*, had scenes between men.)

"Sonny's Blues" was originally published in 1957, so it's now full of historical markers. Sonny gets sent to prison for selling heroin and serves a little more than a year; the Rockefeller Laws, passed in 1973, would have sent him for much longer (and would still). The five-dollar bill the brother hands the local guy by the subway station is given at a time when a subway token was fifteen cents. The Salk vaccine against polio came into use in 1955. The garbage smells that characters keep identifying with slum living are less intensely stinky now, possibly due to plastic bags. Charlie "Bird" Parker is long dead, and the role of jazz in the culture has changed. The scotch and milk that Sonny drinks in the end was a hipster's drink from the 1950s, and when I worked in bars when I was young, every so often an older African American customer would order one.

There are two questions I seem to want to ask of this story now. How have I taken it in as a writer? (Because it seems to me that I have.) And can anything be said about how we read it in this time of Black Lives Matter?

I came to short-story writing a little late, after publishing two novels, and when I was trying to figure out how to do it, I remembered something Grace Paley used to say, to the effect that it often takes two stories to make one. This was helpful to me, because I was having trouble getting enough out of one. And of course I was reading Alice Munro, with her time-leaps, her image of story as a house with different rooms. What Baldwin does here is another form of that—Sonny's story has to be told by way of its impact on his brother. Sonny gets to do the more dramatic, reckless things—he's had a much more interesting life—and the brother absorbs them by way of his own events and makes his own tune out of them. This use of a less daring character to register a more dramatic character's events is a strategy I think I've used. It's not unique to Baldwin (Fitzgerald did it another way in *The Great Gatsby*) but I would like to think that years of reading "Sonny's Blues" left me an unconscious imitator.

The brother is our interpreter, and it's quite a discursive story. He functions as a guide for the reader outside the world of the story, outside 1940s and 1950s Harlem. Which brings us to matters of race. Baldwin uses the narrating brother as a way to bring other circumstances to bear on Sonny's tale. One of my favorite passages is the brother's childhood memory of his parents sitting around after a big Sunday dinner—"And the living room would be full of church folks and relatives. . . . For a moment nobody's talking, but every face looks darkening, like the sky outside. . . . The darkness outside is what the old folks have been talking about. It's what they've come from. It's what they endure. The child knows that they won't talk any more because if he knows too much about what's happened to *them*, he'll know too much too soon, about what's going to happen to *him*."

This appears right before the mother's revelation about the uncle killed in the racist South. The darkness of what the "old folks" have endured is the history of and context for the narrative of Sonny. It's worth noting how skillfully Baldwin includes this—a concrete memory of what was mysterious to the child, a darkness whose origin is felt but not detailed. (The mother's speech has the details.)

This is followed by sections about Sonny as a difficult teenager, though we don't learn until later that he was using drugs as well as cutting school. This high-school-age Sonny has lost both his parents, and the sole member of his immediate family is off in the army. Nowhere in "Sonny's Blues" will you find the word "trauma"—a category of thought prevalent in a later era. "Trouble" is the operative word. The story, which is certainly full of sympathy for Sonny, is investigating the relation of injustice—racial injustice—to personal suffering and the formation of personality.

In the film *I Am Not Your Negro*, an older Baldwin is asked why he once left the United States to go live in France and talks about "the very real danger of death" he knew in the United States. The writer Isabel Wilkerson pointed out in the August 25, 2014, *Guardian*, "The rate of police killings of black Americans is nearly the same as the rate of lynchings in the early decades of the 20th century." This is the atrocious side of why "Sonny's Blues" has not dated.

"Sonny's Blues," written when Baldwin could not have been more than thirty-three, has a magisterial ending, written in a style no author would easily adopt today. Sonny has invited his brother to hear him play in a club. It's plain that the other musicians, "horsing around" and teasing Sonny, view him with great respect. Baldwin builds this long section with its own rise, following the music—Sonny at the piano is at first "working hard, but he wasn't with it" and then, in fits and starts, he makes his way in. Even the allegedly unmusical brother hears how the players listen to each other to improvise (Sonny has been complaining all along of no one listening): "And, while Creole [the bass player] listened, Sonny moved, deep within, exactly like someone in torment." The torment has been the material of the story—suffering, trouble, the rough parts, "what the blues were all about." When Sonny gets to the real depth of his playing, the language elevates— "Freedom lurked around us and I understood, at last, that he could help us to be free if we would listen, that we would never be free until we did. Yet, there was no battle in his face now. I heard what he had gone through, and would continue to go through until he came to rest in earth."

We (I mean writers) don't go in for using that sort of "we" now. Of course, it's not Baldwin's job to be us. I have sometimes wanted to emphasize to readers that the story (positing the quite hopeful idea that art can be made out of pain) is also arguing that the blues are not the same as *complaining*, which anyone can do. In fact, they know this from the route the story has taken them on. The story has its own sort of happy ending—Sonny is really very glad to be praised and sent a drink of congratulation. It's his night. "I was yet aware," the brother thinks, "that this was only a moment, that the world waited outside, as hungry as a tiger, and that trouble stretched above us, longer than the sky."

Joan Silber is the author of the short-story collections *In My Other Life* (2000), *Ideas of Heaven: A Ring of Stories* (2004), and *Fools* (2013), and of the novels *Household Words* (1980), which won the PEN/Hemingway Award, *In the City* (1987), *Lucky Us* (2001), *The Size of the World* (2008), and *Improvement* (2017), which won the National Book Critics Circle Award and the PEN/Faulkner Award. She won the PEN/Malamud Award for Excellence in the Short Story in 2018.

"The Laughing Man" by J. D. Salinger

Elizabeth Spencer

"The Laughing Man" was originally published in the March 19, 1949, issue of *The New Yorker*. It was collected in *Nine Stories* (1953). It is currently most readily available in *Nine Stories* (Little, Brown).

When I reached up to the shelf and pulled down my copy of J. D. Salinger's *Nine Stories*, I noted that it was an old Signet Book edition, selling for 25¢. The pages had yellowed and the spine's glue had given up—pages fell on my lap. Carefully I gathered them up and carefully I read through the stories again.

In the late 1940s and early 1950s, Salinger stories, appearing at intervals in *The New Yorker*, were what we all waited for, devoured on sight, loved to talk about. The language, slightly tilted—precise observations oddly selected—caught up a shimmer of listening and seeing, drawn fresh from the writer's mind; our own minds willingly glowed in answer. Things were like that, we felt; we hadn't noticed. People were like that too! Those speeches with their pouncing *italics*, the careful attention given to shoe sizes, to nail polish, contents of refrigerators and bathroom cabinets, baseball gloves, vacuum cleaners, all the daily baggage of objects we used and lived with.

Interiors abound. We are always in apartments or taxis or hotel rooms or restaurants. Vital talk is going on. How much people smoked back then! Cigarette stubs choke the ash trays, packs are fished out of pockets, out of purses, rung from machines; the cry for matches is as frequent as *goddamns*. Habits of a generation pass before us, but especially active is this bloodhound of a writer who is all the while busy sniffing out the phony and following the faint trail of the true spirit.

But what is this spirit? There are puzzles here and booby traps and dangerous false leads. The rainbow has a foot; softly brilliant colors are bathing it. If only to find it. One reassurance: the writer is seeking too. He is ahead of us, never behind, but not so far ahead we cannot see his heels advancing. In his novel *The Catcher in the Rye* and in the stories, he hasn't grown certain yet. He is more *aware* of the Terrible Traps than of any way to *escape* them.

And all along the way, we were finding Salinger fun to read. So much life is coming out; the wit is up and lively. The turns of phrase were quotable and everybody quoted them. Nobody wanted to miss a word.

From *Nine Stories*, I chose "The Laughing Man" for comment because it touched my heart. Close reading brought up questions; they jumped out of the underbrush like rabbits.

The hero of this tale is John Gedsudski, the "Chief." The narrator is a young man looking back. He was once one of the Chief's hero-worshipping bunch of nine- (or eight- or ten-) year-olds, the "Comanches," whom the Chief, through arrangements with parents, drove out in a rickety bus for sports in the park on Saturdays and holidays. The scene is New York City, Manhattan, pre-war.

Who can get the feel of that huge town better than Salinger? Especially the way it must have seemed to kids growing up there. Nearly all his best stories evoke it. Back then, it had peaceful areas, was safe to play and walk in. Home could be some big airy *four*-bedroom (!) apartment. There were empty streets, and quiet, clean-swept hours, now submerged and all but smothered in gridlock, honking taxis, shouting drivers, horrendous rents, toiling sidewalk crowds, actual danger. In *The Catcher in the Rye*, Holden Caulfield walks at night to a lake in Central Park. Imagine doing that now.

John Gedsudski is from Staten Island, "a shy, gentle young man," a law student, in college days an athlete. Anything but handsome, he is only five-three or -four, with black hair growing low on his forehead, short legs and long torso—ape-like is not quite said. But to twenty-five little boys he is a god: "It seemed to me [says the narrator] that in the Chief all the most photogenic features of Buck Jones, Ken Maynard, and Tom Mix had been smoothly amalgamated."

Each time the game of the day finishes, when all return to the bus, the Chief relates another chapter of the Laughing Man. The boys are enthralled.

Here is the tale within the tale:

The Laughing Man has been cruelly disfigured as an infant. His features remain squashed together: his nose mashed down flat, his head shaped like a pecan, his mouth compressed vertically into a perpetual laugh. Whoever sees his face faints dead away. He wears a red mask made of poppy petals.

The Laughing Man lived in China. An outcast, he made friends with animals and spoke their language. *They did not think him ugly.*

His feats are prodigious. He crosses the Chinese border to Paris and outwits Dufarge, a famous French sleuth, who hates him. He grows rich. He is served by a dwarf named Omba. A beautiful girl worships him. But his greatest bond is to a timber wolf called Black Wing.

Chapter follows chapter, as weeks and seasons go past. The boys hang breathless on the storyteller's voice. They see all New York as an extension of the Laughing Man's territory. They too are his agents, sleuthing tirelessly. The narrator sees himself as "not the only legitimate living descendant of the Laughing Man. There were twenty-five Comanches in the Club, or twenty-five legitimate living descendants of the Laughing Man. All of us circulating ominously, and incognito, throughout the city, sizing up elevator operators as potential arch-enemies, whispering side-of-the-mouth but fluent orders into the ears of cocker spaniels, drawing beads, with index fingers, on the foreheads of arithmetic teachers."

But now comes the moment of complication. First a picture, then a person. The Chief has a girlfriend!

She is Mary Hudson (a graduate of Wellesley) and the narrator can recall only two other girls besides her he would call beautiful. The Comanches reject her at first, but she turns out to be a good baseball player: with every hit she runs at least two bases. She can even steal. Gradually she wins them over, and they take her in as one of the bunch.

But one day she is late to join them, and the Chief, to kill time while waiting for her, spins out another installment of the Laughing Man. The great sleuth is now in trouble. Black Wing has been captured by the Dufarges, his French enemies, who offer the Laughing Man "Black Wing's freedom in exchange for his own." The Laughing Man's devotion is such that he readily agrees and the Dufarges lure him to meet Black Wing "in a designated section of the dense forest surrounding Paris." But it is not really Black Wing; the Dufarges, having "no intention of liberating Black Wing," have brought in an imposter, a timber wolf whose back leg has been dyed white, like Black Wing's. The Laughing Man speaks to the wolf in wolf language, but the imposter does not understand and reveals his true identity.

A pause. Mary Hudson has not come, and all go from the bus to their game.

Mary finally appears, but she refuses to play. When the narrator offers her a mitt, she throws it back; it lands, by accident, in a mud puddle. Timid but desperate, he dares to invite her to come home with him sometime. She snaps a refusal. There is a tearful scene with the Chief, and the girl runs away. The return to the bus is an anxious one.

But it is time for the story. The Comanches are waiting for a last-minute rescue of the Laughing Man, who has been got out of worse scrapes than this. But though Omba the dwarf is on the way from China to Paris with a saving draught of life's blood to revive his master, Dufarge reveals that the real Black Wing, the beloved wolf, is dead. The enemies have killed him. The Laughing Man drops off his mask and dies.

Among the Comanches an awful silence falls. They know without being told that the story, like the Laughing Man and Black Wing, will never be revived.

Leaving the bus, the narrator sees a piece of red tissue paper flapping in the wind against a lamp post. Now is the moment when the angel feather falls to earth. (What if it's only a pigeon's?) That paper, to the boys, signals the poppy-petal mask.

A great story can be circled about endlessly. Is this a love story? If so, why didn't the ugly beast become a prince at the kiss of the beautiful girl? All the material is present for it, but it doesn't happen. Was it unbeknownst to himself that John Gedsudski told his own story?

There must be a difference between a love story and a story about love. Here are two strange love objects. One is Black Wing, a male timber wolf. The other is a girl who insists on playing baseball with a bunch of kids. We aren't told how Mary—a classy girl, Anglo by her name—met John—a weird-looking Pole—only that she appears, joins the crowd, then spurns them. What did she and John talk about? Why did they quarrel? Whatever the reason, Mary Hudson has no intention of going on being a baseball chum. (But once she *thought* she could!) Her last appearance is like the false appearance of the impostor wolf. Black Wing is dead; the original Mary Hudson is dead. The present Mary Hudson is an imposter. The Laughing Man cannot live. This could be John and Mary's story, but it isn't.

"The Laughing Man" is a story about innocence. Love, Salinger seems to be saying, *has* to be innocent, or it isn't love. The innocent lover—ugly, adoring, single-hearted—is the Chief. How masterful he is in the guise of the Laughing Man! A whole nation (China!) adores him. The crime problems of France fall before him. He is famous, all-conquering, superb.

Has John Gedsudski yet seen his own identity in this tale he spins? When does a teller (or a writer—*any* writer) learn that they are somehow, in some way remote or intimately near, talking about themselves? Perhaps John hit on the story when he sensed how the boys worshipped him. Maybe at first he was just inventing a boys' adventure tale—all must have a hero, a superman. Perhaps John did not see how near and nearer the story was growing to himself. And though Black Wing could hardly resemble Mary Hudson—even sex and genus are poles apart—it is the nature of devotion that is identical. Each wears the indelible, the unmistakable mark of the beloved.

Love and innocence can only be defeated by the beloved. The invincible Laughing Man can receive a fatal wound. The Chief as Hero can be destroyed. With cold deliberation, before all of his young worshippers, by means of the story he has invented and spun for them, he destroys himself.

The narrator recalls how the whole troop on the bus fell silent, how little Billy Walsh (the youngest) burst into tears, how his own knees were shaking. His teeth were chattering "uncontrollably" when he returned home, and he was sent straight to bed.

By the time *Nine Stories* appeared in collected form in 1953, *The Catcher in the Rye* had already come out three years earlier. Holden Caulfield had already walked into our consciousness, our conversation, our literature. Holden was a troubled adolescent kicked out of school. We have all been in some ways like him. There is no way not to relate to his pain, his search for honesty, for innocence and love, daunted so often, but sometimes, in rare precious moments, found.

In two future books—*Franny and Zooey*, and *Raise High the Roof Beam, Carpenters and Seymour: An Introduction*—each containing two long stories, Salinger continued to engage us in his and his characters' search at ever increasing depths. At that point his work began to draw critical attack. Though welcomed at first, great success apparently made it suspect. It began to be called precious and narrow, out of the mainstream of American life. Sexuality was called into question—why this adoration of children, of sisters, of a brother dead by suicide? The writer's very devotion to his characters was called excessive.

Time magazine ran a Salinger cover story. In a long article of analysis, a *Time* staff writer probed the writer's life as he had gleaned it. His article raised numerous questions, hinting though not stating that Salinger might be a "minor" rather than a "major" American writer. Why otherwise couldn't he let go his obsession with Seymour Glass, a character who early on, in a short story, had committed suicide? Other critics were calling Salinger "weak," unable to face life's harsh realities. How wonderful to drag down whoever rises high! It is an old American game.

By the time the last two books appeared, Salinger, with who knows what degree of resentment against public curiosity and critical attack, had retreated to an isolated life on a fenced property in northern New England. His only company seemed to be his wife and their two young children. His days were spent in a writing studio; he devoted hours to Zen meditation. Such fragments drifted about in the literary gossip of the time. Had his writing ceased altogether, or was it simply not publishable? Good authority declared that the latter was the case.

At all events, he was gone. Except for a lawsuit he brought against a would-be biographer in 1986, he might as well have departed the planet.

Whatever one's judgment of his chosen way, he was spared the "literary life." No autograph sessions, appearances on television, participation at conferences, membership in prestigious academies, honorary degrees, interviews conducted by telephone with the *New York Times*, inquiries from curious reporters, or questionnaires from earnest students, no consultations with seekers of MAs and PhDs.

He vanished.

But we are not without him. Re-issued many times, his four books now stand together on the paperback shelves of bookstores. The newest editions have pure white covers, a rainbow-colored slash across one corner. There are no quotes, no blurbs, no cozy notes about the author: only his name. At the local library several copies of each book are available. *The Catcher in the Rye* is constantly in demand, but others look equally worn.

At the time Salinger was publishing, American books were loaded with explicit sex. Our anxieties of those days had a lot to do with sexuality, much to do also with those bitchy twins, success and money. Prominence was required. You had to look right, to talk the right phrases, quote the right people, live in the upscale apartment or neighborhood, drink the right drinks and order in the right restaurants, vacation at the right places. The 1960s had not arrived to do their ruthless housecleaning. Salinger from the first smelled out the phony drift of things. Others may have done so, too; a good case can be made for the perceptions of John Cheever among others. But in no other writer has the regard for innocence and the necessity for purity of motive seemed so vital—a matter of the spirit's life or death.

The Glass family, as he lovingly traced them out, find their saint in the dead brother Seymour, who thought deeply about Jesus, wrote Haiku poems, dwelt with life and death as twin faces of the same eternal spirit. The vision grows plainer as we go along, until at the end of the two last books, what is livable and possible is a spiritual perception which carries us beyond apparent endings. Christ is in the Fat Lady; for her we shine our shoes. Christ is latent also even in the "phony," in the average, in common humanity. We must live in a state of constant prayer; we must *watch*. Difficult it may be, but it is the way.

There is no reason for such a writer to continue giving to his readers. We have these four great offerings already. When we read them all again (as I did, going from the earliest straight on to the next), we see how Salinger causes us to search along with him. In doing so, he changes us, and we share moments of finding and changing along with him. He was able to snatch us back from the perilous cliff's edge while we are coming through the rye.

Elizabeth Spencer is the author of the short-story collections *Ship Island and Other Stories* (1968), *The Stories of Elizabeth Spencer* (1981), *Marilee* (1981), *Jack of Diamonds and Other Stories* (1988), *On the Gulf* (1991), *The Light in the Piazza and Other Italian Tales* (1996), *The Southern Woman* (2001), and

Starting Over (2014), as well as nine novels, a memoir, and a play. She won the PEN/Malamud Award for Excellence in the Short Story in 2007, is a five-time recipient of the O. Henry Award for Short Fiction, and is a member of the American Academy of Arts & Letters.

"Girl" by Jamaica Kincaid

Diana Wagman

"Girl" was first published in the June 26, 1978, issue of *The New Yorker*. It was collected and is currently most readily available in *At the Bottom of the River* (Farrar, Straus and Giroux).

The first time I read this story, I read it as my students do. I was a student myself, unmarried, without children, and I laughed and disparaged the speaker—the mother—as my students still do. What a bossy know-it-all, my students say and I said when I first read it. Telling her daughter what to do, not allowing the daughter to make up her own mind and so horribly old fashioned. My students snicker.

Some of them nod knowingly. The young women especially hear their mothers' voices. They recognize the cadence and the chiding, Mother fully expecting her daughter to screw up and already disappointed, unhappy in advance. Although the particulars of the mother's instructions are unique to Antigua and Barbuda, the tone is universal. It's a story about trust, and the mother definitely does not trust her daughter to know what is the right thing to do.

As a young student, I too heard my mother's voice. "Do you hear me?" That was my mother's refrain. When she was angry. When she was telling me I'd made another mistake. Do you hear me? Meaning was I listening? Was she being understood? Pay attention, she was saying, this is important. And in the single line that is the daughter's interjecting voice in "Girl," "*I don't sing benna on Sundays at all and never in Sunday School*," we hear the typical teenager replying none of this is important, Mom, you obviously know nothing about me or my life or how I behave.

In 690 words Jamaica Kincaid tells the trajectory of an entire relationship, complete with expectations of the future, but obliquely. She avoids the traditional storytelling, "Once there was a girl and she lived in Antigua and her mother was always telling her what to do" and does it in voice, in rhythm, in the precise choice of each word. Without being told directly, we know the girl thinks she will never measure up and also that ultimately she will leave her mother behind.

The first time I taught this story, my mother had just died unexpectedly and too young. The story took on new meaning. I know Jamaica Kincaid had a fraught relationship with her mother—that they were close until her much younger brothers came along and then she was expected to quit school and help provide. My mother and I had our difficulties too, and I felt incapable of making her happy. When I read the story to prepare for class I cried. I heard love in the mother's scolding and a deep desire that her daughter be happy and succeed in her life. At that time, I had two small children at home and it broke my heart that my mother wouldn't get a chance to tell them what to do, to boss them around the way she had me. Her advice hadn't been so bad. She knew more than I wanted to admit when I was living under her roof. In the story there are moments when we hear what must have been the mother's life—"this is how to love a man, and if this doesn't work there are other ways, and if they don't work don't feel too bad about giving up"—with a poignancy and sadness. And there are moments of fun: "this is how to spit up in the air if you feel like it, and this is how to move quick so that it doesn't fall on you."

Whenever I teach this story, I follow up with an exercise to write a paragraph of advice in the voice of someone the students know—a parent, an older sibling, a teacher—paying attention to the rhythm and cadence of that person's speech. I tell them to try and make it as real as possible. I sat while they wrote that first time, my first class as a fiction teacher, and thought about my mother. I missed her.

The last time I taught this story, my daughter was heading off to college. We had always been close, but that spring she was doing her best to separate from me. It was difficult and at times painful. I tried to remember it was normal, she needed to put that distance between us, but what I wanted day after day was to sit her down and "give her a piece of my mind." When I read "Girl" in preparation to teach it again, I heard my voice. Different words, but the same cautioning tone, the same worry and concern. I heard the same love, hidden in reprimands and warnings: "the slut I have warned you against becoming." I had to laugh. I had come full circle with this story, from the angry daughter, to the bereft daughter, to the scolding mother.

I will teach "Girl" again this summer for the first time in a while. As I wrote this essay, I realized it has been forty years since I first read this story. Now my children are old enough to be their own people. They have no need even to pretend to listen to my counsel. Now they boss me around and tell me what I should or shouldn't do and what dangers lie ahead. The difference is I know they do it out of love.

Diana Wagman is the author of the novels *Skin Deep* (1997), *Spontaneous* (2000), *Bump* (2003), *The Care and Feeding of Exotic Pets* (2012), *Life #6* (2015), and *Extraordinary October* (2016).

"Fatherland" by Viet Thanh Nguyen

Kao Kalia Yang

"Fatherland" was first published in the Spring 2011 issue of *Narrative*. It was collected in *The Refugees* (2017). It is currently most readily available in *The Refugees* (Grove).

I read Viet Thanh Nguyen's "Fatherland" shortly after I returned from my first official visit to Laos, the birth country of my mother and father, and the land of my buried ancestors. Nguyen's short story was published in 2011, four years before the publication of his Pulitzer-Prize winning first novel, *The Sympathizer*. "Fatherland" was originally published in *Narrative*, where it was the prize winner of the winter fiction contest. The story is a great study of Nguyen's style as a writer (his poised prose, worldly characters), his vast knowledge of Western art and film (his understanding of colonial cultural productions), and his ideas and perspectives on the Vietnamese-American and Vietnamese-Vietnamese relationship (his focus on humanity in times of war and of the peace of its aftermath). The story is narrated by Phuong, a young woman growing up in Saigon, her older half-sister from America with the same name—although she calls herself Vivien after the star of *Gone with the Wind*—and their father, a once-powerful man who now lives as a tour guide of the past. "Fatherland" is a study of identity: who we are, how we present ourselves, and who we wish to be. As a woman whose own life's circumstances have been shaped by the Vietnam War, the same war that resulted in the separation of the characters of Nguyen's short story, although a war fought in a neighboring country, I was interested in learning how fiction might be useful for the experiences I'd just gone through in Laos.

In order to enter Laos and stay safely within the country, I could not go back as I was, a Hmong-American writer struggling to make ends meet, a writer whose work centers on and emerges from the travesties of the war in Laos. I had written two books about the history of my people, the stories of our lives after the acts of war waged upon us by both the Central Intelligence Agency of the United States of America (an organization that commissioned 32,000 Hmong men and boys to fight and die in support of the American cause) and the Communist government of Laos (a government that instituted genocide against my people once the Americans had left the war). In my application for a visa to visit Laos, I wrote that I was a teacher. It was a partial truth, for what writer does not teach in her speaking and the stories she writes, particularly if her home genre is creative nonfiction?

I found myself in a situation not unlike Nguyen's Vivian, although our circumstances were different. In her case, she'd left as a young child with her mother after the war during her father's five-year sentence to a New Economic Zone. After their leaving, Vivien's mother, through a series of letters back to Vietnam, constructs a life for her eldest daughter: a life where she is a successful doctor, a young, independent pediatrician who has traveled the world. In reality, she is a receptionist who has been laid off from her job. She is visiting her father, his new family, and the country of her birth on her severance pay and credit cards. Much of the story is about how she is perceived by her younger stepsister, Phoung, as someone who "bore utterly no resemblance to the throngs of local people waiting outside to greet the arrivals, hundreds of ordinary folk wearing drab clothes and fanning themselves under the sun." Although the small lie on my visa was for the sake of the government in power and its officials, because of the nature of the country, its investment in civilian spies, and the real dangers posed for Hmong-Americans visitors, I could not tell my relatives the truth about my work in America or the life that I was living there. I could not compromise their safety that way. So, I played the role of a teacher in America on an excursion back to Laos, squinting beneath the fiery sun, white skin heating up beneath its rays.

Like Vivien, I used my credit cards to pay for meals for family and friends who believed that in America I was earning a respectable income as a teacher, making a healthy living at a regular job. Like Vivien, I met relatives who remembered my mother and father and who through these memories loved me, people who I had never met, but now could never forget, some who I trusted immediately, and others who I felt sorry for, but each carrying an ocean of story inside of them so heavy at times that the salty water leaked from their eyes upon the sight of me—plump and healthy, born on the side of peace, growing up in the possibilities of America. Like Vivien, I told them, "I don't mind spending money." I, too, wanted to show my family in Laos a good time.

I found myself in a web of perceptions, real and constructed, answering questions about my life on the other side of the ocean, a life that was not up for discussion. I found myself talking to my cousins, born and bred in Communist Laos, about the difference between Sprite and Coke in America and Laos. The Laotian variety had less fizz. Its sweetness was more cloying. I did not like it as much. My Laotian cousins talked to me about how they'd heard stories from people who'd visited America, who'd spent the days and the weeks there missing and yearning for the Coke of Laos. We laughed. It was funny and it was real, and it wasn't enough. In my heart, I wanted to tell them that I was a writer, here—as I was everywhere—listening and looking and feeling for the powerful stories. I wanted to tell them about the mountains in Laos that I had seen—how they were taller than any other mountains I had ever visited—but I wasn't sure if my cousins had ever had the opportunity to visit these same mountains in the place of their birth. So, I talked of aim and squat toilets and the dangers of sunglasses in the Laotian toilet sheds. We laughed. In the sound of our laughter, I hoped that the elders around us, the ones who had lived through a war that many of us had not been born into, found a suitable bandage for those long-ago wounds that had not healed but had festered and hardened during the long span of years apart.

I found myself weeping in "Fatherland" when Nguyen takes the two sisters, Phuong and Vivien, up on a Ferris wheel in an amusement park, where the lake at the park's center becomes "the size of a saucer" and paddleboats float "like crumbs on its surface." The sisters are talking. Vivien tells Phuong that she'd once worked in an amusement park in order to meet boys. Phuong wants to know if she met a boyfriend. Yes, a cute boy named Rod, a kissing partner in a darkened car. They are having a safe, sisterly conversation, and then Phuong shares a secret: she doesn't a want a boyfriend, nothing to hold her back, because she wants to leave Saigon behind, to be sponsored by her sister, to leave for America, to become a doctor and to help people. Vivien weeps. She can't do it. America is hard. Her life is hard. She can't take care of a younger sister. She has to put her life back together, to pay off credit cards and her student loans, to make sure that her house isn't taken away from her. All throughout my stay in

Laos, strangers and family alike asked me to help find sponsors for their loved ones, for their young ones, for themselves, because they wanted a better life, a life that is more like mine than the one they were living in Laos. Each time they asked, I said I would, but in the dark of the hotel room with the buzz of the air conditioner around me, on my thin mattress I wet the pillow with the weight of their requests. I knew no one in America, myself included, who was strong enough to carry another person from Laos into a better life.

Nguyen's "Fatherland" forced a reckoning, a looking at my life as it is in America and the lives of my people in Laos. There are facts that I, like the characters in Nguyen's short story, have to encounter: wars bring on different realities for its survivors, drive us apart in time and space, and create a place of unreality when we meet in moments of peace. Where the wars were once fought on land, air, and water—they now live on us, in us, and around us. We have all become captives in the same globe of unreality, a world shaken again and again so that it can come back to some kind of imperfect rest, far from contentment, far from closure—a world that is fraught with the lies we tell ourselves and each other so that we can continue at this thing called life and love, this network of family across the far oceans.

Through Viet Thanh Nguyen's "Fatherland," I was able to process the knowledge I've carried all my life and encountered in Laos: I would never live my life with all of my family, certainly not as I am. The war had torn us apart. In the apart, in order to survive, to flourish and grow, we've had to become versions of ourselves that we could never carry back to the place where we had been destined to be together. These spaces don't exist anymore. These possibilities are the things that wars kill, and we live in a world full of war. Is there a single human being in the world that we live in now who has lived their full lives through within the reach of all they considered family? Will there ever be again? What is gained and what is lost in these long-distance love stories that grow thinner and thinner generation after generation? These are the questions that Viet Thanh Nguyen's "Fatherland" poses for a writer like me, a first-generation Hmong-American writer trying to tell the stories of what happens to a people, a world, in the aftermath of loss.

Kao Kalia Yang is the author of the memoirs *The Late-homecomer* (2008) and *The Song Poet* (2016)

"The Pura Principle" by Junot Díaz

Mako Yoshikawa

"The Pura Principle" was first published in the March 22, 2010, issue of *The New Yorker*. It was collected and is currently most readily available in *This Is How You Lose Her* (Riverhead, 2013).

How do we read and teach an amazing story that's been written by an author whose behavior seems reprehensible? Can a work of art be separated from the person who created it, and even more vitally, should it? Is it possible—*isn't* it possible—for an author who is demonstrably guilty of sexist behavior to produce a story that's interesting and even edifying about sexism? These are the questions that confront me when I think about Junot Díaz now.

Before Zinzi Clemmons stood up and spoke out against Díaz, I'd heard rumblings from colleagues about him. How misogynistic his work is, how toxic. How the students reading him need to be cautioned: don't write like him; stories should do more than celebrate predators and put down women. These were comments I blanched at and, at times, spoke out against, especially those directed at the writing students: I believe that writing should reveal the different prisms, even or especially those that are flawed and skewed, through which people see the world; many young writers already seem to be laboring under a heavy burden of cultural sensitivity. But for the most part I managed to ignore the rumblings, to treat them as so much background noise.

This was possible because I teach at a school where the students are famously edgy, and because my classes are made up of aspiring young writers—writers who are hungry, as I am, for different voices and new ways of telling stories. With these students, I've had the immense pleasure of reliving my own joy at discovering Díaz's work, the shock and thrill I felt when I picked up *Drown* in the late 1990s, an era in which writers everywhere were emulating Raymond Carver's restraint and repressed style, my amazement at encountering a voice that was profane, intimate, lyrical, moving and oh-so-funny, a voice that effortlessly, irresistibly combined Spanish with English and erudite references with geek pop culture. I was studying literary criticism then and nursing dreams of writing novels, dreams that I couldn't quite acknowledge even to myself, and Díaz's voice changed everything; it showed me not just what language can do, but how immigrants and writers of color could contribute to literature and art, how someday they—or was that we?—might enrich and even transform the cultural landscape.

Still, the accusations against Díaz—that he forcibly tried to kiss Clemmons when she, as a young aspiring writer, hosted him at her grad school program, and that he has been rude, dismissive, offensive, and aggressive to other young women writers—are serious. And in recent conversations I've had with students, a number of them, even those who seemed most clearly enraptured by Díaz's voice and stories, expressed unease at the thought of studying his work in class now, citing the need for sensitivity to students who might feel offended by Díaz's actions; a reluctance to put money in his pocket; and a new discomfort with the characterization of women in his stories.

I'd argue, though, that in spite of my hesitation—*because of* my hesitation, the unease that so many of us feel—the issues that Díaz's case has raised are important and, in this day and age, increasingly essential. The accusations provide an opportunity for discussions that may be fraught and that almost certainly will take us beyond the words on the page, but will prove thought provoking and consequential for all of us.

So the question, to me, isn't whether we should teach Díaz, but how. Which means that we first need to think about how we respond to students who feel outraged by his actions, and what we do if they express scruples about reading and discussing his work.

There's a range of reservations that students might have after all: well-considered and strongly held political convictions based on knowledge of the issues; visceral personal reactions stemming from trauma; and preconceptions based on little more than rumors. If the main issue bedeviling the students is whether the writer should profit from his work, the answer is simple: check it out of the library rather than buying it. If the students' reservations are more general and seem strong and sincere, I wouldn't force them to read the author's writing. Yet if they're open to and capable of rational conversation on the subject, I would invite them to talk with me in private. There I would do my best to persuade them, gently, that they would contribute a lot to the class discussion. Because they *would* contribute—the other students as well as I would benefit from listening to and wrestling with their views as well as their readings of the text.

According to some critics, the problem with Díaz's work is that his female characters are almost all sex objects and victims. Thus we have Virginia Vitzthum, who writes in *Elle* about how excited she was to read "The Cheater's Guide to Love" because Yunior, the brash, women-chasing and none-too-deep narrator of so many of Díaz's stories, is in his forties: "Finally, I thought, I'll meet a woman who isn't summed up as 'big stupid lips and a sad moonface' or 'this one piece of white trash from Sayreville' or 'a big Dominican ass.' But—no such luck." As she explains, "these women look like chumps, because all the men do is cheat on them. . . . We pretty much only see the women as exes, crying and screaming after they've been cheated on, or as new possibilities, cataloged in terms of their fuckworthiness."

I take issue with Vitzthum's reading. But her comments are useful in that they highlight the challenge of creating characters of an oppressed or marginalized group. If a female character of an oppressed or marginalized group is presented as weak, highly emotional, or overly fond of men or sex, many would call that negative stereotyping. But if she's a purely positive character, noble and strong and virtuous, that's just promoting a different stereotype, while creating a flat character besides. The goal, I'd submit, is to write characters who are complex, believable, and real—characters who might make mistakes and have flaws.

Many or even most of the women in Díaz's stories have been betrayed or disappointed by Yunior and other men, that's clear. But that doesn't make them chumps. A good proportion end up walking away, breaking their cheating partners' hearts, and loving someone who doesn't deserve love—well, I'd say that's not being weak, but human.

Even more important, there's a considerable range in how Díaz's female characters respond to their disappointments in love and life. This is in evidence in his oeuvre, but we can also see it distilled in "The Pura Principle." The story features three compelling female characters, all complicated in different ways: as excellent a case as any for the need to continue reading, studying, and teaching Díaz's work.

Told in the first person, "The Pura Principle" recounts the last months of Yunior's brother Rafa before he dies of cancer. Rafa looms large in Yunior's psyche as a figure of almost mythic sexual magnetism and cool, so perhaps it's not surprising that Yunior tells the story of his decline and death through the women who love and mourn him—women who at first glance seem like a gallery of Latina stereotypes.

Tammy Franco, one of Rafa's former girlfriends, had been abused by him. "Bad, too," Yunior tells us. "A two-year-long public-service announcement. He'd get so mad at her sometimes that he dragged her around the parking lot by her hair. Once her pants came unbuttoned and got yanked down to her ankles, and we could all see her toto and everything." This horrifying account is made worse by Yunior's jokey delivery— the public-service announcement crack—and the fact that Tammy, who has married someone else, is "[t]he only one who hung tough" when Rafa becomes really ill: she's a victim who comes back for more abuse.

Or so it seems. To Yunior's surprise, the relationship between Rafa and Tammy isn't sexual; when they sit in her Camry, Yunior watches, waiting, as he tells us, for Rafa "to palm her head down into his lap" for a blow-job, but this never happens. When Yunior asks what they're doing—"Ain't she, like, married to some Polack?"—Rafa gives him a look. "What the fuck do you know?" he says, a seemingly rhetorical question that Yunior answers with a reply that we the readers could echo: "Nothing." We don't know why Tammy goes back to Rafa. Maybe she feels love; maybe forgiveness, pity, or sympathy with a fellow victim. Or maybe she *is* a textbook case of victimization—maybe she's back for more beatings and humiliation, maybe she's intent on saving her abuser. Díaz leaves any and all of these possibilities open; Tammy's motivations are a mystery beyond Yunior's ken, and ours. The image of her and Rafa together in the car, though, perhaps gazing straight ahead—Yunior notes that "It didn't even look like they were talking"—is an evocative one. Sitting next to him, Tammy seems like Rafa's equal, or perhaps even something more; Rafa, Yunior says, is in "the bitch seat." Tammy is hardly a feminist role model. Yet in that she appears in control during these visits and seems to decide when to come and go, she's not downtrodden either: a character who resists easy categorization.

A second and more prominent female character is the eponymous Pura. Rafa meets her when he, to Yunior's stupefaction, takes a job at the Yarn Barn. A recent arrival from the Dominican Republic, Pura has a young son and no papers; in sharp contrast to Tammy, she's selfish, grasping, and heartless, a user and a taker. She pits herself against Rafa's and Yunior's mother, and when she and Rafa marry, Mami, to Yunior's shock—he's in a state of befuddlement pretty much throughout the entire story—kicks them out of the house. Later, when Rafa becomes feverish, Pura asks Yunior to take him to the hospital but doesn't allow him to use Rafa's car, saying that she's lost the keys—a lie, as Yunior knows; Pura's afraid he won't give the car back. She watches as Yunior puts Rafa in a shopping cart and doesn't accompany them to the hospital, telling Yunior that she has to stay with her son; she never visits Rafa, but goes to Mami and Yunior to ask for two thousand dollars, money that she says Rafa borrowed from her.

Even though we don't like Pura—how could we, when she's so scheming and greedy, so uncaring about poor dying Rafa— she's vivid and anything but weak, and even though Yunior doesn't probe her motivations, we can; clues to a deeper understanding of her character are embedded in his narrative. As she tells Yunior, her mother married her off at thirteen to an older man, after which she escaped to Newark only to endure more hardship; now she's "trying to stay afloat, looking for her next break. She smiled brightly at my brother when she said that.'" Yunior questions the veracity of this account and Mami tells him it's "ridiculo," but later he overhears her telling her friends how her mother had almost traded her for two goats; we're left to assume that this litany of tribulations has some grounding in truth.

Then there's how Pura is first described. She's very attractive, Yunior says, but "unlike your average hood hottie [she] seemed not to know what to do with her fineness, was sincerely lost in all the pulchritude"; she's also a "total campesina," with Spanish that Yunior can barely understand. In other words, she's innocent and clueless, a country girl and single mother who can't even make herself understood to other Dominican immigrants: her situation is desperate, which makes her eventual triumph that much more remarkable. Indeed, we can flip the story and imagine it being told with her as the heroine: a tale of a woman who starts out with nothing but is smart and determined, a character who figures out how to survive and take care of herself and her child.

The third important female character of the story is Mami. A woman who loves her elder son more than anything, she seems the epitome of the patient, long-suffering saint of an immigrant mother. She kicks Rafa out, but does nothing to prevent him from stealing from her, thus joining the swelling ranks of women who allow ungrateful, undeserving men to take advantage; worse still, when Pura comes to ask for the two thousand dollars, Mami goes to the bedroom and returns not with a pistol, as Yunior expects and hopes, but a hundred-dollar bill.

The text makes it clear, though, that Mami isn't weak. When she hands over the money, Yunior tells us, "For a minute they stared at each other, and then Mami let the bill go, the force between them so strong the paper popped": she's on to Pura's game, and is every bit her match. So why give her the money? Over the course of the story, we've seen Mami cycle through a raft of emotions—grief, anger, frustration, yearning, and hopelessness—and her decision to give money to Pura is surprising but it also feels *right*; it seems true to her character. Still, the inner workings of her mind in this scene are hard to discern. I'd argue that deep down Mami understands what Pura and her son meant to Rafa; she senses that through them, as through his Yarn Barn job, he was trying to contribute and do some good before he died. But that's just my reading. Perhaps Mami sees that Rafa might have loved Pura, or found some happiness with her; perhaps she thinks that as a result, she owes her. Perhaps she feels sorry for Pura, perhaps she knows that Pura's just trying to survive. Perhaps it's all of the above: just as we can't be sure of why Tammy returns to Rafa, so too are Mami's motivations open to interpretation.

There's more to the story, of course. How Yunior deals with his own grief, and his and Rafa's conversations and relationship. Then there's Rafa himself—his quiet desperation to do something meaningful before he dies, the spirit and fight that he shows in the story's end, which I won't spoil by summarizing. Yet it's the female characters that captivate me. They embody what I believe is one of the ideals of great writing: to capture how complex people are, how capacious and even uncontainable—mysteries not only to those closest to them, but perhaps even to themselves.

Mako Yoshikawa is the author of the novels *One Hundred and One Ways* (1999) and *Once Removed* (2003).

"Honeydew" by Edith Pearlman

Mary Kay Zuravleff

"Honeydew" was first published in the September-October 2011 issue of *Orion*. It was collected and is currently most readily available in *Honeydew: Stories* (Little, Brown).

Within this masterful story, Edith Pearlman tells a tale that is both sacred and profane. Not only that, she keeps flipping the two, sullying the sacred and elevating the profane. She starts by listing the grounds for expulsion from the esteemed Caldicott Academy, located in the fictional Boston suburb of Godolphin. Essentially, "drinking and drugging and having sex right there on the campus could supposedly get you kicked out; turning up pregnant likewise." And then she introduces us to Alice Toomey, hallowed headmistress at the private school for girls. Alice has turned up pregnant from having sex "right there on campus" with a married man, father of the school's most troubled and gifted student. The other girls admire that student, Emily Knapp, for how much she knows about bugs and how little she eats. "This tall bundle of twigs that called itself a girl—Alice's palms ached to spank her." A few times each year, Emily swallows a hallucinogenic drug alongside Mr. da Sola, who grinds the powder from a grub he raises in the Caldicott greenhouse. All this at the school recognized two years in a row for having the Most Effective Director.

Actually, Pearlman's sullying starts earlier than the first line, with the very title. "Honeydew" alludes to the manna from heaven that sustained the Israelites in the desert as Moses led them out of Egyptian bondage, but eleventh-grader Emily Knapp reveals the flip side to what heaven provided. According to Emily, most things can be explained through the biology of the gut, specifically bug guts: "Of course the manna, which Exodus describes as a fine frost on the ground with a taste like honey, was thought to be a miracle from God, but it was really Coccidae excrement. . . . Nomads still eat it—relish it. It is called honeydew."

See what I mean about the sacred and profane? Depending on how you argue it, edible bug poop falling from the sky might well be evidence of the highest or the lowest order. Unless we're all of the same order. As Emily thinks, "Ah, Coccidae. She could draw them—she loved to draw her relatives—but unfortunately the mature insect is basically a scaly ball: a gut in a shell."

And so the story goes. The headmistress having a pleasurable affair is an appalling breach of trust, unless her accidental pregnancy is the link of compassion to her lover's starving daughter. Maybe she's deserving of that Most Effective Director award after all. Mr. da Sola giving a vulnerable student mind-altering powder is a parent's worst nightmare and also sets off a reader's alarm. Real and imagined stories continually show us fragile girls being damaged or abused. But Pearlman's ant-hill is crawling with people who act selfishly but not maliciously. Emily, who keeps only crackers and a box of prunes in her study bunker, hallucinates a feast under the influence of ground moth, and she awakens to pastries Mr. da Sola has made for her. Pearlman's description of Emily's vision renders the profane sacred: "In Emily's repeated dream, she was attending a banquet where she was compelled to crawl from table to table, sampling the brilliant food: pink glistening hams, small crispy birds on beds of edible petals, smoked fish of all colors ranging from the deep orange of salmon to the pale yellow of butterfish."

In an interview about this story, Pearlman explains that for *Orion*, the environmentally oriented magazine that requested a story, "the lovers and the would-be anorexic would have to be vigorously involved in the natural world." This quest led her to ants, who can feed their colony or eschew food completely, along with the ground grubs and the manna in the wilderness, and she gives "thanks to my characters for requiring me to do entomological research."

We give thanks as well. Despite being a physician and an anatomy professor, Emily's father describes his daughter's plight in bug terms: "She wants to become a bug and live on air . . . and a drop or two of nectar. She thinks—she sometimes thinks—she was meant to be born an insect." Although Caldicott is not a boarding school, Emily is given her own little room, a closet outfitted by Mr. da Sola with shelves for her insect specimens, "for the study hall nauseated her, redolent as it was of food recently eaten and now being processed, and sometimes of residual gases loosed accidentally or mischievously." As she "put[s] one of three carrot sticks into her mouth," she thinks about exoskeletons, compound eyes, and the ant's segmented body: "the rear segment, segmented itself, which contained the abdomen and, right beside it, the heart."

Emily lectures her classmates on that intelligent design, how the heart and stomach are together, "and would you believe it the reproductive organs too, well, you probably would believe that." Pearlman captures the mania of young girls to ingest and regurgitate everything about syntax or utopian societies—or the lowly ant, whose collective pouch is likened to a soup kitchen. Alice chimes in to Emily's lecture to say, "Then the larger stomach belongs to the community." And with that, it becomes clear that we are reading a story about appetite. For Alice and Emily, the way to a woman's stomach is through her heart. Emily, starved for love, grows thinner as Alice is getting bigger by the month.

Years ago, my daughter and I were invited behind the scenes of Chicago's Field Museum. There we met a young scholar disappointed by her new assignment categorizing mammals. She had been in the Division of Insects for years, and she lifted the hem of her shirt and pushed back her sleeves to show us larger-than-life-sized tattoos of a praying mantis, katydid, and several beetles inked across her arms and torso. When I asked her what she loved about bugs, she slid open a drawer in museum storage and explained how an entire species fit on a single tray. Clearly awestruck, she waved her hand over the display, saying, "The whole world is there in one drawer."

As I read about Emily Knapp's devotion, I repeatedly thought of that young scholar of insects. She had wrinkled up her nose at mammals, so cumbersome and fleshy; likewise, Emily can barely abide their company. Preferring bugs to people is rare enough in young women, but I also kept remembering the museum drawer that she slid out with such veneration. How like a short story to contain an entire world in its pages!

The truth is, private-school stories are as common as bugs and nearly as classifiable. In lesser hands, snarky narrators collect privileged students who use their wits to get in trouble and their entitlement to get out, or they pin teachers to a board, either for crossing a line or inspiring a lost soul. They sort administrators into those behaving admirably or with hypocrisy. Pearlman's talent is giving them all to us in one story, all in the same drawer, and treating them with honesty enough and wit so we are left to marvel at their nature.

Can you imagine being a fly on the wall and seeing everything with compound eyes? Emily aspires to turn into a giant insect, and the headmistress who feels that her troubled student "should be sprayed, crushed underfoot" has a change of heart when the flutters of motherhood move her to recognize Emily as one of her own. Now, Alice yearns to take her home and "whisper to the misguided girl that life could be moderately satisfying even if you were born into the wrong order." We can't know if that's enough when Pearlman finally closes the drawer, having shown us a world where the sacred and profane exist not only side by side but also within each specimen.

Mary Kay Zuravleff is the author of the novels *The Frequency of Souls* (1996), *The Bowl Is Already Broken* (2005), and *Man Alive!* (2013).